THE
BEGGAR'S
THRONE

by David Falconieri

MacAdam/Cage Publishing

MacAdam/Cage Publishing
155 Sansome Street, Suite 550
San Francisco, CA 94104
www.macadamcage.com

Publisher's Cataloging-in-Publication

Falconieri, David.
The beggar's throne / by David Falconieri –
1st ed.
p. cm.
LCCN: 99-69322
ISBN: 0-9673701-0-8

ISBN 1-931561-57-5
Paperback Edition 2004

1. Great Britain–History – Wars of the Roses, 1455-1485 – Fiction.
2. Great Britain – History – Fiction. I. Title
PS3511.A633B44 1999   813.54
QB199-500572

Manufactured in the United States of America.

10 9 8 7 6 5 4 3 2 1

Book design by Dorothy Carico Smith

ACKNOWLEDGMENTS

Thanks are due to my old friend Charles Cunningham for his support and pre-publishing assistance; to my mother, Diana, for her editing advice and for being there when spirits needed lifting; and special thanks to Michael Igoe for his long hours spent editing the manuscript and for his excellent suggestions and historical insights given over drinks at the Wynkoop.

To Danamarie, my life's inspiration

THE
BEGGAR'S
THRONE

ENGLISH NOBILITY IN 1460

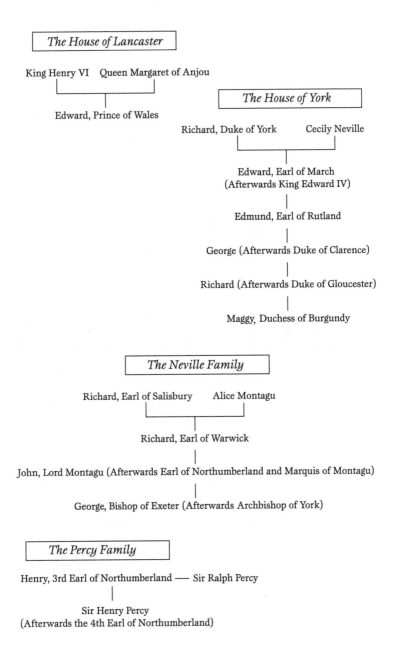

The House of Lancaster

King Henry VI — Queen Margaret of Anjou

Edward, Prince of Wales

The House of York

Richard, Duke of York — Cecily Neville

Edward, Earl of March
(Afterwards King Edward IV)

Edmund, Earl of Rutland

George (Afterwards Duke of Clarence)

Richard (Afterwards Duke of Gloucester)

Maggy, Duchess of Burgundy

The Neville Family

Richard, Earl of Salisbury — Alice Montagu

Richard, Earl of Warwick

John, Lord Montagu (Afterwards Earl of Northumberland and Marquis of Montagu)

George, Bishop of Exeter (Afterwards Archbishop of York)

The Percy Family

Henry, 3rd Earl of Northumberland —— Sir Ralph Percy

Sir Henry Percy
(Afterwards the 4th Earl of Northumberland)

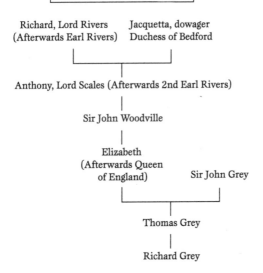

The Woodville Family

Richard, Lord Rivers   Jacquetta, dowager
(Afterwards Earl Rivers)   Duchess of Bedford

Anthony, Lord Scales (Afterwards 2nd Earl Rivers)

Sir John Woodville

Elizabeth
(Afterwards Queen
of England)   Sir John Grey

Thomas Grey

Richard Grey

Supporters of the House of Lancaster

Henry Beaufort, Duke of Somerset
John de Vere, Earl of Oxford
Jasper Tudor, Earl of Pembroke
John, Lord Clifford
Thomas, Lord Roos
John, Lord Fitzwalter
His Daughter: Katherine*
Sir Hugh Courteney*
Roger, Lord Colinsworth*
Robin of Redesdale
Pierre de Brezé, Count of Maulevrier

Supporters of the House of York

John Mowbray, Duke of Norfolk
William, Lord Hastings
William, Lord Herbert
Sir Julian Admonds of Norwich*
Sir Nigel Stafford of Devon*
Charles the Bold, Duke of Burgundy

*Indicates fictional characters

P R O L O G U E

"You say this letter proves your damning charges against the queen?" the bishop asked suspiciously.

"Your Grace, the letter must be presented to the king." The priest started to shake. "The truth must be told."

"Yes, of course it must," the bishop said, casually regarding the rolled parchment on the table between them. It was the queen's seal that fastened the paper together, of that there could be no doubt. "Guard!" he called toward the heavy oak door that led to the hall beyond.

"Why do you summon the guard?" asked the priest, his voice trembling.

"These are serious charges you make against Her Majesty. But I'm sure that if this letter confirms your suspicions you will be exonerated."

Father Stephen stared at the bishop, seeing the lie in his overfed face. Suddenly he snatched the parchment from the table and held it against his breast. "You intend to betray me to the Queen, is it not so?"

"Give me the letter, Father Stephen." The bishop held his hand out to receive it.

The priest backed slowly toward the door. "God forgive me," he croaked, and turned to run from the room.

"Guard, stop him!" shouted the bishop behind him.

Father Stephen ran headlong from the bishop's chamber. He heard shouts coming from somewhere behind that resonated against the stone walls of Westminster Palace. Turning down one hall after another, down several flights of stairs, he ran like a deer from the hounds.

At last, he could run no more and opened the first door that yielded to his push. He ducked inside and closed the door, finding himself in a small bedchamber.

Brushing the sweat from his face, he checked to see that the parchment in the folds of his robe was undamaged. *God forgive me if I sin in this matter,* he thought. *And damn the bishop for his greed.*

He slid behind a curtain that separated the sleeping chamber from a closet and looked down at the parchment again. The queen's seal was still intact, but he knew what it said, having stood over her as she wrote it. "For the sake of our son…" The words burned his memory, so damning were they. He wondered whose sin was the greater, hers for her crime, or his for betraying her trust? *It doesn't matter. The truth must be revealed!*

He jumped at the sound of the door opening, reciting to himself a litany of prayers to control the fear. After a moment of terrifying silence, a woman's voice called sharply.

"Please come out from there at once!" Father Stephen was too petrified to respond. Some movement had betrayed his presence. The curtain was pulled aside to reveal a woman as frightened as he. "Father Stephen?"

"For the pity of Christ, do not call out," he said, grabbing her arm. It was Katherine, a lady-in-waiting to the queen, one whom he knew to be kind and God-fearing. This was someone he felt certain he could trust — but he had thought the same of the bishop.

"What is it, Father?" Despite his best efforts he could not control his shaking.

"There is not much time and the truth must be told. God has chosen you, my daughter, to carry this parchment to the king." He quickly told her what was contained within the sealed document and how he had been betrayed by the bishop. Finally, he placed the parchment in her hands.

"I will protect you by leaving before I am found here. God keep you, my child." He made the sign of the cross slowly before her face, then ran from the room.

Closing the door behind him, Father Stephen ran for his life. Down a spiral stair and through several more doors, he ran through a kitchen, pursued by the nauseating smell of curing pheasant. Pushing past startled servants, he hurried through a set of double doors to a parlor. He paused to catch his breath and to still the pounding in his chest. The far doors crashed open and guards poured through.

"Halt!" yelled the first one.

"My Lord in Heaven, I commend my soul to thee," he mumbled as he was surrounded and restrained.

Back in her bedchamber, Katherine found a chair and collapsed in it. Soon, she knew, the queen would tear the palace apart searching for this letter.

The door opened again and Katherine jumped to her feet. But it was another of the ladies-in-waiting, Elizabeth Woodville.

"Good lord, you look pale," Elizabeth said. "What's wrong?"

"Nothing," she said quickly. Too quickly.

Just then it occurred to her where to hide the letter.

PART ONE

CHAPTER I

The village of Northwood spread thinly along the banks of the River Tyne, the smell of cook-fires lifting in the damp wind. Walking over the muddy, black path that led through the center of town, the miller's second son, Samuel, listened to the roar of the Tyne, swollen to near the top of its banks by a steady rain that had lasted for weeks, and that still drenched the thatch roofs of the simple dwellings.

Approaching the millhouse, he could see through the darkness only an occasional light under a doorsill and the faintest outline of the path before him. He cursed himself for leaving Warkworth Castle so late. Still, in these times of rebellion, he was lucky to get any leave at all, much less a fortnight.

The timber-and-stone millhouse perched on the riverside, the mill and its workings a fixture of his childhood memories. The giant water wheel was locked and still. Samuel stood for a moment listening to the gears straining against the force of the water when a splash made him pause and look into the gloom.

"Is anyone there?" he asked the darkness. No response. As he turned to take the last few steps to the door, a strong hand closed around his ankle and pulled his foot out from under him. Samuel fell like a log onto the muddy path. A dark form pinned his arms to the soggy ground. He struggled against the weight and his own fear trying to free himself — to no avail.

"And you call yourself a soldier?" his attacker asked casually just as Samuel was about to yell for help.

Samuel recognized the voice. "Christopher! Damn you. Get off me, you fool!"

"If you insist," Christopher mocked him.

"What in God's name are you doing out in this weather?"

"I was just walking home from Ethan's when I saw you coming down the path, and I thought I'd give you a proper welcome."

Refusing his brother's offered hand, Samuel pulled himself out of the mud and leaned against the stone foundation of the house.

"Damn you," he said again. "How could you know it was me in this witch's dark?" Samuel knew the answer, of course. Christopher had always had a keen night vision, and this was not the first time he had used it on Samuel.

"Come," said Christopher, "let's go in before we catch our deaths."

"After you, brother." The last word dripped with scorn.

Christopher chuckled and pulled the latchstring. Inside, a warm fire smoldered in the hearth and a single candle burned in the center of a square table. John, the town miller, looked up from where he sat on a three-legged stool as his sons walked through the door. Above his beard, his smiling eyes showed the cares of over forty winters.

"Samuel!" he said. "I had not expected to see you. How is it you're back from Warkworth?"

"The earl gave some of us a fortnight's leave." He embraced his father.

"Samuel!" His sister Sally came from the back room and ran into his arms. "I thank God to see you safely home again."

"I missed you most of all," he said, embracing her tightly.

The youngest of the three children, Sally was dearest to his heart. Christopher, as the oldest, would inherit his father's trade and worldly possessions, leaving Sally and Samuel with only each other. Samuel, in fact, had been sold into the earl's service at fourteen, in exchange for one year's taxes. This was a common exchange and gave younger brothers a more promising future. Samuel trained as an archer for the earl's private guard. He had already seen several actions and had proved a fine marksman.

"You're dripping wet," Sally said. "Give me your cloak." As an afterthought she took Christopher's too.

The two sons sat at the small table with their father. The aroma of stewed vegetables reminded Samuel how long it had been since his last real meal. Sally quickly began dishing out bowls of the stew.

"Where's Emma?" asked Samuel.

"She's at Jeremy's house," answered his father. "It's Edith's time, and

Emma's helping with the birth."

"The midwife said it could be a difficult birth," added Sally, shaking her head. Silence followed for a time. Emma was also expecting, and the dangers of childbirth were legend. John Miller changed the subject.

"So tell us the news from Warkworth," he asked Samuel. "There are rumors of rebellion from every transient and beggar that walks through town. One tells us the king is dead, another that York is taken. One poor wretch came into town so frightened by the rumors that he swore the French were hot on his heels. I just mill the grain the same as each day past. If the wars come to Northwood, God's will be done."

"There is evil news indeed, Father," Samuel told him. "The Yorkist lords that were until now banished to Calais invaded with a large army and defeated the king at Northampton. Poor King Henry is now their prisoner in the Tower. The Duke of York himself has returned from Ireland and claimed the throne."

"I'll not be ruled by a Yorkist king, by God," Christopher blurted.

"Nor will the Earl of Northumberland, for as long as the Percys hold the title," said Samuel.

"These are problems for others," John Miller said. "With this bloody rain we've problems enough right here in Northwood without worrying about which bloody duke would be king. Barely enough grain came in to feed the village through the winter. And the earl is not likely to forgive any of us our yearly tax. He already took his tenth of my sacks of grain."

"You shouldn't have forgiven Thomas of Endstreet his milling then," said Christopher. "It will get around now that the villagers can acquire your services for nothing if times are bad."

John Miller stomped his foot on the hard dirt floor. "If I can't lend a hand to my friends when they hurt, then God forgive me. Besides, Thomas knows when a debt is owed, and I know I'll be satisfied by him when it counts."

Someone approached; the four looked up. The door swung open and Christopher's wife, Emma, stood at the threshold kicking mud from her shoes. When she saw Samuel, she forgot about the dirt.

"As I live and breathe!" she exclaimed. "God has answered my prayers." She leaned in to hug her brother-in-law tightly.

"I am greatly pleased to see you well, Emma. How is Edith?"

Emma shook the rain from her cloak and sighed.

"She is well, thank God," she answered, crossing herself. Sally did the same. "And your friend Jeremy has his son. But it was a terribly long labor and Edith will be a while recovering." She began to clean the hearth, as much to comfort herself as to set the place right.

"Jeremy a father!" Samuel could scarcely believe it. They were both the same age, seventeen years, but now Jeremy already had a son.

"You were telling us the news from Warkworth," Christopher interrupted.

Samuel repeated the news about the king's capture at Northampton for Emma's sake. She could only shake her head in disbelief.

"After the battle, Parliament debated the duke's claim to the throne but could not bring themselves to dethrone poor Henry. Instead they adopted the duke as Henry's heir apparent, and decreed that upon the death of the king, the House of York shall inherit the crown."

"How could they?" exclaimed Christopher. "I can't believe the queen would accept that. The Prince of Wales would be disinherited."

"The queen was not party to the agreement. And neither were any of the northern lords. There will be more fighting, I can assure you."

"And with you right in the front lines, as usual," said Emma angrily. "This fighting will be the ruin of us all, I know it."

"I am an archer, Emma, and we usually get sent in first. But I have learned to take good care of myself."

Emma said nothing but began to cut vegetables with loud chops.

"It's been a long day. I'd better be turning in." Samuel began to feel his long journey from Warkworth.

"You'll find your bed the same as when you left it," said his father. "There's a taper in the cupboard."

Samuel found the candle and lit it using the flame from the one on the table. After saying goodnight, he stepped into the back room, which was divided by curtains into three sleeping areas. After removing his clothes and collapsing onto his straw sleeping pad, he pulled the light wool blanket up and let sleep drift over him. With the sound of the river roaring outside, he felt safe and at home in his father's house.

The next morning Samuel rapped gently on Jeremy's door. He heard no sounds from within and began to worry that something was wrong.

"Is it really you?" The voice came from around the corner of the cottage.

"Jeremy!" Samuel ran to embrace him.

"At last you're back," said his friend. "How long can you stay?"

"Only a fortnight. So I hear you're a father, you dog!"

Jeremy smiled broadly. "I can hardly believe it myself. Emma has already been here this morning to look in on Edith. I swear we are forever indebted to her."

"I'm just glad to hear everyone is healthy," Samuel said, "and I'm sure that's all the thanks Emma needs."

"She told us the news about the king. How is it the earl let you leave in such dangerous times?"

"He felt there would be no more fighting until after the Christmas Holy days and did not wish to feed us all between now and the new year."

"I'm glad for it. I miss your face around here. Everyone is so damn serious. Come, help me fetch some water."

They grabbed two buckets each and headed down to the river. Samuel remembered many such trips when they were growing up. Jeremy's family were farmers, as were most of the other villagers, and they had little time for fun at any time of the year. Scraping a living from the land required that everyone do their share, including the young ones. So the friends found ways of having their good times while accomplishing their chores.

"Are you still the best with that bow of yours?" asked Jeremy. The earl, like most lords, required that all the young men living on his lands be trained in the art of marksmanship with the longbow. If the town needed to provide men for war, they would be prepared. During their training in Northwood, no one in town could match Samuel's skills, though Jeremy came the closest.

Samuel smiled sheepishly. "My captain at Warkworth says he's never seen anyone with a better eye for the bow." He shrugged. "I never put that much effort into it."

"I just pray it serves you well when you need it most." Jeremy had become serious. When Samuel first left to join Northumberland's guard, it had seemed like an adventure to them all, but now that real battles were being fought and lives lost by the hundreds, he feared for his old friend every day that passed.

Samuel could not dwell on such thoughts. "Don't worry, Jeremy. For all we know, there's already been some settlement to the issue and there will be no more fighting." He wished he could believe that himself.

Arriving at the river, they filled their buckets and began the more arduous return journey. It was another overcast morning and every field and road was soaked. The dampness made him feel cold to his very bones. He had never seen the Tyne run so full or fast.

Samuel stared at the path before them. The wattle-and-daub huts of Northwood huddled around the stone church at the center of town, its thick rectangular walls and timber roof seeming the only permanent structure in town, with the possible exception of the mill.

Growing up, this was his world and it had seemed so natural. But now he had seen the great castle of Warkworth and many of the rapidly growing towns between here and there. Now Northwood seemed somehow pathetic. If not for the comforting faces of his loved ones, he'd have fled and never returned.

"Do you want to hold my son?" Jeremy said with a broad grin. Samuel saw that his friend hadn't changed a bit since they last spent time together. He silently wished he could say the same about himself.

That same evening in London, Edmund, the Earl of Rutland, watched from the window of the great hall of Baynards Castle, his father's house, as sheets of rain pelted the ground below. A fire crackled in the massive stone hearth, backlighting the gargoyle andirons and casting a flickering light on the Flemish tapestries adorning the length and breadth of the chamber walls. The waters of the River Thames, made dark by the gloomy evening, swirled past the south wall.

Edmund could not remember another time when the rain had been so persistent for so long. On his journey from Ireland with his father he saw that much of the kingdom's crops had been ruined by flooding, and he knew that many Englishmen this year would lose their perpetual battle against starvation, even if they managed to avoid a marauding army or pitched battle in their fields. He paced between a large oak table in the center of the room and the window, wondering what was taking his brother

Edward so long to arrive. Ever since their father, the Duke of York, had separated them almost a year ago, he had prayed for a safe reunion. For most of his seventeen years he had known only war, and he still saw no end to the deadly cycle. A sudden gust of wind lashed a wave of rain against the window just as the huge wooden doors of the Great Room came open with a fury. Edmund turned to see his brother Edward, the Earl of March, standing with his usual smile wide across his face.

"Edward!" He sprang across the room and embraced his brother, almost knocking him to the ground. "I thank God to see you well!"

"And I, you," Edward said heartily.

"There's not a scratch on you," said Edmund as he examined Edward's face in disbelief. "How is it you come away from Northampton so unscathed?"

"It was as if God held his hands around me during the entire battle," said Edward, crossing himself. He closed the doors to the great room and together they walked back to the fireplace. Edward held his hands over the flames, but seemed to take little comfort from the heat. "I never knew how it would really feel to be surrounded by such tumult. To speak the truth, much of the battle is hard to recall. I was fully engaged, Edmund, surrounded by flashing swords; the air was thick with arrows. There were times, I swear, when I couldn't tell if it was friend or foe around me." For a moment he paused, the visions of blood and bodies mangled beyond recognition hard in his mind. "God's blood, it was intoxicating." He blinked and the smile returned to his face. "The whole time I was wishing you could have been there by my side. What a brace of warriors we would have made!"

"If only Father had let me join you instead of hiding with him in Ireland." Edmund could not keep the bitterness from his voice. "But is it true that Buckingham and the noble Talbot are slain?"

"Their bodies lay by the king's tent when we arrived, hacked and bloodied. As for Buckingham, a well deserved end. But Lord Talbot was an honest man and a great warrior. I still grieve for him." Edward stared at the flames, the fireglow dancing on his face. Suddenly he was angry. "But he betrayed us and went to the queen. Why would he do that, Edmund? We gave him our love."

"These are deadly times, Edward. No one knows from day to day who holds authority over his life. The French wars were easy for Lord Talbot, for there was no mistaking the face of the enemy."

"The king has failed to keep the peace," said Edward, "and he lost all that was gained in France by his father. It is clear that our father must take the throne. He is the only one of royal blood who has the strength."

"Many will call him usurper," Edmund said, "and many more will pay the price for our actions with their dearest blood."

"You speak like a priest. Do you propose to let haughty Margaret murder us all? She is hated by the commons. Were it not for their fondness for the weakling King Henry, the people of the realm would rise as one and send her packing to France from whence she came."

"I despise her and all the Lancastrians as much as you," said Edmund, "but history is our enemy. They who seize power by force spend their lives protecting themselves against others who would do the same. It has always been so."

"Be that as it may, it is too late for regrets. Northampton has sealed our fates and we must take what fortune has given us."

Without responding, Edmund walked to the wall opposite the fireplace. A huge Flemish tapestry depicting two jousting knights surrounded by adoring spectators covered the entire wall.

"And when you become king, as you will one day if Father takes the throne, will we still be friends? Will we still laugh and speak as we always did before?"

Again the wind drove the rain against the window with a loud shudder. The sadness in Edmund's voice had moved Edward. They had been raised together at Ludlow Castle near the Welsh border, apart from their eight other brothers and sisters, and had been inseparable since birth.

"God willing, it will be a Christmas to remember for us all." He thought for a moment. "Do you remember our last Christmas at Ludlow? We hardly knew that a world existed outside our walls even though these wars bedeviled us even then. I never saw so much food in all my life. Even Oliver sickened himself with too much food."

Edward smiled at the thought of Edmund's adoring page. "How is Oliver?"

"He is well and never misses a chance to take advantage of my kindness."

"Edmund, I swear to you that when I am king, I will not change." His brother watched the flames dance over the logs that they slowly consumed and said nothing.

The following morning, in the east courtyard of Baynards Castle, Oliver prepared his master's horse for a long journey. All around him, the frenzied activities of dozens of knights and retainers made it difficult for him to concentrate. They were all preparing to escort the Duke of York and his party to the north. A further escort of three thousand fighting men waited beyond the city walls at St. John's Field, including a much smaller contingent assigned to Edward, whose duty would be to scour the west counties for more troops.

Oliver saw the duke with the Earl of March off near the stable doors, Edward appearing to listen intently to a long set of instructions from his father. Oliver fastened his jerkin against the cold breeze. He was standing ankle-deep in thick mud as he held Edmund's horse by the bridle.

"Good morning, Oliver." He had not noticed Edmund approaching from behind, so steeped had he been in his own discomfort.

"Good morning, my lord," he said, bowing deeply from the waist.

The horse twitched with pleasure at the sight of his master. Edmund calmed him with reassuring strokes and soft words.

"Are you ready for a long journey, Oliver?"

"Very well prepared, thank you, my lord, though I fear the roads will be difficult indeed thanks to all this bloody rain." Oliver looked down on his mud-caked shoes with disgust.

Edmund could not help but smile at the sight of his page so pointedly miserable. "Tell the supply sergeant to let you ride in one of the wagons. There's no reason for you to walk all the way to Sandal Castle on these roads."

"Thank you, my lord!" After a quick bow, he bounded off in search of the sergeant.

Edward, having heard the last of his father's interminable advice, walked over and slapped Edmund on the back. "I wish you were coming with us," he said. With him was his friend Sir William Hastings, who, though ten years older, was Edward's boon companion, sharing his zest for carousing and late-night antics.

"Father insists I go with him," said Edmund, "and there's no changing his mind. But I'll see you at Sandal Castle before long."

"And when we lock horns with the queen we'll be side by side as we teach her where her cares should be," said Edward.

"That may be difficult," interjected Hastings, "since we don't know where the queen is, or even if she's still in England."

"I'll warrant you she's gone no farther than Scotland," said Edward. "The Scottish king would jump at any opportunity to gain territory from English soil."

Hastings shook his head. "I don't think he's got the stomach for it, my lord. He knows we have friends in his court who would make deadly trouble for him if he waged war against us. At most he'll give her sanctuary and maybe a few fighting men, but nothing that need concern us. The French king concerns me more closely, as he will surely send her help, and if it's substantial, she will have a formidable force."

"It would be easy to raise many fighting men against such an army. The common folk hate the French like nothing else."

"I pray you're right, my lord," said Hastings.

"Most of those commoners you're talking about," Edmund objected, "still love King Henry and may not rush to our aid as quickly as you may think. I've seen it wherever we travel. His pious and gentle ways have endeared him to the people. If he had had the sense to marry an English queen instead of a French one, we would not have gotten this far."

"And maybe the kingdom would have been governed better," said Edward, "but instead there has been nothing but chaos for decades."

Turmoil sounded from the gates of the courtyard. They turned to see the Earl of Warwick and his father, the Earl of Salisbury, enter, their huge warhorses exhaling steam as they pranced by. The Nevilles handed their reins to servants and walked over to where the Duke of York was busy giving last-minute instructions to the captain of his escort.

"Our father doesn't seem too pleased to hear the news," said Edmund, watching the lords. Turning to Hastings, he said, "Sir William, I wonder if I might have a moment with my brother?"

"As you wish, my lord." Then to Edward, "I'll see to our horses."

Edward watched him go, then turned to his brother. "What is it, Edmund? You look more distracted than usual."

"I don't know. That's the problem. I just wanted to spend a moment with you before we went our separate ways, I suppose."

Edward looked into his brother's eyes, something he usually knew better than to do.

"I had a dreadful dream last night."

"It must have been bad indeed to upset you so."

Edmund's horse grew restless. "I dreamt you were king, sitting on a great throne, but when you asked for pledges from the lords, they turned their backs as one and refused. You were so terribly alone. I tried to speak but had no voice and no one paid me any attention, not even you. It was if I were not there at all." He shuddered at the memory.

"These dreams are only the manifestation of your fears," Edward consoled him with a forced smile. "There is no truth to them."

Edmund looked at him for a moment, then smiled weakly. "Perhaps you're right." The Neville earls were still talking with the duke. It looked like they were finally coming to some conclusions over strategies, and Edmund felt a renewed fear. "It was good to see you again, Edward," he said. "If even for this short time."

Edward could sense that more needed to be said, and he longed for the time, but at that moment York, Warwick, and Salisbury approached.

"It's just as I feared, Edward," barked the duke. "The northern lords have rallied to the queen's aid and have been raising troops against us. You must leave with haste to the western counties, where I have good cause to hope you will find friends willing to help us. Are you prepared?"

"I shall not fail, Father. I need only take my leave of my brother and I'll be off."

"Your brother will see you at Sandal Castle. Your mission is vital and time is short."

Hastings brought Edward's horse to him and mounted his own. "Your escort stands ready, my lord," he said.

"God's protection be with you, my son," added the Duke of York.

Edward looked desperately at Edmund. They embraced. "Until Christmas, then."

Edmund nodded, and Edward mounted his horse. Just as his brother was about to apply the spurs, Edmund grabbed the halter and for his brother's ears only said, "For God's sake, Edward, don't let them have your soul." Before his brother could respond, Edmund released the halter and slapped the horse on the rump. Edward took one last look back to the gathering in the courtyard and then disappeared into the streets of London.

His father's voice intruded into Edmund's dark mood. "I'm sorry you couldn't go with him, son," he said, "but the business we pursue is vital to the kingdom, and such causes require sacrifices."

Edmund was not about to tell the duke that his inability to join Edward was not the cause of his moody behavior. His father wanted to be king, and good intentions notwithstanding would pay any price for the crown. "I understand, Father," Edmund said and, leading his horse toward the captain of the guard, began making final preparations for the long journey to Sandal Castle.

CHAPTER II

"Lord Clifford, what news from Pembroke and Northumberland?" In the short time Margaret had been Henry's queen she had learned the English language well, but still spoke with a thick French accent that betrayed her lineage. She was attended in the meeting hall of Pontefract Castle by her husband's two staunchest allies, Clifford and Somerset, and by her typically large entourage. She sat on a dining chair as though it were a throne.

The wolflike Clifford, his hand on his sword, spoke to his queen. "Majesty, the Earl of Pembroke has your warrant to raise men in the west and will meet us here with all possible haste, but it may be another month before he can join us. The Earl of Northumberland will join us soon with his northern army. Together with the ten thousand already here, we shall have a formidable strength."

"And my son," said the queen. "Have you seen to his safety?"

"He is closely guarded in the sleeping chambers, Highness," responded Henry Beaufort, the Duke of Somerset. The queen looked away, but Somerset stood his ground.

"My lady, if I might be so bold," the duke continued, "it is my belief that we should strike as quickly as possible toward London. Now — when the rebels are flush with their victory and unprepared for another battle."

Somerset was ill advised to remind the queen of the Yorkist victory at Northampton. Her expression turned sour.

"My lord of Somerset, we will not risk our son's life again unless we are certain of victory. When Northumberland arrives, we will be well prepared to fight again. Besides, if the impetuous Duke of York remains true to form, he will come here to seek us out. And when he does, we shall give the traitors the welcome they deserve." One of her advisors stooped to whisper something in her ear.

"My lady, it is not always wise to allow the enemy to attack on their terms," Somerset pleaded. "Lord Clifford, you must help me to convince Her Highness."

"I will not," said Clifford, "since my mind and hers are one in this matter."

The queen regarded Somerset casually. If only his father still lived, she thought. He had been her greatest supporter and advisor, and she still mourned his death. From the moment of her arrival in this dreadful land, Edmund Beaufort had stood by her and helped her to understand the vagaries of these crude people. *My dear Beaufort. I begged you to avoid that battle.*

She stood, signaling a frenzy of activity among her train.

"My lords, please advise us upon the arrival of Northumberland. For now, we grow tired and would retire." With that, she left the room, her train with her.

Somerset watched her leave. "I pray you're right, Clifford. We both know this is not a popular queen, and given time the rebels are likely to raise many troops from among the wavering noble families."

"Regardless of how they feel about the queen, the people still love their king, and while he is a prisoner in the Tower, their sympathies are with us." He took a step closer to the duke to bring his entire menacing self to bear. "As for the wavering noble families, my father too was slaughtered by the Yorkist traitors. I will be God's avenging angel for all those who side with York. I swear it on Saint Thomas' bones."

Clifford turned his back and strode from the room. A page entered from another door. "Your Grace, the queen asks that you join her in her closet."

The duke nodded and dismissed him with a wave of his hand. *His anger will serve us well,* he thought, *but it will be his undoing before this war is over.*

In private chambers, Somerset waited patiently while the queen rummaged through papers that required the royal seal. She had assumed the right to govern in her husband's name during his absence. The fact the Yorkists did not recognize such authority mattered to her not in the least.

"My lord of Somerset," she said, finally fixing her sharp brown eyes on the duke. "You know our pleasure. Have you found Lady Katherine?" Her advisors continued to hand her papers as she finished signing the previous one.

"I have not, in all fairness, Your Highness, had time to continue the search, being predisposed to find fighting men for the wars instead."

"We know your worth, my lord, of that you may be assured." The duke bowed with thanks, assuming the best of the comment. "However, the apprehension of that girl is most important to us, and despite the need to fight against this cursed rebellion, it remains our primary wish that she be found." She pushed an advisor away before he could proffer another document. Her casual mood shifted to an angrier one. "Without her in our custody, victory over these rebels would be rendered meaningless." Now, even the courtiers fixed their attention on the duke.

"I assure Your Highness I shall redouble my efforts." Somerset wiped a bead of sweat from his brow. "But to find an individual who has disappeared into the common throng in these tumultuous times will not be an easy task."

"Be that as it may, we want her, and soon. Are we clear on that point, my lord?"

"Quite clear, my lady."

"Good," she said severely, "then you may leave us." The duke bowed deeply and left the room. Margaret gazed at the spot he had vacated. *No, young Somerset, you will never be the man your father was.*

Emma and Samuel sat together near the wheelhouse waiting for Christopher. The river was still several feet higher than normal and the torrents of murky water swept past the millhouse at a frightening pace, the half-submerged river willows along the shore bent almost horizontal against the force.

"I can't see how you're going to get down there," Emma worried. A large branch had been swept under the mill wheel by the flood and was jammed between the wheel and its housing. The branch had to be removed — and quickly — or the mill would be paralyzed.

"We'll wade over to the other side and use the sluice wall," said Samuel. "It doesn't look too bad."

The two stared at the water, thinking their own thoughts. Somewhere behind them, someone was shouting for a child. The smell of wood burning permeated the air. "I don't think I can remember the last time I saw the sun," said Samuel, looking up at the gray, misty sky.

"I'm frightened, Samuel," Emma said unexpectedly. "It's not bad enough that I'll soon be going through what Edith just did, but now I have to worry about you as well. Every time you leave, I wonder if I will ever see you again. Do you know what that's like?"

Samuel did indeed. "Every time I pick up my longbow, I remember these woods near Northwood where I spent so many hours alone. I know these trails so well." He stopped for a moment, remembering the smell of damp woods. "Each time I pack up my arrows, I try to remember everyone's face in my mind one last time. Just in case." He hugged her.

She put her head on his shoulder. "You know, your brother worries a great deal about you too." Samuel said nothing, watching in silence as the river boiled over a submerged boulder, creating a whirlpool on the downstream side. Emma lifted her head, suddenly angry. "Why is it so hard for you to believe that? I can see it clearly in everything he does when you're around. He only wants you to respect him for what he is."

"And what exactly is he?" Hardness tainted his voice.

"For one thing, he's your brother." Her disappointment with Samuel showed. "And he feels very responsible for everything that happens to you all."

"You didn't grow up with him, Emma. You don't know what we had to endure."

"Maybe not, but I can't help wondering what was so horrible that you can't put it behind you." She stood up and walked to the stream's edge, letting Samuel think about what she had told him. She pulled her wrap up around her shoulders against the chill in the morning air and looked out over the rooftops of the village. Beyond the thatched roofs, the planting fields stretched away from the town, waiting for the spring tilling. The stubble of last year's crop was still scattered haphazardly over the dark earth. It was all very familiar.

At last, Christopher, John Miller, and Sally appeared from around the corner of the millhouse and came down to the river wall. Christopher was carrying a rope coiled around his neck.

"Are you ready to do this?" Christopher said, surveying the wheel.

"Let's get it over with," said Samuel. He pulled his light tunic over his head and slipped out of his sandals, then took the rope from Christopher and tied one end around his waist. He handed the other end of the rope to his brother and waded slowly into the current.

"Watch your step near the sluice," said John Miller. "It's bound to be slick."

Indeed, it was. Samuel fought to keep his feet on the mossy surface of the sluice as the water became deeper. He had splashed around in this river often in his youth, but he could not remember the water ever being so fast, or so cold. At last he reached the far wall of the channel and climbed out of the water, shivering some feeling back into his numb limbs.

"Off you go, Christopher," John Miller said when he saw that Samuel had finished the crossing. "Do it just like your brother."

"I know how it's done," Christopher glared at his father. Samuel braced himself on the other side and watched as his brother waded in.

Surprised by the icy water, Christopher panicked and tried to quicken his pace, fighting for a grip on the mossy sluice. Almost within an arm's reach of the far wall, still struggling against the current, he lost his footing for a moment and fell backward. Samuel quickly pulled him the last few feet to the wall, and Christopher hauled himself out of the water. On the other side, Emma crossed herself with relief.

The brothers walked along the far wall until they reached the wheel. They could hardly hear each other over the roar of the rushing water. They saw the branch, a stout portion of an ash tree.

"I can't see how we're going to budge that thing," Christopher yelled.

"Let's tie the rope around it and pull it together."

Christopher nodded, and Samuel leaned down over the wall to tie the rope onto the fattest part of the branch. The two men braced themselves on the wall and tugged on the line with all their strength.

The branch would not budge. Finally, they collapsed on the bank, defeated and worn out. And still the water ran on past the frozen mill wheel. The brothers knew the branch had to be dislodged, somehow, or…the alternative was grim. The entire village needed that wheel to move. John Miller still stood on the other shore with Emma and Sally, and the sight filled Samuel with a new strength. He crawled toward the wheel.

"What are you doing?" yelled Christopher.

"Just keep a strong hold on that rope," he yelled back. Taking a grip on the side of the huge wheel, he lowered himself back into the freezing water and stepped precariously onto the branch itself. His father and sisters were screaming from the shore and he knew what they were saying, though he couldn't make out the words, but what he was about to do had to be done.

"Pull!" he yelled at his brother, then began to jump on the base of the branch with all the force he could bring to bear. The branch shifted under him, swayed, then with a whoosh broke free. Samuel's feet flew out from under him, and he was tossed in the swift current, clinging to the wheel with his cold wet hands. He could hear screaming from his family as he struggled to pull himself out. With the strength that comes from desperate need alone, he finally lifted his legs over to the wall and flopped out of the water like a freshly caught fish.

"Are you all right?" asked Christopher, astonished that his brother would take such a risk. He still held the rope tied to the branch, which bobbed in the current beside them.

"I'm fine," Samuel coughed. "Let's get rid of that thing before it gets jammed again."

They pulled it to them and lifted it over their heads to the river side of the wall and let it fly. They watched for a moment as it drifted out of sight.

They crossed back to the near bank, arriving wet and shivering.

"That was a foolish chance you took," John Miller chided Samuel. But Christopher saw the admiration in his father's eyes.

"If you ever do something like that again…" Emma didn't know whether to be mad or happy. She placed a cloak around his shoulders.

"I was there, too," said Christopher.

"Of course you were, husband," she said, giving him his cloak. "We were just worried, that's all."

They all walked back to the house, where Sally prepared hot bowls of stew.

CHAPTER III

Edward, Earl of March, lay awake under his bedspread contemplating the naked young girl beside him. Hastings had an eye for beauty and had found her feeding pigs outside the town of Oxford. Even though it took his retainers a good hour to clean her up, once done she was quite attractive. Edward marveled to himself how the perfect shape of her buttocks was apparent even through the bed covers. And she was marvelous company, the kind Edward liked most: awed by his presence, she had little to say unless responding to questions. But when it came time to please him, she withheld no favors and gladly accommodated his every desire.

Still, in the sobering light of the morning, his lust quite satisfied, he felt strangely empty. He sat up with his arms cradled around his knees, staring intently at a point somewhere in the middle of his tent. Normally, while traveling through the country, he would stay with some noble family as a guest. On this trip he felt more secure sleeping with his escort, as if it were a campaign. It was important for his men to remember that a state of war did exist and he wanted them battle ready.

He heard the men of the morning watch going about their duties, preparing food and seeing to the horses. "Are you risen, my lord?" a voice called from outside the canvas.

"Come ahead, Sir William," said Edward, recognizing Hastings' voice. Shaking off the morning haze from his thoughts, he threw off his bedcoverings, pulled on his linen drawers, and began splashing cold water on his face from his washbasin. Hastings could not help but notice what a fine figure of a man Edward had become. Easily the tallest man in his entourage, he was broad-chested with well-muscled arms and shoulders, flawlessly lean. His sharp blue eyes were framed by thick brown hair that this morning was quite disheveled.

"Sir William! What news this morning?" Edward was pleasant but not as jovial as Hastings had expected him to be, given the evening's activities. He looked to where the young girl had ducked beneath the bedcovers and wondered if she had not been entirely satisfactory for the earl.

"I trust you had a pleasant evening, my lord?" Edward asked.

"Quite pleasant, thank you," he said after a quick glance at the bed. Hastings was relieved. "By the way, what's her name?"

"To be honest, I didn't take time to ask her, my lord. What is your name, wench?" he called over to the bed. A muffled sound came from somewhere underneath the thick covers. Hastings stepped to the bed and pulled the covers off. The startled young girl sat up holding her arms modestly over her breasts.

"What is your name?" Hastings repeated the question now that he had her full attention.

"Letitia, if you please, my lord," she said in a barely audible voice.

"Letitia," repeated Edward, rolling the word off his tongue. "What an unusual name. What does it mean?" He felt every name should have a purpose.

"It was my mother's name, my lord," she responded timidly. "God rest her soul."

"Is she dead, then?" asked Edward.

"Yes, my lord. The black death took her two years ago." Hastings took an involuntary step backward and Edward hurriedly crossed himself with exaggerated reverence. Few earthly terrors conjured up fear as did mention of the black death, a plague that had taken the lives of a third of the subjects of the realm not a hundred years past.

"Two years ago, you say?" Edward glared at her.

"Yes, my lord, it was two years, I swear." Edward and Hastings relaxed with that assurance. Edward pulled a long sleeved tunic over his head and tightened the leather fasteners. Over that he pulled a looser, fur-lined cloak which he fastened with a small gold brooch, shaped in the image of a stylized rose.

"Sir William, it's time we take to the road again. Has our post returned from Gloucester?" Edward had sent several messengers out to the western towns of the Welsh marches requiring fighting men from any who wished to retain the good wishes of the Duke of York. He knew that the queen was also raising troops in the same area using the Earl of Pembroke as her agent, and therefore time was of the essence.

"The post has returned, my lord," said Hastings. "Your father's troops are mustering near Gloucester. Pembroke's whereabouts are still unknown, but these people are loyal to your father, fear them not. The queen's name will invoke little love here."

"I have faith that you're right, Sir William. Where is my confessor?"

"He awaits your pleasure outside. Shall I call him in?"

"He makes my penance more severe when I keep him waiting too long, so I suppose you had better." There was a sound like a throat clearing behind them, which reminded them that Letitia was still in the bed, naked and shivering.

"I suppose you had better get dressed before he comes in here," said Edward. She sprang up and gratefully started pulling on her clothes. "I imagine I'll be saying a few extra Hail Marys on your account anyway, but there's no point making him crazy at the sight of female flesh. I could be on my knees till noon."

"And now you may send in my confessor," Edward said, turning to Hastings. "It's time we get on the road to Gloucester, before the queen's men have a chance to prevail upon these wavering noble families."

With a slight bow of his head, Hastings took Letitia and left the tent. A moment later, Father Dennis entered through the flap. "Good morning, my son. I trust you slept well?" he asked after looking pointedly and disapprovingly at the rumpled bedcovers.

"Very well, thank you, Father. And yourself?"

"Our Lord in Heaven has not granted me the gift of carefree nights, my son. I carry the sins of the world with me, which leaves little time for anything but prayer." Edward wondered if he was about to get one of Father Dennis' long sermons regarding the evils of the flesh. But instead, his confessor said simply, "Come, let us begin. We have much to pray for today."

Edward knelt before Father Dennis and began the long litany of prayer that started every day of his life. As he feared, it was an extra-long session that morning.

"Are you going to the christening for Jeremy and Edith's new baby? Samuel and I are to stand as sponsors." Emma was pleased at the prospect of being a godparent.

It had been two days since the branch had been freed. Samuel had spent most of the time with Jeremy. Emma wanted to see more of Samuel but was disappointed that things had not improved between him and Christopher. She and Sally were now preparing the evening meal, which she hoped Samuel would stay at the mill long enough to share.

"Of course I'll be there," said Sally, a thin smile finally gracing her face. "You know I wouldn't miss it for anything."

After a moment Emma asked, "Is it true what I hear about the Smith's son, Stephen?"

"What have you heard?" Sally asked sharply.

"Only that he takes every opportunity to talk with you, and that he tends to pay more attention to you in church than to his prayers."

Sally was indignant, "I don't know who told you that but it is simply not true. And even if it were, I can't see what that has to do with me."

"Very well," Emma's reply was followed by a heavy sigh. "But I did see you two talking closely at the village garden last week."

The garden was an area near the church set apart from the crop fields on which the villagers grew vegetables such as peas, beans, cabbage, and spinach. A communal effort, they'd found, yielded better crops — though, to be sure, each family still had its own plot around its cottage. Sally spent a great deal of time tending it, not only because she had no children yet to tend, but also because she enjoyed the garden a great deal. Naturally, that was where she frequently talked with the smith's son. And despite her protestations, she did enjoy his company.

There was a disturbance at the front door. Someone was talking and kicking the mud off his feet. Sally was glad for the interruption. She jumped up to open the door and found outside, still working to remove the black mud from their feet, Jeremy and his father, Gilbert, the town reeve.

The reeve was a local farmer selected by the villagers for a term to oversee the earl's work around Northwood. It was a post that was coveted not so much because of the authority it gave but because to be elected was a demonstration of honor and respect from one's fellow villagers.

Gilbert had been elected reeve just earlier that month and was still uncomfortable in the role. Though few villagers had his skill behind a plowshare, in the ways of politics he was clearly a farmboy.

Sally had always liked Gilbert, especially his quick wit and easy smile. She smiled to see him hopping on one foot and scowling at the mud on his other foot.

"Welcome, Gilbert," she said, giggling. "Please come in."

"Thank you, young miss," he said lightly, returning to his dirty task. "This bloody mud will be the death of us," he mumbled. At last they were clean enough to enter, and Emma served mugs of barley ale while the men sat at the table close to the hearth, allowing the heat to chase the chill.

"Where is Samuel?" asked Gilbert.

"He's in the mill with his father and brother," said Emma, stirring the porridge again.

"You'd better call them all. We have difficult news."

Emma looked at Jeremy. "My God. Is it Edith?"

"Edith and the child are both well, Emma," Jeremy quickly reassured her.

She exhaled loudly. "You gave me a scare. What news is this, then?"

"I have to ask you again to call the men here, Emma. It is news they must hear."

"I'll get them," Sally volunteered.

They all sat silently until the miller and his sons arrived from the mill room.

"Gilbert, you have news for us, I'm told." John Miller said as they entered.

"I've a message from Warkworth, an order from the earl himself." He took a large swallow of ale, further heightening the tension around him. He was choosing his words carefully.

"Then tell us," said Samuel impatiently.

"The earl has recalled all his retainers, and that includes you, of course, Samuel. What's more, we're to send him five more able bodies. You're all to be on your way by the time the sun rises again."

Sally and Emma were crestfallen. It meant Samuel would not be spending Christmas with them and, far worse than that, he would in all likelihood be going into battle with the earl. Samuel sat emotionless staring at the table. He did not know why this news had surprised him so. It was

Christopher who broke the silence.

"Did the messenger give any news of what is afoot?"

"He said only that new armies are needed to fight the rebellion."

So the war continues, thought Samuel. "There's no use feeling sad about it," he said. "We have no choice but to comply. Have you found the other five men?"

"Tonight we gather at the church and choose. I should think we'll have enough who are willing. And Jeremy will be one."

Samuel's jaw dropped and the rest stood in stunned silence.

"But he has a new child to care for," Sally finally spoke what the others were thinking.

"He has a duty to the earl, and I won't have it said that I would send another to war but not my son."

"Surely you will have enough volunteers. Edith will need him." Emma was incensed.

"The decision is made. I will see to Edith while he's away. My son understands." Jeremy said nothing but nodded his head in agreement.

"How can you send him into these wars with no formal training?" Samuel could be silent no longer. "These are bloody wars, and he'll not know how to protect himself."

"He'll have as much training as the rest of them, except for yourself, Samuel. And I'm sure you'll look out for him."

Samuel felt a great weight on his shoulders.

"I'm going to the church," Sally said and made for the door.

"Wait. I'll go with you," said Emma. She swung the kettle of porridge away from the flames, and together they left.

Edmund stood atop the barbican of Sandal Castle, a single tower directly over the main gates. From his vantage point he commanded an extraordinary view of the surrounding countryside in all directions. Low clouds scoured the gently rolling hills as they swept slowly to the east, leaving pockets of fog in their wake. To the north, across a low copse and the River Calder, the town of Wakefield lay nestled between two low hills, betrayed only by a handful of thatched roofs. While it was too distant to make out human activity, Edmund imagined the townsfolk there, busily going about their daily tasks.

Edmund felt uncommonly at peace. Behind him, the activities of castle life filled the courtyard. Chickens, pigs, and sundry other animals wandered wherever they had a notion. Hundreds of diverse chores were being performed by dozens of servants.

Edmund saw a man approach dressed in the plush, velvet-lined habit of a bishop. The Bishop of Exeter waved to catch Edmund's attention as he strode toward him along the allure. Edmund bolstered himself for the interruption. Though he liked the bishop, he did not want company.

George Neville was the Earl of Warwick's younger brother, and another high-placed member of that powerful family. When older brothers took all the attractive hereditary titles in a noble house, their younger kin were often left to join the clergy. But in the case of the Neville family, powerful bishoprics were usually available. The bishop was a large man like his brother. Though not honed by years of military combat and not as imposing in appearance, he had the same penetrating pale blue eyes.

"Well met, Your Grace," said Edmund when the bishop arrived on the platform. "Had I but known you wished to speak to me, I would have come down to you." *Or run the other way.*

"Thanks for your greeting, my lord." Edmund kissed the bishop's ring. "You have found a wonderful place to admire the Lord's work," he said.

"I used to spend many hours in a similar place at Ludlow where Edward and I grew up. There was a high turret from where, I swear, you could see all of the Welsh highlands. I can't tell you how many hours I spent there when I needed to be alone."

"I normally would not wish to intrude into another's solitude, but I felt it would be an opportune time for us to talk."

"You are not intruding, Your Grace," said Edmund. "It was a long journey from London and I was only taking a moment to refresh myself."

"I see your father was quite successful raising troops along the way." He gestured at the hundreds of campsites of the billeted troops outside the walls of the castle.

"There are many who always seem willing to go to war for one cause or another."

The bishop let the comment go. "My father tells me French Margaret is holed up nearby in Pontefract, and has offered a Christmas truce."

"Yes, the envoy from the queen came yesterday. Father was only too content to grant a truce, since it will be some weeks before Edward can arrive with his help." Edmund flicked an ant from the parapet and watched it fly out of sight on its way to the moat below. "I pray he arrives soon."

The bishop turned to face him. "Tell me what's troubling you, my son. I have seen a dark mood on you since you returned from Ireland."

Edmund considered his answer for a moment, wondering if he really wanted to confide in this man. "I can't help feeling I'm never going to see my brother again," he said at last.

The bishop seemed to understand. "You must have faith that history will bend to God's will. We who are true to His wishes will be blessed with victory in the end."

"These are not heathens we fight, Your Grace, but our cousins."

"It is for God alone to judge the right and wrong of all things. Being all of us wayward children, we can only do that which we feel in our hearts is true. The grace of God will protect us from folly."

"Can you tell me here, before God, that our cause is holy? To rebel against His anointed king, and to take up arms against the peace? Is that what you came up here to tell me?"

The bishop stared out over the lonely winter-killed fields. "I cannot honestly say if there is a right or wrong in these proceedings, but the loss of our French possessions and the Lancastrians' own inability to make peace among themselves has caused this turmoil in the kingdom, not any actions taken by your father. I believe that you are taking too much responsibility on your shoulders. Times are changing all around us, my son. Even among the common people there is a restless mood, as if the values that have bound us together since the birth of the Savior are no longer sufficient. They seek more from life than ever before; they now expect such things as comfort of the flesh and beauty in this life."

"Is it so wrong to seek beauty and happiness?"

"It is wrong only if one forgets that such things are God's alone to bestow, and the pursuit of such worldliness stands between us and Paradise like a great wall."

"It is a hard life you would condemn us to, Your Grace."

"It is written that the rewards are greatest for those who sacrifice the most." He put his hand on Edmund's shoulder. "Will you not tell what has put you in such a melancholy state?"

"I am honestly not sure I know myself, Your Grace," he answered. "I've had feelings of foreboding; just glimpses of something that frightens me, but there is no shape or definition to them."

"Perhaps you simply fear the outcome of these wars and the possible fate of your family. It is a common thing."

"I do not fear death, Your Grace," Edmund said forcefully. "I only experience these feelings when I'm with my brother, as if the bond between us flows like a river." A thought occurred to him. "Do you suppose a sacrifice would be made in vain if it were made for a cause one did not believe in?"

The bishop looked intently at the young man, puzzled by the nature of his question.

"I would think that would depend upon the motivation behind the sacrifice. One's intentions are meaningless. Unless the soul is pure, all actions will come to ruin."

"But who among us is truly pure of soul?"

"I speak of the purity that comes of faith. He who plunges into the abyss of the unknown for the sake of his own soul need have no fear, for to him, the Lord promises salvation."

Edmund's composure seemed to change as the bishop watched, as if a conundrum eating at his psyche had finally been resolved.

"What is it, my son?" the prelate asked quietly.

Edmund smiled. "I am no longer troubled, Your Grace. " He left before the bishop could say another thing.

Samuel and Jeremy stood before Pontefract Castle, a dark and foreboding place. They and the other thousands of troops that arrived this morning with the Earl of Northumberland were making camp nearby where the army of the Duke of Somerset and Lord Clifford's men had been billeted for three weeks. They were amazed to see the size of the army that the queen had been able to command, given her lack of popularity and the recent defeat at Northampton. There were easily twenty thousand men-at-arms camped here, half of whom had been raised by Northumberland. And these were not the rabble that were frequently gathered during such arraying, but a disciplined army that had been tested by frequent summonses to battle Scottish incursions. They were northerners, formidable fighters.

Samuel had arranged for Jeremy to camp with him and the rest of Northumberland's personal guard. They had already stowed their few belongings at their sleeping pads, and now had the rest of the day to recuperate from the long march.

Samuel and Jeremy left the campsite and the unusually quiet members of the earl's guard behind and meandered toward Pontefract's moat. The bridge to the courtyard was lowered, but the gate was heavily guarded. At the slightest hint of trouble the bridge could be raised in less time than it would take to cross it. The castle was reputed to be the strongest in the realm, though it had never been tested in a siege. Staring up at the impossibly tall battlements, Samuel silently thanked God he would not be part of the army that first tested it. Located at one end of the castle was the stone keep, a massive structure constructed of one semicircular tower after another all the way around. Stretching away from the keep were the main walls of the castle, far thicker and higher than any he had seen before, which enclosed acres of land and were fortified by seven square towers, the largest of which guarded the main entrance and drawbridge. Two outer walls enclosed even larger areas where the troops were billeted.

Samuel looked out over the countless campfires that dotted the fields surrounding the castle, their smoke mingling with the low fog in the evening gloom. So many men, he thought. He began to shiver against a cold that came from within.

"I never knew it would be so wondrous," remarked Jeremy in awe. He had never before in his life left the area around Northwood. "It's much bigger even than Warkworth."

"The more I see of these castles, the less I like to be near them," Samuel said almost to himself.

"And look at all these men! I never thought to see such a gathering of men-at-arms." He counted off more than fifty small fires just in the small area nearest to them.

"I wish you hadn't come, Jeremy."

Jeremy refocused his attention on his friend. "You're afraid, aren't you?" It was not an accusation but a simple observation. "I never thought you were afraid of anything."

"What do you see out there, Jeremy? Do you see their thirst for blood?

Don't be fooled. That's only a mask to hide the fear every one of them feels, and I'm no different. You don't become braver after many battles. You just learn to hide it better."

Jeremy shivered against the night's chill. "Will I be with you when the battle begins?"

"When it begins and when it ends, my friend. I promise you that." Samuel closed his eyes hoping to see the faces of his family, but once again there was only the darkness he shared with Pontefract Castle.

In Pontefract, Clifford, Northumberland, and his son Sir Henry followed a knight past the huge double oak doors of the throne room and into the presence of Queen Margaret. Margaret was seated on the edge of the throne in deep conversation with a man dressed in canonical robes Clifford did not recognize. *No doubt,* he thought with distaste, *a member of the French clergy.*

The queen was dressed for battle in a leather tunic with the red rose symbol of the House of Lancaster emblazoned on the front. She broke off her conversation and held out her hand to Northumberland.

"You are most welcome, my lord of Northumberland," she beamed. The earl kissed her hand.

"I thank Your Highness, and may God protect you and your royal family in these troubled times."

"Rise, noble lords," granted Margaret. "We see in your faces the final victory in this vile rebellion. Lord Clifford, what is the latest intelligence?"

Clifford marveled to himself how relentless this woman could be, and though his personal dislike for her would never change, he had to admire her determination. She was like an arrow in flight; that which stood in her path would surely feel her wrath.

"The rebels are attempting to secure more troops from around the area, but we have intercepted most of their new men for ourselves. They cannot match our numbers."

"Highness, if I may," interjected Somerset. "Sandal is a formidable fortress and we risk a great deal in a frontal assault. We would surely lose more men attempting to breach its walls than the rebels will defending them."

"Do you have a better plan?" she said casually.

"I urge Your Highness still to proceed with haste to London. With our present numbers, we can free the king and secure the throne."

"And leave the rebels to our rear?" Everyone in the room looked to see who had had the temerity to question the duke. Young Henry Percy stood defiantly under their scrutiny, but wondered nevertheless if he should have kept his silence.

"Who is this brash young knight?" the queen finally asked, the severity of her words tinged with mirth.

"Majesty, please forgive the forwardness of my son, Henry," said Northumberland. "He is new to the court and unschooled in when to address his betters."

After considering the young man for a moment, Margaret offered her hand to Sir Henry.

"It may be so, my lord," she said finally, "but he suffers only from the zeal of youth, and we are well served by such courage. Rise, Sir Henry, and be free to render to us your opinion when you feel strongly."

"I thank Your Highness," said Henry as he retreated to his father's side. He did not fail, however, to see Somerset glaring at him.

"Lord Clifford, what say you to my lord of Somerset's advice?"

"Young Henry is right," Clifford asserted in a deliberately loud voice. "We have the chance now to take the traitors and I, for one, cannot wait another year to feel the blood of York on my hands. We can march to London after the rebel York feels the point of my sword."

"We concur," said Margaret. "And do not fear, my lord of Somerset, we have a notion that we will not need to lay siege to Sandal Castle, if York is true to form. Our trap is set from which the rebel duke will not emerge alive. My lords, array your men for battle. Tomorrow before the sun sets, the rebellion will be over."

The queen stood and her train with her. She swept from the room without another word, leaving the four noblemen alone by the throne.

"I pray she is right," said Somerset, "for tomorrow many wives will lose their men."

Clifford did not hear him. His hand was clenched on the haft of his enormous sword, and he looked at no one in particular.

CHAPTER IV

Oliver watched as his master climbed to the top of a flat-topped stone column at the foot of a set of steps and sat looking out over the courtyard. Oliver strode to the foot of the column and sat in silence, hoping his master would notice him.

"Oliver, you need not attend me today," Edmund said tiredly.

"If it's just the same to you, my lord, I have no other matters to tend to, and it's a fair day to be in the courtyard."

Edmund had to smile. A light rain had been falling most of the day and he knew there were any number of places Oliver would rather be.

"I think that I ask too much of you, Oliver," Edmund said. "When was the last time you saw your family?"

"I visited with them once since I was sold into your service, Master, when I was twelve, I think. I remember thinking at the time that they didn't appear to have missed me much. Besides, this is where I'm needed, not there." He stood and stretched his body. "In my estimation, if I had not been sold into your service, I might never have left that little village I was born in. I tell you honestly, my lord, I can't even remember its name." He scratched his head and continued almost to himself, "I wonder if it had one."

A new thought occurred to Edmund. "If we are successful in these struggles and I became a prince, how would you feel about your service then?"

"If that were to be your fate, my lord, I could not serve you any differently than I do now."

Edmund tucked his knees into his chest and wrapped his arms around them. "I don't think that I could be a king," he mused. "I wouldn't like the changes that I'd have to make."

"For some, the lure of such power would be worth a great deal," responded Oliver, shaking the moisture from his hair.

"I don't believe that such people realize the price they have paid until it is too late. Still, I suppose someone has to be king." He thought about that for a moment. "I wonder if King Henry wishes he had been born in that little town of yours that has no name, instead of at the royal palace. Who could possibly envy our great king his prison room in the Tower?"

"Not I, my lord. The kitchen maid's mother is guard enough for me."

Edmund laughed, then turned serious.

"If I should fall in this battle, Oliver, I would like you to commend me to my brother. Tell him that everything I've done was for him." After a moment's hesitation, he added, "And tell him that all I beg in exchange is that he remember well our lives together."

Oliver looked up at his master, surprised by the sudden turn of the conversation. "I do not understand, my lord. And to speak in this way could bring evil fortune." He crossed himself.

"Fortune will find its own way into our lives, Oliver, regardless of our best efforts to control our own destinies. Remember my request."

"As you wish, my lord." Oliver was upset by his master's cavalier attitude toward fate. He should know better than to tempt God, especially when a battle was looming.

"If you wish to marry the young kitchen maid, you have my good leave, Oliver. I would not wish to stand between you and your joy, especially at this time. You are young and should enjoy the advantages of a loving wife and family." Edmund knew that his own future wife would be chosen for him by his father to seal some bargain with another lord. The joys he wished for his page would not be his. "I will even see to it that you have some time together without duties for a while."

"As always, you are most kind, master, but I don't think that I'm ready for a wife yet. The thought of it gives me chills."

"Don't wait too long, my friend," said Edmund softly. "Our youth will be quickly by us."

Oliver was about to inquire of his master's glum mood when their attention was jarred by the clanging of the alarm bell, which set in motion a flurry of activity within the castle. Startled, Edmund jumped up to see the guard in the watch tower furiously ringing the bell. The captain of the watch came out from the base of the main battlement and looked up to the sentry.

"Report!" he demanded impatiently.

"An army, Captain," the sentry shouted pointing to the north. "Thousands strong!"

"Give me a proper report, damn you." The sentry tried to compose himself, and looked out on the field between Wakefield and Sandal. An army was emerging from out of the woods, knights on horses, archers, and a sea of footsoldiers.

"Three hundred horses, Captain," he estimated as he spoke. "And of all other men, between five and six thousand."

The captain was visibly shaken. "How can that be? Give way, you fool." He ran up the spiral stone steps to the allure as the Duke of York and the Earl of Salisbury came out from the great hall, both strapping on their swords. Edmund jumped down from his column and stood at the base of the stairs, followed by Oliver. They all waited impatiently for the captain's report.

"What is the cause for this alarm?" demanded York.

The captain turned at last and reported, "My lords, no less than six thousand fighting men are arrayed without. They wear the colors of Lord Clifford."

"God's blood, this is treachery," cursed the duke. "The queen is sworn to uphold the Christmas truce."

"She has forsworn herself, my lord," said Salisbury, "and she has caught us indeed. Most of my men are gone, gathering food and supplies."

Edmund saw the rage on his father's face, and he knew that the time had come. He prayed for the strength to do what had to be done.

Samuel and Jeremy emerged from the woods before Sandal Castle wondering about Lord Clifford's strategy. Usually, on the day of a battle, the troops would be arrayed at first light to make the most of the day on the battlefield. Since they had arrived late in the day at Sandal, Samuel expected them to make camp and begin the assault the next morning. Instead, as the sun dipped toward the trees, Lord Clifford ordered them out into the open field before the castle, and to stand ready for combat. Clifford was in charge of the operation, with Lords Wiltshire and Roos along to assist. Samuel and the other members of Northumberland's personal guard were assigned to give close support to Lord Clifford, and were in the vanguard of the army.

As they marched around the town of Wakefield, Lord Wiltshire split off from the main army with two thousand men and disappeared into the woods to the west of town. As they approached the edge of the wood in front of Sandal, Lord Roos, with three thousand more soldiers, separated and stood off to east. Clifford, with the rest of the forces, marched boldly out of the woods and stood before the castle.

Samuel and Jeremy stood in the shadow of Clifford's horse wondering about the strategy. There could not have been more than an hour of daylight left, and to begin a siege at this time seemed impossible. But instead of signaling an attack, Clifford sat serenely on his horse and waited.

The Duke of York was livid. That the queen could be a part of such treachery, and during the Christmas week! The drawbridge had been lifted at the first sound of the alarm, and the army outside his walls notwithstanding, the castle was fairly secure. The archers on the walls would be able to cut down hundreds of men if they attempted to cross the moat, making a frontal assault a fool's tactic. But he had not thought to provision the castle against a siege, and certainly there would not be food for five thousand men for more than a few days. At last word, Edward was still weeks away.

"What news?" he yelled toward the sentry post.

Edmund, who had joined the watch after hastily donning his armor and long sword, answered. "They have not advanced. They seem to be waiting for something."

Salisbury, who had just then rejoined the duke after organizing a supply line from the castle dungeons, said, "More than likely they are waiting for some siege equipment. Only Clifford would be so bold as to show his hand before he was prepared."

"We'll see how bold he is," said the duke. To the nearest attendant he snapped, "Summon my guard to their horses and bring me my armor."

Salisbury stared at him in disbelief. "Your Grace cannot be serious."

"I'll not have haughty Clifford stand outside my gates scoffing at me while he waits for more men. Captain, assemble your men!"

"My lord," shouted Salisbury, chasing after the duke, "they have two men for every one of ours. These are dangerous odds."

"They will not be expecting us to strike first. It's the only advantage we have."

At the call to assemble, Edmund told Oliver to prepare his horse and await him with the others in the courtyard. Now as the footsoldiers and horsemen crammed into every available space, they were both waiting for orders. He did not understand why they were assembling instead of preparing for a siege. The call also went out to the troops billeted outside the walls to prepare to join those who were inside at the front gate.

Edmund mounted his horse. "God keep you, Oliver. Stay out of harm's way until this is over, and try to find my brother. He will see to your needs."

"I have you to see to my needs, my lord, and require no other," he said. Edmund nodded and smiled.

They clasped hands and the young earl urged his horse up to where his father was looking over the men from atop his stallion. As everyone stood ready, there was an eerie quiet over the castle. "We are outnumbered, but surprise is on our side," the duke addressed them. "God has blessed our cause with many victories and will not desert us now. Let every man remember that our cause is just, and God's hand will protect you." There was a general shout of assent from the ranks, and York shouted to lower the bridge.

As they issued forth from the castle, and were joined by the rest of York's army, the duke gave a final shout and charged directly toward Lord Clifford's position.

When Clifford saw the bridge begin its descent, he sat high on his horse and craned his neck to confirm the latest development. At the sight of the duke's army gathering in front of the castle, he began to laugh. Samuel looked at him incredulously wondering what the man could be thinking. Instinctively he reached around to his quiver for the comforting feel of his arrows.

As York's army assembled, Clifford shouted, "Archers! Prepare your lines."

Samuel, Jeremy, and the rest of the archers formed two long lines in front of Lord Clifford's vanguard, and nocked their arrows. It was cold enough to make Samuel's fingers stiff, but he knew after the first few volleys he would not even notice.

"Fire at will when you have the range," barked Clifford, spurring his horse toward the rear of the archers, where he began organizing the ground troops.

York's forces were in full charge toward them and would be in range in seconds. No one would have to tell the archers when to fire; each knew within a yard how far his target needed to be. Samuel gauged the speed of the horses, the distance left between them, and drew back his bow. The first volley was loosed by both lines within a second of each other.

The flock of arrows arched through the gray sky. At the end of their graceful flight, they rained death on the charging army, in the midst of which dozens fell to the ground in agony or instantly dead. Before those in the ranks could thank God that they were still alive, the next volley was on its way.

Samuel noticed one knight surrounded by others who held up shields to protect him with each volley. He guessed that it was one of the rebel lords, perhaps even the duke himself. Another rider wearing the same colors charged out in front of everyone as if he wanted to take the brunt of the attack on himself. Samuel thought that he was either very brave, or knew something about fate, and he was about to take aim at that man when Clifford gave the order for the infantry to engage. His job was finished for the moment. He watched as the ground troops streamed by him to join the battle. Clifford himself was riding furiously from rank to rank giving direction and brandishing his huge sword.

After a quarter-hour of furious combat at close quarters, Clifford ordered the troops to fall back, much to Samuel's astonishment. There did not seem to be any advantage being gained by the rebels and it seemed entirely unnecessary to give ground, but like the rest, he complied and began a slow retreat toward the tree line. Just as their backs were hard on the woods, he heard new shouting from off to the east. He looked out over the battle lines to see Lord Roos' force appear from out of the woods to attack the rear of York's army. Samuel realized that Clifford and the queen had planned a masterful trap, and that York, by coming out of Sandal to engage them, had fallen into it.

Edmund watched as his comrades fell around him before they even had a chance to strike a blow. He knew that after the initial volleys of arrows they would be able to close ranks, but getting to that position seemed to take forever. He saw that his father's men were carefully protecting him as was their duty, so he bent his attention to the field between himself and the enemy. He did not look up to see the flights of arrows bending toward him, and as they fell to the ground or struck someone near him, he closed his eyes and spurred his horse forward. When he next noticed his position there was no one between himself and Lord Clifford's army. He drew his sword and was the first of his father's men to engage the ground forces that had come out to meet them, slashing at anything that drew near.

The troops before him began retreating, and he rode in among them with abandon. The daylight began to fade as the battle progressed, and the figures of the enemy seemed, to Edmund, to take on a ghostly pallor. As his pursuit took him close to the trees near the River Calder, Clifford's men stopped their retreat and began to swarm around him. His sword arm throbbed with exhaustion, and he was not sure whether the moisture he felt on his body was from the rain or from blood. He did not hear the new attack from Lord Roos' column, nor did he really feel the impact of the ground when a soldier grabbed his arm and tugged him off his horse. He felt only the sensation of falling into an infinite hole before he lost consciousness.

Oliver watched Lord Roos' men hack their way through the devastated ranks of the duke's army. The final blow came when the duke sounded retreat and attempted a return to Sandal. At that moment, Lord Wiltshire's column appeared from behind the castle and charged over the bridge to occupy the duke's last hope for refuge. York desperately led his last charge into the midst of Clifford's men, and finally was dragged off his horse and hacked to death by footsoldiers. The great rebel had been vanquished, and moments after his death, the remainder of his men surrendered their arms.

Clifford, after confirming York's death, appropriated many of Northumberland's men, including Samuel and Jeremy, and began searching for anyone who might have escaped the onslaught.

"My lord, can you hear me?"

Edmund was not sure what voice came to him from the darkness, which he mistook for the domain of the dead.

"My lord! Please, you must flee or bloody Clifford will be hard upon us."

Edmund's eyes fluttered open. In the early evening dark, he recognized the unmistakable silhouette of his page. The ears that stuck straight out from his head identified him even to one as groggy as he.

"Oliver? How in God's name...?"

"There's no time, my lord. Please rise, we must flee this place. We are close to town and may find refuge there."

Oliver helped the young earl struggle from his armor, now more a hindrance than useful protection. He was mortified at his master's wounds. His left leg was bleeding profusely from a gash in his thigh just above his knee, and the side of his face was badly gouged from the chin up to his temple.

His master a dead weight on his shoulder, Oliver made slowly toward Wakefield, wondering at his fortune. After York's army had left the castle, he had compulsively run after them on foot. He simply could not bear to wait and do nothing. By the time he arrived near the battlefield, bodies were everywhere. A riderless horse came to him when he called it. Oliver mounted and urged it into the fray.

Finally, he caught sight of Edmund charging headlong into the enemy near the wood. Horrified by his master's obvious danger, he galloped after him. But by the time he caught him, Edmund was being pulled from his horse and set upon by a footsoldier. The soldier never saw Oliver come up from behind him at a full gallop, nor did he see Oliver's foot as it crashed into his face. And now, as he cajoled Edmund toward town, he could not believe his luck. That nobody interfered as they made for the safety of a thicket of low shrubs was a miracle in itself.

At last, they reached the bridge that crossed the Calder, on the other side of which lay the town of Wakefield. They were halfway across when fortune abandoned them.

"Hold!" a stern voice called out from behind. Oliver turned, still supporting Edmund, to see Lord Clifford and a small force of men emerge from the woods.

"Run, Oliver. Save yourself," Edmund spoke in a low but urgent whisper.

Instead, Oliver leaned Edmund against the stone railing of the bridge and stood defiantly as he was surrounded by Clifford's men. One took Edmund by the hair and lifted his face, then saw the Falcon-and-Fetterlock emblem on his tunic. "He wears the colors of York, my lord."

Samuel and Jeremy watched Clifford step up to the young lord, who, Samuel guessed, was probably no older than himself.

"My friends, we have found the Earl of Rutland, and indeed a treasonous rebel," said Clifford, murder in his voice.

"Please, my lord, he is badly hurt," pleaded Oliver. Clifford laid him on the ground with a blow of his gloved fist. "Another word, cur, and you'll join him in Hell."

"Clifford, he is nothing to you. Leave him, I beg you." The words came painfully from Edmund.

Clifford returned his gaze to the earl, like a cat to a mouse. "Any friend to a Yorkist traitor requires my attention."

"I am your prisoner. What more do you need?"

Clifford slipped his long dagger from his sword belt and stepped up to Edmund's face. "I require only your life." His eyes glared red with hate.

"I have never done you wrong, Clifford," whispered Edmund.

"Your father killed mine. Do not expect better from me." Without another word, he plunged his dagger into Edmund's heart. Oliver screamed and tried to reach for his master's body as it slowly sank to the ground, but was restrained by two soldiers.

The shock of his other wounds having dulled his senses, Edmund felt no pain while darkness enveloped his mind. His last thoughts were of Edward. *Farewell, my brother. God keep you till we meet again.*

"You bloody butcher!" Oliver screamed from where he lay on the ground, hysterical with grief. Clifford swung on him, his blood streaked dagger ready to strike again.

"My lord!" Jeremy grabbed his arm and pushed him aside.

"Jeremy, don't..." Samuel, knowing the danger in his friend's act, was horrified.

Almost as a reflex, Clifford lashed out with his dagger, the tip of which slashed neatly across Jeremy's throat. The boy fell back into Samuel's arms, hands to his neck in a vain attempt to stop the flow of blood. Unable to breathe or speak, he clasped Samuel's hand for a moment before dying.

The entire scene had played itself out before Samuel as if in a dream. In each moment he had been too slow to prevent this nightmare. Now his dearest friend lay in his lap, his dead eyes fixed on his own.

"He is rightly served," Lord Clifford's voice pulled him from the dream. He wiped the blood from his dagger and slipped it easily into its sheath. "I'll not be corrected by a common cur."

Samuel lost his sanity to rage and leapt toward Clifford with a scream. Two of his fellow soldiers tackled him in midair.

"Don't be a fool!" one of them whispered to him as they struggled on the ground.

Clifford made to withdraw. "Bring the body of Rutland," he barked. "And bring that man to me for punishment," indicating Samuel. Mounting his horse he rode off without looking back.

"That was a foolish thing to do," said one of his fellow guardsmen. "Come, we'll entreat with the earl to grant you leniency."

Samuel shook his head. "Go. I'll be along later." His friend feared the consequences of leaving Samuel behind, but nodded and helped the others with Edmund's body.

When they were out of sight, Samuel sat next to Oliver, who was sobbing in misery. He hoped to give this stranger some small comfort, while hatred seethed within him. *The earl will not grant me leniency, because I will never fight for the House of Lancaster again.*

"Come," he helped Oliver to his feet. "There's nothing here for either of us." He lifted Jeremy's body into his arms and together they walked into town.

CHAPTER V

Bradgate Manor nestled among the Midland hills like a pearl in a shell. Elizabeth Woodville waited impatiently in its great room to say some precious last words to her husband before his long journey. Sir John Grey had been summoned to York by the queen. The Greys were faithful supporters of the dynasty, having fought for the Lancastrians in France and at home generations before that. Elizabeth's mother, the dowager duchess of Bedford, was one of the preeminent ladies of the peerage, her late husband having been an uncle to the king. And since the duchess was French by birth, she was a favorite of Queen Margaret.

"There you are, my love," Sir John said as he entered the room from the great hall beyond. Elizabeth turned from the window and smiled at her husband. They met in the center of the room and embraced passionately, Elizabeth wanting nothing less than to remain here in her husband's arms, the moment frozen for all time.

"I can't bear the thought of you leaving again. How is it that Margaret cannot seem to make a move without you?"

He drew apart, if only to catch his breath. She was a woman of surpassing beauty, with golden blond hair and eyes of deep blue shrouded by long lashes that swept up from her lids and gave her a sleepy, intoxicating appearance.

"I should have left you a note and taken my leave through the back door," he said with a sigh, kissing her again.

"And not had a final embrace to see you on your way? You wouldn't have made it past the first oak." Sir John knew she spoke the truth.

"Nevertheless," he said with a sigh, stroking her hair, "I must leave presently. When we have put down this rebellion, we'll take the children and visit the court in London. Would you like that?" He did not have to ask. London was an enchanted place for Elizabeth, where she had spent several years in the service of the queen

"Then come home soon, my love, because I can't abide the thought of waiting long."

At that moment, Sir John saw several horsemen coming around the last bend of the drive toward the manor. "Riders coming," he said as he separated himself from his wife. "Were you expecting anyone?"

Elizabeth shook her head no, and they both went up to the windows to get a better look. As the riders slowly came toward the entryway, Elizabeth recognized them and began to run to the front entrance. "It's my father and brother!"

The servants of the household began to scurry about, preparing to receive the guests. The steward, Arthur, quickstepped to the front entry, trying to arrive at the door before Elizabeth.

Having just barely beat her, he opened the double doors as the riders were dismounting. Elizabeth's father, Lord Rivers, and her brother, Anthony, Lord Scales, were accompanied by a handful of knights and retainers, wearing chain mail over their jerkins.

"Father!" Elizabeth ran to embrace him.

"Child, it's always my greatest joy to see you," Rivers embraced her tightly.

"We didn't expect you," she said without thinking. Suddenly, she pulled away and looked at her father with concern. "Is there anything wrong?"

"Nothing that an end to this rebellion will not cure. We've been summoned to York, same as your good husband." He took Sir John's hand.

"How did you know that I had been summoned as well?" Sir John asked.

"The same post that stopped here came to Grafton first. He told me you had been summoned as well, and we thought to accompany you to York since there's safety in numbers these days. And I wanted to see my daughter again."

Sir John put his arm around Anthony. "You are both most welcome. Please come in. We'll have a drink before we take to the road."

The house staff attended to their knights and horses, while the

Woodvilles settled into the warm surroundings of the front sitting room.

"Is mother well?" Elizabeth asked.

"She is well and sends her love," said Rivers. "She hopes you will visit while we're away on these civil matters."

"I'll call on her if I can, but I had hoped that John would not be gone too long this time." The steward came in and served wine in silver goblets, then stood off against a wall waiting to refill glasses as they drank.

Rivers told the family all of the news from the battles that had recently torn the kingdom apart. It was a time of great danger, he said, and neither side seemed to be able to gain a significant advantage.

Elizabeth asked quietly, "What would happen to our family if the Yorkists were to prevail?"

There was a brief silence. Finally, Anthony stood, walked to the great windows.

"We would survive," he said. "We would do whatever needed to be done, as we always have."

Such determination had run in her family, man and woman alike, for generations, and at this delicate moment she knew it was time to be strong again. She took up her glass and raised it before her kin.

"To the Woodvilles! God keep us and give us the will to be strong."

They all slowly raised their cups in stern agreement. "And let no one come between us," added Anthony. They all emptied their glasses.

"Come," said Rivers. "It's time we were on our way."

Hastings had become impatient with Edward, who, instead of taking his advice seriously, was thinking about the New Year's celebrations. They had spent Christmas in Gloucester, having raised all the troops he thought possible. The preparations were all made for the trip to Sandal Castle, and now Edward felt he deserved some recreation. But the Earl of Pembroke was in the area with an army loyal to the queen, and Hastings though it urgent that they keep them from joining her forces. Instead, Edward was arguing with a local merchant over how many casks of French wine he could deliver by the next day.

"My men would riot if we had only ten casks," Edward chided the wine-seller. "We need at least twenty or we'll have angry half-drunk soldiers turning the town inside out for more. Is that what you want?"

"My lord, I shall use all the resources available to me, but I have not been able to locate any more."

"I know you'll do your best," he said, and with a wave of his hand dismissed the man, who was thinking as he left the room that it might prove wiser to gather his family and leave town than to try to create ten casks of wine where none existed.

Edward looked over to Hastings and noted his scowl. They were both seated at a table in the great hall of a townhome that belonged to the Earl of Pembroke. Edward had thought it only appropriate to accept Pembroke's hospitality while he was off gathering troops for the queen. Clearly, since Pembroke's servants could not be trusted, he had dismissed them all and substituted his own. Now he felt comfortable for the first time since he had left Baynards Castle. A fire was lit in the stone hearth, radiating heat into the chilly marble-floored room hung with mounted stags' heads.

"Come, William, I promise we'll bend all our efforts to dispatching Pembroke tomorrow. But for now, forget these cares. They are making you melancholy."

"As you wish, my lord, but I urge you to keep your troops from celebrating too much. They will have to be ready to march in two days' time."

As Hastings spoke there was a loud knock on the door. The sentry stepped in, waiting to be recognized.

"Yes, what is it?" asked Edward.

"My lord," he said in an unreasonably loud voice, "a post has arrived from York and wishes to be admitted urgently."

"Let him pass," answered Edward uneasily. Why would there be an urgent message from his father? The last he heard, they were safely ensconced in Sandal and awaiting his arrival. The messenger came in, a small man with a red face, clearly out of breath, eyes on the floor as he entered.

"My lord, I beg you give me leave to speak, for my news is grave indeed."

"You have no need to fear me if you deliver your news truly."

"Your father, the Duke of York, and his army are destroyed!"

Edward staggered and fell back into his seat. Hastings, seeing that the earl was too stunned to speak, interposed himself.

"Destroyed in what fashion? Speak quickly, man!"

"My lord, Sandal Castle was beset by the queen's army under Lord Clifford. When the duke issued forth to meet them, they were routed."

"Issued forth?" Hastings was incredulous. "Why would they leave Sandal, you fool! If you speak falsely, I'll feed your tongue to the swine."

"My lord, I saw the results of the battle myself. As God is my witness, it occurred as I have said."

"My father and brother. What news of them?" Edward's voice was barely audible from where he sat, still dazed. Somewhere he found the courage to hear the answer that he dreaded. The messenger lowered his eyes, loath to be the instrument of such pain.

"Their heads look down on the town of York from the Micklegate Bar, my lord. Forgive me."

Edward's body slumped at the news. Hastings interceded.

"Leave us," he said abruptly. "I'll take the rest of your report presently." The messenger stood to leave, bowing deeply, grateful to be relieved of this duty.

When he had gone, Hastings sat with Edward in silence trying to think of words that would give the earl comfort. Some things, he knew, were simply beyond human capacity. It was Edward who broke the silence.

"William, gather the troops and ready them." It had taken a great deal of effort to say the words without faltering. He stopped to clear his throat, and Hastings could see that anger began to possess his young friend. "Send out the scouts. I want confirmation of Pembroke's whereabouts in three days' time. And send a post to the Earl of Warwick in London. Commend me to my cousin and tell him that we seek to join our commands in London after we have dealt with Pembroke." Edward rose from his chair. He put both hands on the table, leaning heavily on it for support. "My father's death will not be in vain, William. I swear it."

The loss of York's army at Wakefield, Hastings knew, would deal a severe blow to any hopes that Edward would fulfill his father's dream of seizing the crown. More personally, if King Henry were to regain his throne, all of the Yorkists would be branded traitors, and the queen would not rest until they were hunted down to the last man. Making quick contact with Warwick in London was imperative, as the Yorkist hopes now lay squarely on his powerful shoulders. Using his vast resources, it may yet be possible to stop the queen before she could retake London and free the king.

"I'll see to those tasks personally, my lord," he said firmly.

"Go now, William. We must move with great haste. The queen is undoubtedly already on her way to London."

Hastings bowed his head and made to leave. At the door, he hesitated. "My lord, I grieve for your loss."

Edward, his back to his friend, slumped against the table and said nothing. Hastings quickly left the room and closed the doors securely behind him. Inside, Edward's childhood memories of life with Edmund at Ludlow filled his mind, and he was seized by uncontrollable sobs.

When the Earl of Warwick heard of the disaster at Wakefield, he wasted no time gathering his forces. As the dead duke's most powerful ally, he knew he was the queen's next target. His most urgent task now was to secure the City of London. It was fortunate that he already had many troops in the city, the remnants of his victorious Northampton army, but the citizens were growing restless and it was all he could do to keep order. He had already sent to his friends in the eastern counties for fresh troops. It had also been fortunate for Warwick that his brother George, the Bishop of Exeter, had escaped from Sandal Castle; he'd brought a detailed account of the Wakefield debacle in only a few days. Now they sat in one of the spacious halls of Baynards Castle on the Thames.

"I tell you plainly, the roads are still almost impassable," the bishop was telling his brother. "It was only by God's good graces and the help of many God-fearing villagers that I was able to get here so soon."

"Nevertheless," said Warwick, "you are here, and we will make the most of this information you struggled so hard to provide." George did not miss the touch of sarcasm in his brother's voice. "The duke's stupidity and arrogance cost him his life, but I'll be damned if I let it cost us. We might still be able to prevail." He thought for a moment. "In fact, the present situation might prove better for us than before. Edward will turn to us for help — he has no one else — and if we are successful, our influence over the throne will be undeniable."

"You assume that we can defeat the queen, which has now been made unlikely by the fortunes of the duke," said George. "She is not a fool. She knows that you are her last real enemy, and she is on her way here, have no doubts about that."

"She will find me a more able adversary than York proved to be. That, I promise you."

"We must guard against overconfidence, my brother. You also assume that Edward will be as clay in your hands, to be molded as you like. But once a man has attained power he will resist being controlled. Edward will be no exception."

"He is young and inexperienced, but he's intelligent enough to know where his strength lies, and that is with the friendship of the Neville family, as it always has been for the House of York. Fear not, he'll be ruled by our guidance."

The bishop contemplated one of the tapestries that adorned the castle walls. The one in this room depicted several holy crusaders as they uncovered the mystical Lance of Christ in Antioch during the first crusade. George imagined himself in that place, enraptured by the power of such a relic. It is said the lance — no more than a rusty bit of metal — was brought into battle by the newly inspired Europeans as they routed the Muslim hordes in battle the very next day. The bishop reluctantly brought himself back to the present, and looked at his brother's ruddy face.

"I keep wondering about something the young Earl of Rutland told me before his death. Something about making a sacrifice for a cause. At the time, I thought he was referring to his brother, though I'm not sure why."

Warwick was growing impatient with his brother's musings. "It's the dream of all young knights to die for what they believe. He was probably feeling his own mortality before the battle. Such feelings are common among warriors."

"Perhaps," said the bishop thoughtfully. "But I don't think so."

Oliver and Samuel huddled under a yew hedge just outside the first cottage on the road into Northwood. It was a cold night with a damp wind that seeped into their bones and made them shiver. Each breath seem to draw the cold deeper into their bodies as they exhaled uneven puffs of vapor. Three men that Samuel could not recognize in the dark were talking and laughing in the street not more than twenty paces from where they concealed themselves. Unwilling to risk being recognized, Samuel had no choice but to wait until they had gone. A far cry, he thought, from the send-off that he was given when he last stood near this place.

Since the nightmare at Wakefield bridge, Oliver had said almost nothing, responding only to direct questions. Samuel feared that Oliver had lost his will to live when he saw his master slain, and as Samuel had led him gently but urgently away from Wakefield on the road to Northwood, Oliver said only that he must go to his master's brother, the Earl of March. It seemed to be all that gave him purpose. Samuel had to explain that he did not know where the earl was and that they needed a place to hide for a while, for surely Clifford would be seeking them soon. He also wondered to himself what kind of reception the Earl of March would give to a member of Northumberland's personal guard.

On the road to Northwood, Oliver had moved as in a trance, offering no conversation as they traveled by night. They had depended on the rations that Samuel carried in his small belt pouch that was part of his battle raiment, meager sustenance for three days of constant walking. They had slept wherever they found shelter along the road. Only his bow and half-full quiver of arrows gave him any comfort.

Now, so close to his father's house, it was maddening to be forced to wait out in this numbing cold. But this was Northumberland's village, and it was crucial that they not be discovered, as word would surely get back to the earl.

Finally, the three men walked noisily down the road, past the first turn and out of sight. Samuel helped Oliver up and they stepped out into the open. There were three homes on the east side, each with light spilling out from under the doorjamb, which they avoided by keeping low and staying to the opposite side. Around the first turn, the River Tyne came up to just below the lane. Samuel looked to see where the men had gone but saw no sign of them. They quickly crossed over and went down to the river bank where they could go the rest of the way to the mill house well secluded from view.

As the mill wheel loomed before them in the dark, the two exhausted travelers cautiously made their way around the front of the house, looking carefully toward the street for any movement. Satisfied that there was none, they slipped up to the door and listened intently for voices that did not belong. Samuel was adamant that no one but his family should know of his presence in Northwood. Hearing only a quiet conversation between two people, he decided to risk knocking softly. After a moment's silence, Samuel heard the door bar slide and the door opened a crack. It was his father.

"Who's there?" he asked holding a candle over his head.

"Let me in, father."

"Samuel!" His father swung the door open at the sound of his son's voice, and shouted excitedly to someone within, "It's Samuel!"

Samuel ushered Oliver in and closed the door behind. As he looked around, he was relieved to see only his family and no visitors.

Emma and Sally jumped to hug Samuel, and even Christopher came over to give him a quick embrace.

"I didn't expect you so soon," he said. "Can the battle be over already?" Seeing his brother's uneasy looks, he became concerned. "The battle went poorly?"

"Give him a moment," interrupted Emma, leading Samuel to a chair. "Can't you see he's exhausted? You just relax for a bit, Samuel, and I'll get you some ale."

"Who's you friend, Samuel?" his father asked.

"His name is Oliver. He was caught in the middle of the battle and hasn't quite recovered his wits yet." He put his hand on Oliver's arm and continued. "I couldn't just leave him there, alone and half out of his mind."

"Of course you couldn't," agreed Sally. "I'll get you both something to eat."

Christopher had waited as long as he could for the news. He sat across from Samuel while Sally set out two tankards of ale.

"Let's have it. What happened out there?"

Samuel could not keep the bitterness out of his voice. "You needn't worry, brother. We destroyed the rebel duke and left no stone unturned in rooting out all who dared to wear his colors."

Oliver broke down and began to sob in his hands. Emma, seeing his torment, knew that he needed rest to salve some bitter memory. She and Sally took him gently around the shoulders and led him into the back room.

"What happened to him?" Christopher asked.

"He watched as his master was butchered in cold blood at Wakefield bridge," Samuel said angrily.

"War is an ugly thing. Who was his master?"

"The Earl of Rutland."

Christopher's jaw dropped. "The traitor duke's son? Then we are well rid of him. I'm surprised that you'd care what became of any member of that family."

Samuel lost control of his temper. "You're a fool, Christopher," he said loudly, "and you don't know what you're talking about!"

Christopher was taken aback. "You're as insane as he is."

John Miller stood between them.

"Let's not have any more of this." He took his seat again and looked intently at Samuel. "Now then, I think you had better tell us what happened."

Samuel was still breathing hard. He took a long pull on his ale. Emma and Sally rejoined them.

"The poor lad was asleep before I could get a blanket on him. Lord in Heaven, Samuel, what happened to you?" asked Emma.

"Jeremy is dead," his voice cracked and the tears rolled down his cheeks.

"Angels of mercy," whispered Emma, hands to her heart. John Miller placed his strong hand on his son's shoulder.

"Tell us what happened if you can," he said gently.

Samuel needed their understanding more than anything at that moment. Laboriously he recounted the progress of the battle at Wakefield, and finally the horrific murders at the bridge.

"I'm so sorry, Samuel," said Sally, wiping the tears from his cheeks.

"I grieve for Jeremy, as well," interjected Christopher. "But why in God's name would you incur the wrath of a nobleman? It's not our place to question such people."

Samuel spoke through clenched teeth. "I did what I had to do."

"We must make this right," said John Miller. "Tomorrow at first light I'll ride with you to York. If the earl is still there, we'll beg for his mercy and for your reinstatement. We have been loyal subjects. He won't refuse me."

"I will not!" Samuel pounded his fist on the table. "I want no part of the House of Lancaster, and I'll not fight for them."

Christopher was incredulous. "You must make amends, for all our sakes. Where will you go otherwise?"

"I don't know." He was feeling cornered. Getting home had been his only goal, as if he would be secure in the confines of his father's house.

"You're a deserter! They'll hunt you down and punish all of us."

"Christopher!" It was Emma, panicked by the deadly threat to the family.

"Be quiet, woman." Christopher strode to the door, overturning his chair as he stood. "Don't be here when I get back, Samuel, or I'll turn you in to the earl's men myself." Not even stopping to put on a cloak, he stormed from the house.

They sat in stunned silence for a while until John Miller finally spoke.

"We must tell Edith of Jeremy's death."

"I'll go tomorrow and tell her myself."

"I will go, and you will stay hidden here until we find a better place."

"But I…"

"You cannot be seen here. I know this is hard, but I fear that the worst is yet to come. Let me tend to Edith. Go now and get some rest if you can."

Reluctantly, Samuel saw the wisdom in his father's words and nodded his head.

"And don't worry about your brother," John Miller added. "He will not betray you."

Christopher's threat notwithstanding, Samuel and Oliver would not be able to stay at the mill house. It would not be long before Clifford sent out men to find the deserter. John Miller let them sleep for a few hours while he went to Endstreet to seek out his friend Thomas, who had a storage shed behind his house. It seemed a good place for hiding, secluded in a woods and not visible from the road. Thomas was beholden to the miller for not charging him one year when the crops were poor. The miller's generosity had allowed him to feed his family that year. But it was not a simple request the miller made. Most townsmen were loyal to the earl. When he heard that Samuel had deserted, Thomas made it known that he considered his debt fully paid. He also made it clear that while Samuel and Oliver could use the shed, he would not help them in any other way, and would disavow any knowledge of them if they were found.

The miller knew that Thomas would not betray him, but he understood the conditions. He went back to the mill house and let Samuel and Oliver sleep another hour, then woke them before daybreak. They had to be in Thomas' shed before first light, or there would be few who were not aware of their presence.

They spent the next day in the shed, resting in solitude. Toward suppertime, Sally brought them some warm bean stew and ale, which she carefully hid in the basket she used to gather berries during the fall. She had insisted on bringing the food herself. She had to see her brother before these ill affairs took him away again. Approaching the shed, she looked quickly over her shoulder, knocked and entered. Samuel and Oliver were lying on the ground covered by a thin wool blanket.

"You'll catch your deaths on that cold ground!" They both jumped at the sound of her voice, Samuel reaching for his bow.

"Sally, you gave us a scare," he scolded.

"Look at you," she said, coming over to hug him. "How could this have happened?" Her eyes were sad above her smile. "Never mind," she continued, digging the food out of her basket. "At least you're still alive."

"Hullo." Samuel was startled by the sound of his voice. "My name is Oliver."

"This is my sister, Sally," said Samuel, happy to hear him speak.

"Pleased," said Sally shyly. "I know who you are. Samuel told us last night. I was sorry to hear of your misfortunes."

Oliver's eyes dropped to the floor. "Thanks," he said sadly.

They hungrily ate the stew and bread while she sat on a stump of wood. "How long can you stay, Samuel?"

"Maybe another day or two, until we can get our strength back again, but not any longer than that. The longer we stay the more likely the earl will catch up to us."

"The stew is excellent," said Oliver. "Did you make it?"

"Yes," she said, "with some help from Emma," she added begrudgingly. They ate in silence until Sally turned to Oliver and asked, "Do you have family?"

"No, not really. My parents sold me off a long time ago."

"I'm sorry. Do you miss them much?"

"Yes," he answered after a pause. "I suppose that I do. But I've learned to live without them. At least I have —" he stopped and put a hand over his eyes.

"Tell me," Sally urged.

He cleared his throat. "At least I had someone who cared about me. But now—"

"You mean the earl? He meant a great deal to you, didn't he?"

Oliver could only nod his head. Sally took his hand and gave it a comforting squeeze, and Oliver managed a tight smile as he looked at her.

How she had grown, Samuel thought, as he watched Sally and Oliver talk. He regretted that he was missing these years of his sister's life. He wondered that Christopher could not see how fortunate he was.

"I'd better be getting back home," said Sally, still holding Oliver's hand, "before I'm missed."

"Will you be back?" Oliver asked hopefully.

"Of course. I have to bring your breakfast, don't I?" she responded with a smile. After gathering up her basket, she gave Samuel a kiss on the cheek and smiled at Oliver, leaving him dreamy-eyed as she walked from the shed. Samuel looked at him for a moment.

"Glad to see you're feeling better."

As promised, Sally did deliver breakfast the next morning, along with another blanket. This time, saying he had to relieve himself, Samuel left her alone with Oliver in the shed for a while. While outside in the woods, he walked some old, barely recognizable paths he'd walked as a child a hundred times, smelling familiar scents and wondering what had happened to those carefree days. He also noticed that for the first time in a month, there were breaks in the clouds, and the sun was streaking through the openings like gilded shafts. Where a beam lit the woods, the ground shimmered gold.

When he reluctantly returned, Sally and Oliver were holding hands again and giggling over some private joke. It was as if a different person had secreted Oliver away and replaced him in the night. They looked up sheepishly when he entered and Sally withdrew her hand, a little red in the face. Samuel tried not to embarrass her any further.

"How are Father and Emma?" he asked, sitting near her on the ground.

"They're worried about you, and about Christopher."

"Christopher is not in trouble with the earl. Why would they be concerned for him?"

"Because he's torn between two masters, and has lost his way. Can't you see that?"

"I can't imagine why."

"Don't be so hard, Sam. He's too stubborn to tell you, but he was so proud of you when you left to fight. And you know that he thinks our security is tied to the earl's fortunes. When you said you wouldn't support the earl anymore, he was devastated. He didn't know what he was saying."

"Oh, I think he knew exactly what he was saying."

Sally could only sigh. She had done what she could.

"I'd better be going," she said. "I have a lot of chores that have gone wanting since you got back." This time she left them both with a kiss, and a lingering smile on Oliver's face.

As she walked away from the shed, she did not even notice Stephen, the Smith's son, until she heard him speak from somewhere behind her.

"A little late in the season to be gathering berries, isn't it?"

Sally jumped as she spun, so taken aback that she forgot all her rehearsed excuses for being near the woods at town's end.

"Stephen," she was almost hoarse, "please do not sneak up on me like that again!"

"I was just wondering what you were doing out here," he said defensively. "I haven't seen much of you recently." He came up close to her, but she stepped away.

"I do not have to account for my hours to you, Stephen. And now if you don't mind, I have chores to do." She left quickly, leaving him wondering angrily what he had done to deserve such treatment.

As Sally sped toward the mill house, the unmistakable sound of large horses galloping into town came from the east side. She watched in panic as six horsemen in mail and helmets passed her and rode toward the church. She ran into the house screaming for her father.

John Miller told Sally to stay at home and then ran to the square, where the townspeople gathered near the church. When he arrived, the riders had dismounted, and he saw that three wore the Earl of Northumberland's livery. Of those, he recognized the earl's seneschal, Sir Toby Ridgeway, the overseer of all of the earl's personal holdings. He did not recognize the badges of the other three riders.

When Sir Toby was satisfied that he had made an auspicious enough entrance, he cleared his throat loudly and boomed:

"We seek a deserter who hails from this town." That brought the crowd to a buzz. "The deserter's name," continued the seneschal, "is Samuel, son of the miller." The buzz devolved into pandemonium. Everyone knew Samuel and could not believe him capable of such infamy. "If anyone has knowledge of his whereabouts," screamed Sir Toby over the din, "let him come forward now."

John Miller made his way forward to the knights. As he did so, many of the villagers looked away. "Sir Toby," he quaked, "my son has not come home since he left to do the earl's bidding. This news is a dagger in my heart." He knelt before the seneschal, afraid that his entire life and all that he and his father had worked for were about to come to naught.

After a particularly pregnant pause, Sir Toby said, "I believe you to be an honest man, John Miller." He turned to the obvious leader of the other three knights. "Are you satisfied, Sir Hugh?"

Sir Hugh stepped toward John Miller and stared down at him as if he were looking at a spider. A recently made scar marred the left side of his face, disfiguring his mouth into a sinister smile.

"Oh, I trust the miller, Sir Toby," his voice dripping with sarcasm, "but my orders from Lord Clifford are specific. The town is to be searched."

"As you wish, Sir Hugh," said the seneschal reluctantly. "You will all stay here until the search is complete."

"I'll start with the miller's house. The rest of you start with the east end of town and meet back here," Sir Hugh instructed his men.

John Miller was blind with fear, not only at the thought of Samuel being discovered.

As the riders went off to their assignments, a rare insight occurred to Stephen, the smith's son.

Emma and Sally huddled in a corner as Sir Hugh tossed tables and chairs around and ripped down door covers. When finally it became clear that his quarry was not anywhere to be found, he walked slowly to the women and pinned them both against the wall.

"I think you both know where the wretched deserter is. Now why don't you tell me?"

As strong-willed and defiant as Emma could be, the sight of this man with his leering smile filled her with dread, and Sally was simply too frightened to speak.

"We have no knowledge, sir," Emma was finally able to whisper.

For that answer, Sir Hugh sent her sprawling across the floor with the back of his hand. Sally screamed but could not break free of Sir Hugh's grip. Emma lay still on the floor.

"Now will you tell me where he is?" he said, putting his face closer to Sally's with each word. She could only look at him in terror, as words were simply not possible.

"Sir Hugh?" a voice came from the door.

He looked angrily to see who had interrupted his interrogation. Sir Toby was standing just inside the door, regarding Emma with obvious disapproval.

"Yes, what is it?" Sir Hugh was clearly annoyed.

"The men think that they may have found something."

"Very well," he said, then turned back to Sally. "We'll continue our discussion later." Releasing her roughly, he left the house with Sir Toby.

Sally ran to Emma and tried to support her as she struggled to shake the dizziness out of her head. Within a few more minutes, John Miller and Christopher came running up to the mill house. Christopher shouted Emma's name and ran to her.

"What happened?" He was almost hysterical. Emma struggled to her feet with support from her husband and managed to sit up in a chair. She surveyed the damage to her home and tears welled in her eyes.

"This is Samuel's fault," spat Christopher, gritting his teeth. "I'm going to tell them where he is."

Sally grabbed her brother's arm. "No, you can't!"

Christopher shook himself loose. "How can you still defend him? Look at what he's done to Emma," his voice broke as he said his wife's name.

"You will not betray your brother," John Miller said. Christopher stormed from the house.

"Father, stop him, please," cried Sally. John Miller put his arms around his daughter and gently stroked her hair.

"Your faith must be strong, daughter. In the end, it's the only thing we truly possess."

At the first sound of the horsemen riding into town, Samuel and Oliver gathered up their few belongings, tried to erase any sign of their presence, and went into the woods to a place that Samuel remembered from his youth. Samuel had seen the livery of Lord Clifford on three of the riders and knew that capture meant certain execution for them both.

Samuel remembered a pair of large boulders between which a small cave had been worn away by a stream over centuries. The cave was secluded behind one of the boulders and made a good hiding place. While the two of them were quite cramped, it would do until sunset.

As the last light faded over Northwood, Stephen, the smith's son, waited at the river just below the mill. He knew that Sally always came out for the evening's supply of water about this time. When the door finally opened, he watched as Sally came down the path with her bucket. When she was several steps from his hiding place behind a large willow, he stepped out.

"We meet again." Sally, who had already withstood enough horrors for one day, jumped at the sound and clutched at her breast. Stephen was immediately sorry that he had surprised her so. "I'm sorry, Sally, I really didn't mean to frighten you."

"Stephen? How dare you sneak up on me?"

"I said I was sorry. I didn't mean to."

"What are you doing here anyway?" She grabbed her bucket and proceeded to the river bank for the water, knees still weak and wobbling.

"I want you to marry me."

Sally could not find words to respond. She was furious with Stephen for behaving so oddly, and for being so insensitive to what she had been through that day. On any other day she might have been delighted with his offer of marriage, but at this moment she did not even want to speak with him, much less discuss the possibility of spending their lives together.

"Have you taken leave of your wits? Can't you see what's happening to my family?"

"I think that given your brother's behavior, you'd be better off as my wife."

Sally was stunned, then livid. "I'll not marry you now or ever, Stephen."

He stood before her for a moment as his face turned red with embarrassment and anger. Abruptly he turned to leave.

"Very well, if that's what you want," he said over his shoulder. "I have a deserter to report anyway."

"What do you mean?" A hard lump of fear rose in her throat.

"Did you think that I was too stupid to see where you were coming from this morning? I think that the seneschal will be interested to hear about your little morning errand, don't you?"

"Stephen, please don't!" Sally grabbed his arm in a desperate attempt to slow his pace as he continued to climb up to the road. Stephen turned and shoved her back down the hill. Watching as she tumbled and sprawled into the mud near the river bank, he thought for an instant about going down and helping her. She was crying hysterically and still begging him not to go.

"You made your choice," he said coldly. He looked at her for a moment longer, then turned and ran down the road to seek out the seneschal.

Though the stars were out in abundance, it was a moonless night that fell as Samuel and Oliver squirmed to find some comfort in the little cave that had been their hiding place for several hours. When the sun set, it left a cold night, and Samuel knew it would only be worse when they left the cave. He wondered if the soldiers had given up their search. He did not want to leave without saying his farewells to the family, and he was not provisioned for an hour's outing, much less a long journey. In fact, they had between them only Samuel's battle pack, which contained no food, his bow and quiver of arrows, and the clothes on their backs.

He had made up his mind that when it was late, he would slip back into town and try to see his father one last time. It was clear that he could not spend any more time in Northwood. They would have to be on their way. He decided that he would be safe enough if he stepped outside the cave to get a breath of fresh air. Trying not to disturb Oliver, who had somehow managed to drop off into a fitful slumber, he pulled himself out of the cave and onto one of the boulders. His legs were cramped and it took several moments to get the circulation back. He stepped from behind the boulder and looked up at the night's canopy through the leafless limbs of the trees.

He wrapped his arms around himself in a vain attempt to ward off the cold, and decided that it would be safe enough to go back to the shed to find the blankets that they had left in a bundle behind the building. There was an almost imperceptible path toward town that started a few yards away. Since it was only a short distance back, he felt certain that he could find the way there and back without getting lost in the dark. He made his way slowly along the path. When he saw a faint light coming from somewhere ahead, he breathed a sigh of relief.

"Here it is, my lord. This is where they're hiding." The voice came from the shed, not more than a hundred paces away. He listened over the sound of his heart thumping as several soldiers broke down the door and entered. "There's nothing here, Sir Toby," a voice called from inside.

"I swear to you, my lord. This is where they were this morning." Samuel recognized the voice of the smith's son, Stephen. He wondered how he had known where they were.

"Look here, Sir Hugh. They were here all right." The new voice came from behind the shed. Samuel knew that they had found his bundle of blankets and leftover bread. He began to creep back into the woods, taking only four steps before tripping on a raised root and falling with a crash.

"There's something here, Sir Hugh! Something moved right back there."

"You men spread out. The noise came from over there." Samuel did not have to see to know that he was pointing right at him.

"We'd be lucky to find him in this dark, Sir Hugh."

"I'll have him this very night, by God. He won't get far."

Samuel jumped to his feet and bolted down the path, crashing into trees and low growing junipers. "There he goes!" he heard someone yell. After that, he was oblivious to any other sounds except that of his own thrashing through the deep underbrush. Falling or crashing into trees at almost every third step, he was already badly bruised and cut. Finally, not having any notion of where he was, he stopped for a moment to ascertain how close the pursuit was. Gasping for air, he strained to see if there was any sign of the boulders. There was none. The crashing of the soldiers and their shouting back and forth was only several hundred paces away, and growing nearer. As he turned to continue his flight, a pair of strong arms grabbed him and held him tightly enough to constrict his breathing.

"Be silent, traitor," a voice hissed in his ear.

Samuel was too exhausted to struggle and was resigned to capture. But the expected shout for assistance didn't come.

"If you can manage to keep quiet, I'll show you a way out of here," his captor whispered

"Christopher!" Samuel finally recognized the voice.

"Be quiet, you fool, and follow me."

He placed his hand on his brother's back as Christopher led him silently down a slope until Samuel heard the sound of water running in a small brook. They crossed over, sloshing through the icy water, until they came to a ledge that rose steeply from the brook. Christopher pushed Samuel down so that they were both hidden under the embankment. They waited in silence until heavy footsteps came crashing nearby and a voice in the distance yelled, "Sir Hugh, where are you?"

Just above them, and not more than a few feet from where they cowered, they heard a low snarl and knew that someone was listening for any sound. Samuel felt sure that his heavy breathing could be heard clear back to town, and with his heart pounding in his chest he had an almost irresistible urge to bolt like a rabbit. A moment later, he heard heavy footsteps crunch away from the ledge. They listened as the voices and sounds of snapping limbs drifted farther away.

"Let's go," Christopher whispered.

"We have to get Oliver," Samuel protested.

"He's already safe. Did you think I didn't know about your little hiding place? Now shut up and follow me."

Again Samuel followed Christopher and his uncanny night vision, with one hand on his brother's back as they made their way through the dark. After walking some minutes, they came to a clearing where a dark shape stood silently.

"Oliver, is that you?" Samuel ventured in a whisper.

"Thank God in Heaven it's you," Oliver gasped.

"Christopher, for God's sake, where are we?"

"The road south out of town is just over there," he said pointing past a small stand of low shrubs, barely discernible in the dark. He turned and began walking back into the woods.

"Wait," called Samuel. "Where are you going?"

Christopher stopped. "I got you here, now you're on your own. As for me, I hope I never see you again." He turned and disappeared into the woods.

After a stunned moment of silence, Samuel finally gave Oliver a shove toward the road.

"Let's get out of here."

He shouldered his bow and quiver that Oliver had brought with him and made their way out of the woods. Keeping to the road's edge so that they could disappear quickly if need be, they walked quickly to the south.

"I'm sorry, my friend."

"Why," asked Samuel absently.

"I'm sorry that, like me, you've lost everything that matters."

CHAPTER VI

Elizabeth's mother's unexpected visit to Bradgate was both delightful and frustrating. Elizabeth was, of course, always very pleased to see her mother, but to not be given some notice was annoying.

They sat in the front room enjoying the warmth of the sun, which graced the day above a clear blue sky for the first time in a month. Bright rays flooded through the huge windows. The duchess was holding Elizabeth's younger boy, Richard, on her lap attempting to carry on a conversation, while the older one, Thomas, sat on the floor in front of her, amusing himself with a brightly colored cloth ball that his grandmother had brought for him. Elizabeth did not normally permit the children in the front room, but her mother had insisted that they be brought down immediately. Their nurse stood by while trying her best to remain inconspicuous.

"How these children have grown," marveled the duchess, "and to think, this one was just an infant the last time I visited."

Her mother's thinly veiled criticism was not lost on Elizabeth. "Mother, you know that you are always welcome here, but it has been so difficult these past two years. Between John's duties to the king abroad and now in these rebellions, we've not seen much of him here at home." She gazed at Thomas.

Her mother could see the pain in her daughter's face. "It is hard to think of these days ending, isn't it?"

Elizabeth looked at her mother and smiled. "There are times that I wish you did not understand me so well."

The duchess carefully lifted Richard off her lap and handed him to the nurse. "Dearest Elizabeth, you are so young and beautiful," she said tenderly, "but those gifts are illusions that will not serve you when you are sorely tested by fate. You must remember that the common needs that bind us together as family and friends can never be dissolved by events, no matter how catastrophic. If the wars go badly, we will still have each other, always."

"Will we? Our husbands may be out there lying dead in some God-forsaken field as we speak. What would we do then?"

"Death provides us with the only stability that is truly permanent, my daughter. Whether they die on a battlefield or in bed, they will die. But thereafter always will they remain unchanged in us, and that will bring us peace. In the meantime, we can enjoy God's gifts as they are bestowed upon us, and must endure the pain that comes with them. Remember that I once had the prestige of a queen when my late husband, the Duke of Bedford, lived, God rest his soul. As regent of France, he was like a king and ruled that beautiful land. They were heady times for us, but as with all things, those days passed, like a crocus crushed under a late spring snow."

"Did you really rule France, Grandmother?" asked Thomas, looking up wide-eyed at the duchess.

She put her arms out toward him. "Come sit with me, my love, and I'll tell you the story." He jumped up and sat next to her as if he were about to receive a birthday present.

"Our king who has been made a prisoner in the Tower, God protect his gentle soul, came to the throne when he was but an infant. His great and beloved father, King Henry the Fifth, had gone to France to press his claim to the French throne when I was a young lady. The two countries fought long and hard, and the English marched many miles through difficult weather and many skirmishes. At last, King Henry's army was all but exhausted, with few provisions and ever so far from home.

"The king decided that for the sake of his men he would return to England to fight again another day. But their way was blocked by a huge French army with fresh troops and many of the finest fighting men of the realm. There were five French soldiers for every Englishman, and they demanded that Henry surrender and be ransomed back to England in shame. But he would have none of that, and on Saint Crispin's day, in a place called Agincourt, the English army, by the grace of God and under His divine protection, routed the French, leaving many thousands dead on the field, while the English suffered few losses. The French king was forced to accept Henry as his heir and even gave his daughter to him for a wife." Thomas had not taken his eyes off his grandmother while she spoke. And as she paused for a moment of reflection, he sat quietly waiting for more.

"Alas, the great king died a short time later, and only a few months after the birth of his son, who, although he was only an infant, was crowned king of France and England. My first husband, the Duke of Bedford, brother of the old king and uncle of the new, was made regent of France. It was then that with my husband we held sway over that kingdom in Henry's name, and sweet days they were." Again she paused and looked with glazed eyes at her grandson's innocent face. "But nothing lasts forever, as God will have it, and the youth of the king gave leave for corruption among the nobility to flourish. The royal family was split asunder by the strife, and the poor young king was used as a pawn in the struggle between the factions. My husband traveled back to England and was able to make peace for a while because he was well respected. But upon his return to France, the bickering continued.

"Finally, God rest his soul, my husband passed away as well, and with his death, the French began to retake their land, county by county, and the English were too weak from the bitter family fighting to save what the king's father had so gallantly won."

"Is that why he's held in prison now, Grandmother?"

"Partly," she frowned. "The loss of France and the weakness of the king's supporters allowed the Duke of York and his supporters to press their foolish claim to the crown, which derives from an even older struggle between factions of the royal family. If it were not for the tenacity of the queen, it may be that York would be sitting on the throne this very day."

"When did you meet Grandfather?"

She smiled at him and stroked his hair, grateful to be able to tell a happier story. "He was a dashing young knight in Bedford's service, and held himself proudly in many battles with the French. In exchange for his loyal service, he was created Lord Rivers, a great honor for a young knight. After Bedford's death, he asked for my hand, and I could not say no, although my family did not approve." Her smile evaporated as quickly as it had appeared, as if an old wound had been opened anew.

"Why did they not approve, Grandmother?"

"Thomas, that's enough for now," interrupted Elizabeth as she motioned to the nurse. "Your grandmother has traveled a great distance and needs her rest." The nurse took the reluctantly obedient child by the hand and, with Richard in her free arm, left the room.

"Thank you, dear," the duchess said, staring absently out the window.

"You shouldn't be ashamed of what you did for love, Mother. It was the most romantic and noble story I ever heard."

"I married beneath my station without the king's permission. To this day I cannot believe that I acted so rashly, and nobility had nothing to do with it, I assure you. I was fortunate indeed that the king allowed the marriage to stand after I paid a substantial fine." Elizabeth did not miss the hint of a smile that drifted over her mother's face. "And I thank God that you found such a fine match in Sir John, so that you won't have to make the difficult decisions that I had to make."

"I would have done the same thing, I'm sure," Elizabeth said.

"Perhaps you would have," her mother's voice trailed off as she closed her eyes and took a deep breath.

The leafless branches of the oaks outside were suddenly taken by a strong wind and raked against the clouds that billowed up from the south.

"We have company," she said, her eyes refocused on the road where it bent around the last hill.

The duchess opened her eyes and peered intently through the window. "It's a lone rider. Perhaps a post from York." She stood quickly.

"Arthur!" Elizabeth called for the steward as she jumped to her feet. "Arthur, a rider approaches. See to the door." Her eyes never left the approaching visitor.

"Very well, my lady," Arthur said calmly from out in the main hall, the sound of his footsteps making toward the door.

She was not normally so flustered at the approach of a visitor, but when her husband was away fighting wars there was always cause. The rider was in no apparent hurry, his horse in a slow trot as it neared the first oak.

"He wears your father's colors." Her mother had come to stand next to her. "Come. It's a post from your father."

Until they had heard his news, they would not be able to breathe freely. It had been a full fortnight since the men had left Bradgate, and any sort of evil could have occurred during that time.

The rider finally arrived at the main entry and was greeted there by Arthur and a stable hand who took his horse as the messenger dismounted.

The ladies waited impatiently in the sitting room for the messenger to be shown in. When at last Arthur announced him, he entered and bowed deeply.

"My ladies, Lord Rivers commends himself to his wife and daughter."

"Yes, yes," prodded the duchess. "Is he well, and what of Sir John?"

"They are both well and send happy news by this unworthy messenger." As if the sun had broken through an overcast sky, both ladies smiled and relaxed. "The queen's army has defeated the Duke of York, whose head sits upon the gates of York, in penance for his treason."

"Is the rebellion over then?" It was too good to be true.

"As we speak, Lord Rivers and Sir John are marching on London to free the king, and to rid the realm of Warwick, the last strength of the rebels. This is all I know, and what my master bid me tell you."

"Good messenger, this news has given us reason to live another day in the kind embrace of peace."

"I also thank you," added Elizabeth. "And now you must have food and rest. Arthur!" she called out to the hall.

"Yes, my lady," the steward said as he entered.

"Provide food and rest for this good man. And tell the stable to provide a fresh horse in the morning, for he must be off again, back to his master at first light. We'll have letters for you before you leave," she said to the messenger.

"Thank you, my lady," he responded gratefully as he bowed and followed Arthur from the room.

"There, you see, my love?" the duchess embraced her daughter, who was misty-eyed with relief. "God has answered our prayers on this occasion. For now, we can hope to enjoy the present, for only He knows what tomorrow brings."

Outside the windows, the silent wind lifted spirals of dust from the ground and wafted the particles to points unknown.

Edward and Hastings rode forth the next morning from Wigmore Castle in front of a column of mounted knights, followed by some four thousand footsoldiers in ranks three abreast. It had been a frosty night with firewood hard to find. The troops had little rest. As their column advanced, the horses spouted steam from their nostrils and the soldiers welcomed the chance to move. A mile from Wigmore, several riders approached.

"Good morrow to you, my lords." It was Sir Richard Croft, a longtime ally of the Yorkists, and his retainers.

"You are most welcome, Sir Richard," Edward answered. "What can you tell us of Pembroke?"

"The news is good if you are prepared for battle, my lord. Pembroke and his followers are but a few miles south of here where the old Roman road crosses the river. Mortimer's Cross, they call it here."

"We are prepared," said Edward grimly.

Shouts came from the ranks and Edward turned to seek the cause of the commotion. He saw many of his men pointing toward the east, some even breaking ranks in fear. He looked to where they were pointing to see not one, but three suns had climbed over the horizon.

"This is a wondrous thing, my lord," whispered Hastings. "What could it mean?"

"I know not, but the men are breaking ranks. We must do something." He thought for a moment longer, eyes riveted on the spectacle of the multiple suns. "Summon Father Dennis to me at once!" Hastings nodded and rode to the rear of the column, shouting for the men to hold their places upon pain of death.

"It is an evil omen, my lord," someone shouted at Edward.

Edward raised himself up in his saddle and addressed his men loudly. "Do not be amazed, my friends. This is a wondrous good omen of excellent tidings. It is the Holy Trinity that shines down upon us and blesses our cause." He dismounted and knelt in prayer. A murmur of agreement washed over the army as Edward's interpretation was passed down the column, and many crossed themselves.

Hastings returned with Father Dennis mounted behind him on his horse. Edward greeted him from his knees. "Look how the Lord blesses us with this miracle, Father."

Father Dennis was only too happy to concur with Edward's interpretation. He busied himself with the rituals of his faith and ended by sprinkling holy water in the general direction of the soldiers, starting, of course, with Edward.

Satisfied that his men were emboldened by the event, Edward ordered the column to reassemble and continue its march toward Pembroke's position.

Less than an hour later, Edward's scouts spotted Pembroke's army approaching the river from the west.

"This is the only crossing for miles in either direction, my lord," said Hastings.

"If they cross before us, they will be able to defend the crossing with only a few men." Edward pulled his armored gloves from his hands. "We cannot permit that." He assessed the ground before them and nodded his head. "William, array the archers between the river and Pembroke's army. We must prevent them from crossing."

Hastings frowned. "My lord, to place the river at our backs will prevent any retreat. We will be pinned against the water."

"There is no choice. See to the deployment before it's too late."

In the next few minutes, Edward's army had blocked Pembroke's path to the crossing and the battle lines were made. Pembroke concentrated his attack at the crossing in the center of Edward's position, hoping to push his foe until they could not hold the riverbank. When the armies collided, the clash of metal on metal and the din of a thousand screaming men shattered the morning. Bodies fell on the blood-soaked ground by the dozens.

"Commit the reserve to the center," yelled Edward at Hastings, pointing to his sagging line near the bridge. Hastings signaled the troops that had been held back from the initial charge in order that they be available where needed most. With their added strength, the middle held and the tide was turned. Pembroke's troops were largely untried and proved unequal to Edward's army.

When the center gave way, the rest of Pembroke's army broke and retreated to the north and south. Edward's followers pursued them, butchering the stragglers, until they were recalled to assemble again. Edward met with Hastings near the bridge where his men had erected his tent.

"We must keep our forces intact for the march on London," Edward insisted to Hastings. "What news of Pembroke?"

"He was not among the dead or captured, my lord. We can only assume that he escaped."

"He always was a coward." Edward spat.

"We have, however, captured his father, Owen Tudor."

"Then he will take his son's place at the block. Bring him before me for swift judgement. His head shall part with his body before I eat my supper. But first, we shall give thanks to God for his helping hand this day. Call Father Dennis to my tent."

"Your Highness, this pillaging must stop!"

Northumberland was desperate to convince the queen to regain control over their troops, who had been sacking town after town on their way south. He stood before the queen in the lavishly furnished royal tent. In attendance to the queen along with Northumberland were Clifford, Somerset, and Sir Andrew Trollope, the queen's principal captain.

On their way south from York, the queen's friends had assembled an enormous army, sixty thousand strong and growing. As they made their way toward London, the troops had sacked most of the villages that they passed, gathering supplies, looting abbeys for valuables, and raping many women who had not been hidden. They had recently arrived at Dunstable and the queen hastily convened her advisors to discuss their next move. But Northumberland had felt an urgent need to challenge the queen's permission for these incursions against the common townspeople and the Church.

"We are engendering much ill will with this behavior," he continued, "and consequences yet unseen may haunt us if it continues."

"My lord of Northumberland may be right, Highness," Somerset stepped forward. "In times such as these it is not wise to make any new enemies, even if they be commoners. And clearly, we do not want to alienate the clergy, for they have many powerful friends."

Queen Margaret showed no outward signs that she had any opinion on the matter, nor that she was anything but uninterested in the subject of discussion. But all those present knew that she was silently weighing her options.

"If I may, Your Highness?" Sir Andrew continued after getting a nod from the queen. "The army must provision itself. These raids on local villages are necessary to that end. I assure you that we use no excessive force to acquire what we need."

The queen looked at Clifford, true to her practice of hearing everyone's opinion before speaking her own mind.

"Highness, we are wasting time on trivialities. My only concern is the Earl of Warwick, who, I warrant you, will prove a more formidable foe than the late Duke of York." At that moment, a sentry entered the tent and fell to one knee.

"Yes, speak," said the queen impatiently.

"Your Highness, we have just received the expected intelligence that you bade me bring you forthwith."

"Proceed," Margaret showed her first signs of agitation all evening.

"The Earl of Warwick has established his camp at the Town of St. Albans. His main army has positioned itself on the north road, with his archers positioned in the town itself."

The queen's agitation disappeared as quickly as it had appeared. "You see, my lords, he expects us from the north and not from Dunstable to the west. Our little ruse has worked." The lords in the tent were forced once again to look upon their queen with begrudging respect. The ruse to which she alluded was Pembroke's expedition, which she had sent down the northern road with orders to create havoc on the countryside, to create the illusion that the main army was coming from that direction. As a result, it was obvious that Warwick had misdirected his defense.

"My lords," said the queen, "it is time to make preparations for the final victory. Sir Andrew, gather your forces and prepare to break camp this very evening. We will not give haughty Warwick a chance to see his error until our swords are at his throat." She then addressed the sentry again. "You will give the rest of your intelligence to Sir Andrew."

When she stood to dismiss the lords, the sentry said, "Your Highness, there is more you may wish to hear."

"Well?"

"Warwick has brought the king himself to St. Albans."

Margaret wondered at this new turn of events. "Is this sound intelligence?" she asked sternly. She did not like surprises, especially those she didn't understand.

"It is sound, Highness." The sentry's voice was firm.

"Very well. Go." After the sentry left, she looked at the lords, who all appeared as puzzled as she. "This changes nothing," she said after a moment's reflection. "We will proceed as planned. Gather your forces."

After everyone had left the tent, she sat on the throne tapping her painted fingernails on the arm rest. "The Lord save you, Henry," she mumbled to herself, "but stand clear of my way now."

As the Earl of Warwick rode through St. Albans checking on his fortifications, he had a distinctly uneasy feeling. With him rode his brothers, George, the Bishop of Exeter, and John, Lord Montagu.

"John, I'll need you to stay here in town with the archers. You should be able to defend our rear flank should anybody come in from the Dunstable road."

John Neville was a stout man like his brothers, with the same steely blue eyes and muscular build. "You needn't worry about your flank. I'll keep it safe," he said with a broad smile. The sound of approaching horses distracted them. "Look, here comes the duke with our quivering king."

With an entourage of ten knights and trailing footsoldiers, John Mowbray, the Duke of Norfolk, rode up to the Neville brothers escorting King Henry, the sixth of that name to rule England.

Seeing the king, Warwick could not help but feel some pity. Gaunt to the point of emaciation, Henry's thin face was pale and barely obscured by a thin, graying beard. His bloodshot dark brown eyes did not acknowledge the people and events around him. He had not spoken coherently since he was led into London after his defeat at Northampton, and most thought that so many months of privation in the Tower had left his already fragile mind unhinged.

"Greetings, my lord of Warwick," Norfolk spoke in a booming voice. "As you requested, we bring you the king and three thousand of the boldest men of the eastern counties to assist you in this needful time."

"You are most welcome, your grace," said Warwick. As their horses sidled up next to each other they clasped hands in greeting. "I believe you know my brothers, the Bishop of Exeter and Lord Montagu?"

The duke acknowledged them with a slight bow of his head. "I do indeed. And now perhaps you can tell me what purpose is served by the king's presence here?"

"Do you not think it prudent to have the king lead his army against the cantankerous and disobedient queen, who has been acting without his blessing against his lawful heir, the Earl of March?"

It was a clever ploy. Parliament had, after all, named the Duke of York to be Henry's heir, and the king had agreed, albeit under some duress. Now that Edward, the Earl of March, had inherited his father's titles, he was the lawful heir to the throne.

With Henry at the head of Warwick's army, the queen was technically the rebel. Although admittedly transparent, this move might help dissuade some of the noble families and the common people from joining forces with Margaret. Norfolk agreed.

"It is prudent indeed. What arrangements have you made for his safe-keeping?"

Warwick turned to the bishop. "My brother will escort him to the abbey nearby. He'll be safe enough there until he leads our victorious forces back to London."

"Blessed are the meek, for they shall inherit the earth."

Everyone looked at the king, surprised that he had collected his wits enough to say anything. Henry was looking directly at Warwick, his blood-shot eyes piercing and focused.

"Take him to the abbey," said Warwick sharply to the bishop. "He needs rest after his long journey." George took the king's horse by the reins. "And see to it that he is well guarded!" yelled Warwick. The fool king had succeeded in spoiling his mood.

At three hours past midnight, Warwick, who had not slept at all, wondered why he had not heard from his scouts. It was a clear, cold February night with a dampness in the air that gave the chill an extra bite. Knowing that the Lancastrians were nearby, he expected an attack at first light and was well prepared, but the lack of intelligence from his scouts was disquieting. After satisfying himself that the main body of his and Norfolk's forces was well situated to the north of the town, he decided to ride back toward town and check on his brother's disposition. As he approached the first dwellings of St. Albans, three footsoldiers came running up to him, panting and out of breath.

"My lord," one said, "this is one of your scouts."

"Give me your report then, quickly," urged Warwick.

"My lord, the queen's army is nine miles from town and closing on the Dunstable Road."

Warwick's demeanor took a sour turn. "Are you sure it's the main body?"

"Yes, my lord. There is no question."

"You had better be right, or I'll have your liver for my breakfast." Without waiting for a response, he turned his horse and spurred it back toward the north at a full gallop. When he reached Norfolk's tent, he yelled for the duke to come forth. The duke was having difficulty focusing his eyes in the dark when he came out dressed only in leggings and a shirt.

"The queen is coming from Dunstable and is only nine miles off. We must redirect your men to join with my brother in town. If we move now we'll have time to redeploy before daybreak."

"Very well. Captain!" Norfolk called hurriedly. After giving instructions to his captain, he looked disapprovingly at Warwick. "How is it that we have been so deceived?"

"I don't know, but I assure you I'll find out when this is over," he said darkly.

When the men of Norfolk's command were roused, Warwick began to feel satisfied that he had met this challenge successfully. But at just that moment, the sounds of men yelling assailed his ears. It was coming from his brother's position, where the Dunstable road entered town.

He spurred his horse southward again and arrived in town to see his brother's archers unleashing volley after volley into the night. He found John with his sword drawn behind the second line of archers yelling encouragement to his men.

"What's happening?" asked Warwick as he came up on John. "Who are you firing on?"

"It's the queen's whole army, as near as I can tell," said John, wide-eyed with anger. "We were not prepared, but these are fine men. We have repelled their first assault, but they're coming again."

"That fool scout said they were nine miles away. I'll have his bloody head under my foot when this is over."

The earl's men were in chaos. The queen could not have picked a better time to attack. Warwick realized bitterly that if John's archers had not been up to the task, they would already have lost this battle, and even as it was, if he did not get his troops organized, they would soon be overrun.

"You must hold them here," he shouted at his brother. "I'll get you help as soon as I can."

Montagu acknowledged with a wave. As Warwick spurred his horse back to the north, the next wave of Lancastrians was approaching the archers.

Hours of fighting in the dark passed, and Montagu's archers had not budged. The Lancastrians, realizing the futility of continuing the attack in this location, withdrew and regrouped toward the north. Warwick had managed to organize the division of men which had been originally ordered to redeploy and directed them to oppose the queen's army which was now attacking at the north end of town. In the dark, the two sides fought without respite. Little advantage was gained by either.

When the first light glowed over the eastern horizon, the Yorkists had finally gained on the Lancastrians and pushed them out of the town into a large field to the west. Norfolk's men were engaged by another division of the queen's army on the north end of town. Margaret had obviously gathered an army much larger than Warwick had imagined, and its sheer numbers would win the day if one of the three fronts was not won soon. The best bet was John's archers, who were now only guarding the southern approaches to the town against light incursions.

Warwick sent word that John was to fall back on Warwick's position where together they would turn the tide of the battle. Within an hour, he was pleased to see his brother approaching from town. But his hope of a quick victory did not last long. To his surprise, the Lancastrians had broken through the left side of his lines and were slaughtering his men by the hundreds. That side had been well secured by his Kentish men under the command of Lovelace, a gentleman who had fought for the Duke of York at Wakefield and escaped that disaster to fight again here.

Through the din of the battle, shouts of "treason!" could be heard from within the ranks, and Warwick's lines began to crumble. Several soldiers came running up the small lane that was normally used by the townsfolk to cart the hay off the fields that were now drenched by the blood of hundreds. Warwick drew his sword and positioned himself to block their way.

"Hold, you bloody cowards! Stop or I'll take your heads here and now." They pulled up before the earl, sides heaving and lungs gasping for air.

"My lord," said one between breaths, "we do not desert. But the men of Kent and their commander have gone over to the queen, and we are being slaughtered. We sought to find a place to regroup, but they're too close. They are hard on our heels now, my lord. You must fly or you'll be taken sure."

Warwick was devastated. The men of Kent were some of his fiercest fighters and he would have trusted them with his life. More men were running from the carnage, and Warwick motioned for the three he stopped to go on, which they did without hesitating. When John Neville's troops arrived moments later, he knew that it was too late to fight on.

"I'm sorry, John," he said angrily. "We are betrayed and must flee. Come, we'll run north and see if Norfolk has established a defensible position."

With a harried and bloody remnant of their army, Warwick and his brother sped north to where they had first set up the main body of the army, before learning that the Lancastrians would attack from the west. But when they arrived, Norfolk's men were in flight before a formidable division of Margaret's army. Thousands of Yorkist soldiers lay dead and mangled on the field. At the sight of that turmoil, Warwick's men lost hope and began to flee in all directions.

"We must be gone!" yelled John to his brother. "The day is lost."

Reluctantly, Warwick nodded and they spurred their horses to a full gallop away from the slaughter.

King Henry sat on the makeshift throne in Margaret's tent. The queen sat on a suitable chair brought in from the abbey, which she had placed next to the king. Beside her, opposite the king, stood the Prince of Wales, now seven years of age. Northumberland, Clifford, Somerset, and Sir Andrew Trollope were also in attendance, as were many dignitaries normally attached to the royal family. The king seemed dwarfed by the throne upon which Margaret had sat so easily. He was clearly uncomfortable.

"My lords, you have all excelled this day," announced the queen, "and we are deeply grateful for your loyalty." All of the lords bowed to the royal family and mumbled about their sacred duties.

"And now," she continued, "we have joyous matters to tend to." With that she leaned over to her husband and hissed something into his ear.

"Yes, of course," he said quietly. He looked around trying to remember something. "I...I need a sword." The lords looked at one another, attempting to ascertain the protocol in such a situation. Northumberland stepped forward.

"If Your Highness would so honor me, I ask that you use my sword, which has been devotedly wielded in your defense a hundred times this day." When the king hesitated, Margaret spoke for him.

"We would be honored to use such a sword, my lord," she said, with a blistering look to her husband, and motioned him toward Northumberland's sword, which had been laid at the king's feet.

Henry slowly lifted the sword and softly thanked the earl, who bowed deeply in return. Henry stood and asked that his son come before him. The young prince complied. Dressed lavishly in brigandines covered with purple velvet, he bore himself with poise before the gathered gentry. He kneeled before his father, who touched both his shoulders with the sword.

"With this sword I knight thee, Edward Plantagenet, Prince of Wales." The prince stood to thank the king and then turned to the gathered lords, who knelt.

That ceremony being accomplished, the queen was back to business. "And now, my lords, we must march with haste to London, as no other obstacles stand in our way. The dangerous rebels are routed and we must secure the kingdom from further rebellion. Tonight we will stay at the abbey, but at first light our course is set to London."

"Your Majesty," Northumberland did not know whom to address, and therefore directed his eyes to the floor. "Your Majesty, I feel I must again ask that you order the pillaging of towns in this area be stopped. I greatly fear that we will garner much ill will if this behavior continues."

The queen was not in a charitable mood. She had suffered much outrage as a result of this rebellion, and now that it was almost over, she felt that her soldiers deserved any reward she could give them. Besides, the southern lords had not given her the support that she felt they should have, so some pillaging in these southern counties seemed appropriate.

"I have promised the men that they may take the rewards that they so richly deserve. I will not, at our moment of victory, deny them. Sir Andrew, have our losses been listed?" Northumberland stepped back, knowing that there was no point testing her further.

"As pertains to those of noble blood, Highness, only two. Of all others by my rough count, only about a thousand. The losses to the Yorkists numbered in the many thousands, and I was unable to glean an accurate count as a result."

"The two of noble blood that we lost, who were they?"

Sir Andrew referred to a small square of parchment and then responded, "Sir James Luttrell, and Sir John Grey of Bradgate Manor."

CHAPTER VII

Samuel was relieved to find such an ideal place to pass the daylight hours. The wind-sheltering privets put them about twenty paces off the road. They had walked all through the night and were exhausted. Worse, they had not eaten anything since supper the previous night when they had been forced to flee. For now, they would manage, but tomorrow they would have to find food.

And then there was the larger question of their destination.

"I tell you that we have only one option." Oliver was insistent. "We must find the Earl of March. He knows me and will give us shelter."

"He doesn't know me, Oliver, and if he discovers I served under Northumberland, he will not take the time to spit on me."

"Then to whom would you suggest we turn? You're a soldier and I, a page. These are not skills that are highly cherished in any town I know of. And how long do you suppose it will take Clifford to get word out to every village and town between here and York about us? We are still very much in the sphere of his northern friends."

Samuel did not have an answer. He sat back on his elbows and stared absently at the bare tree limbs. The morning light streaked red on thin, wispy clouds. He felt a growing mood of desperation. If they could not go back, and had nowhere to go forward, what was left?

"If we could make it back to York, we could blend in with the locals. And Clifford would not be expecting us to go back there, do you suppose?"

"I think there's little hope of making it that far," said Oliver. "But it may be our best hope anyway."

"Then it's settled. When we get to York we'll do our best to find some labor that will meet our immediate needs, and we'll keep our ears open for news of the earl." Samuel was settling in to a comfortable position. "Of course, you realize that given the result of that battle at Wakefield, the earl may already have lost his head on the queen's block."

Oliver was sitting cross-legged next to him with his eyes on the road through a small opening in the hedge. He sighed heavily.

"If that's true, then God has planned a short life for us as well."

Samuel came to consciousness reluctantly. Oliver was shaking him urgently, but it did not register right away; he had been in a deep sleep, the first in quite some time. As he regained his senses, he saw that the sun was high in the southern sky. Oliver's thin face and protruding ears filled his vision when his eyes came into focus.

"Wha…?" Oliver put his hand over his mouth before he could finish. Signaling for silence, he helped Samuel to his knees and pointed through the hedge toward the road. Not more than a stone's throw away, three men were surrounding a fourth. The victim was surprisingly agile and managed to hold the others at bay for longer than Samuel thought possible against such odds. He wore the clothes of a field hand, with a coarse woolen tunic and loose leggings, gray-brown, and filthy. He appeared to be in his mid-thirties, but his face was lined and timeworn.

At last, one of the thugs managed to trip him from behind. He fell backwards and hit the ground with a loud grunt. The largest of his attackers put his knee on the victim's chest, and reached for a knife sheathed near his hip. Oliver whispered urgently in Samuel's ear.

"We must help him."

Samuel pulled him back down. "Wait, you can't help him by being a fool." He reached for his bow and pulled an arrow from the quiver. He nocked the arrow and peered through the hedge to take aim. The large robber had pulled his knife and had it poised above the victim, ready to strike. With the mindless precision that was honed by years of training, he drew back the string and let loose the arrow. It struck the large man in the chest, easily passing through his ribs and heart.

The highwayman jerked back and then fell forward, dead before he hit the ground. The other two looked down at their partner, then looked toward the direction from whence the arrow must have come, terrified, expecting another deadly strike from out of nowhere.

From behind the hedge, Samuel stood, another arrow nocked and ready, and walked slowly toward the thieves.

"I'll give you both a three count to flee before I loose another one." His voice was as steady as his hand on the string. "And if I see you so much as look back, you'll have one each in your backs before you take your next breath."

Having no intention of testing Samuel further, they looked at each other for half a second, then turned and fled down the road as if the hounds of hell were close on their heels. Their victim pushed the dead man away.

"That was an impressive hit, my friend," he said gratefully. "I thought my time on earth was done for certain."

"I had no choice. He would have killed you." He pushed the dead man with his foot so that he could see his face. "I'm sorry, but I had no choice," he repeated quietly.

Oliver was surprised to see Samuel's remorse. It was not what he expected from a professional soldier. "These were deadly thieves, Samuel. They deserved little better."

"Indeed not. I am Nigel of Devon, and I owe you my life — a debt that I will not take lightly, if I can know your names."

"I am Oliver, and this is Samuel, both from the north counties." He did not see any reason to give the man too much information. "We were resting after a long journey when we heard your distress. It was a lucky thing for you that we were nearby."

"Lucky, indeed," Nigel said, looking carefully at Samuel. "Tell me where you learned such skill with the bow, my friend."

Samuel saw no reason to prevaricate. "I served in the Earl of Northumberland's personal guard."

Nigel's eyebrows raised, several suspicions confirmed.

"He trained you well," he said, after a short pause. "You both look as if you could use some rest and food. I know a tavern in Richmond, a day's walk from here to the south, where we can stay in safety and get a good meal. Do you travel that way?"

Oliver hesitated for a moment, glancing quickly back to Samuel.

"We are headed for York."

"Good. Then it's settled, if you don't mind the company? I know I'd feel safer."

They both knew it was probably their best chance to get a real meal anytime soon, but the risks of traveling on the main road to Richmond during the day were great.

"Have you come from the north, then?" asked Samuel.

"Yes, I had business near the Scottish border and was headed for London when you came across my path, by divine grace."

"Did you not see any riders bearing the colors of any northern noble?"

"I saw no riders of that description," said Nigel, puzzlement in his voice. "Do you seek such riders?"

"No," Samuel hesitated, "we thought we saw them during the night. We were probably mistaken."

"It's not easy to miss such riders, even in the night," said Nigel, scratching his head. "Would you rather wait here for a while to see if they return?"

If Nigel hadn't seen any of Clifford's men on the road north of here, it was possible that they had given up the search. After all, it seemed likely that Clifford needed his resources elsewhere. And the thought of the promised meal drove him to carelessness.

"No," he said finally, "we'll go with you now." A quick look to Oliver confirmed that he was of like mind. Hunger was a powerful motivator.

Richmond was a relatively large town, located almost halfway between Northwood and York. It stood on high ground that rose from a dense wood and was dominated by an eleventh-century castle on the apex of the hill. The town itself had become a regional center for trading goods, and was populated by a rapidly growing class of merchants who took advantage of increasing trade between regions, despite the civil wars.

As the walls of Richmond came into sight, the companions crossed the fields that supplied the town with food and with pasture for their sheep. Small settlements dotted the countryside where farmers and overflow residents of town lived in small wattle-and-daub shanties. Nigel led Samuel and Oliver into the center of town, past a few townsmen who were walking home or on their way to the taverns. The streets were so narrow that the overhanging second stories of the buildings almost touched.

At last, on a narrow alley just off the main street, they found themselves standing before a nondescript tavern.

"I know this place well," said Nigel, opening the door. "We'll be safe enough here."

They stepped into a small room dimly lit by several large wall-mounted candles. A lone patron occupied a table near the hearth, and the room's only other occupant, an old woman with several large warts on her grimy face, sat behind a small bar. The man at the table watched them enter from the corner of his eye as he took a pull on a large wooden mug of ale. Oliver was the last one in. They took a table against the back wall of the room.

"Wait here," Nigel told them, "I'll speak with the innkeeper." After talking with her quietly for a few moments, he returned to the table with a third wooden stool.

"I've used this place many times before," he assured Samuel and Oliver. "Molly minds her own business, sure enough. She's bringing us some of her pottage, which will keep us well until morning." He looked down at Samuel's bow and quiver, which he had placed against the wall behind him. "You had better get that out of sight. It's certain to draw attention. Not many townspeople own one." Samuel nodded.

When Molly returned with the pottage and a loaf of barley and oat bread, they attacked their bowls hungrily. The pottage was a thick stew of beans, peas, onion, and barley sprouts, with salt pork added for flavor. It reminded Samuel of the stews that Emma cooked. He wondered what the seneschal and Clifford's men had done to them, to Emma and to Sally, after his escape. It would be difficult for his father to convince them that he had not been aware of Samuel's presence in town.

The silent man by the hearth stood and made his way to the door. As he pulled a ragged cloak over his shoulders, he paused for a moment to look back at the strangers near the wall, and then hurried out the door. Nigel stared at the door for a moment.

"You said earlier that you were recently detached from Northumberland's guard," he said casually to Samuel. "How is it that he would part with an archer of your skills in such times as these?"

The question made Samuel wary and he regarded Nigel with sharp eyes for a moment before he responded.

"Let's just say we mutually agreed that I would no longer serve him."
Nigel persisted. "And you never told me what you do," he said to Oliver.
"You're asking a lot of questions all of a sudden," Oliver said.

"I owe you both a life and I'll not forget that. But it's always best to know something about the company you keep, not that I haven't figured a few things out already." Samuel was now growing apprehensive and wondered if they hadn't made a fatal mistake. "I know, for instance, that the colors you wear are those of the Duke of York." Until that moment, it had not occurred to Samuel that Oliver was still wearing the same clothes that he had worn at Wakefield, and that those clothes would show an allegiance to the dead duke by their very aspect and color. It should have been the first thing they tended to in Northwood.

"If it's true that my savior here served the Earl of Northumberland," continued Nigel, "and I have no reason to doubt it, you make a curious pair; one a Lancastrian and the other a Yorkist. It is also apparent that you are running from someone."

Both of them were silently weighing their options, which seemed to be limited at the moment. Finally Oliver made a decision for both of them.

"My master was the Earl of Rutland. Samuel came to my defense at Wakefield, much to the displeasure of the butcher Clifford, and as a result we both flee his wrath. Is there anything else you need to know about us?"

"No," Nigel said. "There's nothing more I need to know."

They finished their meal in silence, the tension gone at last, and then went up to the second-floor sleeping room, where straw-stuffed sleeping pads lined the floor. The three were the only tenants. Nigel blew out the candle after they had each collapsed onto the nearest pad. There was a single small uncovered window through which a faint glow of moonlight streamed.

Samuel woke with a start and knew instantly that something was wrong. He shook his head to clear the haze. It was well after sunrise and the light streaked through the window. Oliver was still asleep on the next pad, but Nigel was gone, his pad clean as if no one had slept there. Loud voices came from the street below the window. He jumped up and carefully peered out to see several soldiers talking with the man from the tavern the night before, pointing to the door. It occurred to Samuel that they had only seconds to flee the building, and if the tavern did not have a back door, it was already too late. He pounced on Oliver and yanked him off his pad and on to his feet.

"They're right outside!" he said desperately. "Come on."

They plummeted down the narrow steps and into the passage between the main room and the proprietor's quarters. They paused for an instant at the foot of the steps and saw Molly standing between them and the front door. She nodded toward a curtain to their left, and then walked to the door to answer the pounding.

They had no choice but to trust her, and ran through the curtain. They were in a small storage room, the air pungent with the musty odor of dried foodstuffs. The sight of a door at the far wall gave them an opening of hope. Samuel rushed over and cautiously opened it a crack, peering with one eye out on the street. What had happened to Nigel, he wondered. Had he betrayed them? Had they been fools to trust him so readily? Behind them, crushing footsteps were rushing up the steps.

"Check in there!" a loud voice yelled.

Samuel knew they were out of time. Caution to the wind, he pushed the door open and pulled Oliver out into the street. They were on a side alley. To their right, soldiers were entering the tavern. They ran to the left, coming to an abrupt halt as four armed men came around the corner, swords drawn.

"Halt!" an iron voice called.

They turned and ran back the way they had come, but five soldiers had just poured out of the door to the tavern's storage room. Samuel desperately sought another way but there was no place else to turn. A huge man with a hideous scar down the left side of his face stepped through the door, carrying Samuel's bow and quiver. The scar deformed his mouth into a permanent smile.

"We have them, Sir Hugh," said one of the armed men ebulliently. Sir Hugh cowed him into silence with a quick look.

He stood over the frightened young men, dominating the low street by his mere presence. After a moment he spoke to Samuel, indicating the bow, which he contemplated somberly.

"You left your signature in a body by the road north of here," he said.

"The arrow had Northumberland's markings on it. Rather careless of you."

Samuel silently agreed. It had been a terrible oversight not to remove the arrow from the thief before they left. Without warning, Sir Hugh laid a blow with the back of his gloved hand across Samuel's head, sending him sprawling into a wall and then into a heap on the ground. Two of the soldiers picked him off the ground and brought him back to his feet.

"That's with the compliments of Lord Clifford. He is looking forward to administering your punishment personally." Samuel spat blood, unable to clear his head. If it were not for the men holding him, he would not have been able to keep his feet. "Put them in irons," Sir Hugh addressed the soldier next to him. "We leave for Pontefract immediately."

They dragged Samuel and Oliver out into the main street, and fitted them with ankle irons as dozens of curious townspeople watched and jeered. When both were securely chained, they were led to a double horse-drawn wagon with iron posts at each corner. There were already two people huddled in the front corner, both chained to one of the posts. More than a dozen soldiers stood by, all dressed in the colors of Lord Clifford. Samuel stumbled a few feet from the cart, failing to properly judge the length of the chain that connected his leg irons. Oliver reached out and supported him.

They were both roughly lifted and tossed into the back of the wagon. The horses startled and before they could be controlled by the driver, moved several feet ahead. The motion caused one of the prisoners in front to look up, and Samuel's heart sank when he recognized them both.

"Sally!" It was Oliver who choked out her name. Next to her was John Miller, so badly beaten that he was hardly recognizable.

"God and his ministers bear me witness, they will answer with their dearest blood for this outrage!"

The queen was livid. She paced the marble floor of the St. Albans Abbey as Northumberland and Somerset looked on. Gazing absently out a small window in the back wall of the Abbot's private chambers was King Henry, who did not appear to be interested in the events that had so possessed his wife. The royal party had commandeered the abbey for their temporary residence after the battle.

"Our envoy, Sir Robert Whitingham, had apparently convinced the Lord Mayor to surrender London," explained Northumberland, "but the townspeople, fearing that the city would be looted, began to riot. To make matters worse, two knights in Your Highness's service, Sir Baldwin Fulford and Sir Alexander Hody, unbeknownst to us, took some men to the gates of the city and demanded its surrender. When they were refused, they immediately began pillaging the area, confirming the worst fears of the citizens. They poured out of town and put the knights' men to flight. Now, the mayor and citizens are galvanized against us and have vowed not to admit the royal family under any circumstances."

Although Northumberland feared just this sort of setback when he warned Margaret about the pillaging, he knew this was not the time to remind her.

"Your Majesty, one thing is certain," added Somerset, "an attempt to take London forcibly when the gates are closed against us would surely meet with failure."

"We are aware of that," she snapped. After taking several more paces across the room, she spun. "We gave no permission to attack the city. How did this occur?"

"Majesty," responded Somerset, "it is difficult to control every contingent of a large army. We have already begun to see desertions now that it is perceived that no further…um, extra remuneration will be forthcoming to the soldiers."

"That sniveling mayor and his henchmen must know that we shall have their worthless heads on the gates of the city for this."

"Yes, Highness, but you must remember that the Yorkists owe the city a great deal of money, and the mayor and citizens who made those loans know that they'll never see their money again if we prevail. They also know that the Earl of March is on his way here with an army, and that has given them hope."

"Then after we have dispatched the earl, we will deal with London." She turned her back and signaled for them to leave. But Northumberland sensed that it might be a good time to spring his bad news.

"Your Highness, there is more you should hear."

"Well?"

"Our latest intelligence confirms that Warwick has not fled to Calais as was assumed earlier. Instead he has joined the remains of his army with the earl's at Chipping Norton and is headed this way as well."

This was bad news indeed. Warwick would add considerable strength to March's army, and while she beat him once, she did not like her chances a second time with her tired army, especially this close to London, where Warwick commanded many resources.

"Leave us," she said with a wave of her hand. They both bowed and left. Northumberland thought that for the first time since he had met her years ago, he had heard resignation in her voice.

As Margaret stood staring at the door through which her supporters had just left, she felt a hand on her shoulder. Henry had joined her.

"Perhaps it would be wiser to withdraw," he said softly. "There will always be another day."

"Oh, my dear husband," she said putting her hand on his, "if only you could have been stronger, we would not now be so desperate."

"I did what I thought was best for the realm. Perhaps some day you will see that."

She shook her head. "But our son. What of him? He is all that we have in this wretched world that is still pure. How could I stand by and let him be discarded like the day's kitchen waste?"

"Don't you think I thought about that?" he whispered.

She turned to face him and put her hand on his cheek. "I have no notion of what you think these days, my king," she said sadly and then found the abbot's most comfortable chair and sat heavily. She was so tired, but there was still so much that had to be done. "I know what your people think of me," she said, her French accent thicker than usual. "I know that they hate me, and it's only their love for you that gives us any hope at all, but you were never meant to be a king, my husband. We both know that. Someone had to make the sacrifice and take up the burden that you refused. I do not regret doing that, and I never shall."

Henry looked out the window again. Cold air had returned to the land and the abbot's garden was covered with frost. A finch landed on a stone bench, resting from the continual search for food.

"It was so easy to let you do that," he said finally, "and to retreat to my holy studies. And to my madness," he added after a pause. "But I see now how unfair that was to you, only now that it is too late. Can you ever forgive me?"

She reached out to him, too tired to get to her feet. He put his head in her lap. As she stroked his thinning hair, she could not think of anything that she would have done differently in their life together, and that thought gave her comfort. From the very first day that she was escorted into his presence, she knew that life at the English court would not be easy. When she was proposed as a bride for Henry, the French king, Charles VII, demanded that the English cede any claim to the provinces of Anjou and Maine to the French throne as payment. This was a heavy price in the minds of most Englishmen for a French queen, and many of the most influential barons were enraged. The fires that had consumed the factions of the House of Lancaster since the death of Henry's father erupted with renewed fury. Margaret had learned quickly who her friends were and moved to strengthen her new husband's position.

"Perhaps we will yet prevail, but for now I think that you are right. We'll go back to York and strengthen ourselves." She hugged his head to her breast. For these few moments at least, she did not have to be strong.

Edward regarded the courtyard of Baynards Castle sadly. His army had marched into London like conquering heroes, escorted by throngs of townspeople, all shouting jubilantly and welcoming his arrival. After mingling with the impromptu gathering of city officials that had assemble before Baynards, Edward separated himself and escorted Hastings and Warwick into the courtyard. It was here, he remembered bitterly, that he last bid farewell to Edmund. He pulled his cloak higher around his shoulders to ward off the cold of this early March day. Still, it was good to see the walls of Baynards once again.

This jubilant entrance into London was the culmination of a very successful journey. After his crushing victory at Mortimer's Cross, he began the return trip to London, only to hear the disappointing news of the Earl of Warwick's failure at St. Albans. He quickly sent several messengers out to locate the defeated earl with an entreaty to join the remainder of his troops with Edward's. Word came back that Warwick had indeed salvaged a respectable force and was in the process of gathering more men, and that they would meet at Chipping Norton, which happened as planned two days later. The cousins had no choice but to march with diligence to London and face the queen. Neither of them imagined that the people of London would prove such a formidable foil before the Lancastrian army.

Edward ushered Hastings and Warwick into his father's riverside castle. He was flush with excitement and new hope. Handing overcoats off to servants and demanding ale of the butler, they settled into the great hall where a blazing fire burned in the hearth.

"I tell you that there will never be a better opportunity to press your claim, my lord." Warwick was insistent on directing Edward's thoughts. "The people of London will support your right to the crown because they have burned their bridges of reconciliation with the queen."

"I would be king of England, cousin, not of London," said Edward.

"To be sure, we must deal with the queen," Warwick answered impatiently, "but this would be an important first step. The peers and commoners alike must regard you as their king, not just the Earl of March, or they will not support us."

"I must agree, my lord," added Hastings. "What happens here will carry great sway throughout the realm. If you are proclaimed king, we will assuredly carry greater authority with us when we march against Margaret."

"But we can't wait here to convene a Parliament," said Edward. "It is imperative that we march against her before she gathers too much strength."

"Your father said the same thing before he chased her north," said Warwick soberly.

"My father would be king today if he had waited for me before engaging Clifford. I will not make the same mistake, you may be assured."

"Be that as it may, we have the time to meet with the mayor and aldermen. We will gather a large crowd at St. John's field with many of my men scattered about to assure a friendly response to our entreaties. My brother will deliver a forceful sermon extolling your virtues and claim to the throne, and after we get an acclamation from the crowd, we will have the Archbishop of Canterbury crown you at Westminster."

"Can you be sure that the archbishop will side with us?"

"He will not deny me," Warwick responded.

Events were moving faster than Edward had anticipated and that made him uncomfortable, but he could not deny that as king he could force those of the nobility who had not taken sides to do so. To shun him as an earl meant that they could lose their lives, but to defy him as king meant that they could lose all of their estates and titles as well, a fate truly worse than death.

"Very well, good cousin. Proceed with your plan at first light. We'll stay here in London for a few days longer, but after that I'll brook no further delay for our journey north. Sir William, you will devote your time here to making preparations for our next encounter with haughty Margaret."

"As you wish, my lord," said Hastings.

Edward looked into the roaring fire and watched as the flames leaped from the logs and disappeared up the chimney. He had no illusions that this forced ceremony would actually make him king. But still, it was a giddy feeling. With the heat of the fire full on his face, he closed his eyes and tried to remember Edmund's face.

Two days later, events unfolded exactly as the Earl of Warwick had predicted, and Edward found himself surrounded by every dignitary within a day's ride of London in the great hall of Westminster Abbey. Assisting the archbishop was George Neville, the bishop of Exeter, and the Earl of Warwick himself. Together they had placed on Edward's shoulders the royal robes with ermine collar and escorted him to the king's chair, where the golden circlet used to crown many kings before him was placed on his head.

The archbishop then heard Edward's oath once again, in which he swore to keep the realm justly and to maintain the laws. Edward, for what seemed to him the hundredth time in the last two days, repeated his claim to the royal seat. After hearing the loud acclamation of all those in attendance, he was handed the sacred scepter, and every lord present knelt before the new king to pay him homage. Finally, Edward made offerings before the tomb of Saint Edward the Confessor. When he returned to the throne, he was proclaimed King Edward, fourth of that name.

After the festivities in the abbey were over, the lords and prelates retired back to London and the tower room of Baynards Castle, while various heralds proclaimed the news of the coronation throughout the City. Now Edward knew it was time to reward those who had backed him, whose support he would continue to need if his throne was to become secure.

"My most gracious lords, prelates, and friends," he said as he rose from his seat. The revelers came to an abrupt silence as they waited on the words of their new king. "We thank you all for your loyal support and promise you that you shall reap the rewards thereof. We all recognize that the struggles are not over yet, and to that end we must be diligent, but for now let it be known that we hereby create our cousin of Warwick our chamberlain, and his grace, the bishop of Exeter, our chancellor." Both positions guaranteed membership in the king's inner circle of advisors.

"Now if it please you, we will retire, as we would be fresh to make our necessary preparations for war with bloody Margaret."

Everyone in the room rose and bowed as Edward left. Warwick also made his egress with his brother after receiving congratulations for their new positions. They made their way out to a large balcony that overlooked the city.

"You see, George? Our fortunes grow with each day, and the young king will grant us further boons as well, when I request them."

"I do not share your taste for power, my brother. My desire for strong leadership for our country has driven my actions thus far, and God strike me down if my motives become less pure."

"Yes, yes, of course." Warwick hated it when his brother began to preach. Especially now that he was on the verge of attaining that for which he had longed ever since these wars began: the power to match his wealth.

"And I see that I must warn you again not to underestimate Edward. Did you not see how the commons and nobles alike admired him? He wears the crown like he was born to it, and royal robes lie on his back with ease." The bishop turned to his brother. "And I need not remind you that he was successful in battle when we were not."

Warwick stiffened at the words but otherwise showed no emotions. "His youth and inexperience will keep him under our sway until we can strengthen our position. Soon we will be ensconced in every important position in the kingdom and, regardless of how our new king feels about it, too strong to defy."

"As you say," said the bishop with a sigh. He was growing tired of the verbal sparring, which, in any event, did not seem to be doing any good. "First there's the small issue of dealing with Margaret's army. If we survive that test, then we can debate what is best for the kingdom."

CHAPTER VIII

Lord Rivers held his daughter, Elizabeth, in his arms while she wept, her body limp from consuming grief. Sir John had been her life. The news of his death at St. Albans left her empty and desperate. Around them stood her mother and her brother, Anthony, as well as the steward, all with drawn faces hoping that words would come to console her.

"Be comforted, my daughter," said Rivers at last. "He loved you dearly, and died defending the realm. What more could a knight wish? His sons will stand tall in the shadow of his memory as they grow to manhood."

The duchess took her daughter away from Rivers and led her into the sitting room.

"Bring aqua vitae," she said to the steward, who nodded grimly. Anthony could not sit still for long and began pacing in front of the windows as the rest sat in silence.

Elizabeth wiped the tears from her face with her napkin.

"What shall I tell the children?" The steward returned, and the duchess helped Elizabeth sip some of the mild liquor.

"The truth, Elizabeth," said her father. "You must tell them how their father gave his life for his king, as is every knight's duty. And he died most bravely, leading the final charge against the Yorkist positions."

"But what has been gained?" Anthony blurted out. "The queen has abandoned our gains by retreating back to York. And now Warwick has crowned his puppet, Edward."

"I am certain that this is not the correct time to discuss this, Anthony," said the duchess crossly.

"No, I want to understand what has happened." Elizabeth sounded determined. "If my husband has died in vain, then I wish to know why."

"Do you see, Anthony?" scolded the duchess. "Now you've upset her, and for reasons that escape me."

"Mother, please don't treat me as a fragile flower," said Elizabeth.

"She has the right to know, Mother. As king, Edward has the power to have us all declared traitors and confiscate all of our titles and estates. Sir John's children would have nothing."

"I can't believe it will come to that," interjected Rivers. "The queen has not surrendered, only gone back to York to regroup." He was addressing his comments to Elizabeth more than to his son. "We will join her there and, as I know that God will protect our cause, we will be victorious. Margaret has strong support in the north."

"Every time I hear assurances of victory we seem to be drawn further into this senseless war," Elizabeth said sourly. "And you continue to promise us that the next battle will be the last."

"It is true that this rebellion seems to have the many heads of Homer's serpent," Rivers answered dejectedly, "but it cannot last forever, and in the end we must prevail."

"We must indeed," the duchess said sharply. "The fate of the Woodville family wafts in the midst of this storm, and we had best find safe harbor if things go awry." She had seen too many families like theirs vanish into oblivion after ending up on the wrong side of similar conflicts. "When the vultures circle after the last battle, it won't be our carcasses that they pick over. We have been through too much to come to such an end." She wondered if her husband had the strength to find the right path for the family through these dangerous times. His pleasant and easygoing personality did not lend itself well to such hard decisions.

"It has been so long since a strong king has governed," said Anthony, "that many of the great houses have suffered no restraints upon their activities. These wars between York and Lancaster are only the culmination of many squabbles between the magnates. If we prevail, will this change?" It was a troubling question.

"We can only hope for a victory on the field, and then we will be in a better position to work for a more stable government," said Rivers. But he did not exude confidence. He saw that Elizabeth was staring into space with no light in her eyes. "Bring our cloaks," he called to the steward.

"Elizabeth and I will walk for a spell in the garden."

He helped Elizabeth to her feet and into her cloak. They walked into the manicured hedgerows of the Bradgate gardens. In the summertime when the roses were in constant bloom, perfuming the warm breezes that wafted off a man-made lake, the gardens were a delight. At this time in early March, however, there were no flowers and the trees were without life. But the evergreen hedges still defined the paths and the twigs of the trees made delightful patterns against the midday sky. A mist rose off the lake as if shielding some dark secret in the opaque waters. Rivers held Elizabeth's hand as they wound to the left of the waterless fountain beneath the main stairs.

"I have not faced death as you must now," Rivers spoke softly, "and I pray each night that all of the family will long outlive me, which would be good and natural. To be honest, I have doubts about the House of Lancaster. They have flaws and strengths, and they look after their own as do we all. But regardless of who sits upon the throne, our honor as a family must be maintained at any expense, and I know that Sir John believed that with all his soul."

They arrived at an ornately carved marble bench on the shore of the lake, commanding a sweeping view of fields and hills beyond. They sat and let the sun warm them.

"Do you remember," continued Rivers, "that day when you were so much younger — only nine or ten years old, I believe — when Lord Fitzwalter brought his daughter to Grafton?"

"How could I forget that insufferable brat?" said Elizabeth with a scowl. "And I was ten, she some years younger."

Rivers had to smile as he remembered the visit. "She spent the better part of a fortnight denigrating you and trying to make you feel inferior. You were quite miserable having to entertain her, I knew that. But you still kept her company without complaining."

"I thought that she would never leave," said Elizabeth. It had indeed been one of her most vivid childhood memories. The girl's name was Katherine, and she had been raised to feel superior to most. It shamed Elizabeth to remember that she had wished at the time that her father had carried the status of her mother's first husband, the Duke of Bedford, instead of a simple baron. But Elizabeth had been firm in her resolve to maintain her dignity.

Katherine and her father were traveling home from London, where Lord Fitzwalter had spent some time at court as a member of the king's Privy Council. While in London, they had taken delivery of an exquisite porcelain figure of an angel, which Fitzwalter had ordered all the way from Venice for his daughter on the occasion of her birthday. The flowing, half-unfurled wings were so delicately crafted, they appeared as soft as a swan's, and if she died and found herself in heaven, she was certain that she would never see a face so beautiful. It was the present of a lifetime and Katherine wasted no time having it unpacked long enough for Elizabeth to be amazed by its beauty. Indeed, Elizabeth had never seen anything quite as stunning.

"What ever possessed you to go riding that day?" asked Rivers.

"Katherine insisted, and I was not about to let that wretchedly pompous girl claim that she was better trained in horsemanship. We were not far from Grafton before the thunder started, but she continued on." Elizabeth shivered, remembering the look of the sky that afternoon.

"I did not know you had been so foolish."

"Still, if she hadn't tried to cross that ravine, we'd have been all right. Its banks must have been yards above the channel. But when the lightning struck, she was the one to be thrown, not I. It was the loudest noise I had ever heard. I found Katherine at the bottom of the ravine. Her horse bolted back to the stable."

"That's when we knew something was terribly wrong. When we set out to look for you, the rain began to fall in sheets."

"When I slid into the ravine after Katherine, it was obvious that her leg was broken. She could not put any weight on it at all. I had to drag her up that embankment by myself. By the time you arrived to help, I had carried her for an hour."

"It was a miracle, we all agreed. And Lord Fitzwalter could have not been more grateful." Rivers shook his head in silent amazement.

"She didn't talk to me for the rest of the time that she was with us, and she never left her room, not even to eat. I was so happy when they finally left."

"But she left you that porcelain angel as thanks. She evidently learned a great lesson that day."

"I still can't believe she did that."

"I was never so proud of any of my children as I was of you that day."

She took his big hand in hers and squeezed it.

"I feel so empty," she said, leaning against her father.

"It will pass. You must be strong, as you always have been."

"Please be careful, Father, when you go to York. It would be too great a burden to lose you as well."

"I will return, I swear it," he said with conviction. The sun dipped behind a billowing cloud that raced across the sky, and the light breeze turned noticeably colder. The mist shifted slowly over the lake. Rivers stroked his daughter's golden hair and closed his eyes. "You never go anywhere without that angel, do you?"

Elizabeth took a deep breath. "Katherine and I served together as ladies-in-waiting for Queen Margaret two years ago, before these wars broke out. When I told Katherine that I had the angel with me, she didn't even want to see it. I never could understand her, but I was sure that she loved that angel dearly."

CHAPTER IX

The flickering glow of a torch and an occasional moan coming from somewhere beyond the iron grill of his cell door were Samuel's only connection to the outside world. He had no way of knowing how many days had passed since they had been left within the bowels of Pontefract Castle, but he guessed that it must have been many nights based on the number of times bread and water had been shoved through the bars. Samuel and Oliver sat over his father as Sally slept on the stone floor, its hardness eased only by a thin layer of filthy straw.

John Miller was dying. His wounds had not been tended, and Samuel doubted it would have made any difference. His face was badly swollen, and he frequently coughed blood. It was certain that several ribs were broken. On the awful trip from Richmond, Sally had begged for help but was threatened into silence. It was apparent that Sir Hugh was quite content to see John Miller dead for what he perceived to be unpardonable crimes against his authority. Inflicting additional anguish on Samuel was a bonus.

On the trip to Pontefract, Sally was able to tell them that it was only through the intervention of Sir Toby that the entire family was not imprisoned with them. Apparently, he wanted to ensure that Northumberland was not deprived of his only miller in Northwood, and it was simply too distasteful to drag the pregnant Emma into the wagon in chains, so she was left behind as well.

Now, as Samuel sat next to his father with his back to the uneven stone wall, he could not comprehend the course of events that had led his family to these dire straits. His family had been ripped asunder, and his father would most likely die because of him.

"I think this damn place is where I belong."

"Stop blaming yourself," chided Oliver. "You did what you thought was right."

Samuel did not, at first, respond. The occasional moan that came from out of the blackness beyond seemed to emanate from within himself. "When I was with Northumberland's guard, the captain told us a story about this place. Apparently it was here where King Henry's grandfather murdered his cousin, King Richard, and usurped his throne. Aren't we lucky, getting to suffer the same fate as such a great king?"

"Are you there, son?"

"I'm here, Father."

"Water," he croaked painfully. Samuel groped in the dark for the bowl that they were keeping full of water for him. He held the bowl to John Miller's lips until he had managed to swallow a mouthful. It appeared to give him the strength he needed to speak.

"Don't blame yourself for this. It's a burden you need not bear."

"Father." A lump swelled in his throat. "Can you ever forgive me? Every time I follow my conscience, we come to harm. Did you know I killed someone on the road south of Northwood? I tried only to save a man's life from a murderous thief, but in the end I managed to get Oliver caught along with myself. And the man I saved probably betrayed us."

"How can you know what lies in the heart of another man?" his father responded with obvious difficulty.

"How can I ever forgive myself for what has happened to you and Sally…"

"Samuel, listen to me. I…I'm very proud of you. Never forget that." His voice trailed off and his breathing became shallow and rasping.

"Father?" Samuel leaned over the pallet.

John Miller coughed violently and shuddered in his son's arms. With his last strength he whispered in Samuel's ear. "Never forget…" His last breath left his body as a painful sigh.

Samuel pulled his father's limp body up and hugged him tightly. He began to sob.

At last, thought Edward, when Warwick finally entered camp. It had been a lengthy journey northward for his men, but Warwick needed the time to raise troops in the midlands, and while waiting for his cousin to join him Edward had been busy as well. The latest intelligence had the queen's army at about thirty thousand strong, a formidable force that Edward was determined to match. Now with Warwick's men, they were close — about twenty thousand in all. And the Duke of Norfolk had promised more men from the eastern and southern counties, who were to arrive soon. Edward had Warwick and Montagu escorted to his tent while he and Hastings reviewed the camp's fortifications.

"These Nevilles are powerful men, Sire," Hastings said. "I fear that one day you may need to prove that you are their master."

Edward watched the sunset paint red streaks on the underside of the thickening clouds. Another storm was brewing.

"I pray this will be our last battle, William," he said wistfully. "How long do you think it will take us to reach York?"

"Two days, my lord. We will have to pass around Pontefract first, which will slow our progress."

"Very well. We will proceed at first light. We cannot wait on the Duke of Norfolk any longer. Send a runner to inform him to make haste for York. We will surely have need of his services there."

"As you wish, my lord."

"And William," Edward looked tired, but the youthful spark of defiance never left him, "we will deal with the Nevilles when occasion gives us leave. Have no fear, my friend."

Hastings bowed his head and spurred his horse back toward the royal tent. *I hope so, my young king, for I have grave misgivings.*

Heavy footsteps and the clanging of iron against stone fractured the monotonous silence of Samuel's cell. He had been drifting in and out of consciousness ever since Sally assumed the vigil over their father's body. She had said nothing since John Miller's death. Both he and Oliver had attempted to get her to eat, but except for a few sips of water, they had not been successful.

The dim light became steadily brighter. Three soldiers carrying torches stopped before their cell.

"Come out, all of you," one said, loudly unlocking the swing bar that secured the iron gate. Samuel attempted to stand and found that he was almost too weak to get to his feet. Oliver was having the same problem, and Sally had not moved.

Two of the soldiers entered the cell with their torches, almost blinding Samuel with the intensity.

"No!" screamed Sally when one grabbed her arm.

"Leave her," said Samuel. He was appalled to discover how weak he had become. He took Sally gently by the shoulders and lifted her to her feet. "There's nothing more you can do for him, Sally. Please, you must be strong."

With her head buried in Samuel's chest, they stumbled toward the gate.

"You too, old man," said the guard, kicking the pallet again.

"He's dead, you fool," said Samuel savagely.

The guard held his torch over the body. "Why wasn't I informed?" he barked at the other guards.

"We had no knowledge of this, sir," one responded.

"Would it have made any difference?" said Samuel bitterly.

"Bring them, quickly."

He stormed past them and led the way through long stone lined passageways and up several flights of stairs. In their depleted state and with chains on their ankles, they walked with great difficulty. Finally, at the top of a long flight of stairs, the lead guard flung open a door and the light of day flooded the narrow flight. The prisoners covered their eyes as they were pushed out into the central bailey of Pontefract Castle.

"Stay here," ordered the guard. Samuel, Oliver, and Sally huddled together at the base of the high parapet wall. The prisoners trembled in the cold wind, clothed only in filthy rags that had not been changed in weeks. As he grew accustomed to the light, Samuel knew enough about castle operations to know that preparations were being made for a siege. Oliver had come to the same conclusion. Looking at each other as if to gain a silent confirmation, they also knew that in a state of siege, prisoners were usually executed in order to save the resources of the castle. He put his arm around Sally and pulled her close.

He wondered who the master of Pontefract was, and what army would consider a siege of this formidable keep, but the activity in the courtyard was unmistakable. Food and munitions were brought in across the drawbridge in large wagonloads. Twice the normal complement of lookouts plied the gate and guard posts, and armaments were piled in sheltered locations where they would be easily accessible. From among the rumble of activity, a cart arrived, driven by a surly man who leered at them as he pulled the horse to a halt. He broke into a sinister half-smile that revealed the few black teeth left in his mouth.

"His Worship says put 'em in," he said, almost unintelligibly.

They were lifted into the cart and chained to the corner posts, and Samuel knew that the end of a rope was waiting for them at their destination.

"Why are you bringing my sister?" Samuel asked one of the guards. "Sir Hugh said she would serve his household."

"No!" cried Sally, clinging to him. "I will stay with you. Please don't let him take me."

"Sally, please," Samuel was desperate. "You don't understand."

"Fear not, churl, she will indeed serve me before we're finished." Samuel spun to see Sir Hugh's hideous permanent sneer. "Lord Clifford wishes to see to your disposition personally, and I have the honor of escorting you to him where he waits in York. But your dear sister is mine, never fear. And I promise you I shall use her well." At the last words, Sally shrunk closer to Samuel, praying that the nightmare would end soon. Sir Hugh signaled the wartish driver to follow him. The drawbridge was lowered, and they rolled slowly over the moat and onto the road beyond.

They rode for an hour over rutted, muddy terrain as a light snow began to fall. Sir Hugh and another knight rode before the wagon as they slowly made their way northward. Behind, three footsoldiers and another mounted guard followed, all wearing the colors of Lord Clifford. They crossed an ancient, narrow stone bridge over a small stream into a dense thicket of stout trees. Between Pontefract and the bridge the land had been stripped of its trees centuries ago to make way for the fertile farmland that now lay fallow under winter's grip.

Several miles beyond the bridge, a tree had fallen across the road; it would have to be moved to let the wagon pass. Sir Hugh looked at the trunk for a moment, checked the area on either side, and ordered the men in the rear to come forward. They straddled the tree and hefted it high enough to free it from the mud and began to slide it toward the side of the road. Samuel paid no attention to the activity until he heard a familiar whine and thunk that made him jerk his head up over the rail of the cart. He had just enough time to see the guard behind them fall off his horse when another whine and thunk caused him to spin around to see that Sir Hugh had an arrow through his shoulder just beyond where the breastplate of his armor ended. And then chaos erupted from the woods.

Six men engaged the footsoldiers, who had finally collected their wits enough to drop the tree and draw their swords. Shouting orders to the others, Sir Hugh's personal escort grabbed the reins of his master's horse and together they jumped over the tree and fled north, Sir Hugh hanging on with his good arm. The driver of the cart screamed something unintelligible just before an arrow entered his belly and emerged from his back. He fell off the driver's seat groaning in agony as he hit the ground.

While the struggle boiled around them, Samuel ducked back under the rail of the cart and held Sally to shield her. Oliver struggled against his chains, thinking that this might be their chance to escape before the bandits turned their attention to them, but the posts of the wagon proved too stout. Moments after it had begun, the three footsoldiers were dead, and the bandits began to strip the bodies of any valuables.

"I told you I take my debts seriously," said a voice from the back of the cart. Nigel of Devon climbed into the wagon and smiled at Samuel and Oliver, then began to unlock the chains that held the three. "It's a good thing that this guard had the keys to these chains and not one of those two that got away."

"Nigel?"

"Yes, my friend, it is I. Did you think I deserted you?" The last of the chains were off and Nigel and his henchmen helped Sally down from the cart. "I see that you need nourishment," he said. "Our camp is not far from here, and we have fresh venison. Come," he said to the others, "help them. They will need their strength in the next few days."

In the town of York, Queen Margaret and Lord Clifford were alone in an antechamber of the mayor's townhome, confiscated by the royal party for the duration of the campaigns. A page had just delivered the latest intelligence from Margaret's formidable spy network, which had not failed to keep her one step ahead of her enemies ever since the rebellion had started. This time, however, the news could have been better. She had not thought it possible for Edward to gather a strong force this quickly and to have them arrayed and marching northward. Yet the intelligence had him only a day's march from Pontefract at last word, closer by now. Still, she was also well arrayed and could put more men in the field than he, so it was not as bad as it could have been. But the boldness of this young son of York had surprised her, and that was cause for concern. She had never underestimated an opponent before.

"It would be better for us if they were delayed as much as possible," she told Clifford, "and we can think of only one way to accomplish that. Take a small detachment and destroy the bridge over the River Aire where the road crosses south of Saxton. It is too deep for crossing with all their supplies and armaments."

"It would not be a difficult thing for them to rebuild a suitable bridge once they see that the bridge is out, Your Highness," replied Clifford.

"By then we will have our forces deployed in very favorable positions, and will be ready to end this rebellion once and for all. Inform Captain Trollope that we wish to see him."

Clifford noted the fatigue in her voice. He knew that he would have to be strong indeed to keep them from losing the kingdom to the bloody Yorkists.

"As you wish," he said.

Nigel's camp was well hidden, a few miles to the north of the ambush. The smell of venison cooking over a small pit fire reminded the three prisoners of their hunger, and large portions of the roasted animal were given to each of them once they had been settled next to the warm fire. Samuel and Oliver ate heartily, and even Sally forced herself to eat, although she had said almost nothing since their rescue.

"I'm sorry I wasn't able to help you when you were captured, my friend. You must believe that. I would not wish for my worst enemy to be within the clutches of that villain, Sir Hugh Courteney, of that you can be certain. That night, after you fell asleep, I kept thinking about that man who had sat by the fire in the tavern. I'd seen rogues with that look on their face many times before. So I slipped out quietly and went to find a henchman of mine that lived down the street a ways. It took me a while to find him, as he was unfortunately not with his wife that night, if you have my meaning. When I finally found him, he told me, as I suspected, that from my description the man sounded like a notorious informer for the local magistrate. What I hadn't counted on was that Clifford had already put the word out on you two, and the local authorities surrounded the house before I could get back to warn you. I'm sure you can figure the rest out."

"Who are these men?" asked Samuel. "And for that matter, Nigel, who are you?"

Nigel nibbled the last bits of meat off the bone and tossed it into the woods.

"I am what you see before you," he said, holding up his hand as Samuel was about to berate him. "And I am in the service of King Edward."

Samuel could only stare at him blankly. "Who is King Edward?" he asked.

"While you were imprisoned, Edward, late called the Earl of March, was proclaimed king in London, and we are all sworn to serve him, as we did his father before him."

Oliver became interested. "I served the House of York all my life and I never remember having seen you before."

"You served York's son. I served his father as a scout, and as such I kept to the shadows always. I kept him informed as best I could about the state of the realm, me and henchmen like these you see here."

Oliver seemed satisfied. "I must see him. I have a message for him."

"What message could you have for the king?"

"From his brother," he said softly.

Nigel remembered that these men had been present at Wakefield.

"You may very well get your chance. I expect the king's entire army to come up this very road within the next two days."

"How do you know that?" asked Samuel.

"It's my business to know. And I'll tell you more: There will be a great battle here soon. The Lancastrians are preparing their forces nearby, and Edward is coming to settle the issue. Within two days' time we'll know who will rule this land."

Edward and Hastings sat atop their horses in front of the main column of the king's army. They had passed through the town of Pontefract, out of arrowshot from the castle, not concerned that the great keep was in hostile hands, and headed out of town on the north road over the same path that Samuel's prison wagon had traveled the day before. Now they waited in the woods for word from his forward scouts. By now he figured that the vanguard detachment had reached the town of Saxton and, in accordance with their orders, would be sending word back regarding news of the Lancastrian army. He was beginning to become concerned when he heard the sound of hooves pounding down the muddy road from the north. It was the forward scout, who pulled his horse up short of the king, dismounted, and knelt.

"Your Majesty, the bridge across the Aire has been destroyed. There is no passage here for your armaments."

The news was not tragic, but it meant delay. He turned to Hastings. "Have the work crews report to the front. We must have a usable bridge back up by tomorrow morning." Hastings acknowledged his orders and sped back into the ranks.

"Is there news of Margaret's army?" Edward asked the scout.

"I arrived at the river with your vanguard, Sire, and, finding the bridge destroyed, was not able to scout the north side." Edward was about to dismiss him when the scout added, "There is one, however, who claims to have such knowledge whom I passed on my way here. He is being detained by your guards." Heavy wagons and dozens of burly footsoldiers began to stream past Edward on their way north to the river, followed by Hastings, who urged them forward.

"Go quickly and tell the guards to hold that man. We will attend them soon." The scout bowed, jumped on his horse, and sped north past the work crew. Edward gave the signal to his captain and the entire army continued its march in the same direction.

His main column came up to the forward camp in less than half an hour, not far from the place where the road crossed the River Aire. There, a contingent of his personal guard stood watch over a group of rough-looking men. He was delighted when he recognized the first one.

"I had not dared hope to see you again after all this time, Nigel!" he said with a grin.

"Your Highness does me honor," said Nigel.

"I should have known it was you when the scout said somebody could tell me what was happening on the other side of the river. Tell me how does it look?"

"I would that I had better news for you, Sire. The former king and queen are residing at York, and their army has by now camped on all the best locations above the Dintingdale Valley just south of the town of Towton, eight miles north of the river. The Duke of Somerset, the Earls of Northumberland, Devonshire, and Westmoreland, Lords Clifford, Rivers, Scales, and Andrew Trollope are all with them."

It was a noble gathering that Margaret had assembled against him, but Edward had expected it, and they had passed the point of no return years ago in this affair.

"My lord, there is one here who says he must speak with you. I owe him much and beg you to allow him to approach."

"Very well, he may approach."

Nigel turned and signaled for one of the filthiest men behind him to come forward. It was not until he had come to within two steps of the king and knelt before him that Edward recognized the young man. "Oliver?" said the king incredulously, appalled by his deplorable condition.

"Yes, Master," said Oliver, "I am honored that His Majesty remembers me." Nigel released his breath. He could now be sure, for the first time, that Oliver's story was true.

Edward saw the shackle sores on Oliver's wrists.

"Why has this man been imprisoned?" he asked Nigel.

"He was captured by Clifford's men after Wakefield, my lord."

"Master," Oliver interrupted, "I have a message for you from the Earl of Rutland." Edward stiffened. The grief of his brother's death was still an open wound.

"We will hear it in our tent," he said softly. "We will send for you."

"Master!" Oliver was persistent. "My friends are part of the message." He pointed to a man and a woman in equally deplorable condition.

Edward turned to his personal guard. "See to it that they are all bathed and that their wounds are tended. Give them suitable clothing and bring them all to our tent."

With a motion to his captain, the army resumed its northward march.

Edward had dismissed everyone from his tent except Hastings and a personal guard after Nigel, Oliver, Samuel, and Sally had been escorted into his presence. The army was camped on the south shore of the River Aire while the work parties were busy building a bridge to replace the one that had been destroyed by the queen's men. The weather continued to deteriorate as the night approached, with increasing winds driving icy snow flurries hard before them. Edward listened quietly as Oliver told him the story of Wakefield, and Samuel watched the king slump in his regal chair as he heard the story of Edmund's murder. For the first time he noticed that Edward was only a year or two older than himself, not yet even twenty.

"On the road you said that Edmund had given you a message," Edward said after Oliver had finished the tale.

"Forgive me, Master, but I thought it best to tell you of his final hours. It was only this, but he made me swear to tell you. He said that if he was to perish in battle, to commend him to his brother and to say that everything he did that day, he did for you. He bade me to remind you of the days at Ludlow and all things that were good therein, for he remembered them fondly and knew that you could find strength in those memories."

His brother's message from beyond had left Edward in a trance. The memories of his childhood with Edmund would always hold a sacred place in his soul; how could he ever forget them? What was it that Edmund had told him that day at Baynards when they parted for the last time?

"Edmund," he whispered.

"My lord, are you well?" asked Hastings. Edward waved him away and asked Oliver to relate the rest of the story of their flight from Wakefield and subsequent events.

"You," said Edward, addressing Samuel, "come forward." Samuel came from behind Oliver and knelt. "We are grateful to you for saving the life of Oliver and our good servant Nigel of Devon. How can we repay you?"

Samuel thought for a moment. It was not every day that one could ask a boon from a king.

"I wish only a safe haven for my sister, Your Highness," he said, "for she has been sorely abused by your enemies."

Hastings was about to berate Samuel for being overly presumptuous, but Edward silenced him with a wave of his hand.

"I will see that she is carefully guarded until the battle is over. If God wills that we are victorious tomorrow, she shall be escorted back to Northwood and safely deposited with her family. Would that be satisfactory?"

"Yes. Your Highness is most gracious." Samuel looked at Sally, who said nothing.

"Your Highness," Oliver stepped forward, "I ask that I be allowed to accompany Sally to Northwood, if she will have me."

"You have our good leave. Sir William, see to their comfort and that our promise to these good subjects is fulfilled." Hastings could not help but feel that the request was beneath him, but he bowed and escorted them from the king's tent. Before they had gone far, one of Edward's personal guard came up behind them and took Samuel's arm.

"The king requires that you come to him again."

Sally wrapped her arms around her brother. "No," she said desperately. Samuel, knowing that he could not deny the king, handed her to Oliver.

"It will be all right. Oliver will look after you." Reluctantly, she let go and Samuel returned to the king's tent.

Edward was still on his chair, deep in thought as Samuel entered.

"Your Highness has sent for me?" The king looked up and motioned for him to stand.

"You did not say what you would have from me for yourself."

"I need nothing for myself, my lord. Your Highness has already been most gracious."

"Do you not seek retribution for what has been done to you and your family?"

"If you are successful tomorrow, my lord, I will have all the retribution I need."

"We understand. But the problem remains that success tomorrow is not guaranteed, though we pray to God that he favors our cause. What would be your answer if we asked you to join our personal guard? To hear Nigel speak, you are skilled with the bow, and such men will be sorely needed." Samuel did not immediately respond. "We could insist," Edward added, "but feel that we owe you at least the option of refusing, and if you do, you have our leave to go. But consider this: You will never get a better chance to avenge yourself on Clifford and Northumberland."

Samuel honestly did not feel the need in his heart for revenge, but he also knew that if Edward were to lose the next conflict with the Lancastrians, he and Sally could find themselves back in the Pontefract dungeons before long, and the thought of that was too terrifying to contemplate.

"I would be honored to join your guard, my lord," he said, bringing a quick smile to the king's face.

"Splendid," said Edward. "We shall notify the captain. He will see to your provisions."

As Samuel left the tent, he hoped that Christopher never found out about his new job. Things were bad enough between them already.

The next morning brought with it a strong southerly wind that drove a light snow before it. The late March sky was gray and low over the River Aire as Edward's workforce put the last touches on the replacement bridge. Samuel stood in his new colors, refreshed by a good night's sleep and a hearty breakfast of salted pork, wheat bread, and a tankard of ale. The king's personal guard was well fed. Ready to join his new brothers in arms, he said his farewells to Oliver and Sally.

"I love you, Samuel," she said, embracing him. "Please come back to us." Samuel could not find words to respond. She returned to her tent, not able to bear the pain of the farewell any longer.

"You can depend on me to take good care of her," Oliver said, taking his friend's hand.

"I know it," Samuel said.

"I want you to know before you go…" he struggled for the words, "that I appreciate everything you've done for me, and…and that I'm proud of you as well."

They embraced for a moment, and then Oliver followed Sally back into the tent. Samuel lingered for a second or two, then headed to the mustering area for the king's guard.

Shouting came from the river. The captain of the king's guard, Sir Julian Admonds, swiftly organized his men and led the rush to the bridge. When they arrived, there were men fighting on the bridge and arrows were flying in both directions across the river. To Samuel's horror, he saw Lord Clifford's men attempting a crossing. Hastings was down on the bank directing the troops.

"Hell's fire!" yelled Sir Julian. "Did it not occur to anybody that a bridge can be used from both directions?" Samuel nocked an arrow. Sir Julian set them on top of the first ridge along the road to the south. His first duty was to protect the person of the king, and if any of the enemy made it across the bridge they would have to pass his position.

Edward and Warwick came over the ridge with their men and fell headlong into the fray. With Edward in the thick of the battle, his guards had to become footsoldiers. Sir Julian led them down the ridge to within range and directed their arrows against the men on the bridge.

The bow felt good in Samuel's hands. His aim was still true and his shots hit their mark each time at this close range. He saw Warwick take an arrow in the leg, which caused him to withdraw with some of his personal guard. Clifford's men gained the south side of the river, and Edward's men began to fall back.

Clifford had waited patiently all night while the rebels rebuilt the bridge. He knew he could give them a proper surprise as soon as their work was completed.

Now the moment had arrived. The queen had ordered him to rejoin her forces after he had destroyed the bridge, but he had seen a chance to catch the rebels and perhaps put an end to their leaders while their entire army was stretched for miles along the road leading to the bridge.

When first light broke, he ordered his men across and led them with his huge sword flashing red with blood.

They finally cut through the soldiers on the bridge and poured over the south side. He saw Edward in the thick of the fighting and turned his horse in that direction.

Samuel had never been instructed in the use of a sword — did not even have one. Instead, he withdrew up the ridge to gain a vantage point. Sir Julian watched him depart, and with a scowl waded into the enemy.

Upon reaching the ridgetop, Samuel surveyed the battle, which had grown much closer now that Clifford's men had gained the south side. In fact, they were all now within range of his bow. Searching desperately, he finally reacquired sight of Lord Clifford, dangerously close to the king. He nocked his arrow and gauged the distance to Clifford himself. When he loosed the arrow, he was confident of his aim, and indeed, his arrow did strike its intended target. Unfortunately, Clifford turned at the last moment and the projectile bounced harmlessly off his breast armor.

Even from his distance, Samuel could tell that the strike had startled Clifford, but his attention was not distracted from the fighting around him. Samuel let another arrow fly.

The second arrow passed through Clifford's throat and halfway out the back of his neck. Still holding his huge sword, he fell from his horse.

Without Clifford's inspiration, his attack quickly fell apart, and the remains of his troops fled across the bridge toward Saxton, closely pursued by Edward's vanguard. When he saw that the battle was done, Samuel slowly descended from the ridge. The king was standing over Clifford's lifeless body.

"He does not appear so menacing now, does he, my friends?" said Edward, turning him with his foot. "But now is the time to press our advantage." He had raised his voice so that everyone could hear. "Captains, gather your men. The way is clear to finish French Margaret!" A loud cheer went up from the men, who all gathered in their units and began to cross the bridge.

After a new vanguard had formed across the river, Edward and the Nevilles — Warwick's leg bandaged but not badly wounded — crossed the bridge. The entire army was soon passing through Saxton and into the Dintingdale Valley just south of the town of Towton. A tributary of the Warfe, the River Cock, ran along the left side of the valley in a deep ravine that meandered around several wooded loops, while a broad plateau rose to the right side of the valley. As they passed through town, Sir Julian rode up next to Samuel and dismounted. Leading his horse by the rein, he walked next to his new recruit.

"That was the best arrow strike I have ever seen back there, lad. To strike an armored horseman in the neck at that range is nothing short of a miracle." Samuel smiled in acknowledgment. "I wanted you to know that before I tell you this: I'll not have my men acting on their own whims. This time, you very well might have saved the king's life, so I'll not gut you like a fish and leave you for the crows. But if it happens again, you'll not get another warning. Do you understand that, lad?"

Samuel was taken aback by Sir Julian's words, which were spoken in an almost friendly manner, but he knew with a single look that there was no prevarication in the portly knight.

"It will not happen again, Sir Julian. I swear it."

He thumped Samuel on the back. "I believe you." He mounted his horse and looked down once more. "Where did you learn to handle a bow like that, lad?"

"It came naturally to me when I was being trained. The captain of Northumberland's guard said I had an eye for it."

"I'm glad you're with us now, lad," he said, trotting off to the front of the column.

Samuel shivered against the cold wind that drove a hard snow before it, coming up the valley from behind them. He began to make mental adjustments for how the wind would affect the flight of his arrows. The ranks in front began to break and spread out across the narrow valley. Then for the first time he saw the queen's army, and the sight of it made him tremble even more. As Nigel had reported, they had indeed occupied the strategic plateau that commanded the road as it wound past Towton and points north. To his experienced eyes, it appeared that Edward's army was outnumbered by several thousand.

Word came from the front to prepare for an assault. Samuel had expected as much, as there would be no other way to dislodge Margaret's army. Sir Julian came back to organize the guard. When he had them together, he addressed them from horseback.

"The king has ordered us to accompany him on the left flank. Follow me and stay together."

Edward's army advanced in three ranks, the standard battle tactic of the day. The king gave the Nevilles charge of the center and right flank and, taking command of the left himself, began the march up the valley toward the enemy's positions. As they reached the foot of the plateau, the archers were ordered to advance to within range and fire. It was at this point that the archers were in the greatest peril — their counterparts had the strategic advantage of greater height. On this day, however, the wind came howling up the valley directly into the faces of the Lancastrians, causing their arrows to fall short while the Yorkists' arrows flew to their targets. The charge was ordered, and the main army began its arduous ascent. Because the Lancastrian archers could not reach the enemy, the Yorkists gained the ridge top and the two front lines of the huge armies collided with the sound of thousands of weapons crunching together.

Bodies fell by the hundreds between the two armies, the heaps of dead and wounded creating a barrier between the lines. Soldiers coming from the rear ranks found it necessary to climb over the piles of bodies to continue the engagement, and all the while, the snow drove up from the valley floor, a curse to both sides. The battle line began to fragment as soldiers sought to find ground that was clear of bodies on which to better stand and fight.

Samuel and the guard stayed close to the king, some wielding deadly battle-axes or short swords and some, like Samuel, firing arrows at short range when they could find clear targets. Samuel had to scavenge for arrows to keep his supply, a task made easier as they ascended the ridge because of all the Lancastrian arrows that had fallen short in the wind. The battle at the top of the plateau raged on for two hours until the sheer number advantage of the Lancastrians began to take its toll. Some of Edward's ranks on both flanks began to break and flee, a condition that Edward knew well could be highly contagious.

He broke off his fighting and ran his horse behind his troops' lines shouting encouragement and attempting to shore up lines where they were weak. Warwick was doing the same on the right side, and while they were losing ground on all three fronts, at least there was no wholesale flight, which would have spelled the end for the Yorkists. But ground was still being lost and soon they would have their backs to the slope of the ridge.

Running out of room to maneuver, Samuel could feel the desperation of those around him. He had run out of arrows and could find no others, and he looked desperately for anything to use as a weapon. He saw to his right a battle-ax that was still held by a dead soldier and ran to take it as a Lancastrian spotted him and moved to attack. The dead man's clutch on the ax was still strong, surprising Samuel as he pried the dead talons from the haft. He freed it just in time to deflect a deadly blow from the blade of the Lancastrian, but the force knocked him to the ground. In that position, he would not have been able to protect himself from the next strike, but instead of delivering the expected death stroke, the Lancastrian collapsed to the ground next to him, the left side of his skull missing. A man whom he judged to be even younger than himself took Samuel's arm and pulled him to his feet.

"Come on," he yelled, "there's a place over here where we can rest." Samuel gratefully followed him to a tree away from the battle line, where they both collapsed. "Sir Julian taught me to take a quick rest whenever the opportunity lends itself. My name is Stanley. You're the new recruit, aren't you?"

"Samuel," he nodded in affirmation. "You saved my life."

"We are in the king's guard together. It's our duty to look after each other," responded Stanley between deep breaths. "But we can't stay long. It doesn't look as if things are going well for the king."

The battle continued to rage in the driving snow, which had already covered the thousands of dead in the field with a white sheet. There was very little room left between the Yorkist army and the slope of the plateau, below which ran the River Cock, and it was only Edward's valiant leadership that kept his ranks in order.

"I see Sir Julian," Samuel pointed to where their captain was swinging his sword with abandon, accompanied by other members of the guard. Samuel felt shame that he was resting through the battle. "I'm going to help him," he said, getting to his feet slowly, disappointed that his muscles were so slow to respond.

"We'll go together," Stanley said. "We can watch each other's back."

Samuel nodded his assent. Together they ran deep within the thick of the battleline and fell upon the Lancastrians together. Protecting each other like a unit within the ranks, the guardsmen fought on, protecting the king who was himself in the midst of the fight, his armor and valor an inspiration to them all. Somehow, the line held fast to the edge of the ridge.

Another hour of desperate fighting had passed when the Yorkists were surprised to find that their right flank was gaining ground. In fact, the troops found new hope when the battleline began to swing around to the north and west, the king's position at the anchor point. As the battle progressed, the Lancastrian left flank continued to disintegrate, more and more of the Lancastrian soldiers from that area breaking ranks and fleeing to the north or down into the Cock Valley to find refuge. It was then that a young captain rode up to the king.

"My Liege, the Duke of Norfolk commends himself to Your Grace, and although he has taken ill of a sudden and was not able to make the journey himself, has sent his best men to assist your holy cause, and we place ourselves at your service." Norfolk's men had already fallen on the unsuspecting and exhausted left flank of the Lancastrian army, explaining its collapse and the resulting shift of the battleline.

"You are welcome to the fray, captain," yelled Edward over the battle din. "Instruct your men to push the enemy as far as they can toward the river."

"As you command, Sire."

Renewed by the excellent tidings, Edward spurred his men on. Some time later, it was the Lancastrian army that found itself on the edge of the plateau looking down at the River Cock, and seeing many of their fellow soldiers fleeing, the rest of the army followed suit.

Closely pursued by the victors, the Lancastrian soldiers tried desperately to find a way to the north. Attempting to cross the Cock, they were cut down by the hundreds until a bridge of dead bodies dammed the water. Using their dead comrades as steppingstones, the queen's men gained the west bank and continued their flight toward York, but the Yorkists remained on their heels the entire way. By late afternoon the Dintingdale Valley and the road to York were littered with the bodies of Lancastrian soldiers, their blood deep in the mud and snow. Miles downstream, where the Cock emptied into the River Wharfe, farmers saw the waters run red.

At the edge of the plateau over the valley, Samuel watched as Yorkist footsoldiers pillaged the bodies, seeking valuables that would make the risk of their lives worthwhile. Exhausted by sheer effort of hand-to-hand combat for so many hours, he found that he could not mourn for so many lost souls, though there was a time only a short number of years ago that he would have wept to see such carnage. He stumbled by himself among the piles of dead not knowing where he should be, when he noticed the glitter of a finer suit of armor. Stumbling over the dead and injured, he noticed a knight of some stature under several other bodies. There was something familiar about the colors...

He pushed the bodies aside and looked with horror at the face of Henry Percy, third Earl of Northumberland, staring up at him with dead eyes. Eyes that accused him of treason against he who had trained and fed him for the past three years and should therefore have expected loyalty from him. Samuel fell to his knees and buried his face in his hands.

A strong hand rested on his shoulder. Sir Julian regarded him sadly.

"I know what you must feel, my boy. The earl and I fought together in better times, and if there were a nobler knight than he, I know not who it would be." He motioned for some of his men to come near. "Come and bear this noble soldier gently to the king, and tell him for me that it is his enemy, Northumberland. Go." When they had carried the body off, he helped Samuel to his feet and walked with him to a clear area where the guard was gathering to give thanks for their victory. They passed dozens of bodies and wounded men, many moaning in their final death struggle.

"You must realize that greater men than you or I are faced with the same difficult decision these days. Who can tell anymore where honor begins and duty ends? We used to live by the code of Arthur and all seemed so clear, but now we travel roads that lead us into hell everywhere we turn."

Samuel stopped and turned toward him. "I did not learn from the same teachers as you, Sir Julian. I was taught to obey and to be happy with my station in life. And I was. Until I left Northwood and saw how those nobler than myself lived." He turned and continued walking. "Now I have no place I can truly call home."

At the gathering of the king's guard, Father Dennis led them in prayers of gratitude. Beyond, bodies were carried to waiting wagons, where they were heaped by the dozens and loaded away to mass burial sites somewhere to the north of town.

CHAPTER X

Lord Rivers knelt before Queen Margaret, worried that the news from Towton would send her into a fury. Instead, she simply sat on her throne apparently oblivious to his presence. All around her, servants of the royal household were making frantic preparations to leave, packing only what a few wagons could carry. It was essential that they travel swiftly, as the Yorkists would surely be in pursuit.

"Clifford, Northumberland, and Trollope, all dead?" asked Margaret in disbelief.

"Yes, my queen," he said sadly.

"The very props of our throne are gone then." Suddenly her vision focused. "Who is tending to our son?"

"The Duke of Somerset, Majesty."

"We have only one place left in this world where our bones will be safe from the vultures of war. Attend to my husband and see that he is not detained by his musings. We must depart for Scotland this very hour, and pray that God will find us safe haven in that desolate place." She left the room, attended only by her French priest, the departure barely noted by those who were busy packing trunks.

Rivers' son Anthony came in to find him, and Rivers took him aside.

"She has decided to flee to Scotland."

"As we knew she would. Are we still in agreement?"

"We are," responded Rivers with conviction. "We will gather with the family at Grafton and await our fate."

"At least if we're to die, it will be in our home and not in some dreary moor of Scotland. I will not run from Edward like a rabbit from the fox."

"Let's away then, and leave the former king and queen to their destiny." An hour later, the former royal family and their escort slowly slogged out of York over roads thick with mud, defeat, and death. King Henry followed his wife and son on his white stallion, a gift from the Duke of Burgundy when Henry was a young man visiting Paris. He had named it Gabriel after the Archangel. He leaned over and stroked the horse's neck.

"Fear not, my constant friend," he whispered in its ear. "From dust were we made, and dust we shall surely be." Snow drove against their backs, the wind pushing them northward.

King Edward and his army arrived at the gates of York two days later. Warwick and his brother Montagu rode at the front of the column with the king, Samuel and the guard immediately behind. The citizens of York, being understandably apprehensive about how the new king would treat them, turned out en masse to welcome their new monarch with all the pomp they could arrange. As the king and his party approached the gate, it was opened before them and the mayor stepped forth from the crowd of dignitaries to greet them.

"My gracious king, we welcome you to our fair city and beg that you forgive any favors that we bestowed upon those who once called themselves king and queen. We are but common subjects and cannot easily refuse those who arrive at our gates with puissance."

Edward was about to respond when he saw the wall over the main gate, called the Micklegate Bar. There, the rotted, empty eye sockets of his brother Edmund's face stared down at him from a pike. Next to Edmund was his father's and that of Warwick and Montagu's father, the Earl of Salisbury.

"Take them down!" ordered Edward. He was furious.

The dreaded look of retribution shook the mayor to his soul. Not realizing to what the king was referring, the mayor strained to see what had angered him. When it dawned on him that the heads of the great Duke of York and his kin had not been removed from the walls where the queen had placed them, he suspected that his life might pay the forfeit for the oversight. He jumped to his feet and frantically directed some of the townspeople on the wall to retrieve the heads. When they had been carefully lowered and placed in caskets before the king, Father Dennis was summoned to say the last rites. Edward knelt and prayed in silence.

To his chagrin, Samuel realized that he was becoming accustomed to such barbarism. Only a few years had passed since he was an innocent young boy playing in the glades of Northwood. He thanked God that Oliver and Sally were not here to see this. They were in the rear of the column, which would take another day to arrive.

"Carry them with dignity to York Minster," commanded Edward after he had finished his devotions. "And bring me the remains of Lord Clifford. His head shall replace these, and there it shall remain until God takes the wall down from under it."

They marched to the cathedral, where mass was said for those who had perished and thanks given to God for their glorious victory. Afterward, food was brought from all over town to feast the king's party, who celebrated a hard-won crown. Samuel slept with his new comrades of the king's guard, hoping that Edward would remember his promise to a poor peasant family and see Sally and Oliver safely back to Northwood.

For the next three weeks, the king stayed in York while contingents of his army marched through Yorkshire subduing pockets of resistance and exacting tribute and oaths of loyalty from the towns and nobility. Disturbing news arrived from the north that Margaret and Henry had reached the court of James III of Scotland, and that she had been promised military aid by the Scots. Edward summoned Nigel of Devon the morning that the news arrived. The king had commandeered the bishop of York's private townhouse, a splendid manor located on a high promontory on the edge of town. Nigel was brought without delay to Edward, who was busy at that moment discussing strategy with Warwick and Montagu.

"Nigel," the king's face lit up at the sight of his favorite scout. "We hope that you've enjoyed your stay in York as much as we have?"

"Indeed I have, Your Majesty, though I must confess that I would like to return to my home. My wife has not seen me for months."

"We plan on returning to London soon, and when we do, you'll have our good leave to return to your family with our best wishes. But first we would hear your advice on an issue that causes us great concern. Come, walk with us." Arm in arm, Edward led him over to a map on a table.

"The Lancastrian pretender to our throne has ceded Berwick Castle to the Scots for their promises of aid," he pointed to a spot on the eastern shore just south of the border between the two kingdoms. "My blood boils at the thought of Berwick in Scottish hands, but the vile deed is done. You were my eyes on the Scottish border until just recently. What do you think are the chances that James will make war on us?"

"My lord, as you know, James does not have the support of many of his greatest lords. In my view, it will be difficult for the Scots to muster a force of any real size, but I would not disavow the possibility of a small Scottish army being augmented by troops from France. However remote the possibility, we should be prepared."

Edward thought for a moment as he stared at the map. "We agree. The Castles of Northumberland are still held against us, and could provide safe havens for any such incursion. Until we secure the northern counties, we must be vigilant." He led Nigel to where Warwick and Montagu had been carrying on a private discussion. "My lords," he addressed the Nevilles, "it is our wish to acquaint the realm with their new king, and we therefore propose to return to London after visiting as many of the midland counties as time will permit. However, we cannot leave the north unguarded. We therefore propose to leave you both here as guardians of our realm until the Northumbrian castles have been secured. The army is at your disposal, as we will need only our guard and a few others."

"A wise policy, my lord," Warwick said. "We will bring these castles under your sway with all possible haste, and will meet you back in London when the deed is done."

"Now Nigel," said Edward, turning back to the scout, "return to your family. You have our leave with our thanks."

"If I may be so bold, Your Highness, may I speak of one more matter?" Edward nodded his consent. "If you will recall, the commoners who saved my life — and did you great service at Towton, I have heard — are still here in York awaiting the assistance that you promised them."

"I do recall that, and confess that I had forgot them. What is it that they wish of me?"

"Only safe passage to their village in Northumberland, my lord."

"I will dispatch two of my personal guard to accompany them, but they must return within the fortnight. Make that clear to the captain. Come with us now and enjoy some of the bishop's wine. He has an excellent collection." As the king and Nigel left the room, the Neville lords bowed their heads until they were alone.

"This is good, John," said Warwick. "While the king is out of the way taking his tour of the realm, we will shore up the kingdom for him. By the time we finish here, he will know that he cannot rest without us guarding his borders."

"I like these northern lands," said John. "It may even be that I will convince the king to grant me some of these castles after we have secured them."

"With me in London directing the king's policies, and you in the north to secure our power, we will do well indeed. Everything is proceeding as I have hoped, by God, and I will see to it that you get your northern castles."

"I tell you this: I do not share the king's concern for the Scots. They haven't the stomach to tangle with us, and French Louis must guard his kingdom from the Duke of Burgundy. Poor Margaret, she will find no help wherever she turns."

"And we will sleep well with that knowledge. Come, let's share some of the bishop's wine with our new king."

"We both know that it's best this way," Samuel said, and wished that he really believed it. The country between York and the River Tyne was still perilous to travelers, especially those who favored the new king. Due largely to the loyalty of the Percys to the House of Lancaster, the north counties were not pleased to have a Yorkist on the throne, and many of the towns and villages were still quite hostile and restless.

Samuel could have chosen to be one of his sister's guards to Northwood, and Sally had pleaded for him to join them. But he knew that his reception in Northwood would be icy indeed, and he could not bear the thought of facing Christopher. Perhaps some time after the wounds had healed, but not now.

"But Emma will have her child soon, and you know she wanted you to stand as sponsor at the baptism," Sally pleaded.

"The king has only granted the use of the guard for the trip, so I couldn't stay if I wanted to. Besides, I really doubt that Christopher would allow me that honor anymore. And the two guards that volunteered to go with you are real fighters; you'll be safer with them than you would be with me." He put his hand gently on her mouth as she tried to object further. "I really wish things could be different, you know that. Please tell Emma that I miss her and will try to see her soon. Here comes your escort."

Two soldiers approached leading four horses by the reins. Both guards wore tunics bearing the king's new emblem, a Sun-in-Splendor, a representation of the sign they had received from God at Mortimer's Cross when three suns appeared in the sky before the battle.

Sally hugged her brother like she would never release him, before finally allowing herself to be placed on one of the horses. Oliver asked the guard if he could have a moment with Samuel before they left. He took Samuel aside as if he were too embarrassed to be overheard by anyone else.

"I know that I will have to acquire the favor of your brother when I get to Northwood, but yours is the opinion that I value." He cleared his throat and looked at his feet. "If she will have me, and at a time when she has recovered from these horrible days, I would like to make your sister my wife."

Samuel did not understand how he had not seen this coming. All the signs were there from the moment they met, and it likely would have happened before now if his own actions had not caused such pain for them all. He did not know if Oliver would be a good husband to his sister, but he had to trust in her judgment.

"I think Father would be pleased," he said smiling. "And I know that I am." They embraced and Oliver jumped lightly onto his horse, as did the guards, their journey home beginning with the first step of the lead horse. When they had drifted slowly out of sight, Samuel turned to join his new comrades. *And may you both find the peace that I have lost.*

When King Edward and his entourage left York, he left behind the Nevilles and the bulk of his army. The king's party journeyed toward London, wending its way slowly through many of the midland and eastern communities including Lichfield, Coventry, Warwick, Daventry, and finally Stony Stratford, only a short ride from Grafton Manor, the home of Lord Rivers.

Rivers and his son had arrived at Grafton to find Elizabeth already arrived from Bradgate. When they had learned of the Yorkist victory, they waited in dread to hear their fate.

The dowager Duchess of Bedford, however, had all her life been one of the ablest politicians of the Lancastrian court. When she heard that the king would stay in Stony Stratford for several nights, she sent word to him that Grafton Manor was at his disposal. And to the amazement of her family, he had sent word back accepting her invitation.

As the royal party arrived, every servant of the household stood lining the front of the manor. Lord Rivers and his wife waited in the center flanked on one side by Elizabeth and on the other by Anthony. The king was accompanied by Hastings, ten mounted knights, and forty men-at-arms. Edward pulled his horse to a stop in front of the Woodvilles.

"Lords Rivers and Scales, step forward. Before we soil our feet on the dirt of this place, we will hear your oaths of loyalty."

Lord Rivers spoke first. "My Liege Lord, I swear by the blood of the Blessed Virgin that from this day forward, my life and worldly means are Your Majesty's to dispose of." Anthony followed with the same oath.

"Rivers and Scales, know our judgment. You have professed your loyalty, and we are convinced. Know all men here present that we pardon your recent assistance rendered to the pretender Henry and his family, and that we seek no further retribution against you or your goods."

"His Majesty does our house a great honor with his visit," the duchess said as the king took her hand and kissed it. Once having been a preeminent lady of the realm, she was entitled to some respect, even from a king.

"Your invitation honored us," he said, looking over to Elizabeth. "And may we be given the pleasure of an introduction?"

"This is our daughter, Elizabeth," said the duchess.

As Edward took her hand, he looked closely at her face. Her deep blue eyes and cascading gold hair held his gaze as he kissed her hand. There was something sad about her. Something...

"Will it please Your Majesty to come inside?" Rivers' voice pulled him away.

Edward reluctantly turned from Elizabeth and was led into Grafton Manor. As the dust cleared from the entryway, the first buds of the lilac shrubs swelled under a warming spring breeze.

P A R T   T W O

CHAPTER XI

Christopher meandered past the produce stands, hawkers, beggars, servants, and shoppers along the market street of York. The dense summer air was filled with the odors of frenzied human activity, foul and sweet aromas mixed into a sensory soup that made him loath to inhale. The quiet village of Northwood had not prepared him for such an olfactory assault.

The town of York showed little resemblance to the old Roman frontier fortress from which it sprang. From here, the legionnaires had once patrolled as far north as Hadrian's Wall, the northernmost boundary of the empire, and the grid pattern of the central town was a tribute to the ancients' rigid sense of form and function. Since then, however, the narrow streets had been crowded with one- and two-story wood and stone cottages that hung over the streets, obscuring the well-ordered Roman plan.

Three years had passed since the Millers had been forced to abandon Northwood. Sally had returned safely from the clutches of Sir Hugh, which Christopher had considered a miracle. But when the news of the earl's death and the attainder of his properties by the usurper, Edward, reached the townsfolk, the Miller family was no longer welcome in Northwood, no matter Christopher's unwavering loyalty to the Percys.

When Oliver had requested his blessing to marry Sally, Christopher was not, at first, inclined to give it. However, at the strong insistence of Emma, he reluctantly agreed. The parish priest of Northwood consented to marry them even though the townsfolk wanted no part of the family, and no one outside of the family except for Emma's good friend Edith attended the simple ceremony. A few weeks after that, they packed up their worldly possessions into a large cart and left their past behind. Using their assets, the fruits of John Miller's life's labors, they built a new millhouse on the east shore of the River Ouse in York. Oliver had eagerly assisted Christopher and had proven to be an excellent worker. Together with their wives, they had created a new home out of the ashes of the past.

The period right after their arrival in York had been an especially trying one for Emma. The death of John Miller had been a terrible blow, and Christopher's unrelenting resentment of Samuel was also a source of pain. She gave birth to their first child, Sarah, after a long delivery, three weeks after their arrival, and while it was not the best time to be hampered with an infant, Christopher was greatly relieved that both mother and child had come through the ordeal with their health intact. Last winter a second daughter, Alice, had been born. Christopher had a hard time disguising his disappointment at not having been given a son this time, but Alice was proving to be a delightful child.

Sally had also given birth four months ago to her first child, a boy that Oliver insisted they name John, after the man who had selflessly sacrificed his life to help them after Wakefield. Christopher admitted to himself some envy over Oliver's son, but they had become friends since the move to York, and he cherished his role as uncle to young John.

Christopher made his way around the frenzied activity of the market street, finally turning on to one of the numerous side streets. The small street was dominated by a large alehouse where he had spent increasing hours during these last few months. It was a good place to grumble about the state of the realm to many who were sympathetic to his way of thinking. The kind of gathering that made a man feel secure. He entered a large room containing dozens of tables. To his left he saw the man he sought sitting alone, and he felt his heart quicken. Trying to act inconspicuous but feeling as if every eye in the room were focused on him, he wended his way past scurrying barmaids and noisy tables filled with men playing cards or games, or just shouting and laughing in pairs and threes. Arriving at the table, he sat down and looked around.

"For the love of God, Christopher, don't look so damned guilty," Simon Johnson said from across the table. "If you act like you just slept with the bishop's favorite tart, someone's bound to start asking questions." Christopher returned a nervous smile and settled into his chair. A barmaid put a mug of ale down before him without saying a word and continued on about her rounds.

Christopher took a long pull of the thick brew. Simon spoke in a casual voice that was neither too low or too loud, but calibrated to match the general din around them. "Good news," he said, rubbing his nose. "I spoke with my contact, and he's agreed to let you join us. Of course, he'll want to speak with you first, before he makes a final decision, but you're as good as in, I'm sure of it."

Christopher was excited and frightened, and to his chagrin, he began to shake. Perhaps he wasn't ready for this after all.

"When do we start?" He tried to control his voice.

"You'll be contacted when it's time, and not a moment before. You must be ready to leave at once, whether we come tonight or a year from now. In the meantime, go home and go about your life as always, and speak to no one about this. Do you understand?" Danger was implied.

"I understand," Christopher said firmly with a new resolve.

"God knows how young Percy has fared after three years in the Tower," said Simon, rubbing his nose again. "If only Henry would come out of hiding, it would give us a leader to fight behind."

"Most think that he's in Scotland still."

"Many of the northern castles are still held in his name despite the best efforts of the Nevilles to possess them. This gives us hope." Simon decided it was time to change the subject. "Now tell me, how do your daughters fair?"

For the rest of the evening their voices melded with dozens of others speaking of life's common dramas.

CHAPTER XII

Edward pulled his horse to a stop and listened intently to the sound of the thrashers off in the distance. The woods around him were thick, making vision difficult beyond a few dozen feet. His entourage, including Hastings, had fallen behind, which gave him a moment to enjoy the humus-laden aroma of the woods and the warm summer breeze as it rustled through the leaves. He could hear the thrashers to his left and right as they flushed the deer before them toward a pre-arranged spot at the end of a long swale between two low ridgelines. He had hunted before in Whittlebury Forest, near Grafton, and knew it well.

Three years had passed since his accession to the throne. He had known from the start that a crown taken by force would need constant vigilance to keep, and the residual civil unrest from the wars would not disappear quickly. But the nobility, and especially the common people who had longed for stable government for many years, were becoming enamored of their handsome young new king, who at the ripe age of twenty-one dispatched his royal duties with ease and grace.

To be sure, the northern castles had proven to be more obstinate than he could have imagined, and the brothers Neville had spent many lives and resources trying to wrest those counties from Lancastrian hands. The irritating presence of Henry and Margaret in Scotland was a constant source of trouble, and it was the very threat of an invasion that gave the northern castles the will to continue their resistance.

"Sire!" Hastings' voice boomed through the trees. Edward looked to see the rest of the hunting party approaching with diligence. "Sire," Hastings repeated as he pulled his horse to a stop. "It is folly to ride in these woods without your escort. I need not remind Your Grace that they are frequented by the most unsavory villains."

Edward smiled at Hastings' concern. After the battle at Towton, he had elevated Hastings to the peerage by creating him Lord Hastings and also made him his Chamberlain, the closest of the king's councilors. If it was possible, they had become even more constant companions since Edward had won the crown, and Hastings had continued to locate all of the finest young wenches available in the realm to fill his nights with pleasure.

"Forgive me, William," said Edward with a smile, "but a moment of solitude is the one thing that a king craves above all else, being so rare. Come, let's go forward or the bucks will escape the trap."

The king's party moved forward, listening for the sound of the horn that would signal the thrashers that the trap must be sprung. They slowly meandered along a narrow path that led into the drainage where Edward's men would drive the game before them, ducking under and around limbs.

"Does your wife resent me for taking you whoring so frequently?" Edward asked unexpectedly.

Hastings shrugged his shoulders. "She understands that the weakness in men requires them to seek the comfort of strange arms occasionally, my liege. It suffices her to know that she will bear my heirs."

"Perhaps you're right," said Edward. "But a king must be more circumspect over his choice of brides, for the woman I marry will bear the heirs of England."

"You are still young, my liege, and there is no need to rush into a hasty decision. Many foreign princes will offer their daughters to you in order to bind our peoples in friendship. It is an opportunity not to be taken lightly. The new king of France has already offered his sister, the Lady Bona, to Your Grace. A treaty of friendship with Louis XI sealed with such a marriage would be highly beneficial."

"I do not trust Louis, William. He turned on his own father and sided with the Duke of Burgundy during their recent struggles. Such a man has no honor. And now that he's king, he has turned on Burgundy and attempted once again to crush the autonomy of that great dukedom, which has been our ally for many years. No, I would not trust Louis to keep his promise if there were profit for him to betray us."

"The Earl of Warwick has been wooed by Louis and appears to have taken his side in that struggle, Your Highness. It would be wise, if I may be so bold, to keep a watchful eye on the Nevilles in this matter, and let them know your mind."

Edward reflected for a moment. "No, I think it best not to let the Nevilles know too much about our policies. We still need their strength and it would not be prudent to argue with them about these matters."

They rode in silence for a few moments while Edward contemplated his too-powerful cousin Warwick. "I think, William, that we can take advantage of Warwick's friendship with the new French king."

The hunt had gone well, and there were deer slung over the horses of several retainers. On their way back to Grafton, Edward and Hastings led the party along the wooded path through the dense underbrush, dodging low branches and talking loudly of plans for the evening. The woods before them opened into a large glade, and the late-day sun streaked through the canopy illuminating the forest floor. The glade was dominated by a single large oak with branches that stretched seventy feet from the ground. At the base of the trunk stood a figure wrapped in a body-length cloak with a hood, and two small children held close. Hastings quickly motioned for the escort, some of whom rode directly to the figure with drawn swords.

"Who are you and what is your business in these woods?"

The cloaked figure took a step forward and pulled the hood back. Edward's attention was assured as locks of golden hair cascaded from the hood and a beautiful face that he recognized from somewhere came into view.

"You need not fear me, my lord," the woman said confidently to Hastings, falling to one knee. "I am a gentlewoman and seek only the honor of a word with the king."

Hastings was indignant. "The king does not grant audiences in the forest. Be gone."

The woman looked directly at Edward. "What I ask is a small thing to so great a king. "

Hastings signaled to his men. He was not in the habit of debating with subjects.

"Take them," he called to the nearest soldier.

"Wait!" said Edward sharply, wondering where he had seen her before. He was captivated by her beauty, and the radiance of her deep blue eyes. The boldness and fearlessness that she displayed before Hastings intrigued him. "Who are you, my lady?"

"If it please Your Highness, my name is Elizabeth Woodville, daughter of Lord Rivers."

Edward remembered his short visit to Grafton Manor after the battle at Towton, and his meeting with the Woodville family. He had gone there at the invitation of the dowager Duchess of Bedford, who, he knew, still had many friends in his court. If he could befriend her, she could help him turn old allegiances from Lancaster to York. And he remembered her beautiful daughter, who at the time was mourning the death of her husband.

"William," he said finally, "it is our pleasure that we speak with the Lady Elizabeth for a moment. Withdraw with your men." Hastings withdrew to the edge of the clearing, but had the area encircled. Such chance encounters gave him an uneasy feeling.

"Now then, my lady," said Edward, dismounting. "Rise and tell us what you would have of us."

Without getting to her feet, Elizabeth signaled for her children to come and kneel next to her. "My gracious lord, I seek a boon which only you in your great wisdom and kindness may grant. And lest you think it ill of me, I ask this boon not for myself but for these fatherless children you see here before you. Through no fault of theirs, their father died in battle against Your Majesty. In your wisdom, you took my husband's lands and goods, but now I implore you to think of these children, who have been dispossessed of their inheritance for their father's acts, and grant them the boon of returning Bradgate Manor to them."

She's enchanting, he thought, mesmerized by her sleepy eyes.

"Please rise, my lady," he responded at last. "Suddenly your boon has gone from a request for a word to a larger request for a grant of land."

"The two are as twins, Your Highness," she said. "For one could not be requested without first gaining the other."

Edward laughed. "How did you know that we would be hunting in these woods today?"

"It is the duty of loyal subjects to know when the king is near. In case services are needed."

He laughed again. "Or perhaps when the king may be of service. You are an unusual woman, Lady Elizabeth. We will think on your request. But this is not the place to grant boons. You may inform your gracious parents that we will dine with them tonight." He took her hand and kissed it, lingering for a moment on the soft, flawless skin, then jumped on his horse. "Until tonight, then, my lady. Hastings!" he called over his shoulder. "Provide the Lady Elizabeth and her children with a safe escort to Grafton. We will dine with Lord Rivers and his wife tonight."

Hastings was surprised by the sudden switch in plans, but bowed his head and gave the appropriate orders.

With two guards to escort her, Elizabeth rode slowly back to Grafton. She did not know if she had accomplished anything, but at least she would have one more opportunity to ply the king for the return of her beloved Bradgate. To entertain the king on such short notice would put an immense burden on her family and servants, but she knew that the king was testing them, and she would not fail.

A visit by the king required that not only he but his entourage of retainers and courtiers be fed and entertained. On this visit, the king brought with him a party of twenty, a relatively small contingent.

The dowager Duchess of Bedford was no stranger to such occasions, and knew what needed to be done. Pigs, hens, and eggs were hastily procured from nearby farms, extra help was assembled to staff the kitchen and stables, and wood by the cord was brought from storage to fuel the kitchen stoves and hearths. The supper was served without incident and Elizabeth was relieved to see that the king appeared to enjoy himself. She could not help but notice that Edward gazed at her intently when he was not engaged in ribaldry with her father or others of his party.

When at last the repast had been completed, Lord Rivers invited the king and his company to the Great Room for entertainment by the musicians, but Edward had other plans.

"We thank you, Rivers, for the fine meal." Addressing his men, he spoke loudly. "We implore you all to go in with Lord Rivers and to enjoy his hospitality. As for us, we ask leave to walk with your daughter in the gardens."

"Our daughter has my good leave to go with you, Sire." He could not, of course, refuse.

Edward escorted her into the garden, which was blooming with lilac and mock orange. Three of Hastings' men stood near the back wall of the manor, always vigilant. They walked around to the lake where Elizabeth and her father had sat that cold afternoon three years ago when she had heard the news of her husband's death. Edward took her hand and kissed it gently.

"I wanted to tell you how lovely you look this evening." Elizabeth noticed that he had dropped the royal plural. "In fact, I had a hard time keeping my eyes off you."

"You did not appear to be trying very hard in my estimation, my lord," she said, looking out over the lake.

Edward smiled. He was drawn to this woman in ways that he had not hitherto known possible, and he had bedded more women than he could remember.

"Tell me, sweet Bess, do you admire me?"

"You are my king," she said.

"You know that's not what I mean."

"I understand you well, my lord." She looked into his eyes. "And I am your loyal subject."

Edward turned from her and after a moment's reflection, he stood and watched the sun vanish below the horizon. He wondered to himself if anyone would ever speak to him like a normal person again.

"Please, Bess, tell me what you're thinking. I left my crown back with your parents."

Elizabeth decided to take him at his word. She realized there was risk, but something in his face and demeanor gave her the courage.

"My lord's crown is not so far away that he cannot retrieve it if he wishes. Forgive me, but I won't be one who shares the pleasure of your evening company, and is bade farewell on the morrow without further regard. I have been a gentleman's wife and would be so again, if God so desires."

Edward took her hands. Looking hard into her eyes, he could not fathom his fascination with this woman. Few of his subjects would dare question his motives as she had just done, but instead of angering him, she had succeeded in captivating him further. She appeared to him as through a fog, distant and yet alluring beyond belief.

"Is that what you think? I had hoped that you would feel as I do at this moment. What can I do to open my soul to you so that you'll see more?"

"The answer to that, my lord," she said tenderly, "is within yourself."

"I don't understand. Is it your lands that you wish?"

"Forgive me again, my lord, but perhaps now it is you who are misinterpreting my motives. While it is true that I cherish Bradgate, I refer now only to my reputation. I know that many consider my family to be of lesser blood, but we are proud and have always been loyal to the throne. I would not be an evening's entertainment."

Edward took a moment to think. "Perhaps I have assumed the worst of you," he said with a thin smile. "I can only open my heart to you and ask that you trust me when I tell you that I have never felt the way I do now in the presence of any other."

Elizabeth smiled. She had been treading dangerous ground with the king, but if the events of the last few years had taught her anything, she knew that the safe path rarely led to desired destinations. She was flattered by the attentions of this handsome young monarch, but the danger of disappointing or angering him lurked behind every word. By confronting his hunting party in the woods, she had only wanted to convey her desperate wish to have Bradgate restored to her. But now the encounter seemed to have garnered entirely unexpected results, and she feared that the disposition of the outcome hung on how the conversation ended this evening.

"You are the king, my lord. Your every act carries with it great consequences. I believe that I do now know your heart in this matter, but I still have fears that will not be easily quelled."

"I would only rule your heart, Bess, if you let me. Tell me what you fear." Elizabeth felt a sadness in his voice that did not seem related to his words.

"I fear that Your Highness does not know enough about me to speak of love. My children know that their father died while fighting against you; it is not easily forgotten."

Edward took her hands. "What has gone before cannot be changed, and though I regret that the path which brought us here is ridden with many dead, including your late husband, I thank God that He has seen fit to bring us together on this evening."

Elizabeth could not hide the fact that Edward's attentions were stirring emotions in her that she had not felt since the death of her husband. The touch of his hands sent chills through her body that she struggled to control. Edward, sensing her receptivity, gently pulled her to him.

"I wish to see you again, sweet Bess, if you'll have me."

She felt the strength of his desire as their lips grew closer.

"I hope the days will be short until then." She shivered violently as he kissed her deeply, pulling her firmly into his body. She had not hoped to feel this way again in her lifetime, and they lingered in each other's arms.

CHAPTER XIII

The rutted, muddy streets of Durham were still familiar to Samuel, though several years had passed since he had seen them. A scant fifty miles from the great northern castle of Warkworth, he had made several journeys to Durham on the earl's behalf during his apprenticeship, and had always enjoyed the sparse northern woods through which the road wound. Durham was also not far from Northwood, and occasionally his father had escorted wagonloads of milled grain to the markets here for the earl, sometimes bringing Samuel along.

Now he was enjoying a moment's respite from his duties, having accompanied the king northward with the guard. For three years he had enjoyed the favor of Sir Julian, who had taken it upon himself to train Samuel in various skills of war, especially in the use of the short sword. Sir Julian was a strong advocate of versatility, and wanted his men to be capable in whatever skills were warranted by any situation. Now Samuel felt comfortable wearing his sword belt, and was confident in his ability to use his blade, though he still preferred to face an enemy with a full quiver on his back and a bow in his hands.

The streets he remembered had not changed much over the years. The hustle of activity and overbearing aromas recalled many old, forgotten bits of memory, which now rolled through his mind like gusts of wind through the winter woods. Even the faces all seemed strangely familiar. The only person he didn't recognize was himself.

His body, while still quite thin, had grown strong and sinewy through the constant physical exertion of his training and occasional combat, and by the natural transformation to manhood. His thick, curly black hair hung

in locks to his shoulders, which were covered by a leather jerkin emblazoned with the king's Sun-in-Splendor symbol. But it was his face that had
changed the most. Still clean shaven as he preferred it, the cares of many
battles and the traumatic events of Wakefield and Towton had left their
marks. It was not the eyes of a twenty-year-old man that gazed upon the
ramshackle houses that lined the streets of Durham, but those of one who
had seen too much for his tender years. Somehow he could not shake the
feeling of being alone.

"Samuel!" The sound of his name from somewhere out of the crowd
startled him, and he spun on his heels to see who could be calling. He saw
an arm waving and a head bobbing above the crowd. Recognizing his friend
Stanley, he normally would have been pleased to see him, but at this
moment Samuel was fighting the urge to run and hide. He waited, however,
until his friend caught up, breathing heavily after what must have been a
significant exertion. Stanley put his hands on his knees, taking a moment
to catch his breath.

"I thought I'd never find you," he said at last. His reddish hair and light,
freckled skin seemed all the more pale in contrast to his tunic with the Sun-
in-Splendor emblem of the king's guard.

"I didn't know you were looking for me," Samuel said. "Come, you look
like you could use some water." He took Stanley's arm and led him to the
public fountain that sprang from the wall of a stone building in the town's
central square. Stanley splashed the water on his head and drank mouth-
fuls between hurried breaths. When it looked like he was recovered from
his run, Samuel clapped him on the back. "So what brings you to such a
state?"

"The guard has been summoned to the king, and we should be there
now!"

"What's wrong?"

"We're to take part in the investiture. Haven't you heard?"

Samuel shook his head and relaxed. Another ceremony, he thought with
annoyance. He did not relish the thought of standing around as ornamen-
tation while another of the nobility was granted some high honor or post
that did not concern Samuel in the least.

"What investiture?" he asked absently.

"The king's brothers, of course. I cannot believe that you don't know."

Now that Stanley reminded him, Samuel did remember something about the king's youngest brothers returning from Burgundy where they had taken refuge during the past several years. Now that Edward felt secure on the throne, he had sent for his mother and brothers. The dowager Duchess of York returned to Baynards Castle in London, where she took up permanent residence to be closer to the royal court. The boys, on the other hand, were sent directly to the king's presence.

"Yes," said Samuel with a sigh. "I do remember, now that you mention it. The ceremony is today?"

"It's to start at sunset, but we're required to be at the bishop's manor house now, so that proper preparations can be made. Sir Julian sent me after you with solemn warnings about being late."

"Very well, then. We'd best be off." They walked quickly along the busy street, doing their best to avoid the mud, spinning and dodging the densely packed pedestrians.

"You never told me what you thought of Sir Julian's tale," he asked Samuel as they ducked under the canopy of a fishmonger's wagon, the pungent odor of eel turning their stomachs.

Samuel thought for a moment about the story Sir Julian had told to a group of the guard the night before while they were at supper. It was a banquet sponsored by the king for his guardsmen, over which Sir Julian presided as the king's representative. The old knight had spent much of the evening relating the ancient tale of Roland, a knight in the service of Charlemagne while the emperor was fighting the Moors of Spain some six hundred years ago. Roland had been assigned to lead the rear guard of the army. Another knight, jealous of Charlemagne's favor toward Roland, betrayed Roland to the Moors, who attacked the rear guard with an army that far exceeded Roland's in size. Instead of blowing his horn and calling for Charlemagne to come to their rescue, Roland engaged the enemy, thinking it far nobler to risk his life and those of his men. While he and his men fought bravely and inflicted disproportionate losses on the Moors, in the end he could see that victory was not possible, and only then decided to blow his horn. But it was too late. By the time Charlemagne answered the call, Roland and all of his men lay dead on the battlefield, a loss that sorely grieved the great emperor.

While Roland's mistake was plain to them all at the banquet, Samuel could not surmise why Sir Julian had chosen to tell that story on that occasion. He hid his ignorance behind a quick shrug of his shoulders.

"I think it's plain that he was trying to tell us something."

"I guessed that much myself, you lout," Stanley gave him a shove into the path of a large man who was walking in the opposite direction. Samuel barely managed to avoid a collision. He lunged back and grabbed Stanley by the tunic and they struggled against each other, both trying to avoid being forced to the muddy ground. Several passersby, angered at being jostled and bumped, cursed them as they crashed into the side of a building. Finally releasing each other, they slumped onto a short foundation wall, laughing and panting from the exertion.

"Don't worry about them," said Stanley defiantly to the scowling faces in the crowd. They both knew that as members of the king's guard they did not have to live by the same rules as the commoners. He made a mock lunge at a woman who looked especially disapproving, and with a yelp, she scurried down the street, yelling curses back at him as she went. Again, they laughed with glee.

"It's good to hear you laugh again, Samuel. You should do it more often."

"I grew up near here, did you know that? It still all looks pretty much the same after all that's happened."

"You speak like an old man, my friend. How much did you expect things to change in your short life?" Stanley laughed, but Samuel's face did not change. Stanley saw a chance to learn more about his friend. "Where is your family now?"

"The last I knew, in Northwood. Just a day's ride to the north of here."

"Perhaps Sir Julian will give you a few days to visit."

"I don't think I'd be welcome," Samuel said absently.

"It sounds like a story I'd like to hear."

"It's not one I care to tell." Samuel jumped to his feet. "Come on, we're going to be late."

Stanley quickly caught up. "Everyone in the guard knows that it was you who killed Clifford, and with an arrow shot that's practically legendary. Sir Julian said that you had some score to settle. What did he do to you?"

"Sir Julian tells more stories than he should," said Samuel. After walking silently for a while longer, he spoke again. "I had the temerity to question Clifford's honor after the battle of Wakefield, having watched him needlessly slaughter the defenseless Earl of Rutland. After that, his men hunted me down and took me, my father, and sister prisoner. My father was beaten so mercilessly that he died shortly after. The rest of us were rescued by the king's men, but my brother was devoted to the Percys and blamed me for everything. My joining the king's guard only made matters worse."

"I doubt it not," said Stanley under his breath. "Why did you join if you knew that it would alienate your brother?"

Samuel thought for a moment. "I'm not really sure, but it seemed like the right course at the time. Besides, it's what I was trained for, isn't it? I didn't really see a life for myself back in Northwood. It just seems as if every time I try to do the right thing, those closest to me suffer the most, so if I were you, Stanley, I'd keep my distance."

Stanley grabbed his arm, stopping their rapid pace toward the bishop's Manor House.

"If that's the cost of your friendship, then I'm willing to pay." Samuel had not expected such kind words, and could think of nothing to say. Stanley smiled, then pushed him down the street. "If I get punished for being late on your account, you'll be sorry, I swear."

They ran the last few blocks that separated them from the bishop's house, darting and dodging around every obstacle. As they turned the last corner and the iron gates came into view, a woman carrying a basket full of onions and herbs stepped out from around the corner and, unable to check his speed, Samuel collided with her, sending them both headlong to the ground, scattering the contents of her basket. Dazed at first, then simply angry, the woman glared at Samuel.

"Do you not know that others use these streets as well?"

Stanley stood smiling while Samuel scrambled to gather the woman's basket and its contents. He apologized profusely and helped her to her feet, handing the disheveled basket back. His actions had disarmed the woman, who had to smile at his embarrassment.

Samuel looked at her for the first time. An attractive woman in her early twenties, she had brown hair in one long braid. She bore herself proudly, more like a noblewoman than the kitchen hand she was.

"Come on, Samuel. We're late as it is," urged Stanley. Samuel did not seem to hear him.

"My...name is Samuel," he stammered.

"Your friend has already told me that," she said. Positioning her basket on her shoulder, she brushed past him and continued down the street. "Please do be more careful in the future."

"Will you please come on," urged Stanley more persistently as Samuel watched her disappear around the corner.

"Do you know her, Stanley?" he said, grudgingly allowing himself to be pulled toward the iron gates of the bishop's home.

"For heaven's sake, man, she's a kitchen maid in the bishop's service. Kate, I think her name is. Have you not seen her toiling there?"

"No," he said wistfully, "I haven't." They entered past the gate toward the rear where the guard was camped. There's something about her, thought Samuel. *Something...*

The great hall of the bishop's manor was lit by a dozen torches. Samuel and the rest of the king's guard were arranged in single lines along both walls, except for Sir Julian, who stood below and slightly to the right of the throne. All of the guard wore the gold-and-black tunic with the Sun-in-Splendor symbol. Samuel stood somewhere toward the center of the room on the right side, from where he was able to see the entire room. Stanley stood next to him. Countless dignitaries and courtiers mingled, carrying on dozens of conversations. Samuel easily recognized the brothers Neville, who stood near the front of the room by themselves. The Earl of Warwick and his brothers George, the Bishop of Exeter, and John, Lord Montagu, had become the principal power of the kingdom and the staff of the king's party. Warwick and Montagu had only recently returned from the north after having contended with the Lancastrians, who were still holding the great castles of Bamborough, Dunstanborough, and Alnwick, as well as Berwick Castle, which had been treacherously deeded to the Scots by Margaret in exchange for their support. Samuel also recognized their host, the Bishop of Durham, who was talking to two magnates that he did not recognize. It felt hot under his heavy leather tunic.

Two sentries on either side of the huge double doors at the end of the room lifted their horns and loudly signaled the impending arrival of the king. The doors swung open and the sentries went to their knees. The first to enter were two pages bearing the lion and Fleur de Lis crest of England

and the king's Sun-in-Splendor symbol. After them, the king himself entered, followed by Lord Hastings and two young men dressed in the royal purple velvet and floor-length capes, who Samuel assumed were the king's brothers, recently arrived from Burgundy. The ranks of noblemen and courtiers bowed deeply as he passed. Upon arrival at the dais, the king took the two steps up and turned to face the room. He wore around his shoulders a velvet cape with ermine collar. On his head he wore a simple gold coronet, and in his right hand he carried the symbolic staff of office. Two pages lifted the cape from his shoulders and arranged it on the throne behind him, upon which the king finally sat. Hastings and the two brothers stood to the right of the throne, opposite the Nevilles.

"My lords of Warwick and Montagu," said Edward, "you are welcome back to our court." Both bowed their heads in silent response. "Tell me now what news you have from the north."

"Your Highness, she who lately called herself queen has a small force of French mercenaries and English traitors, and they are locked still behind the walls of our great northern castles. We continue with our siege and given time we will smoke them out like rats. The puissance that Your Highness brings will spell the end. I had also hoped for help from the noble Duke of Norfolk, but I regret to inform Your Highness that the duke has joined his ancestors and will never more answer a call to arms."

Edward was crestfallen. After the Nevilles, Norfolk had been the strongest of his allies, and he had always felt more secure knowing that someone other than the Nevilles could assist him if needed.

"We mourn the loss of our great kinsman," he said after a moment. "Lord Hastings, you will give our respects to his heir, young John Mowbray, and tell him we weep for his loss." Hastings acknowledged with a bow of his head. "As for the northern castles, we commend the actions of our cousins of Warwick and Montagu and instruct all our loyal subjects to assist them with any need. My lord of Kent, you and Scales will accompany them in this campaign." He was speaking to the two noblemen that Samuel had not recognized next to the Bishop of Durham. The Neville brothers looked at each other momentarily, but made no comment. The Earl of Kent was a longtime supporter of the House of York and a kinsman to the Nevilles. But Scales was a Woodville, and had fought for the Lancastrians. Warwick did not understand why he was being included in this task.

The king offered no explanation. "And now to the business at hand, which we have anticipated with great joy. George and Richard, stand before us, and we shall hear your oaths!"

As the two young men stepped to the foot of the throne, Samuel found it difficult to believe that they were born of the same parents. The eldest, George, was blond and tall, and stood as if he were himself the king. His brother, Richard, three years younger, was dark and small.

After both had given the king their oaths of loyalty, Edward stood and put his hands on their heads. Samuel could not help but notice the difference in the expressions worn by the two youths. Richard seemed in awe of his majestic brother and gazed up at him with excitement. George, on the other hand, looked uncomfortable and acted as if the attention were commonplace.

Edward addressed George first. "Know by all men here present that before God and His ministers, we create our brother George the Duke of Clarence, and grant him all the appurtenances and powers attendant to that title." He then placed a circlet of gold on George's head as a symbol of his dukedom. Turning to Richard he said, "And know by all men here present that before God and His ministers, we create our brother Richard the Duke of Gloucester, and grant him all the appurtenances and powers attendant to the title." Richard was then also crowned with the gold circlet of office. "My lords! Welcome these new dukes to our court." The young dukes turned and were greeted with applause. "Come, my lords, and let us repair to the banquet hall and celebrate. My heart is full of joy today!"

Samuel was relieved to hear that his services were not required at the banquet and was released for the night. Being anxious to attend breakfast in the morning, he retired without the usual carousing common to evenings with the guard.

The next morning Samuel was awake with the dawn and took unusual care washing at the pumphead. He had been careful not to wake Stanley, who usually accompanied him to breakfast, because on this occasion he had no desire for his company. He could smell the cooking fires from the kitchen hearths, and wondered how the bishop could afford the immense cost of hosting the king and his train. Walking quickly to the side entrance of the kitchen, he looked timidly through the door. There, behind a large kettle, stood Kate. He watched for a moment as she strained to stir what seemed a thick and difficult stew, her hair still in a single long braid which bounced as she moved. He was mesmerized by the shape of her breasts, which pushed their round form against her apron.

He stepped in, trying to look more assured than he felt. "Good morning to you, Kate," he said at last.

She smiled casually. "Samuel, is it?"

"I'm pleased that you remember."

"Am I likely to forget a person who knocked me to the ground?"

Samuel blushed. "No, I don't imagine that you would."

There was an awkward pause. "So what is it that you need at this early hour, young man?"

"I was...I wonder if you'd like to join me after your duties this evening?"

"What exactly were you thinking you'd like me to join you for?"

Samuel blushed again. "I just meant for a walk in town, if that's agreeable with you."

An unwelcome voice came from the doorway.

"So there you are." It was Stanley.

"It is agreeable with me," Kate said quickly. "You may meet me here when we put out the cooking fires." Then she raised her voice. "Now help yourself to the rolls over there. I'll not be serving you." Samuel smiled broadly and with light feet walked over to help himself to a freshly baked roll. When Stanley joined him, he didn't have to ask what had caused Samuel to fail to wake him that morning.

Samuel had been waiting patiently for quite a while before Kate finally emerged from the kitchen. She smiled tiredly when she saw him.

"I hope I didn't keep you too long. It's not an easy task to feed the king's party, and we're all going mad trying to keep up."

"I can only imagine," he said sympathetically. "I know a place down along the river that's very peaceful this time of day. Would you care to see it?"

"Should I call the housekeeper to watch over us?" Samuel blushed, and Kate laughed. "I suppose I can trust a member of the king's personal guard."

The River Wear had an abundant flow by the time it reached Durham. The waters reminded him of home.

"I feel like I'm intruding," Kate stood beside him. The sun was just setting below the horizon, and the dim light made her seem mysterious. He could feel the warmth of her body. "I should know better than to come to a place where a man has found solitude."

Samuel was amazed by her insight. "Forgive me, I sometimes drift when I should be more attentive. Tell me about yourself. You're not like any kitchen maid I've known before."

"Oh? And what strikes you as different about myself?"

Samuel laughed. He loved the way she went directly to the point. "I think you know what I mean," he said softly.

Her face shimmered in the last glow of the day. "And you're not like any soldier I've ever known."

"Oh, but that's what I am, born and bred," he said bitterly. "It's all I've ever known, and all I'm likely to know hereafter."

"I don't believe that."

Samuel took her hand and led her down a narrow footpath that followed the bank of the river, ducking the ghostly willow branches along the way. The stars made their entrance onto the darkening dome above them, lending a misty glow to the river waters as they rippled past. He found his favorite spot, atop a low bluff, and they sat with their feet dangling over the edge of the rocky face above the current. The night breeze wafting gently past, Samuel felt a comfort that he had not known for many years. He began telling Kate stories of his youth and of growing up in Northwood, and even retold some of the events of the past couple of years, including the horrifying stay at Pontefract and the death of his father.

"Well," he said at last, "now you see that I am just a common soldier after all."

She put her warm hand on his arm.

"I only see a young man who has taken a great many burdens on himself that are best shared with others."

"You still haven't told me anything about yourself."

She turned away. "There's nothing much to tell. I grew up just south of here to a large family of farmers. I did my family duties and worked hard until I was fifteen when my father began looking desperately for someone to whom I could marry. But the thought of working as plow ox for some-one else for the rest of my life did not appeal to me and I ran away to this town, thinking that things would be better. As it turned out, the bishop took me into his service and he treats us well enough. At least I have some time to myself occasionally so that I can go on walks with handsome young men like yourself." Even in the dark, she could tell that Samuel was blush-ing again.

But there was a quality to her voice that did not seem warranted by the story, an unmistakably sad tone.

"I think we had better return before it gets too late. I wouldn't want peo-ple to start talking about you." As he turned toward her, he found her lips pressed against his, a kiss that lingered gently into the night.

CHAPTER XIV

"**M**y lord of Somerset, what news from the king of the Scots?"

Three years of exile had not broken Margaret's spirit. Her tireless efforts to secure help from Scotland and France had borne some fruit, even if the reacquisition of the English throne still appeared most unlikely. But she had sworn to fight to restore her son's birthright until the day of her death.

As for Henry, he accompanied them everywhere but rarely spoke, and at times relapsed into his witless stupors. Margaret would have grieved for him had she the time, but the mission that drove her every breath took precedence. For now he would have to content himself with his biblical studies and daydreams, the contents of which she could only imagine.

Since the deaths of Clifford and Northumberland, her power had been reduced to a fragment of its former self. The Duke of Somerset and the Earl of Pembroke had remained loyal through all their tribulations, but they had never commanded the wealth and resources of her fallen lords. Louis of France had been maddeningly reluctant to provide men and funds for her cause, mainly for fear that Edward and his ally Burgundy would join forces and war against him; he knew that he had not the strength to withstand a joint attack. He did, however, allow her good friend, Count Pierre de Brezé, to join her cause with a small band of men that he had raised with his own funds. His presence had been a godsend to her, not only for his strength but for his unquestioning support. Sir Ralph Percy, the late Earl of Northumberland's brother, had also joined them, helping with the defense of Bamborough Castle.

Now if only the Scottish army would arrive, they could begin the next phase of the campaign. Margaret had taken up residence at Dunstan-borough Castle, where her supporters now gathered to discuss strategy. She had converted the great hall into her throne room, where she sat with Henry.

"Your Highness," said Somerset, "Edward has arrived at Durham with an army, and Warwick will most likely wait to join him before advancing on our positions. As for the Scots, we have heard that they were dispatched from the king's court a fortnight ago, but their exact location remains a mystery."

Margaret became agitated. "We have told you that we will not expose our son to the dangers of a battle with the usurper. We must have assurances that the Scots will arrive before them."

"If it were in my power to do so, Your Majesty, it would give me great pleasure, but the vicissitudes of the Scots will not permit it."

"Flee. Flee, good wife. Bloody Warwick comes." It always startled the court when Henry spoke. "And he will prove more true than all the Dukes of Somerset."

Somerset was visibly shaken. "My Liege, I protest my loyalty!"

"Peace, gentle Somerset," interjected the queen. "The king has not been himself, and we know you to be a true subject." She glared at Henry. "My lord, you have mistaken yourself. It is Warwick who is your enemy, not Somerset."

His face was devoid of expression. "Flee, good wife."

"Peace, my lord," she said sadly. "We are safe here for now." Her assurances did not seem to comfort him, but he withdrew back into himself. Margaret attempted to restore some decorum to the gathering.

"My lords, we must have some intelligence of the Scottish army. Send all the scouts that we can spare and bring us certain news."

Not a day's ride from Margaret and Dunstanborough Castle, Warwick and his brother John were at Warkworth Castle, preparing to send a large column of the king's soldiers toward the former queen. Though Edward had taken ill at Durham, he had already sent his army to join with the Nevilles weeks before, and had sent instructions to the brothers to begin the siege of the Lancastrian-held castles at once.

John marveled at Warkworth's commanding position on the cliffs above the sea. "This castle has a most pleasant seat, don't you agree, Richard?"

Warwick was more concerned with the activities in the courtyard below them.

"I like it better since we wrested it from the Percys," he said gruffly.

"I think I shall ask the king for this castle when we've disposed of Margaret and her Frenchmen."

"If that's what you want, I'll see that he gives it to you."

"You seem very confident that he's willing to do your bidding."

"He owes us for his throne and he knows it. Without our strength, even these petty Lancastrian incursions would be a serious threat." Below them, columns of men were forming up just outside the castle moat.

"If the rumors are true about a Scottish army coming this way, it may not be a petty incursion."

Warwick dismissed the notion with a wave of his hand. "The Scots fight better among themselves than against English armies. We have more than enough power to siege the castles and repel the Scots."

"How will you deploy the men?"

"We'll send the king's men with Kent and Scales to direct the siege of Alnwick. It's the nearest castle and I'll be better able to keep a close eye on them. You, brother, will take your men to Bamborough, and I will make haste to Dunstanborough. We'll dispatch daily messengers to each other. We can always break off from one place to assist the other if a Scottish army does dare to invade."

"I'll be off then. Good fortune to you, Richard, and we'll meet again when this business is over."

Left to himself, Warwick watched as his brother assembled his men and made preparations to leave. *Once and for all, we must dispatch this bothersome Margaret, so that we can keep a closer watch on the king and his court.*

Somerset bowed as the queen entered a small sitting chamber where she liked to speak with her supporters away from Henry.

"What news, my lord," she asked impatiently.

"Highness, it is certain that Warwick and Edward's army have arrived at Warkworth. They may already be deployed toward us."

"And the Scots?"

"I regret that there is still no word."

Margaret made a quick decision. "We and our train will depart from this place, and await news at Berwick. My lord, we entrust you with the defense of our castles until the Scots arrive to assist you."

"I will hold them against the devil himself, my lady."

"May God grant you His protection."

After weeks of siege on the castle, Warwick could feel the growing desperation of those inside Dunstanborough. And from the accounts of the messengers, it seemed things were going equally well at the other two castles. At Bamborough, news came that the defenders were already eating their horses. It was late October, and the cold weather would also prove harder on the defenders than on his troops, who were being constantly replaced with new recruits from Durham and the surrounding country. And as yet there was no sign of a Scottish army. A messenger approached his tent. He was no more than a boy, likely come to serve with one of the knights as a page. He knelt and waited to be recognized.

"Well?" Warwick asked.

"A message from within, Your Worship," he said. "The Duke of Somerset wishes to discuss terms for the surrender of Dunstanborough Castle."

"At last," he dismissed the boy with a quick wave of his hand. To one of his attendants he said, "Arrange a parley with Somerset for this very afternoon. Go." He pushed the man out of his way and addressed another. "Send word to my brother at Bamborough and tell him we expect to join him within a week." He smiled with satisfaction.

Lord Montagu was delighted the day Warwick rode into camp before Bamborough Castle. The additional troops, he was sure, would bring a quick end to the siege, and he was growing weary of these incessant broils. For three years now he had been fighting, and there were other pursuits that he hoped to enjoy. But he could not pretend to hide his surprise at the sight of the Duke of Somerset riding at Warwick's side, as if he had been a longtime brother-at-arms instead of the detested enemy that he was. When Warwick dismounted, Montagu embraced him warmly but did not take his eyes off Somerset.

"My brother, you have among you a detested enemy. How came this to be?"

Warwick slapped him on the back. "Come. Let's retire to your tent and speak of these matters. I have a strong thirst for some grog."

Montagu's tent was the model of simplicity, containing only a sleeping pad and a round table with four stools. The dirt floor was covered with a plain red carpet, which showed the wear from dozens of campaigns. He and his brother sat quietly while a page served them with a pitcher of grog and two wood cups.

"And now," said Montagu impatiently, "tell me why that traitor is not in irons and on his way to the block."

Warwick emptied his mug and poured himself another.

"As a condition of yielding the castle, he begged the king's forgiveness and it was granted. Against my advice, mind you. But the king has consistently shown a desire to forgive these Lancastrian swine, the reason for which escapes me."

"But Somerset was the worst of them. And I'd rather run him through where he stands than turn my back to him."

"You need not lose sleep over that fool, John. We'll keep a close eye on him, but he has no following and will not pose a threat to anyone. I asked that he prove his loyalty by joining us on this siege, and of course he agreed, so I'll know where he is for the time being. But he's not the only one to whom the foolish king has granted clemency."

Montagu knew what was coming. "Pembroke?"

Warwick nodded. "The treasonous cur refused the king's offer of forgiveness, but was granted safe leave to return to Scotland anyway."

Montagu was incredulous. "It cannot be! He'll foment rebellion in the north for the rest of his life. How could the king be so blind?"

"He must have felt that it was worth the price to get possession of Dunstanborough. I must confess, I'm not sorry to see the castle in our hands this easily. If sending him on his way saved me months of sitting before that damned castle, then let him go. We'll see his head on the block soon enough."

Montagu saw the logic in his brother's argument. Letting his anger slip, he poured them both another round.

"Then I assume the king would allow us to use the same tactic here?"

"If wretched Percy wishes to throw himself on the king's mercy, he would be free to go. Somerset has the king's orders to offer him clemency. He felt it would be more convincing coming from a Lancastrian."

"Good. If so, we'll join Kent and Scales at Alnwick, and put an end to this nonsense sooner than I had dared hope. But I tell you plainly, brother, I swear that I'll not rest until I see Somerset's head on the block as well."

"Let us drink to that," said Warwick, raising his mug. "What is a king's pardon to us, after all? Come now and let's offer Percy the same pardon."

Alnwick Castle had been garrisoned from the beginning by Margaret's French mercenaries, and Warwick knew that this would be the most difficult castle to take, given the hatred the French felt for Englishmen. It had been relatively easy to convince Sir Ralph Percy to yield Bamborough and accept the king's pardon, but Warwick was not pleased that as a condition of the surrender, Percy had been allowed to remain in charge of both Bamborough and Dunstanborough. However, the two castles had been possessions of the Percy family for generations and, given Sir Ralph's oath of allegiance to the king, it was a logical boon to grant.

From their position atop a low hill, two arrow-shots' length from the ramparts of Alnwick, Warwick, Montagu, Kent, Scales and Somerset defiantly glared at the men on the walls of the castle. As the enemy soldiers went about their business on the allure behind the crenelation, Warwick wondered to himself if those within felt the weight of impending doom as they measured his irresistible force.

"Lord Scales," he called. "How do you estimate their rations?"

Anthony Woodville had always hated Warwick. There had been animosity between the Nevilles and the Woodvilles ever since Elizabeth refused to marry a Yorkist ally who had been suggested to her by the late Duke of York and Warwick. Instead she had married John Grey, a Lancastrian supporter. Only the unfortunate fate that had seen a Yorkist claim the throne left him in his present position of having to bear taking direction from this conceited earl.

"They were not able to properly secure supplies for a long siege, my lord," he said. "I would estimate their rations to be very low." Warwick nodded and said nothing.

"We have news that Margaret and Henry have fled to the north looking for safe passage to Berwick," added Montagu. "It is likely that the French have given her a few boats to ease her trip north."

"May ill winds greet them all the way," said Warwick, not really caring what became of them. His attention had been diverted to a rider that galloped furiously toward them, already past the first line of sentinels guarding the north. Upon arrival, he spoke loudly without waiting to be recognized.

"Arm yourselves, great lords, the Scottish army is on my heels, not more than an hour's ride north."

The news stunned them all. Several yelled questions, which the scout tried his best to understand and answer. Finally Warwick silenced them with a shout.

"Under whose banner do they ride?"

"They carry the colors of the Earl of Angus, my lord."

"It is logical," said Montagu. "Angus is the only one who would dare raise an army for Henry. We had best not underestimate him."

"I have no intention of doing so, John. What do you estimate their force to be?"

"Five thousand strong, my lord." The answer brought scowls from the gathered lords. The Scots had managed to surprise them with an army twice the size of their own.

Warwick tightened his resolve. "By God, we will not yield what we have fought so long to achieve. Gather the troops in defensible array." He pointed to a low, marshy area to the west of their position. "We will make our stand in that sheltered place. Hurry, my lords. There's not much time."

Somerset rode with Scales and the others to help array the troops. When they were out of earshot of the Nevilles, he leaned over to Scales and smiled broadly.

"The earl doesn't seem so haughty all of a sudden."

Scales nodded. "May the Lord save an arrow just for him."

The north wind blew a foreboding chill into the Earl of Angus. He had thought ill of this excursion from the start, and indeed it had been particularly trying from the day they had set out. Count Pierre de Brezé had appealed to his honor by reminding him of the promises that he had made to Margaret a year before, and it would simply not have been right to refuse her assistance. But he had felt the hand of illness on his soul since the journey had begun, and on several occasions had to stop the progress of the army to allow himself to recuperate. When at last Alnwick Castle came into view, it was through tired eyes that he surveyed the field.

"My lord," the count addressed Angus, "we have a clear advantage of numbers. We should not hesitate. Perhaps you would permit me the honor of leading the troops." He knew Angus was in no condition to do so.

Angus ignored him. "Why have they abandoned their positions along the high ground?" With the freezing rain on his face, Angus felt a wave of nausea coming over him and fought to maintain his composure. The scouts came back and reported that the English were fortifying their position in the low area.

"My lord, we must press our advantage now!"

"I tell you, I fear a trap," Angus managed to say with some conviction. A messenger arrived from behind them. "Speak," he commanded.

"My lord, Queen Margaret and King Henry have gained sea passage toward Berwick and are not within this castle."

"What?" Angus turned angrily toward Brezé. "You told me we were riding to her defense and now I find that she has fled?"

"My lord," pleaded Brezé, "surely you see that she had to protect her family?"

Angus shook his head to clear his misty vision. A new wave of nausea gripped him.

"I'll not risk the lives of these brave men for nothing," he said, waving at the ranks behind him. At that moment he wanted nothing more than to be off his horse and warm within his own castle. "My lords," he yelled as he spurred his horse around, "let us withdraw. If Henry leads us back, we'll return. Until then, away!"

Brezé was apoplectic with anger, but argument was futile. As the army began its retreat, he wondered which evil spirit sat on Edward's shoulder that granted him such good fortune.

At dawn the following day, the French garrison commander surrendered the castle without condition. His men were starved half to death and the departure of the Scottish army had so demoralized them, they would have most likely murdered him. The garrison was given safe conduct to join the retreating Scottish army, and Warwick entered Alnwick Castle in celebration. It was time to rest from a long campaign that had seen the final expulsion of the Lancastrians from all the northern castles except Berwick, but that castle would be regained someday as well, Warwick was certain. He would leave his brother here to maintain order, and make haste back to the king's court, where he could turn his attention to more interesting matters of state.

The once king and queen of all England, Henry and Margaret, with their son, the ten-year-old Prince of Wales, and a small party of Frenchmen boarded four carvels near Bamborough with hopes of reaching Berwick Castle to the north in a matter of a day or two. But they had encountered rough seas from the first day and now the wind, howling from the east, whipped the waves into monstrous swells. Henry stood with the captain near the wheelhouse, having left Margaret amidships huddled with the prince. Henry grabbed the captain by his cloak and yelled over the wind.

"I cannot leave my kingdom! Take us back."

The captain struggled with the wheel as if fighting demons for control.

"My lord, these are dangerous seas," he yelled back. "I could not put you ashore even if I had the desire."

Henry was persistent. "The ship is lost. I see its ghost in the waves. Take me back before it's too late!"

"I tell you plainly, my lord, this madness endangers us all." He pulled Henry's hands off and pushed the king to the deck. "If we live, I'll answer to the hangman!"

A wall of water crashed against the boat and washed over the deck, taking several of the soldiers over the opposite side. The carvel took a deep plunge into the swell as water rushed through hatchways into the bowels of the ship. Henry looked to see where his wife and son were drenched from the last wave and clinging desperately to each other and to a lifeboat that was sheltering them in the center of the ship.

"I see the ghost," he mumbled to no one in particular as he swung under a railing and jumped down to the main deck. A French soldier tried to stop him, but another wave crashed against the deck at the moment he released his hold on the rigging, sweeping the guard into the sea before he saw it coming. The captain could not see what had become of the king, but had all he could manage trying to keep the ship from foundering. The next moment, he watched in amazement as feeble Henry emerged from behind a staircase and slowly made his way to where Margaret was still clinging to the life raft.

"My wife," he yelled at her, "we must be off this ship. I have seen its ghost in the waves."

Eyes wide with terror, she assisted him under the life boat, desperately seeking the shore line.

Another surge of water washed the deck, dumping more sea into the hatchways. The carvel began to founder. Two of the crew joined them under the life boat at great risk from the waves.

"Your Majesties, we must release this boat into the water. It's our only chance," one of them yelled.

"Yes, yes," said Henry, "we must release the boat!" But Margaret was close to hysterics and could not stand to lose their haven. Before she could say anything, another wave crashed across the deck and drenched them again. By then the sailors were releasing the tie-downs.

"My son, my son," yelled Margaret.

"I'll be all right, Mother," the boy assured her as a sailor pulled him out from under the raft.

"Hurry, we must be off before another wave hits. The ship is going down!" He helped Margaret out from under the boat and Henry followed them. The last tie-down was released and the sailors used pulleys to lower the boat over the side, then assisted the royal family in. The sailors looked around and yelled for anyone who could join them before releasing the last line. Three of the French soldiers had been near enough to make it.

They drifted away from the ship as it took another deep dive into a swell from which it did not fully recover. The bow of the boat stayed submerged. The sailors were able to keep the small boat turned into the swells, and they rose and fell with the sea but did not take water. The carvel slipped bow first into the sea and disappeared. The other ships were nowhere in sight. Margaret sought desperately for the shoreline and found it, much closer than she had dared hope.

"Can we make it?" she asked pointing to land.

"If God and the sea are willing," one of the sailors said as he pulled on the oar. "But we have to find a safe place to ride out the storm away from those rocks, where we can get ashore."

"I will stand again on my kingdom," mumbled Henry to no one in particular. He had become remarkably calm and serene.

For the first time, Margaret reflected on her husband's recent penchant for prophesying the future, and it occurred to her that several of his predictions had come true.

And Henry did indeed walk upon the soil of his kingdom again. Two hours of backbreaking rowing by the sailors had landed them on a small beach between rock outcroppings that sheltered them as the storm blew over.

The next day they took to the sea again in their small boat, which when rigged with its sail cut swiftly through the waves. They sped up the coast, guests of a strong but friendly west wind, the relatively short distance that remained between them and Berwick Castle. There they were well received by the Scottish garrison, and were once again masters of at least this one place. The news of the surrender of all the northern castles was a crushing blow, but even worse news greeted them. Their principal ally in Scotland, the Earl of Angus, had died, and the army that he had promised them was dispersed. If that were not bad enough, Somerset and Percy had accepted Edward's pardon. As she hugged her son to her breast, Margaret knew she had lost all of her great allies, her remaining possessions on the carvel, and her husband to madness.

CHAPTER XV

Samuel walked without direction. He absently pulled his collar up against the cool evening air, passing several people without noticing them. His mates were at their favorite tavern as usual, but he had no desire to join them.

He was thinking about Kate and how he would see her again. He could not ask her to follow him around from camp to camp, but there was no telling when he would be near here again.

A strong hand closed around his mouth while an arm around his waist pulled him into an alley behind the main street. For an instant, Samuel thought it was Stanley and tried to free his mouth, but a blow to his stomach by a second person took his breath. Another blow brought him to his knees, gasping for any air at all. One of his attackers took him by the hair and pulled his head up. Samuel could see only a dark outline of a face before him, a black shape silhouetted by the dim glow of starlight. A throaty voice hissed at him.

"Tell Kate we want the letter or we'll kill you both. Do you hear me?"

Kate! What could her connection be to these thugs? Samuel did not have time to consider an answer before the toe of a boot crushed against his ribs. He sprawled on the ground, pain stabbing through his body. Another blow to the ribs was all that he felt before consciousness drifted away, furious that he had no way to protect Kate.

"He couldn't have gone far," Stanley guessed.

He and Sir Julian looked helplessly down the main street, but saw no sign.

"Are you sure you saw him come this way?"

"I'm sure. And only a few minutes ago." They continued down the street, checking side alleys as they passed them. "He's been very distracted these last days. I suppose that love will do that to you."

"Murder! Help, for pity's sake, help!"

The voice came from somewhere beyond the next alley. The guardsmen ran toward the voice, which kept up the cry: "Murder! Murder!"

They arrived at a side street where six or seven people, one of them holding a torch, were gathered around a hysterical older man who was still repeating his horrible message for anyone who would listen.

"Give way, in the name of the king!" Sir Julian barked as they arrived. The gawkers, relieved that someone of authority had arrived to take control, parted. Sir Julian saw a man dressed in the king's colors lying perfectly still, face down in the muck of the alley. "Sweet angels of mercy," he pleaded as he knelt to inspect the victim. Samuel's face was caked with mud, and blood oozed from his lips. Sir Julian lifted him by the shoulders and put his ear to his mouth. "He breathes still. Help me with him!" Stanley and James lifted his lifeless form carefully. "Quickly, to the bishop's palace. It's close by." With Samuel between them, and Sir Julian holding him in the middle, they made their way to the palace, where they sent for the bishop's physician who lived within.

Samuel was laid on a bed of straw in the stable, the closest shelter from the main gates. Sir Julian knelt beside him and listened again at his mouth.

"There is still breath within him," he said at last. "Go, one of you and get water, another blankets. And be quick!" he snapped as they hesitated. "Someone find Kate and tell her what's happened here."

"I'll go," said Stanley.

When the water arrived, Sir Julian cleaned the mud and blood from his face and was horrified to see how pale Samuel had become.

"Where's the bloody physician?" he cursed. A few minutes later, they heard footsteps running toward them and looked up to see Kate standing at the door. Afraid to enter, she paused, as if waiting for someone to speak her worst fears. "Come close, Kate," said Sir Julian softly. "He still has breath within him, but I know not for how much longer."

Kate slowly walked to where Samuel lay unconscious. She knelt next to him and put her hand on his cheek.

"What happened?" she asked.

"We found him like this in the street, Kate," answered Sir Julian. "If an old man hadn't stumbled on him, he'd still be there now." They heard another set of running steps, and James entered, out of breath.

"The bishop's physician says he will not tend to a commoner, and to find the town physician."

Sir Julian cursed under his breath and left the stable with long strides. In the silence that was left, Kate stroked Samuel's hair as the tears ran down her face.

"You cannot leave me so soon, my love. Please, Lord, do not take him from me now." Wiping the tears from her face, she began humming a tune. Stanley began to weep.

Minutes later, a distressed voice could be heard from outside.

"I tell you, the bishop has forbidden me to treat others. A price will be paid for this outrage!"

In through the door came the bishop's personal physician, assisted roughly by Sir Julian.

"You will care for a member of the king's guard, or I'll hang you by a rafter here and now." Realizing that the bishop would be little use to him at that moment, the doctor stooped to look at Samuel.

"Step aside, woman," he said, nudging Kate away. Removing the blanket that covered Samuel, he began his inspection. When he got to his torso, he paused, then said, "Cut this shirt away, quickly!" Stanley took his knife from its sheath and cut Samuel's shirt up the middle, allowing the physician to separate the sides away from his ribs. Kate gasped at the sight. Two angry red and purple welts had been raised over the ribs on his left side. The physician scowled as he probed. "He has several broken ribs, and there is unquestionably damage to his lungs. He must not be allowed to move until the ribs have had a chance to heal."

"Then...he'll live?" asked Sir Julian.

"The damage does not appear to be severe, and his breathing is steady. He should be fine, but he must remain still, or more damage may occur."

He stood, still quite agitated. "Now I must return to the bishop's quarters before I am missed."

"There is nothing more you can do for him?" Sir Julian looked sharply at him.

"I swear, there is nothing more that can be done. He should awake shortly, and then you must restrain him. And now, good night." He left in a huff, his dignity having suffered enough.

Sir Julian ordered that a pallet, the kind used to carry the injured from a field of battle, be brought from the supply room, and then had Samuel carefully placed on top and tied down with leather straps. He ordered Stanley to move Samuel to his personal quarters. Kate grabbed his sleeve.

"Please, I must be with him."

Sir Julian nodded his agreement.

When Samuel opened his eyes to see Kate he felt a peaceful haze begin to clear. The realization that he could not move his arms brought back the memories of the night before. He attempted to raise himself up but a sharp pain restrained him.

"You must lie still, my love," whispered Kate.

Samuel waited until the searing pain had subsided. "Where...?"

"You're in Sir Julian's quarters."

"Who did this?" Every word was an effort.

"We don't know. Your friends found you in the street. Now please," she touched his lips with her forefinger, "try to rest, my love."

"They told me...they wanted...the letter." Kate froze in horror when she heard the words.

"What?" she stammered.

Samuel was desperate to tell her what little he knew, but the effort had exhausted him and he began drifting back into sleep.

"Tell...Sir Julian..." was all he could manage before falling back into a deep slumber.

Kate felt his cheek and began to shake from fear. *What have I done?*

After four weeks of rest, Samuel could finally move without discomfort. He and Kate had taken their favorite walk along the river the day before, and, moving slowly, he was able to negotiate the rough terrain without difficulty. On this morning, Kate had brought his bread and porridge as usual and was sitting with him in the stable. They had gone there to be alone.

Sir Julian had relieved him of his duties until he had healed, but moved him from his private quarters when he could see that Samuel was no longer in need of close observation. But today there was a sense of urgency that interrupted his leisurely convalescence. The king had also recovered from his illness and was preparing to return to London. The time had come to make hard decisions.

Before the attack, Samuel might have been content to leave Kate here to wait for him. But now he was afraid for her safety and had no intention of leaving her in Durham. They had not spoken much of the attack, but the mysteries of it burned his thoughts. The guard had investigated the incident under Sir Julian's direction, but no sign of the attackers had surfaced. The motivations behind it remained a mystery.

"I'm going to resign from the guard and stay here with you," said Samuel, his mouth tightly drawn.

Kate took Samuel's hand in hers. "Perhaps that would not be the best course of action. Now you have the protection of your friends, but that would vanish if you left to stay with me."

"I've thought of that, but I cannot see another way. I assure you I can protect us. I will not be surprised again, I promise you that."

"I know that, my love, but you are only one man and these are dangerous men."

"What would you know of them?"

"I know only that these were not common thieves, or they would not have said what they did."

"Are you sure that some past lover does not still harbor feelings for you and is jealously trying to discourage me?" Kate became angry, her response quiet but sharp.

"There has been no such person in my past, I assure you."

Samuel put his hand on her arm. "I didn't mean it to sound that way.

I'm sorry. I just can't bear the thought of you being in danger on my account. Enough people have suffered because of me."

Kate leaned over and kissed him gently, and smiled at the sheepish look on his face. She pulled him down into the straw, where a long embrace brought shivers to them both. Pulling his tunic off, she ran her hands gently across his mended ribs. They kissed again, long and deep.

"I've never…been with a woman," Samuel confessed in a whisper.

"Nor I with a man," she said.

The noonday sun warmed the stable and sprayed light through the roof and walls. Samuel lay next to Kate, their naked bodies together on the soft bed of hay.

"I love you, Kate," he whispered in her ear as he gently stroked the flawlessly smooth line of her hip. To his surprise, she pulled away. "Did I do something wrong?"

Kate put her hand on his cheek. "Of course not, my love. I have never known such happiness."

"What is it then?"

"Don't you see? This will only make our lives more difficult, our choices more agonizing." Samuel rolled onto his back. Sunlight sparkled through the holes in the roof.

"I may have a temporary solution to our troubles, if you are agreeable." He paused for a reaction, but Kate only waited. "Last week Stanley agreed to ride to Northwood to see what had become of my family. He found that they had left there for York shortly after the battle at Towton."

"You want to return to your family?"

"Not me, Kate. You. I'm sure that Oliver and Sally will keep you until we can decide what we need to do, and you would be out of harm's way for a while."

"You would not come with me?"

"If I knew you were safe, I could stay with the guard until we find more answers."

Kate pondered the issue for a moment. "Do you have any idea where they are or how I'd find them?"

"No, but I'll ask Sir Julian to let me go with you, and if they're anywhere in York, we'll find them."

"It would give us a bit more time to make some decisions," she mused. "Very well, my love. It's off to York with us then." She pulled him back on top of her, savoring the feel of his chest pressed against her breasts. "Hold me, my gentle love. God only knows when we'll know such happiness again."

Two days later, the bishop's palace was a command center. Horsemen galloped in and out, and carts loaded with provisions rolled out of the gates in a steady stream.

"I'm sorry, lad. I have no choice in this matter. Our duty to the king requires that you remain with us." Sir Julian, seeing the panic on Samuel's face, took him by the arm and pulled him over to where they could speak in private. "Old Henry and his wife have managed to raise another army, God knows how. The king requires our services and I can't let you go."

Samuel felt like a trapped animal. "I must resign the guard, then. Kate cannot make the journey alone, especially after what's happened. You know that as well as I."

"I do indeed, lad, but that changes nothing. And you can forget your resignation. To quit now when battle looms would be seen as desertion. You'd be clapped in irons or worse, as sure as I breathe."

Samuel slumped against the cold stones of the palace wall. There seemed no way to protect Kate, and he wasn't even sure that he'd see her again. He measured the distance to the main gate and considered his chances if he made a break for it, but he knew Kate would not be safer if he were a fugitive. He felt Sir Julian's hand on his shoulder.

"Look here, lad. Go and have her gather her things. I'll send my page with her on the journey. He's a strapping boy and will guard her well, and it's all I can do for you." Samuel knew that Sir Julian was offering a great deal.

"Thank you, Sir Julian. I'll tell her now."

Sir Julian smiled and gave his arm a squeeze. As Samuel ran off to the kitchen, the old knight was almost glad that his own youth had long ago expired.

CHAPTER XVI

Emma could not hide her concern as she felt her daughter's fevered forehead. The grinding, rumbling sound of the mill wheel, as familiar to her by now as the sound of her own heartbeat, filled the room. Their new mill house was more spacious than the one in Northwood, and had been built with their new family in mind. In the last winter, Oliver and Sally had built a small cottage next door. Emma pulled the sheet up further around Sarah's neck.

Sarah let out a soft moan and turned on her side, and Emma adjusted the blanket. Christopher entered carrying a basin of water and a cloth. He set it next to Emma on the floor.

"Is there any change?" he asked, and saw the answer on his wife's face. She confirmed his assessment with a motion of her head while rinsing the cloth in the cool water and placing it on Sarah's head.

Christopher took her hand, giving it a gentle squeeze. He could think of nothing else he could do to ease their suffering, and it was the most frustration he had ever felt.

A soft knock came at the door. With a last glance toward Sarah, he walked into the front room and spoke through the door.

"Who's there?" The intrusion was unwelcome.

From the other side came the soft answer, "Oliver."

Christopher slid the bar from its hook and walked to the hearth without saying a word. Oliver opened the door and stepped in. The cooking fire that lit Christopher's face was the only light in a room that otherwise reflected the gloom of its lone occupant. Oliver warmed his hands over the hot bricks.

"I came only to see if there was anything that I could do. Sally wanted to come as well but the children are not yet asleep." They had agreed to keep Alice until Sarah was well again, not wanting to risk any chance that she would catch the same affliction.

"No," Christopher said without taking his gaze from the flames. "Just tell Alice that we'll see her tomorrow."

"Has there been any improvement?"

He glanced quickly at Oliver and shook his head. "We have no answer for this affliction but to pray and wait." Pausing for a moment, he said, "You've learned the milling trade well, Oliver. You could open your own business if you wanted and be independent of us."

"It is not independence that I desire. I'm surprised that you don't know me better by now."

Christopher shrugged off his answer. "When you first came to us I treated you poorly. I just wanted you to know that I misjudged you, and that I'm sorry."

"Those were difficult days and you had much to deal with. I've never given it a second thought."

"Still, I should have trusted in my sister's wisdom. She was born with my father's good sense." Oliver could not resist the opportunity.

"Your brother deserves the same trust."

"It was he who broke the trust between us, not me," Christopher snapped. "He had all the opportunities, to fight alongside the earl and be admired by all the townspeople. Instead, he betrayed us and caused us to be rejected by our neighbors and friends. Can you really expect me to forgive him the death of our father?"

Oliver tried to control his temper. He took several deep breaths.

"You can't believe that he caused your father's death."

"Who else? If it had not been for his choices at Wakefield, my father would still be alive."

"And I would undoubtedly be dead," said Oliver quietly.

Christopher stared defiantly into the fire, but Oliver knew that he had made his point. "Tell me, why did you save us that night in the woods if you felt this way?"

"That whore's son, Sir Hugh, abused my wife. I had to get some measure of revenge."

"Is that the only reason?"

"I told you it was, didn't I?" he snapped the response. "Look, with the whole town against my brother, I couldn't just stand by and let him be caught."

"The price for keeping your trust, if that's what you choose to call it, was higher than you could possibly imagine."

"All things that we value come at a price, Oliver. He made his choice."

"For which I owe him dearly."

Christopher thought for a moment. "I know that, and I've never held your loyalty against you, have I?"

"No," conceded Oliver. "But Emma and Sally need Samuel back in their lives. Can't you see that they have paid a heavy price for this feud as well?"

"It is not a feud, Oliver. And as far as the women are involved, Samuel is welcome back if that is so important to them. But don't expect me to act the loving brother, because I'll have none of him."

At that moment, Emma came into the room and made a loud "shhhh" sound. She spoke in an angry whisper.

"Sarah has finally fallen to sleep. For pity's sake keep your voices down!" She walked to the door and wound her wrap around her shoulders. "I'm going to check on Alice, I won't be long. Look in on Sarah and be quiet." With a quick look and approving nod at Oliver, she left the cottage and closed the door quietly behind her.

"I'm going to sit with Sarah," said Christopher, leaving Oliver alone by the hearth. The small flames crackled in the dark.

At first light the next morning, Christopher and Oliver received a large new order of wheat to be milled. With Oliver's help, five wagonsful were unloaded into the mill storage room, while Christopher carefully logged the amount. He had sworn that he would uphold his father's high standards of honesty, and worked hard to earn the same good reputation. He looked toward the garden where Sally was tending to this year's crop of onions, cabbage, carrots and other vegetables that would grace the stew pot through most of the winter. Little John, now two years old, and Alice, just over one, were with her.

Happy as he was to see these children flourish, he wondered what would become of them if he was to leave for a while. And, above all, he wished that Sarah could be out there playing with them.

"That's the lot of it, Christopher." Oliver came from behind and tapped him on the shoulder. Christopher nodded and went to settle with the farmers, while Oliver took his turn watching Sally and the children.

Christopher rejoined him in a moment and they both stood watching in silence until Christopher cleared his throat.

"I think you could run this mill by yourself, don't you?"

Oliver looked at him. "Why would I wish to do that?"

He shrugged. "I only mean that you could if you had to."

"I suppose so. But it would not be my preference." He rubbed his ears.

"It may be that someday I wish to take a journey for a while, and if I do it would be nice to know that I can count on you to take care of things around here."

"Where would you go?"

"I don't know." Christopher began to regret bringing the subject up. "Who knows what the future could bring."

Emma called his name from the door and ran to embrace him.

Christopher was immediately apprehensive and pushed her to arms' length.

"What happened?"

"God be praised, my husband. The fever has broken and she asks for food."

As if the weight of the world had been lifted, he took Emma to him and hugged her tightly as she sobbed with relief. Sally, who had seen her come out of the millhouse, looked to Oliver for an answer. His smile confirmed her hopes.

It was not surprising that they did not notice the two hooded figures that approached from the road until one of them spoke.

"I hope we do not intrude."

Christopher stepped forward. Their long hooded outer garments fell full length to the ground, hiding their appearance. It was difficult even to see their faces. Sally's first impulse was to check the children. John and Alice were still where she left them, oblivious to the newcomers.

"What do you want?" asked Christopher.

"We seek Christopher the miller. Are you he?"

"I am."

The strangers looked at each other, nodded, and then pulled their hoods back. The speaker was a young man of strong stature, the other, a lovely woman in her early twenties with long brown hair and dark eyes that glowed with intelligence. It was she who spoke next.

"Forgive us for this abrupt intrusion, but there is need for us to be cautious. We have traveled far to find you."

"Very well," said Christopher. "But you still haven't told us what you wish of us."

"I bring a message from Samuel," she said.

Christopher said nothing.

"Please, is my brother well?" asked Sally.

"He was well when we parted," she said, "and still with the king's personal guard." Christopher's jaw dropped. When he saw that everyone was looking at him, he spun on his heels and went into the millhouse. Emma watched him go, then turned to the strangers.

"You must be hungry. Please come inside and rest."

The man addressed himself to Oliver. "If I may, sir, I need only a night's rest and then I'll be off again back to Durham. My master bade me return with haste after I saw the lady safely to you."

"If you wish," he said. "You can stay in the storage bin."

In the main room of the mill house, the strangers helped themselves to generous portions of Emma's stew. They introduced themselves as Kate and Harold. Kate told the story of their journey, which had taken ten full days, thanks to all of the troop movements along the main roads to the north. Kate had succeeded in disguising her sex as a precaution against the hazards of the open road.

"But why did Samuel send you to us, knowing well the perils of such a journey?" asked Emma.

"He feared that I would not be safe if left alone in Durham, and he was given no option but to leave with the guard."

"As usual, he comes to us when he's desperate," Christopher snarled from the corner of the room.

"You needn't mind my husband," Emma told her, glaring in his direction.

Sally had been studying Kate intently. "Do you love my brother?" she asked.

Kate felt uncomfortable at first, but seeing the hope in the sisters' faces, she knew she could be open.

"With all my heart."

"You are welcome to stay with us as long as you wish," said Oliver. "I just hope that you can put up with young John's antics," he added as he picked the boy up off the ground.

"I will earn my keep. You will not find me averse to work, I can promise you that."

"Come," said Sally. "I'll show you to our home."

That evening, Christopher was feeding Sarah the first solid food that she had been able to take for three days. Emma had prepared a thick soup with turnips and pork, a rare treat. One of the farmers had traded the leg of a freshly butchered pig to Christopher for services rendered and they had been eating of it for several days. Christopher had not spoken much with Emma since that afternoon when Kate had left with Sally. The last thing he wanted was for Emma to be angry with him, but there was so much he had kept inside for all these years that he had no notion of how to explain himself to his wife.

A soft knock came at the door, and Christopher immediately became annoyed, certain that it was Oliver. He set Sarah in the chair and walked to the door. It was his friend Simon. At first he was just surprised, since it had been several months since he had seen him last. But something in the way Simon looked made him swallow hard. Christopher looked behind him for a moment and then stepped outside, closing the door.

"It's time, Christopher," said Simon.

"You...you mean now?" Christopher was dazed.

"We leave this very moment. You'll need nothing from your home; we'll supply you with clothes and food."

"But I need to make arrangements," said Christopher, almost pleading.

"We can't let you do that, Christopher. It's too dangerous. We must leave at once, with you or without you. Decide now."

Christopher thought about Emma and what she would think. But this was the chance that he had wanted all his life, and he knew it would never come again.

"Give me a few moments," he said. "I can't just disappear. If you can trust me to join you, you can trust me to be discreet." Simon nodded his head.

"Be quick about it, my friend, or you'll not find me here again," he admonished.

Christopher went back into the mill house and found Alice where he had left her. He picked her up and kissed her on the head as she squirmed in his arms, moisture coming to his eyes.

"Emma!" he called toward the back hall. "We must speak."

She came in, and knew right away that something was wrong.

"What is it?"

Christopher carefully handed Alice to her mother.

"Sarah is well?"

"She has no sign of fever, God be praised. Tell me what's wrong."

"I'm taking a trip and I don't know when I'll be back."

"A trip to where?" She was stunned.

"I can't tell you that, but I should be back within a few months."

"Months! Christopher, for the love of God, tell me where you're going." She was becoming desperate.

"Tell Oliver that he must run the mill in my absence. I'm sure he will do fine. With Samuel's woman you'll have plenty of help."

She grabbed him by the sleeve. "Christopher, tell me where you're going! Do you expect me to live for months without knowing whether you're dead or alive?"

"I'm sorry, Emma, but this is something that I must do. Please try to understand. I must leave now."

"Now?" Emma was on the verge of hysteria, but Christopher had already grabbed his cloak and was on his way out the door. "Christopher!" Emma screamed out the door as he hurried out. She ran after him with Alice crying in her arms. "Christopher!"

But to no avail. She watched her husband disappear into the night, like a nightmare from which there was no awakening.

CHAPTER XVII

The rumors of the Lancastrians massing an army in the north proved to be false. Messengers intercepted the king's army on its way north, to confirm that Margaret had been unable to muster any kind of unity from within the Scottish nobility after the death of the Earl of Angus. Edward decided to once again entrust the bulk of his army to the Nevilles, who were to remain and provide a constant vigil.

In this rare moment of calm, Edward decided that it would be a good time to accomplish a task that had already waited too long. After spending some nights in York making preparations, Edward and his train rode to Pontefract Castle. There in a modest, temporary tomb rested the bodies of the king's father and brother Edmund.

The stay at Pontefract was a short one, just long enough to exhume the bodies and place them in splendid new caskets, elegantly carved to befit their noble inhabitants.

Samuel was forced to watch the procession from the courtyard wall of this dreaded castle, where his own father had died in his arms. The cold memory chilled him as he waited for various ceremonies to conclude in the bowels of the dark keep, and as time passed, he found it increasingly difficult to maintain his post.

Without warning or word to anybody, perhaps because he had made no conscious decision, he found himself running down the stairs. In the courtyard he saw the door through which he and his family had been dragged that horrible day. Inexplicably drawn to it, he walked through the open door and down into the dungeons that were barely illuminated by torches affixed to the damp walls. The smells made him queasy, but he continued, as if pulled by ghosts, down to the cells. The place appeared to be deserted.

He did not know how, but Samuel knew which cell had been theirs. He swung the unlocked iron grate open and stepped in. The cell was completely empty, and did not even contain the platform on which his father died. He shivered from the cold. I'm proud of you, he could still hear his father's voice. Sitting on the cold stone step by the grate, he wrapped his arms around himself and shook uncontrollably.

The sound of sobbing gently disturbed the solitude. For a moment he wondered if it was real or imagined. He peered down the dimly lit corridors straining to hear. Turning a corner, he saw at the end of the next corridor a well-lit room, and the sound of sobbing was surely coming from there. He suspected that he should flee, but he needed to see what was in that room. When he reached the door, he was astonished to see two elegant coffins, and between them with a hand on each, the King of England weeping with grief.

"Hold!" the order came from behind. Samuel leapt against the wall opposite the door. "What is your business here?" Lord Hastings, Sir Julian, and several guards confronted him. When Sir Julian recognized the intruder he cursed under his breath.

"What means this rude interruption?" the king demanded from the doorway, wiping tears from his face.

"I beseech Your Grace's pardon," said Hastings, mortified that this man had somehow slipped passed his vigilance, "but I found this man at the door. I know not how he got passed us."

"If I may, Sire," interjected Sir Julian, "he is one of your guard and poses no threat to your person." Hastings glanced at him, silent condemnation in his look, somewhat surprised that the old knight could allow one of his own to stray so egregiously. The king looked at Samuel, who had fallen to his knees, paralyzed with fear.

"Speak. Why have you disturbed our solitude?" His tone was angry but somehow solicitous.

"Fo...forgive me, Your Highness," responded Samuel as if each word might be his last, "but I had no knowledge that Your Grace was in that room." His eyes were trained on the stone floor, not daring to look up.

"How did you get past my guards?" demanded Hastings.

"I came through a door on the courtyard. Please, my lord, I wanted only to see the place where my father died."

Sir Julian stepped up. "His father did die in this place, Sire."

"Take him," Hastings motioned to the guards.

"Wait," the king stepped forward. "Sir Julian, is this not the man who saved Nigel's life before Towton?"

"The very one, My Liege."

"Withdraw for a moment. We would speak with him alone." Reluctantly they obeyed. "Rise, soldier, and come in here where we can see you better."

Samuel stood and steadied his wobbling knees by supporting himself against the wall. He followed the king into the chamber and waited silently to be addressed.

"How did your father come to die in this place?"

"Lord Clifford's men beat him and brought us all here to die, Sire. My father died many nights later in a cell near here."

"Clifford," Edward repeated the detested name through clenched teeth, his hand on Edmund's coffin. "It would seem that we have something in common." It was not his place to say anything, but Samuel knew that he might be able to ease some of the king's pain.

"I was with Your Highness' brother the night he died." Edward stared at him.

"You saw him die?" he asked painfully.

"Yes, Sire. It was quickly done, but he was most noble in his final moments. His last act was to beg for the life of his page, Oliver."

Edward turned away from him and stood quietly. Samuel could see his shoulders tremble. Again, he knew that it would have been most prudent if he remained silent, but bitterness possessed him for an instant and it was too late.

"It was in wishing to grant Your Highness' brother's wish that I caused my father's death in this place."

Edward turned and stared at him, not knowing immediately how to react to such forwardness.

"Yes, I remember now. Oliver said you protected him while he came to me with his message." Edward walked back to the coffins and rested his hand on Edmund's again. "What is your name?" he asked.

"I am Samuel of Northwood, Your Highness."

"Hastings!" the king shouted, turning to face the door. Hastings and Sir Julian came within seconds. "Take Samuel of Northwood and restore him to his post. He has our pardon for disturbing our devotions. Now leave us and see to it that we are not disturbed again."

When Edward found himself alone again he stood over Edmund's coffin in silent vigil.

"It seems that you were right, my brother," he said softly. "How many have paid the price for our quest?"

The next five days were spent on the road, the king's entourage slowly wending its way southward toward Fotheringay, the funeral chariot bearing the bodies of the king's father and brother drawn by six horses and draped in black trappings decorated with the ducal arms of the House of York. At each day's end, mass was celebrated with all the townsfolk who came to mourn with their king. The fifth day saw the procession reach its destination, the church in Fotheringay, which had always been one of Edward's favorite places, and in which vaults had been prepared under the chancel to serve as the final resting place for his kin. A final mass was celebrated, attended by thousands of people, followed by a lavish supper for poor and noble alike.

Until the bodies had been placed in the vault, Samuel had been one of the select guardsmen given the duty and honor of standing sentry over the caskets. The appointment had been made at the insistence of the king himself. It was an appointment that Samuel cherished, for he knew in his heart that his father's memory lay in the vault with these great lords.

"Forgive me, Sire, but I feel duty-bound to advise you that it may be more prudent to keep the Nevilles closer to court." Lord Hastings was outwardly calm, but his voice betrayed an uncommon agitation.

Edward stood in the center of his dressing room as his valets prepared him for his morning audience. He was not looking forward to the daily chorus of supplicants who demanded his attention. But today he had decided that it was time to hear from the French ambassador, who had been craving an audience since he had arrived at court almost a month ago. Edward had made a point of keeping him in limbo, wanting to demonstrate to King Louis, and his own people, that the French king did not carry any special significance in the English court.

Upon hearing the news of the arrival of the French ambassador, the Earl of Warwick had taken it upon himself to leave the northern army in his brother John's quite capable hands and to return himself to London. Warwick had repeatedly tried to convince Edward that he should abandon England's old ally, the Duke of Burgundy, in favor of a treaty with the King of France, and now he was angered by Edward's cavalier treatment of the ambassador. But Edward was not inclined to abandon Burgundy, and also saw this as an opportunity to deal with his too powerful ally, Warwick. With his typically disarming smile, Edward bent his attention to his old friend Hastings.

"I can't see any harm in letting Warwick think that he's making important decisions for England, while we continue to do what we feel is necessary here. I don't like him here in London, and France is the only place I can send him where I know he will readily agree to go without suspecting that we're manipulating him."

"Sire, such games are not well played with men like Warwick." Hastings would not allow himself to be distracted by the young king's easy manner. "If you anger him, he would make a formidable enemy."

"Enemy?" Edward raised his eyebrows. "Who would he support for the throne if not me? The Lancastrians would rather see him dead than accept support from him. No, William, Warwick is stuck with me and he knows it. It would gain him nothing to become my enemy."

"Such men find ways to be destructive when they feel slighted, Your Highness."

Edward sighed and smiled again. Hastings was the kind of friend a man could not rule without, one whose loyalty was unquestionable and whose devotion to duty was a rock upon which a monarch could stand.

"I assure you, William, I will not be careless with my Neville cousins. Now come, and let's dispense with today's business so that we can begin the hunt. By the way," he added as he dismissed the valets with a wave, "I wish to pay a call on Grafton Manor again. The woods in that place are most pleasant."

Hastings knew that the woods were not the only draw to that manor, and did not like the fact that Edward was spending so much time with Lord Rivers and his family of reformed Lancastrians.

"As you wish, my lord," he responded.

Edward hesitated for a moment. "I've decided to grant the Lady Elizabeth's request to restore Bradgate Manor to her and her family. I think they have suffered enough for their past loyalties."

Hastings could not hide his disappointment. He had hoped that the king would deed Bradgate to him, instead of giving it back to the Woodvilles.

"Come, William," Edward pounded him on the back, "for you I have much greater rewards than a manor house. Let's get to the business of the day and then be off." Hastings could not deny that his rewards had already been great. But as they left together for the throne room, a splinter of resentment toward the Woodvilles began to fester.

While they waited for the king to make his entrance, the Earl of Warwick and his brother, the bishop of Exeter, stood toward the front of the throne room alone. Around them in small groups were dozens of courtiers, all embroiled in significant conversation among themselves.

"I tell you this, George, to see the Duke of Somerset so brashly standing in this room galls the very fiber of my soul." Warwick's eyes were fixed on the duke where he stood across from the Nevilles, speaking to Lord Rivers. "And it doesn't surprise me to see that he speaks with Rivers. Old allegiances are hard to forgo, and I plan to watch them both very closely."

"I'm sure that the king has them here at court for just that reason," responded the bishop.

"And yet he takes the traitor on his hunts and gives close ear to his counsel, as if he fought by his side all these years. Clemency is one thing, but this blind faith in such scoundrels is dangerous policy. Somerset has always gone the way of least resistance, and he will again if circumstances dictate."

"You could be right, but can you really be concerned about that insignificant duke?"

"I care only that he could be a part of some treachery, and I don't like having to watch my back, or the foolish king's for that matter. And do not underestimate our former queen. As long as she breathes she will foment rebellion, and use whomever she must to put her whelp on the throne."

"That is true enough, but the king keeps the duke at court at all times. He is the least of your worries."

"I hope you're right, George. And since you spend most of your time here, I expect you to keep an eye on him as well. We can never have enough information when trying to keep a king under control."

"You can rest easy. Nothing happens here that escapes my scrutiny. Will the king receive the French ambassador today?"

"If he doesn't, he'll hear a mouthful from me. This is a golden opportunity for us to mend our relations with Louis, especially if Edward marries his sister, Bona. And if we broker that marriage, we'll stand to gain the strong favor of Louis as well."

The bishop raised his eyebrows. "You have an insatiable appetite, Richard. Beware that you do not overestimate yourself. If we drop our support from the Duke of Burgundy in favor of this alliance with France, Louis may prevail against our old ally, and gain a strength that could pose a danger to England."

"We do not need Burgundy to protect ourselves against the French. He proved useful before mad Henry lost most of our French possessions, but without them to protect, our future course is better struck with Louis."

A flourish of trumpets sounded the imminent arrival of the king. The double doors at the rear of the throne room were opened by two of the household servants, and Father Dennis, the king's personal confessor, entered carrying a cross before him. He was quickly followed by several of Hastings' men and then by Sir Julian and Hastings himself, and then Edward.

Seeing their king, murmurs spread through the room. Edward was resplendently dressed in a silk tunic of gold covered by a white velvet surcoat held together with a long chain of heavy gold links. Over everything was the sable-lined robe distinctive of his office. Even the Earl of Warwick, no stranger to fine raiment, was impressed by this handsome young king and his regal way.

Edward sat and surveyed the court before him in silence.

"Our cousin of Warwick, since you are in London instead of with our northern army, we can assume that our border is safe." It was more of a statement of fact than a question, but Warwick would never have allowed the thinly veiled insinuation that he was somehow in dereliction of his duties to go unanswered.

"Your Highness' northern counties are indeed secure, and Lord Montagu remains in constant vigil to assure that they stay that way."

"Very well," the king said. "Lord Hastings, fetch hither the ambassador from King Louis." Hastings bowed and left the throne room. "Lord Rivers, we intend to recreate ourselves, after our business here is concluded, with a hunt tomorrow near Stony Stratford. We would avail ourselves of your hospitality at Grafton Manor."

Rivers bowed. "Your Majesty is most kind to do us the honor."

"My lord of Somerset, we would be pleased if you would join us." The king's tone was one of insistence.

"I would be honored, Sire," the duke said.

The doors opened once again, and Hastings led the French ambassador to the throne, where he knelt. François Lascombes was well known in France as a scholar and close advisor to Louis XI, and always bore himself with impeccable dignity. Whenever Louis required sensitive understanding of those with whom he would do business, Lascombes usually was sent to gather information. This new English king was an enigma to Louis, and it was imperative that he understand Edward's motivations and desires, for such knowledge was the foundation of victory in any struggle for advantage.

"What news from our cousin of France?"

Lascombes rose and responded in a lilting accent.

"Great king, my master has sent with me, as a token of his esteem for Your Highness, two of the finest Spanish stallions from his royal stable. He has learned that Your Highness is greatly fond of the hunt and hopes that these fine animals will serve you well. They are in the courtyard now, if it please Your Grace."

"We thank our cousin of France and will receive them when our leisure serves us better," said Edward.

"Further, Your Majesty, my master requests to know your intentions regarding the offer of his sister, the Lady Bona, to be your queen. She is well loved by the king, and a more virtuous maid will not be found in our fair land."

"We doubt it not," said Edward. "Advise your master that we intend to send an embassy to negotiate that, and other pressing matters, and will do so before the month is out. My lord of Warwick, you will be our voice to the French king, as we know that you are fond of that fair realm."

"I am indeed, Sire, and am most pleased to obey."

"An excellent choice, Majesty," Lascombes interjected. "My master has long wished to meet the great Earl of Warwick in person." Warwick gave a slight nod of his head in acknowledgment.

"Lord Hastings, see the ambassador on his way with gifts for Louis of France." Lascombes bowed deeply and left with Hastings. "My lord of Warwick, we wish you good fortune on your journey, but mark us well: Make whatever bargains you feel are in our best interests, but make no assurances of our final agreement without our prior consent. We are not yet sure of Louis' intentions and have some reservations about his sincerity."

"Sire, I have had some communications with the French court and I am satisfied the king is strongly desirous of peace between our countries."

"Perhaps. But mark you well our admonitions, nevertheless. And now, what further business comes before our court today?" he asked the heralds. "We have plans for the hunt at Stony Stratford, and we wish to be off at first light."

Upon hearing Edward's plans, Lord Rivers hastened back to Grafton to prepare for the king's hunting party once again. While he appreciated such royal attention, these visits were becoming expensive, and Rivers spent much of the trip from London calculating ways to find additional money. On the other hand, he was mystified by the king's affection for his daughter. It seemed incomprehensible to Rivers that the king would make Elizabeth his queen, given the fact that there were higher-born ladies in the realm, and his daughter would not carry the benefit of any foreign alliances. He remembered his own marriage, of which the great families had disapproved. His future wife had been married to the uncle of King Henry, a great duchess whose only weakness was to love a lowly knight in the duke's service. Could it be that King Edward was similarly smitten with Elizabeth? He dared not hope.

Trotting up to Grafton Manor's elegant front entry, he was met by three servants. His wife greeted him with a kiss, and they sat together in the great room before the hearth while Rivers sipped wine quietly.

"Once again, we are to be visited by the king, my wife. It seems that he has taken a special liking to your hospitality." The duchess sighed as she thought of the work such a visit would require.

"I don't believe that he visits us for any service that this old lady has to offer," she said. "But I'll let the kitchen know that they will be spending the night again." Rivers put his arm around her and finished his glass, motioning to the waiting servant for more.

"Tell me, is it possible that the king's intentions toward our daughter could be honorable?"

"He has made improper requests of her, to be sure, but she has denied his desires. And yet he returns again to our house."

The light from the great leaded windows was growing dimmer as they spoke. "These attentions of the king could gain our family great advantages," Rivers mused as servants brought in the candelabra.

"Do not be deluded, my love, into thinking that we would be accepted so easily." The duchess could not hide her concern. "Such power is illusory, and comes with its own dangers. I fear that we could lose more than we gain. Remember that Margaret is still out there somewhere, and I know her well. I did not spend all that time in her service without learning much about her motivations. She will not rest as long as there is breath in her body to regain the throne for her child."

"Still," said Rivers, "there are ways to protect ourselves should the need arise. It would require that we have some control over the decisions of the king, and a queen could easily wield such influence."

"Perhaps," sighed the duchess. The flickering light of the candles played on the walls and furniture, shadow imps that danced for a moment and then were gone.

The following day, the king arrived in the morning with his usual complement of twenty retainers and most of his personal guard, along with Lord Hastings and the Duke of Somerset. Also in the king's company was Father Dennis, his confessor, who did not usually accompany Edward on these occasions, but who was happy that the king was paying more attention to his spiritual self. The hunt took most of the day, and at twilight the banquet was served.

Samuel, who had accompanied the king, was not happy to be at Grafton. His worry for Kate was growing with each passing day, and had not yet been able to separate himself from the guard. He hadn't heard a word from her since Sir Julian's page returned with news of their safe arrival in York. But Sir Julian had assured him that if no news was heard from the Lancastrians soon, he would grant a leave for Samuel. So he waited while the king hunted for sport, and his own anxiety grew. As Samuel and the rest of the guard took turns eating in the kitchen and standing duty watch, the king and his party finished their meal in the dining chamber. Rivers noticed that Edward was not his usual outgoing self, which was, of course, a cause for deep concern.

When the servants had cleared away the last of the food, Edward stood and said loudly, "My lords, it has been a long day and we wish to retire. Lord Hastings, make ready to return to town."

The abruptness of the announcement took everyone by surprise. A mad scramble ensued to assemble the king's escort. When everything had been prepared, Edward took Hastings aside.

"William, I wish to have some conversation with Lord Rivers. Take my retainers and your men back to town and I'll join you there shortly."

Hastings was beside himself. "My lord, my duty forbids me to leave you here. If you wish to stay —"

"I will keep my guard here with me," Edward interrupted, "and will be perfectly safe. You have your instructions."

Hastings bowed his head and left the room, mystified.

Outside, Hastings' men were preparing the king's horse and Sir Julian was forming up the guard. Samuel was standing near Sir Julian when Lord Hastings approached.

"Sir Julian," said Hastings, "the king will remain here longer. My men and I are ordered back to town, but you shall remain here with the guard. And mark you well, if harm comes to the king your head shall pay the price of failure." When Hastings' contingent had galloped out of sight, Sir Julian spoke to Samuel in a low voice.

"Something is amiss, lad. This is damned strange." Then after a pause he started to deploy his men in positions around Grafton Manor. No harm would come to the king on his watch, Hastings' threats notwithstanding.

Back in the great room, Edward was alone with Rivers, his wife, and the Lady Elizabeth. On this evening Elizabeth wore her golden hair down about her shoulders. and the candlelight shone through the silky strands like sunbeams through an angel's wings. Her long, light pink gown cascaded over her form in such a way as to leave Edward weak-kneed with desire. He addressed himself to his host.

"Lord Rivers, it cannot come as a surprise to you that we have long admired your daughter. Though the cares of state have abused our time and kept us from her side, we have thought of little else. Therefore, if she will consent to our loving request, we wish to make her our queen and wife." Rivers and his wife looked at each other. If Elizabeth was surprised, she did not show it.

Rivers was the first to speak. "Forgive me, Sire, but the suddenness of this announcement has left me speechless. Of course, Elizabeth is yours if she so desires, and may your union be blessed above all others."

"What say you to our suit, sweet Bess?" Edward had not taken his eyes off her. Lord Rivers' permission being a mere formality — he would not deny his king — Edward waited for Elizabeth's answer.

"I too am surprised by this gracious offer, my lord." She was choosing her words carefully. "Is this truly what you wish in your heart?"

"My words would be a poor messenger of my heart should I profess my love in so unsuitable a manner." Elizabeth noted that he had dropped the royal plural. "Let me rather show you that my heart is lost to you completely."

"How would you do that, my lord?"

Edward smiled. "Lord Rivers. Send for Father Dennis, who, if he has marked our command, is waiting in the kitchen."

Rivers bowed and left the room. Elizabeth's drooping eyes opened wider. Rivers re-entered with Father Dennis.

"To show you my heart's true nature, I am prepared to make you my queen here and now, if only you will consent." Father Dennis was seized by a coughing attack, which only the king's stern look managed to quell. The look of disbelief, however, did not leave so easily. It was the duchess who responded, and she was not pleased.

"Your Highness, a queen-to-be deserves a royal wedding and the trappings her new office requires. This sudden wedding with no witnesses would appear unseemly."

"Sire," Father Dennis finally found his voice, "to perform the sacred rite of Holy Matrimony for the king is a privilege that the Archbishop of Canterbury has expressly reserved for himself." In the back of his mind, Father Dennis could easily see the archbishop finding a way to have him reassigned to some God-forsaken parish in the bogs of Ireland.

While listening to the others, Elizabeth had not taken her eyes from Edward. Her handsome young royal suitor appeared almost as an expectant child, innocent and full of the happiness that marks the untainted. It was at that moment that she realized that she truly did love him.

"I will be your wife, my king. And yes, let the ceremony be now, before the crush of state and suspicions of corrupted souls spoil the moment." Edward pulled her tightly to himself as if to create a oneness that could not be sundered. Pressing his lips against hers he felt the warm response of her body.

"Father Dennis," he said as their lips but not their bodies parted. "Prepare for the ceremony. We will be wed before the hour is done."

"As you wish, Sire," Father Dennis said with a heavy sigh.

The ceremony was simple, with Sir Julian and the Woodville family the only witnesses. True to the king's wish, it was over within an hour.

Sir Julian had been as amazed as the rest when he heard what was to be performed on that evening, but stood obediently through the service and said nothing. And after the ceremony, he joined with all others present, on pain of swift retribution, in swearing that he would reveal to no one what had transpired here this evening until the king was ready to make the information known to the rest of his subjects. While the reasons for this secrecy were not made known to him, Sir Julian had been around long enough to know that this wedding would not sit well with many of the nobility.

Back in the town of Stony Stratford, the Duke of Somerset stood before the door of his inn and watched as a fitful Lord Hastings took his leave to wait for the king at the main road by the entrance to town. He marveled that Edward could have such a faithful friend in such times as these. A king was more likely to be surrounded by opportunists and self-serving scoundrels, like those who had poisoned the court of King Henry.

"A word with you, Your Grace."

Somerset spun to see the source of the voice behind him, amazed that one could approach so silently. With his hand on the hilt of his sword, he saw a short man, wrapped in a hooded brown cloak that concealed most of his face except for a crooked smirk.

"Can we leave this public place for a moment? I know that Your Grace is a busy man, but my message comes from a queen."

Somerset motioned for the man to follow him and slipped into an alley between the inn and the adjoining stable. Not wanting to turn his back to him, the duke motioned for him to go first as he made a pretense of checking the street to see if anyone was watching. Satisfied that they were secluded enough, he grabbed the small man by the cloak and pushed him up against the wall of the stable.

"How dare you approach me in a public place? I should have your throat ripped from your neck for placing me in such danger." The small man did not seem frightened by the duke's threats. The smirk never left his face as he responded.

"Please forgive me, Your Grace, but the urgency of my news required that I take bold steps to contact you." Somerset released him and tried to regain his composure in the face of this little man's arrogance.

"Reveal to me your message and be quick about it."

"It is only this, Your Grace: The queen has gathered a new army near Berwick and is marching toward Bamborough Castle as we speak. She instructs me to tell you that she values your friendship and will welcome you back, if it please Your Grace." Each time he said Your Grace he made it sound more like a curse than an honorific. "That is, unless this life as the king's lapdog satisfies you."

Somerset's first reaction was anger, but then he realized that the epithet was probably accurate. He turned his back on the insolent man and took a minute to gather his thoughts. Clearly he would never regain his former prominence under this Yorkist king, and it was even more apparent that the Nevilles would rather see him dead than to grant him the respect to which his high office entitled him. He was snubbed at court and, the friendship of the king notwithstanding, his wealth and lands were barely enough to sustain him.

"How does the queen expect to gain access to Bamborough?"

"I am permitted to tell you this since the deed is already done. Sir Ralph

Percy, whom the usurper foolishly placed in charge, has ceded the castle to the queen. She has only to arrive with her puissance and the gates will be opened to her."

Somerset knew that if this news were true, Margaret would have a strong base from which to renew her attack on the northern counties, where support for Edward was still weak. From such a base, and with Warwick safely out of the way in France, Margaret could prevail.

"I must put my affairs in order here and then will follow you to Bamborough."

"Forgive me, Your Grace, but surely you understand that I am to escort you myself now. The queen has entrusted to me your...safety." Somerset looked at him for a moment, the implications clear.

"I assume then that you have horses waiting."

The little man pointed toward the back of the stable building, and Somerset walked in that direction. Horses were being held by another man dressed in a similar hooded cloak, who handed one set of reins to Somerset. As the duke mounted his horse, the little man sheathed the dagger that he had been holding under his cloak, and mounted his own, a little disappointed that he had accomplished his mission.

On a bluff above a river somewhere in central England, a small castle kept watch over a modest series of planted fields and an insignificant cluster of hovels in which the field hands lived. Night sat heavy on the land, the smell of rain thick in the air and deep in the soil. Within the master's quarters of the castle two men sat in a torchlit room with roughly cut stone walls and sparse furniture. A pitiful flame in the small hearth provided extra light but little heat. The master of the castle, Lord Colinsworth, was a young man in his mid-twenties with fair hair and pale blue eyes, and a complexion that gave him the appearance of illness even when he was not. His late father left him the castle and lofty title, but little silver or land with which to support himself. Many merchants in town were better off than he, and as a result he hated to even leave the walls of his modest inheritance, lest people see him and scoff. His self-imposed exile had given his bitterness ample time to age until it defined his very existence.

"How can you be certain that she is in York?" he asked the other man, who was standing in a dark area of the room near the fire.

"My men followed her from the day she left Durham," was the quiet response.

"But why would she leave? And who was the person with her?"

"We are not certain but it was a serving man, from the colors of his tunic. What man he serves we could not ascertain. As for why she left, it could be that the attack on her man frightened her away."

Colinsworth slammed his hand down on the table. "My instructions were specific," he said angrily. "You were only to see that she got our message, not to frighten her out of town."

The dark shape seemed to shrug. "We underestimated the nature of their relationship. They seem to be in love." Disdain dripped from the word.

"This matter has been bungled badly. Do you at least know where she is in York?"

"I do."

"What do you know of the man with whom she's been?"

"I only know that he serves in the king's personal guard."

"The king's..." Colinsworth was stunned. "Why didn't you tell me this from the start? The guardsmen will be seeking retribution for an attack on their own."

"You needn't concern yourself with that. My men know how to cover their tracks, and the Guard has enough to do trying to keep the Yorkist on the throne. The queen is still giving them fits in the north."

"The stakes are high in this for us both. If we succeed, I can leave this God-forsaken place and take my rightful place among the peers of the realm, and you'll have your place with me assured. But if we are discovered prematurely, you'll find yourself wandering the squalid back streets of York again where my men found you."

The large man took a step forward, allowing the glow from the fire to illuminate a face with a hideous scar that curled his mouth into a permanent sneer.

"Do not threaten me, my lord," he growled. "You haven't the courage to back it."

Perhaps it was because Sir Hugh had blocked the fire, but to Colinsworth it suddenly felt much colder.

Henry and Margaret sat in a private chamber with the king of the Scots, James III, a slight man with a suspicious nature. He had traveled to Berwick Castle to dispatch a troublesome debt to the French king.

For a hundred years he and his predecessors had relied on the French alliance to keep the English king in check, so that an uneasy balance of power could be maintained. If England invaded France, the Scots would pillage in the north of England, and if the English invaded Scotland, the French would lend troops and financial aide.

Now, Louis of France had required that he assist the Lancastrians and James felt honor-bound to comply even though most of his nobles had counseled against it. Concerned about renewed hostilities with Edward, and without the recently dead Earl of Angus to lead them, they were in a weakened position. Still, the debt to Louis needed to be paid.

"We have little support among the nobility," James said. "I can only give you a small force to augment the meager following that has arrived from France. If the northern lords of England are truly inclined to your cause, they will join you when you march south."

"We do not presume to question your support, my lord," responded Margaret impatiently. "However, if we are to convince the northern lords to join with us again, we must have some hope for success. What you have offered is unlikely to sway them."

"Nevertheless, I have extended my private resources as far as I dare. If Edward turns his revenging eyes to us, we will be sorely pressed to defend the realm."

"A king's duty is to his people," said Henry.

James was unsure what he meant.

"It is indeed, my lord," he responded.

Margaret glanced at her husband. As usual she could not depend on him to help. "You could ask for the lords to gather so that we could make a personal entreaty. I know that I could persuade them to contribute to our rightful claim."

James shook his head. "They will not come, my lady. Unless Edward directly threatens us, they will not stir from their castles. I have already asked."

Margaret sat back in her chair, resigned to her situation. Both Louis and James had offered a pittance of help, for such was always the fate of the beggar. For now she would do her best with what she had, and pray that more troops could be gathered from the feckless lords of the north.

CHAPTER XVIII

The sheer number of people in the rebel camp amazed Christopher. He had expected a small and secret group of fighters, but instead, he found hundreds of ragged men jostling for a patch of ground to call their own. The steady drizzle of late summer rain had turned the encampment into a muddy quagmire.

Simon Johnson escorted Christopher past the throng, leading the way to one of the few tents. A large man with rotted teeth and a bushy red beard was standing guard. He recognized Simon.

"Greetings, Gregory. I have a new recruit to see Robin." The guard looked him over.

"I'll have to search you."

Christopher nodded in understanding and allowed himself to be searched. When Gregory was satisfied, he told the two men to wait and disappeared into the tent. Reappearing after a few moments, he motioned them to enter and held the flap aside as they passed. Inside, an unimposing man sat at a table in the only chair, reading a parchment with interest.

"Greetings, Robin," said Simon. "I bring the new recruit that we spoke of." The dark man looked up from his parchment and Christopher got his first good look at him. The clean-shaven face was one of a middle-aged man with a noble bearing, but at the same time not a face that demanded attention in a crowd. His manner was one of disarming confidence.

"You are welcome among my little band of rebels. Like the rest of us, I assume you have precious few skills that will serve us in a battle?"

"I'm afraid I bring only a strong desire to do what I can," Christopher said, "but I must say that from what I've seen, this band of yours does not appear so little."

The man laughed. "It is gratifying to see that so many of the common folk agree with what we're trying to accomplish. The men call me Robin of Redesdale, which while not my real name does have a nice ring, don't you agree? That's all you need to know of me, and you'll know even less about our actions except for those in which you are directly involved. Do you understand?"

"Yes," said Christopher. "But just so there is no misunderstanding, what exactly is it that you're trying to accomplish?"

"Quite so," Robin nodded. "It's a fair and wise question. We are all dedicated to a single goal, and that's to see Sir Henry Percy released from prison and returned to his rightful place as Earl of Northumberland. We know that we have the support of most who live in the northern counties, and if this Yorkist king refuses our just demand, then we'll fight for King Henry, whom we know will do right by the House of Percy. Are you with us, Christopher?"

"With all my heart," he said firmly. While he could not shake his pangs of guilt for leaving Emma and the children, this speech of Robin's had regenerated his resolve to be a part of making the country right again.

"Good! Then I can tell you the excellent news that I've just received," Robin nodded toward the parchment that he had been studying so intently when they first arrived. "The queen has gathered another army near Berwick Castle and fully intends to press her cause. I will raise as many able-bodied men as I can and join her. Tell me, Christopher Miller, can you swing a cudgel?"

"As well as the next man, I expect."

"Then Simon will get you one. I've always thought that a man with a smart cudgel is worth two of the king's footsoldiers. See that he's given what we can spare, Simon, and then get some rest. You'll be needing all your wits before long."

They left the tent and found a small fire where several wild fowl were being roasted on a spit; the men at the fire invited them to share. Afterwards, they walked around the encampment and Simon introduced the new recruit to dozens of people. Christopher was surprised to discover the many walks of life represented by these men: farmers, tradesmen, merchants of all kinds. Later, they found an open spot under a tree to rest.

"Who is this Robin of Redesdale?" Christopher asked.

Simon looked up sharply. "It's best you don't ask too many questions about Robin, my friend. I can tell you only that he's nobly born and a kind and gentle man. He will always treat you right if you do your job and keep a mind to your own business."

"But is he one of us? From the northern counties?"

"He is. They say he's related to the Nevilles, but contended against them and sided instead with Northumberland before the earl was killed at Towton Field. Now he's left only with his honor, and with those few of us that he can raise in secret to help the earl's heir." Simon realized that he'd probably already said too much. "That's more than you need to know about Robin, so let us not speak of him again."

Christopher nodded, understanding that in such a group as this, it would take only one informer to sabotage the entire operation. He changed the subject.

"Was it hard for you to leave your family?" Simon looked out at the dozens of men who were milling around in the rain, all with their own hopes and motivations for being here.

"It was," he answered at last. "My wife was sad to see me go, but I always told her that the day would come, and she expected it." He watched as Christopher fidgeted with a stick. "I gather by the way you left that you hadn't told your wife anything about what you were planning?"

"No. And now I regret that. I can't get her face out of my mind, but I do not regret my decision to join." The last was spoken with a certain lack of conviction. "It's just...well, the children will need their father and now I won't be there."

"The missus and I were never blessed with children, so I wouldn't know about that. But you'll tell them when you return that the world is a dangerous place and if we consider ourselves fit to live in this kingdom, then such sacrifices are sometimes necessary. They'll see the logic in that when they grow to be men themselves."

Christopher grimaced. "They're both girls."

"Well then," Simon was surprised, "their mother will give them what they need. I'm sure that she's a most capable woman."

"Yes. She is," he said sadly.

Simon slapped him on the back. "Cheer up, friend. With luck, this business will soon be done and you can return to them before they know you're gone. Now let's rest. Like Robin says, we may not get another chance for a while." Pulling a thin wool blanket over his shoulders, he rolled over and closed his eyes.

Christopher leaned back against the tree and stared up at the densely leafed branches. *I should have confided in her,* he thought bitterly.

The Duke of Somerset knelt before Margaret and Henry, the former king and queen of England, thinking quickly of how best to explain his defection to the Yorkists. Also present in the audience chamber of Bywell Castle was Sir Ralph Percy, brother to the late Earl of Northumberland, who had already been forgiven by Margaret for capitulating to Edward. That had been an easy act for Margaret, since Sir Ralph had quickly surrendered Bamborough and Dunstanborough Castles back to the Lancastrians when they arrived at the gates.

Margaret regarded her son, the eleven-year-old Prince of Wales, and then the duke. If times had been better, she would have seen his head perched on the castle ramparts within the hour, but this was no time to turn away anyone who could be of use. She knew that she would have to pardon his defection, but first she would watch him squirm.

"Majesties, I profess and swear to you both, before God Almighty, that my allegiance to Your Highnesses has never wavered, but that my actions were necessitated by the evil fortune which befell us all, and by the failure of the Earl of Angus to fulfill his oaths. I decided then that as long as Your Highnesses lived, it was my responsibility to keep my head and live to fight for the House of Lancaster again."

Margaret's stony expression did not change. Shifting her attention to Henry, she wondered what he thought of their having to stomach the platitudes of traitors. She remembered then that Henry had predicted Somerset's treachery right before they lost all of the northern castles. But now the king sat quietly staring at the floor. She sighed heavily and then turned to the prince.

"Edward, what think you of this noble duke's plea for forgiveness?"

He was surprised by his mother's request for advice, but did not lose his composure.

"While I deplore his past actions, I know his grace to be an honest man, and welcome his return."

Margaret was pleased. At such a tender age, he already understood well the difficult decisions required of diplomacy, and when it was wise to make convenient, if distasteful, alliances

"We agree," she said. "Rise, my lord of Somerset, and receive our pardon."

The duke stood and kissed the queen's offered hand. "I thank Your Highness. You shall not have cause to regret this kindness."

"We know it, my lord. You shall take command of our vanguard when our troops move forward, which will be soon." The words amazed Sir Ralph Percy and the soldiers in the room. Command of the vanguard was a critical position, and not one commonly granted to a general of questionable loyalty. Somerset bowed his head.

"I will dispatch the duty with all my ability, Your Highness."

"We doubt it not," and with a wave of her hand signaled that the audience was over. Somerset bowed again and left the room. Percy was the first to break the silence.

"Forgive me, my lady, but this is a dangerous appointment."

Margaret lifted her hand to silence him. "The duke will not betray us again, you can be certain of that. He knows that the usurper would have his head if he tried to go back now, and in the vanguard, he will be too busy fighting for his life to hatch any traitorous plots. And you will be with him, Sir Ralph, just to be sure."

Henry chuckled softly, a sound that drew everyone's attention. "Percy and Somerset; Somerset and Percy." The words seem to amuse him. "Together they will fight and together they'll be true, but no red eyes will cry when together they shall die." The blood drained from Percy's face, and he crossed himself involuntarily. At the sight, Margaret stood.

"These are the musings of a distracted mind, my lords, and should not be heeded. Give way and let the king rest. He has had a most difficult time, as have we all. Prepare the troops as planned. We will march at first light."

Relieved to be dismissed, the courtiers filed out and left the royal family to themselves. Margaret sat, exhausted, and closed her eyes, as if to create a better reality. She felt a hand on hers and opened her eyes reluctantly to see Henry's face close to hers.

"I am sorry, my love, but I thought it would be right to let him know."

Margaret looked at him lovingly. "Let him know what, my husband?

That you are possessed of some kind of evil power? Can't you see that you will take the resolve from his soul if you persist with these rantings?"

"It is his duty to die for his king. He has no right to hope for salvation except from the Lord Everlasting."

Margaret pushed him away. "Until the Lord takes him, I need him at his best," she said sternly. "And it behooves you to give him a reason to put his life in harm's way, not to sap his strength when he needs it the most. If you must make these…prophesies, I will thank you to make them privately to me. If not for my sake, then do it for the sake of our son."

The prince sat silently, wishing that his father had the will to be a great king.

"Yes, please, Father, to reclaim our rights we must stand together."

Margaret put her hand on her son's head. "Fear not, my son. I swear to you that we shall be masters of this realm again."

"Yes," agreed Henry sadly. "We shall."

That same day, a sunny afternoon in early May, Lord Montagu gazed out over his troops, happy at the sight of so many fine men-at-arms. And King Edward himself had promised to bring even more from the south within a few days. Standing outside his tent, he inhaled loudly, enjoying the sweet aroma of lilac in the air. Since his brother, the Earl of Warwick, had been sent to France, he had controlled the entire expanse of the realm from York north to the Scottish border, and once again, he had high hopes that the former king and queen would be finally defeated. His intelligence had placed the Lancastrians carelessly gathered near the town of Hexham, not more than a few hours' ride away. He intended to strike at once and not wait for the king to bolster his numbers.

Watching as the army prepared itself for the march to Hexham, he relished the feel of the warm spring sun on his face. The sweeping flatlands of Northumberland beckoned to him as if he had spent his entire life there. Small clumps of trees dotted the landscape as far as the eye could see, and the rare sight of a cloudless sky all the way to the horizon lifted his spirits.

When his captain informed him that the troops were arrayed and ready for the march, he mounted his horse and gave the order to begin. Montagu rode just behind the vanguard, at the head of the great body of the army, and set a quick pace. He could not wait to engage the enemy once again.

The valley of the River Linnel, a tributary of the Tyne, stretched south from the town of Hexham, not far from the ruins of Hadrian's Wall. Somerset and Percy enjoyed the pleasant weather that had blessed the country. The midafternoon sun stood high overhead with an uncommon warmth. Percy sensed the duke's unease.

"Why are you so restless today, my lord?" he asked.

"We do not have the kind of intelligence that served us so well in our past engagements, and I know Montagu is out there somewhere. Perhaps even Edward himself. We must be well prepared when next we meet."

"You need not fear our intelligence. The scouts will find them."

"This may be our last, best chance to gather an army large enough to unseat Edward. I do not wish to squander it."

"And the fact that Edward has a large price on your head is also a great motivation, I'm sure."

Somerset squirmed. "The Yorkists have no special love for you either, my friend." Wishing he were someplace else and away from Percy's company, he knew that his path had led him to increasingly darker choices, and now it seemed that his life was controlled by the puppeteer. A courier rode in and quickly dismounted.

"My lords, an army approaches from the south, two thousand strong, by the captain's estimate." Somerset walked back and strained his eyes to the south, but saw nothing.

"How far?"

"They are fast upon that hill, my lord." He pointed to a place that was not more than a few arrowshots away.

Percy grabbed him by the shirt. "How could they get that close without being seen?" He was furious.

"They must have captured the sentry, my lord."

Percy had all but lost any outward calm. Somerset felt cold fingers of fear close around his heart, but his first thought was for the queen and the Prince of Wales, who had foolishly accompanied them on this march.

"Go, and tell the queen's guard that she must flee to Bywell Castle. Thank God the king is there already. Go, I say!" He pushed the courier toward his horse, and began ordering the captains to begin a hasty deployment. "They will have the high points before we can get there. Our only hope is to array along the bluffs near the river, and wait for them to attack. If we make them come to us, we'll be fighting from a stronger position." He looked to the south and saw the Yorkist army taking up positions along the hilltops. "Quickly! Before all is lost."

"I would venture to guess that we have caught them smartly, eh, Captain?" Montagu watched as the Lancastrians scrambled like ants in the valley below.

"They have a difficult position to defend, my lord."

"You have a penchant for understatement, my friend. Let us press our advantage. Take half the army and push them against the river from there." Montagu indicated a long ridge that formed a horseshoe around the enemy's position. "When they are all contained I'll attack their center and you need only ensure that they do not escape."

"As you wish, my lord." He bowed quickly and was gone.

Montagu watched as his captain attacked the flank of the Lancastrian position and, slowly, by virtue of better position and superior numbers, began to shove the defenders against the river. Neither army had a large contingent of archers, so the battle was waged mostly by footsoldiers in hand-to-hand skirmishes. Where mounted knights attacked each other, the fighting was more furious. When the time was right, Montagu signaled his men forward to join the fray. His fresh troops stormed down the hill with swords brandished, yelling loudly as much to bolster their own courage as to frighten the enemy. Colliding into the center of the Lancastrian position, his men cut and hewed through hundreds of bodies and soldiers, struggling to clear enough room to swing their weapons. Montagu saw Percy not more than an arrow's shot away and began to cut his way through the dense resistance. This was a prize he wanted for himself.

Seeing Montagu approach, Percy was only too delighted to settle the score on the field of honor. He also steered himself toward a meeting with the hated Neville. As they came within shouting distance, Percy leapt his horse over a wide gully, and in the height of the jump was pierced through the thigh by an arrow. When the horse landed, Percy fell with a crash to the ground. Before the footsoldiers could get to him, Montagu arrived to see Percy squirming in pain. He ordered his men to take Percy to his tent, then waded into the battle again. The Lancastrians were soon splashing into the river in an attempt to flee the thrashing swords of the enemy, and were being cut to pieces by the hundreds.

Before long, the battle was over, and the Yorkists were robbing the dead, pursuing fleeing remnants, and killing mercilessly. Somerset had also been taken alive and was escorted to Montagu's tent with Percy. Montagu searched desperately for the royal family, but found no trace of them, much to his disappointment.

At his tent, a page helped to remove his armor and he took a moment to survey his injuries. He found only a gash on his sword arm, which the page wrapped tightly to stop the bleeding. He silently thanked God for seeing him safely through another battle. Stepping into the tent, he saw Percy lying on the floor, struggling to remove the arrow from his leg, and Somerset sitting on the only stool, staring at the ground.

"Help him with that," Montagu pushed his page toward Percy. Pouring himself some ale, he offered some to Somerset, who refused. A scream from Percy indicated that the arrow had been removed. "Where are Margaret and Henry?" he asked.

"Your king and queen are safely dispatched to fight another day," answered Somerset. Percy groaned from the floor.

"Perhaps," said Montagu, carefully regarding the duke. "Captain!" he called toward the tent flap.

"My lord?" the captain asked when he entered.

"Form details to search for Margaret and her whelp. I want no stone unturned between here and Newcastle!" Margaret had to be captured, or these battles would never end.

"Yes, my lord," the captain bowed and was gone.

"You will both be my guests until orders come from the king regarding your disposition. Is there anything you desire?"

"Only to be removed from your presence," responded Percy tightly.

"I happily grant your request." Montagu motioned to the guards. He fell heavily onto his stool and emptied a tankard of ale. A good day's work, he thought, *but the prize has somehow slipped my grasp again.*

Queen Margaret had been relaxing with her son in the royal tent when news of Montagu's arrival reached her. She had accompanied the army this far, feeling that the men needed some strong leadership for a change, and she wanted the prince to learn what was required of a monarch. Not wishing to be encumbered with Henry and his demoralizing pronouncements, she had insisted that he stay behind in Bywell Castle.

But the worst had happened: The Yorkists managed to surprise them. She would not risk the capture of her son. She had quickly ordered the largest escort that could be gathered in a few minutes, a contingent of ten soldiers, and rode with all possible haste back to Bywell. At first, it looked as if the journey would be a safe one, but fortune, once again, deserted her. A company of fourscore men summoned from Newcastle by Montagu met them on the road in a dense wood.

The gallant sergeant who commanded Margaret's escort had swiftly ordered the queen's small party to fall back to a narrow bridge that crossed a steep channel. There he yelled to the queen to flee into the woods while he held off the Yorkist troops. Two men accompanied her while the other eight held the bridge in a suicidal bid to grant Margaret time to escape.

With the two soldiers, Margaret and her son fled deep into the woods. The captain of the Newcastle men gave chase but lost the fugitives' trail in the dense underbrush. Finally, he decided to give up the search.

For most of the next day Margaret's party wandered through the woods. But when hunger began to demand action, Margaret determined that they would have to risk the road once again. She guessed that they were no more than a day's walk to Bywell, where they could gather a larger escort that would see them safely to Berwick Castle.

Finally, as the woods thinned and the road curved over the top of a flat ridge, Bywell Castle came into view in the distance. The sight filled Margaret with hope for the first time since their speedy departure from Hexham, and taking the prince by the hand, she quickened their pace. She did not realize that the footsteps behind her were not those of her escort.

She heard the sickening sound of an ax that severed the spine of one of her guard. As the other guard saw his partner fall to the ground he had time only to yell "My lady!" Margaret spun around to see a ragged man draw his knife across the poor guard's throat. Three more men dressed in rags and filthy beyond anything she had ever seen before came from a place of concealment behind a hedgerow and walked toward them. She drew the prince to her and stood staunchly before them, knowing in her soul that her time in this life was undoubtedly past. Her thick French accent was steady and strong as always.

"The hand that spills our royal blood will rot in damnation!" Two of the brigands were looting the bodies of the guards while the other two surrounded the prince and his mother.

"You won't mind handing over your purse, will you, Mum?"

"We are the queen. We have no need for a purse."

He pointed to her hands with his blade. "Then you'll have no need of them rings either. Let's have 'em."

She spat at him while removing her rings and tossing them on the ground before her. The man in front dived for them before they stopped rolling. It was more wealth than he had ever seen, or would ever again see in his miserable life. The other two had not acquired any such treasure from the bodies of the guards and came up to join the scramble. A particularly pale man held out his hand.

"Let's see 'em," he demanded of his compatriot.

"Get your own."

Without warning, the pale man leapt at the other, clamping his hands firmly around his throat, holding him in a death grip until no life remained. Finally releasing the body, he began digging in the man's pockets for Margaret's rings. The scuffle and noise had masked the sounds of new footsteps, and as the brigand held the rings up in triumph, the glittering jewels were the last sight he would ever see before an arrow pierced his heart from behind. His body landed with a thud on the ground atop his own victim.

Three new men had emerged from the woods, all well armed. At the sight of them, the brigands took to their heels and disappeared into the woods. Margaret suspected that she had merely been delivered into the hands of a new set of thugs. But to her surprise, they knelt.

"Your Highness need fear no evil from us. We are sworn to protect the House of Lancaster and are pleased that we arrived in time. My name is

Christopher, and your servant."

"With whom do you serve, brave soldiers?"

"With Robin of Redesdale, Your Highness. We were marching to join you when we heard news of the battle near Hexham. Robin overcame one of Montague's search parties and learned from them that Your Highness was somewhere in these woods." Christopher smiled. "I grew up near here. We were lucky to find you before those thieves did you any harm."

"Rise, brave men. We thank you for your aid, but we must make haste to Bywell yonder." She pointed to the castle that stood so tantalizingly close on the nearby ridgeline.

Christopher escorted them until they were close enough to be spotted by the castle watch, which, upon seeing them, sent an escort for the rest of the way. Back among those who accepted her station, Margaret was once again able to feel like a queen. Christopher and his fellows were fed and allowed to rest until Lord Roos, one of the queen's original followers who still lived to attend her, entered the kitchen. He addressed Christopher.

"The queen informs me that you serve one who calls himself Robin of Redesdale. Is this true?"

"It is, my lord."

"I know him well. Tell me, what is his strength?" Christopher did not know if he should be speaking about Robin to someone whose loyalties he knew nothing about.

"He is...well attended, my lord."

"Come, come, man. If I were a danger to him I would not have been with the queen for all this time." But he understood Christopher's dilemma. "You need not tell me where he is, but I must know if he has a following that we may depend on when next we have an opportunity."

"You can depend on us, my lord! We are not fighting men by trade, but we know where our duties lie, and will dispatch them to the best of our talents, by God's will."

"What are you called, my friend?"

"I am Christopher Miller."

"The queen bade me thank you for your services, and though she has nothing of value with which to repay you and your friends, she will not forget your service to her. Now go and rejoin Robin, and tell him from Lord Roos that we will have need of his services again, that I swear."

"I will, my lord."

Leaving the confines of Bywell Castle, the three men reentered the woods to avoid any detection by Montagu's roving bands. As they slowly picked their way through the trees back to Robin's camp, Christopher was haunted by the memory of Margaret and the prince alone and surrounded by cutthroats. Even under those conditions, she had held herself most nobly without fear. He could see why despite the desperation of her cause, people still knelt before her and died for her when asked.

The next day, Lord Montagu entered the prison tent where the Duke of Somerset and Sir Ralph Percy had been carefully guarded. Behind him stood two men-at-arms with the king's Sun-in-Splendor emblem embossed on the breastplates of their armor.

"Henry Beaufort, Duke of Somerset, and Ralph Percy, Knight of Northumberland, you stand condemned of high treason against the person of the king and the realm. Do you wish to speak before I pronounce the sentence which has been ratified by His Majesty?" Montagu held a scroll with the king's seal.

From the time of the battle's end, both of the condemned men knew their inevitable fate. Having been pardoned once by the king, there could be no expectation of leniency this time. Percy struggled to his feet, his leg still almost worthless. But he straightened his back and spoke loudly.

"Montagu, it is you who are guilty of treason against the anointed king of England, and everyone here present knows that my soul is pure in this matter."

Somerset, emboldened by Percy's words, stood next to him. "Pronounce your doom, Montagu. We have nothing to say to you."

"Very well," Montagu was unimpressed, "then hear the sentence of your king. You have been judged guilty of treason and high crimes against your liege lord to whom you both swore loyalty. This very morning you shall be taken to the block and presently beheaded. May God acquit you of your crimes. Take them!"

The walk to the wagon that would convey them to the block was slow, as Percy limped in pain on his useless leg. It was another pleasant day, the sun high in the morning sky, and Somerset, trying with great effort to show no signs of fear, thought that it was a fine day to meet his maker. They rode to the center of the town of Hexham, where many townsfolk and the hooded executioner awaited them before the block. For the sake of these witnesses, the charges and sentence were read again. Percy was the first to face the executioner, whom he forgave before he knelt. The stroke of the ax was swift and brought gasps from the onlookers, to whom such spectacles were like a carnival. Percy's body was thrown in the wagon and Somerset was led to the block.

"God save King Henry!" he yelled to the crowd, and was pleased to see at his last moment that many of the villagers nodded in agreement. He forgave the executioner and placed his head on the block. He did not hear the gasps from the crowd.

Samuel accompanied the guard and King Edward into York, barely able to contain his desire to run from his duties to look for Kate and his family, even though to do so when the army was preparing for battle would be treason. Still, Samuel was prepared to do just that when word arrived of Montagu's quick victory, and the king, not wishing to add to his already considerable debt, dismissed his followers. As the army dispersed, the guard accompanied the king into town where Edward had made arrangements to stay at the palace. Sir Julian insisted that Samuel stay until the king was safely escorted but promised he would have permission to leave that evening.

The king was met by Lord Montagu at the palace and ordered his court to assemble immediately. Sir Julian hastily made the arrangements for the security of the great hall, and all of the dignitaries within the city of York were summoned to attend. Montagu's brother, the bishop of Exeter, and the king's brothers, Clarence and Gloucester, were present, as were Lord Rivers, the king's new father-in-law, though that fact was not yet known, and Lord Scales. Along with the Archbishop of York and the aldermen and mayor of the City, the group made a colorful spectacle of nobility.

When the king was seated, the archbishop, a man of eighty years and barely able to hold his crosier, gave a blessing and thanked the Lord for the victories that he had given his anointed servant on earth.

Edward then addressed the gathering. "We thank you all for this most gracious welcome to York. We have asked you all to attend us here on this glorious day to recognize with us the deeds of our well beloved cousin of Montagu." Shouts and cheers greeted Montagu them.

The young Neville lord bowed. "My gracious liege, I bring you even greater news than that of Hexham Field. Couriers have arrived from the northern castles of Bamborough, Bywell, and Dunstanborough, to confirm that they have all yielded to Your Highness' mercy and are securely held by my men. Moreover, I have most reliable information that Margaret has been wafted back to France from whence she came, penniless and without aid. Your Highness may rest easy that the northern counties have finally been wrested from the Lancastrian traitors!"

The room buzzed with exclamations of surprise and satisfaction. For five years the Lancastrians had maintained a strong threat in the north, but at last the struggle was over. Edward held up his hand for silence.

"My lord of Montagu, stand near and hear the thanks of a most grateful monarch. Because you have most nobly and bravely defended our throne, may you never again be called Lord Montagu, but from this time forward, you and your issue shall be revered as the Earls of Northumberland!"

Montagu and the others stared in stunned silence, barely able to believe what had just occurred. The Earldom of Northumberland was among the richest of the realm, and bestowed power upon the holder second only to the king's in the northern counties. It was a reward of great value for which he had not dared hope.

"Your Highness is too kind," he said finally. "I have done only what my duty demanded of me, and nothing more."

"You have spoken truly, but it is our pleasure to see that such service is appropriately rewarded." Edward stood. "Rise, my lord of Northumberland!" He embraced his cousin. Addressing the room, Edward let his voice rise above the murmuring. "Those who would boldly wreak havoc on the peace of our realm have been vanquished. We decree this evening a celebration in honor of the new Earl of Northumberland, and any who so wish may sup with us tonight!" A cheer went up from the crowd as the king descended from the throne and made his way through the adoring onlookers, sweeping from the room, attendants at his heels.

Samuel did not cheer as the king departed. He knew that this appointment would devastate Christopher. Now, more than ever, he had to find his family and take Kate to a safer haven, though where that might be he had no notion. Sir Julian was speaking with some men he did not recognize. The old knight had treated him like a son, and Samuel hated to leave his service, but he felt certain that his mentor would understand.

Shortly after, in a different, private room, the king's brother, the Duke of Clarence, sat with the Bishop of Exeter sipping wine from pewter cups. Clarence, now nineteen years old, seemed unhappy. The bishop regarded him with his usual penetrating gaze.

"I see little reason for your mood, my lord," he prodded the young duke. "It would appear to me that your brother's hold on the throne has never been so secure, though I would not have expected it five years ago when we so boldly declared our intentions." Not acknowledging the bishop, Clarence only withdrew further into himself. The cleric was not satisfied to leave it. "If I did not know better, I should guess that you're displeased with the king."

"What makes you say that?"

The bishop knew that his arrow had struck the target. "Unlike your younger brother of Gloucester, who is joyous when the king is near, you are moody. I have seen the signs of jealousy before, my young friend, and the marks of it are on your soul."

Clarence was defensive. "I have no reason to be jealous, Your Grace."

The bishop was not convinced. "You were not raised with the king and Edmund, were you?"

"I did not have that honor," he said bitterly.

"And you therefore felt set apart from them?" Goading him was easier than he had expected.

"I have the same blood in my veins as my dear brother, and yet he has treated me like any other of his followers. He has not entrusted me with any important duties or honors."

"Such rewards must be earned, my lord."

Clarence glared at him. "Not when you have royal blood in your veins! Were he to die tonight, I would be king."

"That is true. But such a tragedy is unlikely. I should think that you would be better served enjoying your new rank and prestige as the king's brother and a royal duke of the realm."

"I shall determine how best to spend my time, Your Grace." Finishing the wine in his cup, he poured himself more and drained another half.

"And I tell you that if Edward expects me to be his errand boy, he had better think again of my worth, for I'll not have it."

"We are all errand boys to the king, my lord. Such is the way of things." A page knocked on the door and entered.

"My lords, the king inquires after you both and craves your company."

"We will come," said the bishop, dismissing him with a wave.

"You go, Your Grace," said Clarence. "My royal brother will dine most contentedly without me for a while."

"As you wish, my lord. But a word to the wise: A man's strength is carried in the arms of his friends, not in his own hands." The bishop paused for a moment to allow his warning to sink in, and left the young duke staring into his empty mug.

At about the time that the dignitaries were gathering at the palace, Sally was washing clothes at the riverbank. She had one eye on her washing and as usual the other on John, now three years old and, much to his mother's distress, in constant motion. Recently, however, her new friend, Kate, had helped in so many valuable ways to ease her burdens. And John had developed a strong affection for Kate as well, to the point where Sally dreaded the thought of her ever leaving. But Kate's presence also gave her great hope, for she knew that it was only a matter of time before Samuel would return to them, if only to take Kate away with him. And seeing Kate so well adjusted to her new surroundings might convince him to patch up his differences with Christopher and stay where he belonged.

The thought of Christopher spoiled her mood and she pounded a shirt hard against the washing rock. His departure had left Emma in a perpetual state of melancholy, so much so that Sally was concerned for her health. To be sure, she still cared for the girls and performed her chores as always, but it was habit that gave no joy as it used to, and even their conversations were brief and without warmth. Oliver had also been overwhelmed by the new responsibilities that had been so unexpectedly thrust upon him. Though he proved equal to the task, he resented the unnecessary burden.

"Sally!" Kate's voice beckoned to her from the road. Sally looked up to see her waving and hurrying past the front gate. Sally put her last article of clothing in with the rest of the washed items and stood up slowly, stretching her tired back. "Sally!" Kate repeated as she drew near. "King Edward is here! At the palace," she said, trying to catch her breath.

Sally understood well the significance. If the king was in town, Samuel was as well, and her heart leaped at the news. With Christopher gone, at least for a while, Samuel would feel welcome at home. His presence could even bring some happiness back to Emma.

"Did you hear me?" Kate shook her out of her reverie.

"Yes. Yes, we must get word to him somehow."

"We'll go to the palace ourselves," said Kate. "I'll bring these clothes in and tell Oliver. You bring John to Emma and I'll meet you on the road. Don't just stand there, woman!" Pushing Sally toward John, who was playing near the river bank, she grabbed up the clothes basket and hurried toward the mill room where she knew she would find Oliver.

Oliver insisted on joining them. There was nothing in the milling business that day that he considered more important. Kate waited impatiently as he disengaged the huge wheel and secured it, then placed several full sacks of milled wheat in carefully arranged areas so he could keep track of where each one belonged. Just when Kate was at the end of her patience, he nodded that he was ready. Swinging the front door open, he saw standing before him a large man with a hideous scar down the side of his face that disfigured his mouth into a permanent sneer. With him was another man, face obscured by a full beard and mustache, dressed in filthy clothing and holding several lengths of rope. They appeared to have been traveling for weeks. Without warning, the filthy one pulled a short club from his cloak and struck Oliver on the side of the head. He fell to the ground unconscious.

Kate screamed and tried to catch him as he fell, but Sir Hugh was on her almost as quickly, putting his hand over her mouth to keep her quiet. Before he could get a secure grip his hand came too close and she bit his finger with all her strength. He screamed and struck her on the chin. She collapsed to the ground in a heap. He gripped his hand in agony while his partner stooped to look at the girl.

"If she's dead, we won't be paid!"

"She's not dead, you idiot," he hissed. "Keep your mouth shut and bind her." Responding to the commotion, Sally came running through the door. Recognizing Sir Hugh, and seeing Kate and Oliver motionless on the ground, she started screaming and turned to run. Sir Hugh leaped to catch her before she could bolt, and after a momentary struggle managed to tie a rag around her mouth.

"This is a pleasant surprise!" he said, voice dripping with venom. "I had not hoped to see you again, my sweet."

"You know this wench?" his partner asked in surprise.

"Oh yes. We're old friends, aren't we, my dear?" He pushed her toward his partner. "Bind her well and get them both on the horses."

"What are we doing with this one? We'll have our hands full enough with one."

Sir Hugh grabbed him roughly by the tunic. "Do as I say or I'll gut you like an eel."

Not doubting Sir Hugh for a moment, he swung Kate over his shoulder like a sack of grain. Securing her over the back of one of the two horses that were waiting by the river bank, he came back and did the same with Sally. Sir Hugh took a last look around and then mounted his own horse. As they spurred their horses toward the road, Emma ran to the mill house and saw Oliver unconscious on the floor. Frantically searching for Sally and Kate, she heard horses as they came around the front of the mill house. Running out, she saw Sally still struggling, bound across the horse's back. Screaming Sally's name, she chased after them, but only in time to see them ride out on the road and disappear to the south. Falling to her knees, she could only sob hysterically as the sun set in the west.

Samuel reached the mill house two hours later. He had hoped to see Sally and Emma, speak civilly with Christopher for a while, and then take Kate somewhere where they could be safe. Perhaps things would go well enough for him to spend a comfortable night here with Kate before taking their leave in the morning. Seeing the mill house brought a sense of pride to him, as hearing the news of his family's good business had done earlier in the day when he inquired of them. Think what he may about Christopher, this was an accomplishment, and Samuel was once again jealous of his brother. Perhaps with Kate he could find this kind of happiness somewhere.

He knocked softly. There was no answer and he became concerned when he heard the sound of children crying from within. When there was no response to his second knock, he decided to try the pull string. He felt the latch lift from the inside and swung the door open.

The room was mostly dark, a taper on the eating table providing the only light. No fire smoldered in the hearth. Very strange for Emma to allow that, Samuel thought. It was then that he saw them, on the floor by the hearth. A figure sat cradling the head of another, like the Madonna with the crucified Christ in her arms. A cold shiver crawled up his spine.

"Emma? What happened here? Where's Kate?" He was not even sure that she heard him as she stared vacantly into space. "Emma!" he shook her shoulders. She blinked and looked at him, trying to focus as if waking from a deep sleep.

"Samuel? Is it really..." He could hardly hear her.

"Yes, Emma. Where's Kate?" He was frantic with fear for Kate but could see that it would be fruitless to push her any harder.

"Oh, Samuel. She's gone. They're all gone." And with that she broke into sobs. Now terrified with apprehension, Samuel turned his attention to Oliver. He had a nasty lump on the left side of his head but was at least breathing. Samuel wondered for a moment how Emma got him in the house, then saw a bucket of water near the cooking area and, ripping a swath of cloth from the bottom of his shirt, dipped it into the bucket and began to wipe blood from the wound.

"Who are you?" Samuel almost jumped out of his skin at the sound of the voice. A small boy stood bravely before him, watching him with large innocent deep brown eyes, clutching a coverlet in his hands.

"My name is Samuel. Who are you?" he asked gently as he continued his attempts to revive Oliver.

"I'm John. What's wrong with Daddy?"

Samuel's heart swelled as he realized that this little man was Sally's and Oliver's child. And his name was John!

"Your father took a nasty bump on the head, John, but I think he'll be all right. Do you know where your mommy is?"

"No."

Oliver began to stir. At last, Samuel thought as he lifted his friend's head.

"Can you hear me?" John came and stood beside him, looking down at his father. Oliver's eyes blinked open.

"Samuel?" he asked. When he saw his son, he tried to rise, but a sharp stab of pain and a wave of nausea laid him down again.

"Don't try to move," scolded Samuel. "You've taken a blow to the head and it's still bleeding." He dabbed at the wound some more until it looked as if Oliver had regained some of his faculties. "Can you tell me what happened here? Where are Sally and Kate?"

"We were coming to find you…" Oliver was fighting the waves of nausea. "Two men came to the mill as we were leaving. It's all I remember."

Samuel was gripped by a new panic. Kate! Had the ones who attacked him in Durham caught up with her here?

"He took them, Samuel." Emma had finally collected herself enough to speak. Perhaps hearing that Oliver was not seriously injured gave her some renewed strength. "The devil himself. The one with the scar, I saw it as plain as the horns on his head."

"A scar?" Samuel asked in horror. "The one who killed Father?"

"The same, Samuel." She gripped his hand with unexpected strength. "He's the devil's own child, and he took them both to the south."

"Emma, where's Christopher?" For the first time he realized that his brother was also among the missing.

"He left us, Samuel. Left his work and his children too, and we haven't heard from him since. I imagine he joined his friends and went to fight for the Percys."

The fool! Samuel thought. It all seemed unreal as the story became more incredible. What curse was on his family? Something Emma said came back to him.

"Emma. You said children. Where are your children?" He was almost afraid to ask.

"They're in the back, afraid to come out," piped John. "Do you want me to get them?"

"Could you please, John?" Samuel smiled at him. The child smiled broadly, glad to be of some service, and ran into the back room. A moment later, he returned followed by two timid little girls, one about John's age and the other perhaps a year older.

"It's all right, my angels," said Emma. "This is your Uncle Samuel." Samuel was glad that Emma seemed to be regaining some control. To Samuel she said, "This is Alice and this one is Sarah, my first-born."

Sarah came up to him and gave him a hug. "Mommy, what's wrong with Uncle Oliver?" she asked.

"I'm fine," Oliver was able to reassure her himself. Samuel felt a lump in his throat as he looked at the children.

"How much I've missed," he said, squeezing the tears from his eyes. "This is all my fault."

Samuel was frantic to follow after Kate and Sally at that moment, but his family needed him. He could not leave Emma and Oliver like this. Reluctantly, he realized that little more could be accomplished that evening. He saw everybody to sleep, and although his rest came fitfully, it would be enough. He awoke finally to the comforting sounds and smells of Emma's cooking in the kitchen, which considering her state the night before surprised him. When he entered the kitchen, a smile lit her face and they embraced long and hard. Emma blinked to hold back the tears.

"When I awoke I was afraid that you had only been a dream."

"I did you all a great wrong to stay away so long."

"That's over. When you come back, it will be for good." She had summed up what Samuel was feeling and it filled him with joy, if only for that moment.

"I have one last debt to pay, and then, I swear, I will return for good." She put her hand on his cheek.

"I know you will."

"It's time we got started, my friend," a voice came from behind. Oliver, head wrapped in a bandage, was standing in the door, the color back in his face, what little of it was normally his. Samuel looked at Emma, and she shrugged her shoulders.

"We'll close the mill, and I'll be all right. It's time you realized that you are not alone."

"But what about you, and the children?"

"We'll get by," she said with conviction.

Samuel hugged her again. "And what about you?" he asked Oliver. "Are you sure you're well enough to take what will surely be a difficult journey?"

"You need not fear for me, Samuel. There's too much at stake for me to be feeling sorry for myself."

It felt good to be home again. "Let's eat and be gone. The trail grows colder by the minute."

After a hearty breakfast, they said their farewells to the children, promising them that they would return with the rest of the family soon. Emma had prepared as much dried meat and other provisions as she could find in the house and helped them pack their shoulder bags. And as she watched the last of her family disappear down the south road, she promised herself that she would not cry again until her family was reunited.

CHAPTER XIX

Edward knew that the time for reckoning was upon him, but he needed to bolster his courage before he made his announcement. It had been six months since his secret marriage to Elizabeth, and the secret had been well kept. Of those at the ceremony in Grafton Manor, he knew he could trust Sir Julian with his life, and Father Dennis was only too happy to delay the announcement and the certain wrath of the Archbishop of Canterbury, whose authority he had usurped by performing the wedding. And of course the Woodvilles would obey his wishes to delay the announcement until the time was right.

But now, he was growing tired of seeing his wife only on the rare occasions that he could contrive an excuse to travel to Grafton, and, most of all, he missed the feel of her arms around him at night. To be sure, he had not been without the wenches that Hastings brought to him, but the company of such women left him feeling empty and alone. On the rare occasions that discretion allowed a visit to Grafton, his new wife had left him fulfilled beyond anything he had ever imagined possible. Elizabeth had become everything he had hoped: a person to whom he could speak freely and share all his confidences, with whom he could be himself, not a king.

He sat at the head of the long council table in a high room of the White Tower. His cousin, the Earl of Warwick, had returned from his embassy to France with the expected offer by King Louis of his sister, the Lady Bona of Savoy. Warwick had been seduced by Louis' flattery, Edward was sure, and now the earl would expect Edward to follow his advice and form this alliance with the French.

As Edward fidgeted and wondered how best to handle breaking the shocking news, the others were engaged in an animated discussion over how to handle the Duke of Burgundy if the English allied themselves with King Louis. Lord Hastings seemed the most upset.

"I tell you, my lords, that Burgundy, whatever his faults, has kept the French throne weak by his opposition for years. To abandon him now will only strengthen Louis' hand, and that is why this offer is made."

"Lord Hastings," said Warwick, "we are no longer the divided kingdom of the House of Lancaster, and we have no need for the aid of the self-important Duke of Burgundy to fight our battles for us. I for one would rather have Louis as an ally. Burgundy has shown his disdain for us, and must be punished for his impudence. This wedding would put him in his place."

"The French king has only one goal," persisted Hastings, "and that is the consolidation of Burgundy under his dominion. Once he has realized that goal, he will not have any use for us, and will consider the sacrifice of his sister coinage well spent."

"It would be a more popular decision with our own people to side with the French in this matter," said Northumberland.

"Our people have no love for anyone who lives across the channel," Hastings reminded him. "They want only to repossess the lands won in battle and to see our king on the French throne."

"I fought at the side of the Duke of Bedford when those lands were won," Lord Rivers interjected — the accusation that nobody else in the room could make such a claim apparent — "and I also wish to see His Majesty walk as monarch on the French soil that we fought so hard to possess. An alliance with Louis at this time would snuff that dream which our people hold so dear to their hearts."

"The people's hearts are bound by their purse strings," responded Warwick, more than a little annoyed. "If we help Louis regain the low countries from Burgundy, we will have the freedom to reestablish our Flemish markets. That being done, the merchants will quickly forget Burgundy and his pompous arrogance."

"Your Highness, what is my royal brother's wish in this matter?" asked the Duke of Gloucester, who at the age of seventeen was still somewhat reluctant to bandy opinions with these great lords. Having boundless admiration for his brother, he felt that it was time for a decision to be made, lest they get the impression that the king was not in control.

Gloucester had begun to endear himself to Edward, not by worthless flattery but by clearly supporting Edward's decisions, no matter where they led. It was the kind of support that he would have expected of Edmund had he lived. Richard was the very image of their father, dark in complexion, black hair, and much shorter than the other three brothers.

"My lords, we cannot marry the Lady Bona."

Warwick was stunned. Never did he imagine that Edward would go against his wishes. Why had he sent him to France to negotiate the marriage?

"We have decided to marry the Lady Elizabeth Woodville, daughter of Lord Rivers." The silence that followed reminded Edward of the time when he sat before Edmund's casket in the dungeon of Pontefract Castle.

Warwick was the first to speak. "Your Highness is very merry to jest with us like this." He was hoping that he was right about Edward's amazing announcement.

"We do not jest, my lord. We have decided."

"My Liege," said Hastings, "the Lady Elizabeth is a fair and good woman, but she is beneath your royal dignity." Rivers flushed with anger but said nothing. His own wife, he knew, had been told the same thing when she chose to marry him, but now he knew that he was father to the queen, and these haughty men would be forced to respect him.

"Your Highness, you must reconsider this decision," Warwick was beside himself, realizing that his own reputation as the power behind the throne was at stake.

"It is too late for any reconsideration. We have already wed."

Another stunned silence. The color had drained from Hastings' face. He appeared to be angrier even than Warwick, not comprehending how the king could have made such a decision without his knowledge.

"Who performed this ceremony, My Liege?" The calm voice of the bishop of Exeter spoke for the first time that afternoon. Edward knew that the bishop was contemplating the possibilities of an annulment. He moved quickly to dash any such hopes.

"The ceremony was performed by our confessor, Father Dennis. And there will be no annulment, Your Grace, you may be certain of that. We will send letters to the French king with our thanks for his offer. Now it is time to bring our new queen to court and make arrangements for her coronation. Lord Hastings, you will see to those arrangements. Lord Rivers, we would have further words with you in our chambers."

After a moment during which they all sat in silence, Warwick signaled to his brothers. As they were leaving, Clarence also stood.

"My lords, may I join you?" Warwick looked at the bishop, then nodded, leading them out of the room.

Three weeks later, on Saint Michael's Day, Elizabeth was escorted to Westminster Abbey by Clarence and Warwick. There, in the presence of the king and as many of the magnates of the realm as could be gathered, the Archbishop of Canterbury performed the coronation of the new queen of England. Her sons by her first marriage, Thomas and Richard, now eight and six years old, were present, as were her father and brother, Lords Rivers and Scales, and, of course, the dowager Duchess of Bedford. Also present were her other brothers, John and Lionel, and her seven sisters, all occupying positions and duties of honor during the ceremony. Father Dennis was also present but played no role in the mass that followed the coronation.

He had not been able to avoid the archbishop before the ceremony, and was asked calmly by His Grace whether he was aware that the right of performing holy matrimony for the king belonged to him alone. Father Dennis did his best to assure the archbishop that he had been given no choice and begged forgiveness, which his grace was not inclined to give, making it clear with his silence that should the confessor's duties to the king ever be terminated, he had better find a quiet monastery far from His Grace's presence to live out the rest of his life.

Unlike Edward's coronation feast, arranged in such haste four years earlier, the new queen was treated to a gala. In the great room of Windsor Palace, the dignitaries came to pay homage and swear allegiance to the queen and to any offspring that would bless her union with the king. Edward watched as Elizabeth handled her role with ease and dignity, as if she were bred to the position. Her low-cut, intricately embroidered gown stirred his lust as he watched her receive the favors of noblemen and priests throughout the evening, and though he was anxious to have her alone in their chambers, he would not deprive her of a moment of these ceremonies.

Throughout the evening it was apparent that the old nobility did not approve of their new queen, though they tried hard not to offend the king. All, that is, except for Edward's mother. Cecily, the dowager Duchess of York, made her entrance late, well after everyone else had given their oaths, and the room was hushed by her presence. The matriarch of the House of York, wearing a train longer than the queen's, moved immediately to where Edward sat on a raised dais with his new wife. The king rose to greet his mother with an embrace. Elizabeth glared at her, her hatred obvious to everyone. The lords and ladies watched the proceedings waiting for the inevitable confrontation.

"I regret my tardiness, my lord," she said at last, "but since I was not consulted regarding this evening's plans, my preparations were delayed." Edward was hurt that his mother would behave so poorly before the peers of the realm and was tempted to return the favor, but decided that he would be better served by ignoring her rancor.

"We are pleased to have our mother here," he announced. Looking disappointed, she extended her hand to the queen.

"I must call you daughter. You are welcome to our family." Her lack of sincerity was apparent, and Edward knew it was time to redirect everyone's attention. He signaled for the musicians to play and led Cecily to the table of honor, where the dowager Duchess of Bedford was already seated. Without even acknowledging her presence, Cecily took the chair closest to the royal podium, the highest place of honor.

Elizabeth's mother was not about to take a backseat to this great lady. The Duchess of Bedford had once been the preeminent lady of the realm and knew how to handle this self-important woman.

"I never had the chance until now to welcome Your Ladyship to our family," she said quietly, so that no one else could hear. Cecily recognized Jaquetta's presence for the first time.

"I will never be a part of your family," she snarled.

Jaquetta had gained the reaction she had hoped for. "Nevertheless," she smiled. Then casually, "Doesn't the queen look resplendent this evening?"

"As well as one of her breeding could," she said contemptuously.

"And yet from that breeding shall spring future kings of England." It was her trump card. "And from yours as well, of course, my lady." The latter was said superficially to give deference to Cecily as the king's mother, but they both knew she was reminding this haughty lady that her breeding would soon be mingled with that of the Woodvilles.

Cecily had no answer and simply turned away. She was furious at Edward for this union but knew there was nothing she could do. She decided she would have no further part in her son's court. If he wanted to see her again, he would have to come to her. No further words passed between the two ladies that evening.

It was well into the early morning hours when the king stood, silencing the revelers. He was giddy from too much wine, but still in control of his faculties.

"My lords and ladies," he announced as the room waited in silence. "It is customary for the king to grant favors at such an august event. True to that custom, we have decided to advance two of our most trusted councilors and kinsmen this very evening."

These were the words the courtiers had been waiting to hear, and they bristled with anticipation in the hopes that the king's largesse would fall on them. "First, we have received word from His Holiness in Rome that he has approved the appointment of our cousin and Chancellor, the Bishop of Exeter, as Archbishop of York." All eyes turned to the new archbishop and polite applause and congratulations were heard. The appointment of George Neville as archbishop elevated him to a position equal to the dukes of the realm, inferior within the hierarchy only to the king himself.

"I thank Your Highness for this honor and pledge to be equal to your trust and that of His Holiness." The new archbishop bowed.

"We know that you will, Your Grace." Edward hoped that this appointment would ease some of the animosity his marriage had created within the Neville family. "Second," he continued, "in honor of our new queen, and to further demonstrate our love for her and her kinsmen, we create Lord Rivers, her father and our trusted councilor, Earl Rivers, and bestow upon him all the rights and honors appurtenant to that title." Again, polite applause from the court, but without the enthusiasm that had greeted the archbishop's appointment, and that fact was not lost on the king, nor certainly on Elizabeth. It was clear that the old nobility of the realm had not accepted the Woodvilles as their equals, and the elevation of Lord Rivers to an earldom would not change that. Nevertheless, the newly created Earl Rivers bowed and thanked the king with all the dignity of his new rank.

Shortly after the announcements, Edward and Elizabeth left the celebration and retired to the royal quarters. Their outer garments were removed by the servants, who were then dismissed, leaving the royal couple alone for the first time in what seemed to Edward an eternity. Without a word, he took his wife in his arms and reveled in the feel of her body against his. Kissing her, he felt her passion as if it were a separate soul leave her body and enter his. They fell back onto the bed and struggled to remove the final barriers between them, his lips never leaving hers. The union of their bodies, free from worldly hindrances, brought an ecstasy that neither of them could have expected, and their love and youth gave them the stamina to sustain that moment until the early morning light broke through the windows. Only then did sleep take them both.

The following day, the king and queen prepared for the king's general audience, servants of the wardrobe bringing in one opulent garment after the other until the royal couple had decided on items that pleased them. Elizabeth was trying to choose jewelry from among dozens of pieces arrayed before her on a velvet shelf, trying on several pieces and then tossing them back and selecting others.

"Did you see their faces when you elevated my father?" she spoke more to herself than to Edward, her tone more worried than angry. "I fear that we have many enemies in your court, my king." Edward, having completed his outfit with a large emerald-encrusted gold ring, sat in a plush chair and admired his new queen.

"Come now, wife. These magnates you fear have been my loyal subjects for five years now, and I trust every one of them."

"Surely you can see that the Nevilles have their own best interests in mind, not yours. And now, with an archbishop in their ranks, they have more power than ever, which you can be sure they'll use without hesitation when it serves them best."

"I am aware of my cousins' power, but their strength is derived from supporting me, and they know it. I've given them much largesse and many duties that will keep them feeling important, and as long as that remains true, they will all be happy enough and I will gain the benefits of their military and financial strength, without which I need hardly remind you I would be hard-pressed to maintain my present position."

"I am not without eyes, my husband. I know something of the royal court, despite my sex, and I know where our power lies, but you must see that we cannot allow the present situation to continue. Our marriage has caused Warwick to lose face here and especially abroad. In another man this would not be cause for concern, but in Warwick it is a clear danger. You must take steps to protect yourself."

"And what, my clear-sighted queen, would you have me do?"

Elizabeth made her last selection of jewelry and dismissed the servants with a wave of her hand. This was her chance to unfold her plan to the king.

"We must form other alliances to offset the power of the Nevilles. Between us, we have many unwed brothers and sisters with whom we could forge alliances through marriage. The Earls of Kent, Arundel, and Huntingdon, and the Duke of Buckingham are all young and unwed, and I have an eligible sister for each of them to take as wife. None will refuse if you require that it be so, and think of the resources of all those families at our beck and call should we need them to offset the power of the Nevilles."

"Not to mention the added prestige of the Woodville family if your sisters held all of those families captive."

Elizabeth was not amused. "I should think that you would be pleased to put an end to the tongue-wagging about how you married beneath yourself. If members of my family are countesses and duchesses, so much the better!"

Edward knew all too well that his relationship with the Nevilles was precarious at best, and he had long wished that he could depend on others if he needed them. While his brothers would provide that someday, they were still young. If only Edmund were alive, he thought sadly.

"We had better get to our audience," he said, rising from his chair. "Your idea has merit, my queen, and I shall consider it with care."

"A final thing, my lord. For how long must I endure your mother's superior looks and hateful disrespect? I am the queen and you must not permit this to continue." Edward had dared to hope that the topic of his mother's behavior would not come up, but he knew better.

"If I know my mother," he said with a sigh, "we will not see much of her at court."

"I hope not. For both of our sakes."

As they left the room and their entourage joined them, Elizabeth felt satisfied. There was little doubt in her mind that Edward would do as she suggested. She could be very persuasive if the need arose.

Henry the Sixth, who forty-two years before had been crowned king of England and France at the tender age of nine months, knelt in a small chapel in Waddington Hall, the home of Sir Richard Tempest, staring at a candle he had just lit. He exhaled loudly and wondered if his wife and son were safe. He had refused to leave his kingdom and was taken instead to the Scottish court, where he stayed for two months. Margaret begged him to go with them to France, but may have been relieved when he refused. It was going to be a struggle to convince the peers of France to lend aid to her cause, but if they saw that Henry was not of sound mind, it would have been impossible. Perhaps Henry knew that.

But after two months, King James asked Henry to leave Scotland. Relations between the Scots and Edward's England were improving, and James had decided that to be entertaining the deposed king at his court was no longer politically advantageous. Henry had left as he had arrived, alone and penniless, and he wandered south back into England in anonymity. He had taken shelter and food from monasteries as he wended his way into Yorkshire, and probably would never have been recognized had he continued that way. But the family of Sir Richard Tempest had always been ardent supporters of the Lancastrians — Henry had personally dubbed Sir Richard a knight many years ago. Whether from the need for a friend or the wish to be recognized as something more than a beggar, Henry had knocked on the door of Waddington Hall one night and insisted on seeing the master of the house. Sir Richard, dazed by the absurdity of seeing his former king standing at his door in such an impoverished state, invited him to stay, but hurriedly dismissed all but his most trusted servants until he could gather his wits and determine what to do.

That was one week past, and now as Henry sat in the chapel, he wondered what God had in mind for him. His fate had been odd indeed, to be a king and a beggar, and he smiled at the realization that he cherished his situation, though he would certainly not wish it on anyone else. It was far better to be a beggar than to have innocent people war with one another over his miserable carcass.

"Am I disturbing you, my lord?" a voice came from behind.

Sir Richard stood at the door. A thin man with a tightly trimmed beard and mustache, he always appeared edgy, as if he suspected everyone to be an enemy, and now with the former king in his house he was more nervous than usual.

"Not in the least, good knight," said Henry. "Please come and sit for a while."

"My lord..." Sir Richard was not sure exactly how to proceed. "My lord, I must know your intentions. You must realize that your presence here endangers my family, and it would go very ill with all of us were it to be discovered that I was harboring a known fugitive."

"A known fugitive! And from the king's justice, no doubt?" The words startled Sir Richard. "But this was a head that sat beneath a crown," Henry said, encasing his head with both hands. "And the head still thinks, therefore, I think, it still dwells among the quick." Henry stood and crossed himself before the altar, the meaning of his words lost on his host. He lowered his voice and checked around the room, as if to see if anyone were listening. Frightened, Sir Richard followed his example. "You wish to know my intentions, good knight? I shall tell you directly, and let there be no dissembling between us, for you have sheltered me from my own people and fed me. I intend to live until my time is called, for truly I have no choice in that matter, and it will be the dust of a beggar that you bury on that day."

"Forgive me, my lord," Sir Richard tried to move away from Henry, who had moved uncomfortably close to his face as he spoke, "but I do not understand these musings. Surely you know that I have done all I can for you, without placing my family in desperate danger?"

Henry walked back to the altar and knelt. "Indeed I do, brave knight. Tonight I will dine with you and then be gone at first light, if that meets with your liking." Sir Richard quietly exhaled in relief.

"It does, my lord."

That night after dinner, Henry and Sir Richard's family sat at the long table within the great room of Waddington Hall. Conversation had been rare that evening as everyone felt the tension. Candles flickered around the room, illuminating the withdrawn faces around the former king, who thought he could see the souls of each shifting with the movement of the light.

"My lord," Sir Richard broke the silence, "I have asked my groomsman to accompany you to your next destination, and I've selected a horse for your use. I trust it will serve you well."

"I am in your debt," said Henry with a slight bow of his head.

"Not so, my lord," said Sir Richard with a defiant look toward his wife. "My duty would permit no less." A servant entered, obviously frightened.

"Master, riders approach! They are already at the front gate." Sir Richard jumped up and mustered his courage. His wife glared as if to say she had warned him.

"Go, ask their business and report back here." The servant bowed and left the room. "Ellerton!" he called loudly at the door. In a moment a young man not out of his teens entered breathlessly, still fastening the laces on his shirt. "Get the horses ready, and be quick!" Ellerton bowed and ran from the room.

"Perhaps my time has come this evening." Henry mused, not showing the slightest hint of concern.

"Your time will not come in my house, my lord," said the knight angrily. Loud voices could be heard from the main door, and after a moment, the servant returned.

"My lord, a Sir Thomas Talbot demands that you surrender the person of Henry, late calling himself king." The boy was ashen-faced.

"We are betrayed!" said Sir Richard's wife, terrified.

Five men entered the room without any further announcement. The leader said in a loud voice "Take him!" pointing at Henry. Sir Richard noticed to his horror that one of the men was his brother, John. Before another word could be spoken, John pointed to Henry.

"You see, Sir Thomas, my brother has held the traitor here until he could be apprehended. I hope you will report us favorably to the king."

Sir Richard had to think fast. With a quick look to his wife and then to Henry, who was waiting expectantly for his host's response with an amused look on his face, Sir Richard confronted the intruders.

"Thank God you got here in time."

Sir Thomas did not believe either man, knowing that the Tempest family had always been friends to the House of Lancaster, but he had instructions only to seize Henry.

"The king shall hear of your service," he answered coldly. "Bring the prisoner to the horses."

A guard pushed Henry roughly before him. When he moved past Sir Richard, Henry paused. "The king shall indeed remember your service, sir knight." And with a smile on his face that chilled Sir Richard to the bone, he walked with his captors to the waiting horses without.

In the passage leading to the rear entrance of Waddington Hall, Ellerton listened to the progress of events in the great hall, angered by the treachery of the Tempest family. Taking care to remain unseen, he quietly made his way out to the back where two horses were saddled and waiting. Taking a moment to consider his next move, he jumped lightly on the nearest mare and spurred the animal toward a narrow path through the woods.

In the meantime, Sir Thomas and his men placed Henry on a horse and started down the path that led to the south road. One of the guard held the reins of Henry's horse as he rode alongside. Two of Sir Thomas' men rode behind the king, one carrying a lighted torch. The rest of the guard rode before the king, one forward rider carrying another torch to light the way. It was a damp and thickly overcast night and the path before them disappeared into a black oblivion, the forward torch illuminating only a few yards ahead. A screech owl rattled the silence, leaving the men apprehensive and jumpy, reacting to every rustle heard from the black woods. The sound of a twig snapping to his left startled the rear torch holder so that he held his light as far to that side as he could. For a fleeting moment he thought he saw the ghostly image of a face watching them from within the trees.

"Sir Thomas, there is someone… "

At that moment, something exploded toward him and knocked the torch from his hands. His horse reared when the flame glanced over its flank, throwing the guard to the ground, where he landed heavily, too dazed to realize what had happened. Before he even recognized the danger, the second of the rear guards was hit in the head by something he never saw and fell from his horse.

By the time Sir Thomas grabbed the torch from the guard in front and returned to the rear, he saw only the two rear guards on the ground, their horses prancing nervously nearby, and no sign of Henry. From out of the darkness to his left he heard the sound of horses galloping away.

"This way. Quickly!" He shouted at the remaining two mounted guards.

They forged into the woods, but it was not long before they lost any hint of where the former king and his rescuers might have gone. Sir Thomas knew that to roam the woods in the pitch black of the evening was futile.

"We'll go back to Waddington and spend the night," he said reluctantly, "and find the trail again in the morning. Go and fetch those two fools. I have no desire to look upon their incompetent faces again this evening." The guards left to find their fallen comrades without saying a word, not wanting to anger the knight any further.

Henry had little notion of what had just happened, but he knew that he was free from the captivity of Sir Thomas and in the hands of someone else who was leading his horse through a dense thicket of low growth. There was nothing to do for the time being but to cover his face against the low branches and wait for his fate to unfold. Some time later, when it was clear even to Henry that there was no longer any pursuit, a voice came from out of the dark.

"Are you well, my lord?"

"Who asks?" Henry was still enveloped by darkness and could see nothing.

"My name is Ellerton, until this evening a servant at Waddington Hall."

"I am well. At least, as well as a beggar may expect. May I ask your intentions toward me?"

"My lord, I wanted only to free you from those men. Having done that, I have no further plans."

"I assume then that you do not act on orders from your master?"

"No, my lord. Though I may hang for it, I could not bear to see such treachery."

There was a brief silence in the darkness. "Let me feel your face, Master Ellerton." The young servant felt along the horse until he found Henry's hand in the darkness, and let the former king feel his head and face. "It is an honest face, and one that promises only sadness. But that is the cross that I must bear. Help me from this horse, Master Ellerton. We will need to wait until first light to continue, I think you will agree."

"I do, my lord." Helping him from his horse, Ellerton supported Henry for a few steps until they found a tree trunk that would provide a resting place for the evening.

After securing the horses, Ellerton rejoined Henry. "My lord, what did you mean just now...when you said a face that promises sadness?"

"Have you not heard, my young savior? I am mad, and given to pronouncements that have no meaning. A beggar in my own kingdom. Do not concern yourself with such rantings, but be assured that events will unfold as God wishes."

"Are you really mad, my lord, or do you hide your true self behind this mask?"

A short hesitation. "My state of mind has proven more formidable to rule than the ship of state. But I am content. Do you wish that you were born a king, my friend? I wish that I had been born a beggar, for then I would take pride in the begging, and the king would be content to let me beg in peace. I would have had the right to protect my soul against the wrongs of the world, and gladly shoulder the responsibility for so doing. But I was born a king and therefore I'm mad, that being the only way I could keep from selling my soul."

Ellerton thought for a moment before responding.

"Then, for your sake, my lord, I am glad that I was born a lowly servant."

Henry reached through the dark, found the boy's hand, and squeezed it. "I swear that your sacrifice will not be in vain."

Ellerton did not know of what sacrifice poor Henry was referring, but at that moment, he was certain that he had made the right choice and was at peace with himself.

They did not speak again, and rested until the first light of the new day broke. Ellerton, who was well acquainted with these woods, thought it best to bring Henry to an abbey that was isolated enough for their purposes, not more than four hours distant. They would surely grant two beggars a place to stay for at least a few days. Ellerton knew all of the trails, knowledge that had served him well the night before when he took a shortcut to catch Sir Thomas' party and then escaped along a narrow path that could be discerned even in daylight only by one who knew of its existence.

The next day's journey was uneventful and even enjoyable to Ellerton. He had not understood why he had taken such bold action the night before, but he was pleased at the way things turned out. He had even had time to gather some dried venison from the kitchen before he ran out of

Waddington Hall, which they enjoyed eating at midday. The weather was still overcast, but it was comfortably warm and there was no rain. The sound of the woodland creatures going about their everyday activities fascinated Ellerton as they rode slowly along. Henry had said almost nothing since he awoke that morning, and looked as though he carried a great weight on his shoulders, but was pleasant enough when Ellerton spoke to him.

When at last they arrived at the abbey, Ellerton rang the bell at the gate, greatly relieved to have arrived safely. They decided to leave the horses in a nearby glade where they would have ample forage for days. It would be hard to explain how two beggars had come to be in possession of two such fine and expensive animals. A monk answered the bell and, quickly surmising what they needed, listed to them duties and observances that would be expected while they were under the auspices of the abbey, as if he had recited them a hundred times before. They were led to the kitchen where they were fed bread and ale, and then shown a place to sleep in a large room off the barn where the sheep were brought for shearing.

After helping to feed the chickens and doing some general cleanup around the pens, they attended a mass celebrated by the abbot himself, and then ate a supper of porridge and bread. When they were finished eating, the abbot entered the kitchen, a place where the monks were not accustomed to seeing him. He allowed each of the beggars to kiss his ring. When he came to Henry, he paused.

"What is your name, my son?" he asked looking at him carefully.

"My name is but a quince to one as important as yourself, Father," responded Henry without looking up.

"Nevertheless, I would know it."

"I am called Henry, Father."

The abbot looked at him for a moment longer and then moved on to bless the others.

"Do you think he recognized you?" Ellerton whispered. With a blank look, Henry shrugged his shoulders.

Sleep came easily that night to Ellerton, who fell into a slumber so deep he never knew that a king watched over him throughout the dark hours, replacing his coverlet when it fell off during a restless turn. When the cock signaled the start of the new day, Henry had not slept at all.

They were ushered into the chapel for morning mass, and then brought once again into the kitchen for the early meal of bread and ale. After eating they were given assignments around the abbey and its grounds; Henry and Ellerton were told that their help was needed in the south pasture. Led by several monks out of the main gates and down a path through the woods, they climbed slowly toward some high ground. The clouds had given way to a misty morning through which the sun felt warm on their faces, promising a pleasant day to come. Ellerton noticed that Henry had not spoken at all.

"My lord," he said quietly, "are you well?"

Henry exhaled loudly. "Does your father yet live, Master Ellerton?"

The question took him by surprise. "Yes, my lord, he is a gentleman's steward in southern Yorkshire. At least, he was the last time we spoke several years ago."

"I never met my father," Henry mused. "I was less than a year old when he died, but I heard that he was a formidable man, and beloved of his people."

"I have heard the same, my lord."

"Still, I always wondered why, if he was so magnificent, he could not have extended the courtesy to have at least lived long enough to teach me the ways of being a king. It would have been a simple thing for so great a man, don't you think?"

Ellerton shrugged. "Even the greatest of kings must follow when God summons, my lord. I'm sure he would have preferred it otherwise."

"Do you really think so?"

"It is said he was a most devout Christian, my lord, and I doubt it not that, had he the chance, he would have enjoyed teaching you what he could." The need to comfort this poor man was compelling.

They reached a level place in the woods, near several boulders. From somewhere came the sound of a horse snorting. Henry grabbed Ellerton and pushed him up the path.

"Run, my friend, run!"

Ellerton stood in a daze, surprised by Henry's outburst. Five soldiers stepped from behind some of the boulders. Sir Thomas stepped forward and drew his sword, pointing toward Henry. Ellerton watched as if a dream was unfolding. Without thinking, he leaped toward Sir Thomas with a scream, perhaps hoping Henry could escape during the distraction. The knight spun on him as he closed the few feet between them and impaled the boy on his sword, which protruded several feet from his back. His thick blood quickly covered the knight's hand. Sir Thomas withdrew the sword and Ellerton fell to his knees clutching his stomach, face as pale as a lowland fog.

Henry rushed to Sir Thomas and pushed him aside. The knight hesitated for a moment, then sheathed his sword. Henry knelt before the boy, who was cold as death and shivering violently. He put his arms around him and hugged him closely, tears hot on his cheeks.

"I am truly a beggar now, my lord," Ellerton whispered through clenched teeth. "Is it not so?"

"As true a prince as ever there will be."

Ellerton struggled to smile, then went limp and exhaled his final breath. Henry laid him gently on the ground, closing the boy's eyes and bringing his lifeless hands to rest on his blood-soaked shirt.

One of the monks pulled on Sir Thomas' arm. "We were told you would wait at the pasture. It was the abbot's specific instruction that the abbey not be defiled in this manner."

"Express our regrets to the abbot and give him the king's thanks," responded Sir Thomas. Then pointing to Henry, he commanded the guards.

"Take him. And I trust he will not escape again."

As Henry was led to a horse, he passed near a monk whose arm he took with a grip firmer than the monk had thought possible for such a feeble man.

"If God's love still occupies some cranny of your soul, you will give him a proper resting place."

"We will tend to his remains, my lord," the monk said softly, shamed by what he had seen. "As God is my witness."

Henry released him roughly. The former king was helped onto a horse and as they began their journey toward London, he watched the monks gently lift Ellerton's body and carry him back to the abbey.

The news of Henry's capture spread rapidly through the kingdom. He was quickly escorted to the outskirts of London, where the Earl of Warwick arrested him in the king's name and led him through the streets of the city. To Warwick's consternation, there was little of the jeering and heckling that would normally come from the crowds when a great enemy of the king was captured and paraded through town. But Henry had long ago endeared himself to the common folk with his pious nature and gentle demeanor, and the sight of such a man in so pathetic a state left few with a desire to taunt. Since his last words to the monk after his capture, Henry had not spoken and had only stared vacantly at the ground before him, even as he was brought to the Tower and left once again in his royal prison. When the iron door was closed behind him, the featureless stone walls embraced him as a mother would cradle her infant, and he was content.

At Windsor Castle, Edward received the news of Henry's safe imprisonment in the Tower with relief. While he held no ill feelings toward the wretched former king, he knew that his own position on the throne was now much more secure. Even if it were true that rebellion could still be fomented in his name, Henry's presence in the Tower under Edward's close control made that possibility much less likely, especially since Margaret and the former Prince of Wales were hopelessly exiled in France.

When Warwick arrived at Windsor Castle with the official news of Henry's disposition, he found the king already in the company of Gloucester and Clarence, Hastings, Rivers, and Warwick's brothers, the Archbishop of York and the Earl of Northumberland. While they were gathered in the throne room, it was an informal meeting without all of the usual courtiers and other servants and guards.

"My lord of Warwick, we thank you for these glad tidings," said Edward after Warwick had made his formal report. "It is a day to be remembered not only for the safe dispensing of the former king, but we have also been informed that the queen will give birth within the week, news that we hope will gladden the hearts of all Englishmen."

The announcement of the impending birth of a royal heir was always cause for celebration, as it gave hope for stability in the royal lineage.

After the congratulations and blessings, Clarence, who alone did not seem thrilled by the news, took a step forward and addressed the king.

"Your Highness, allow me also to express my pleasure at this blessed news. May God grant that it be a male heir. But if I may be so bold, now seeming a good time, may I ask a boon of Your Highness?"

Edward looked at his brother, wondering why he would choose this time to ask for a favor. He would have expected his brother to wait until they had more privacy.

"Ask your boon."

"Thank you, Sire. I ask that you grant me permission to marry. The Earl of Warwick has graciously offered the hand of his eldest daughter, Isabel, and the offer likes me greatly."

Edward was stunned by the request, as it confirmed his worst suspicions that his brother had formed an alliance with the Nevilles. Isabel was one of only two children, both daughters, fathered by the Earl of Warwick. As such, Warwick was in effect offering Clarence half of his immense wealth. It was a rich inducement for a brother to turn away from his own. The king glared at his brother. Before he could respond, the herald entered and announced that a messenger had arrived with urgent news. Edward signaled for the messenger to enter. A man who seemed too old and frail for his duties entered.

"Your Majesty, I bring news of two great souls who have parted with their mortal bodies. The first, the noble Duke of Norfolk, so quickly follows his father to his reward, and the second being the Duke of Burgundy, who a fortnight past gave up the ghost at Bruges."

The news of the death of two great allies was disconcerting to the king, and taken together with his suspicions regarding his brother had left him feeling vulnerable. Norfolk had only two years ago come to the title at the death of his father, who had served Edward at the battles of St. Albans and Towton. As for Burgundy, his death had been expected for some time, and Edward was convinced that Burgundy's son, Charles, would continue the old duke's animosity toward the French king and maintain the alliance with the English, but nothing was ever certain when great titles passed into new hands. Feeling overwhelmed by all the turns of the past day, Edward decided that some discretion would be advisable.

"My lords, we wish to withdraw and weigh these matters within ourselves. You will all attend us again in the morning."

Feeling the need to confide in someone, he walked quickly to a seldom-used wing of the royal quarters where an elaborate suite had been prepared for the queen's confinement in anticipation of the birth of their first child. He found Elizabeth in her large bed, attended by several women who went to their knees as the king entered. Sitting on the edge of the bed, he ordered them all out.

"How does my queen?" he asked, stroking her long, disheveled golden hair.

"I am tired of this condition, my lord, but I am content. I have prayed all day that God will deliver you a son." Edward did not seem to react to her words. "What news have you that creases your face so sternly?"

Edward did not at first wish to burden her, but he needed to air his thoughts. He took a deep breath and unfolded to her the events of the morning. After finishing, Edward found himself pacing while his queen chose her words carefully.

"This marriage must not be permitted, my husband. Forgive me, but your brother has been seduced by the Nevilles and would be a dangerous tool in their hands."

"I cannot believe that he would betray me." Edward was agitated. He knew she was right, but resented that she would assume the worst anyway. "The death of Norfolk leaves us with no other friends of significant strength with which to balance the power of the Nevilles."

"Give my father and brothers more authority. They will be your strength, my lord."

"Perhaps, but it will be a while before they would be a match for the Nevilles."

"The wealth of the Duke of Norfolk would speed that process."

"What are you saying?"

"The duke left only an infant daughter to be his heir. The dowager duchess of Norfolk needs a husband, and my brother John needs a wife. Our course seems clear enough."

"But she's twice two times his age!"

"We do not need fruit from her withered womb, only access to her wealth."

Edward was about to dismiss the idea out of hand, but instead turned and looked out the window slit. It was a fair day and the gardens of Windsor Castle were alive with blooms of every color, made more brilliant by the afternoon sun. Could it be that even now that his greatest enemy had been imprisoned, the threat to his throne was greater than ever? Such tactics as suggested by his wife seemed beneath his dignity. But the truth in her logic was undeniable. She put his hand on her stomach.

"This is our future, my husband. Do you want him to wander hopelessly through life like Margaret's son?"

Her words stung. "Lest you forget, it was I who put them there."

"I remember well, my husband. I was her lady-in-waiting, and I know exactly how she felt when your father claimed the throne. I will not permit that to happen to this child, though the effort take my last breath."

Edward took her in his arms. "Do not fear my love, I would never let that happen." *The Tower has no room for another mad king.*

The next morning, the Lords of the Privy Council were assembled once again in the throne room of Windsor Castle. Edward kept them waiting while he carried on a lengthy conversation with Lord Hastings. Finally, he nodded and Hastings withdrew to his place among the other peers. Edward knew he would need all his wits about him in the next few moments.

"Our brother of Clarence, we have carefully considered your request of marriage to the Lady Isabel, daughter to our cousin of Warwick, and regret that we cannot grant our permission."

"May I ask why, Your Highness?" He was seething.

"We have decided that it would not be in the best interest of the realm. Be content, my brother. We shall see that you are well bestowed." Clarence was not satisfied, but nothing could be done at the moment. The king's word was final.

"We have also decided that Lord Hastings and Earl Rivers shall be dispatched with haste to the new Duke of Burgundy for the purpose of offering him the hand of our sister, Maggy, to solidify our pact of friendship."

It was Warwick's turn to flush with anger. "Sire, this hasty act is ill advised! The French king will consider it an act of war."

"With Burgundy at our side, Louis will not dare to defy us," Edward said.

Warwick spoke in tightly controlled words. "I must protest that the negotiations that were so carefully crafted with the French are to be dismissed without further consideration."

"My lord of Warwick, we have recognized your efforts and granted you great privileges in return. Be content that you will always be close to our heart, but in this matter, we have decided to go another way, which should not be taken to mean that we value your advice less."

"I thank Your Highness for those words, but they ring empty in the face of your actions."

"We have made our decision, my lord. Do not presume more than you should."

The tension in the room was palpable as the two men stared at each other like gamecocks in the fighting pit. But in the end, Warwick was intelligent enough to know that this was not the time to challenge the king.

"Forgive me, Your Highness," he said with a smile. "I am a passionate man when honor is at stake."

"You are a valued advisor, my lord," said Edward. "And always will be, if it is your will to be so."

In the courtyard of Windsor Castle, the three Nevilles and Clarence stood in a cluster. Nearby, several pages held their horses. The morning brought another in a long string of fair days. Warwick tugged on his thick beard.

"My lords, the king has been ill advised in these matters. The Woodville family has taken possession of his wits, and I cannot sit idly by and allow them to warp his mind."

"You are too cross, Richard," Northumberland chided. "It may be that the Woodvilles have overstepped themselves, but the king has good cause for his decisions and has followed a reasonable course, even if we disagree with it."

"Our reputation is at stake," said Warwick. "We have been the very pillars of his throne and are therefore owed deference in these matters."

The archbishop had been watching Clarence carefully during the conversation.

"What is your feel for these matters, Your Grace? The king is your brother, and we would therefore be ruled by your judgment."

"You saw how he rejected my request for marriage without discussing it with me. The queen bears no love for me, and it was surely her envenomed advice that has ruled the king. The same fate awaits you all if we do not act now."

"And what would you have us do?" The archbishop was clearly testing the young duke. Clarence hesitated, looking back and forth between the Neville brothers.

"I...have no plan, but you have my pledge that you can count on me, whatever is decided." There was a moment of tight silence, then Warwick clapped him on the back.

"Perhaps the wrong brother of York sits on the throne. Come, we will talk more on these matters."

"Richard," Northumberland took Warwick's arm as he turned toward his horse. "I warn you that a move against the king would be foolhardy. He is popular and has treated us well, and this talk is treasonous on its face."

Warwick regarded him sternly. "No one said anything about moving against the king, my brother."

"I know you better than that, Richard. We have fought many battles together and I have no wish to oppose you, but be warned, I will not be part of any conspiracy against the king."

"Nor would I want to see you on the wrong end of my sword, John," smiled Richard. Then he said, more sternly, "But I cannot stand by and do nothing while our honor is impugned and the realm is led astray by the upstart Woodvilles. We put the House of York on the throne to save our country from poor government, and now we see that the same mistakes are being made again. Our course must be corrected before it's too late. Can't you see that?"

"I see only that your pride is injured, Richard, and you have allowed that to poison your mind. And as for you," he said to Clarence as he mounted his horse, "the time has come for you to learn the meaning of honor." Without another word, he spurred his horse and left them where they stood. After a moment's thought, Warwick slapped the duke on the back again.

"Pay him no mind, Your Grace. He has become complacent and too satisfied. It remains to us who have the courage of our convictions to risk the present for the future of our kingdom." Not sure if he had convinced the young duke, he added, "And remember, my daughter will be yours if we succeed." Clarence smiled and nervously nodded his head. "Good, then we understand each other." Warwick had regained his mood.

"Without John our course will be more arduous, Richard. You must at least convince him to remain away from court for a while." The archbishop could not hide his concern.

"I will see to John, you needn't be concerned. He will not oppose me."

I wish I could be sure, thought the archbishop.

CHAPTER XX

"What is this town?" asked Oliver.

"I believe it's Lincoln," answered Samuel. "I remember hearing about its walls."

They had been following Sir Hugh's trail for two weeks now and had reason to believe that they were drawing closer.

"Have you thought about what we'll do when we catch them?" asked Oliver.

"Whatever presents itself, I suppose."

"Just as I feared," Oliver said glumly. "I can't help remembering what happened at Richmond." The thought of that terror-filled morning discouraged him greatly.

"It was different then," Samuel offered. "We were outlaws and running from our own shadows. Now I wear the king's colors and I won't allow him to escape justice."

"But we're still commoners and he a knight of the realm. The townsfolk will side with him, not us. We cannot confront him openly."

Samuel ran his hands along the string of his bow, gaining courage from the feel of it.

"I have no intention of openly confronting him, but I won't hide in the hedges again either. We will know when we've found him before he knows that we follow, and if we're not careless, Sir Hugh will dine with his master in Hell that very night."

Oliver heard the hate in his friend's voice and did not like it.

"We must remember that we're here for the women, not revenge."

Samuel stiffened in anger, but Oliver's gentle demeanor disarmed him in an instant. He thought about Sally and Kate in the hands of that demented knight, and nothing else mattered except getting them back. Looking at the town in the distance, he sighed heavily.

"You're right, as usual, old friend," he said, and took his quiver and bow from his back, loosening the ties to his tunic. Slipping the king's colors over his head, he wrapped everything together and put the bundle under his arm. "It's best we enter town like the peasants we are," he said with a smile. "I'll hide this bundle somewhere near the walls before we enter the gates."

Oliver nodded in agreement and they started down the road. The day was approaching late afternoon and a gentle summer breeze wafted the pungent odors from Lincoln.

"You seem to have adjusted well to your new life," said Samuel. Oliver stomped his feet to clear the dust that had gathered from the road.

"I suppose so, but I never before felt so helpless as I do now. I keep thinking that I've failed our family and that I should have done something to prevent this."

"It is you who has been the truest member of the family, my friend. My brother left his responsibilities on your shoulders to follow his own misguided sense of honor, and I sent my troubles to you and made you pay a very dear price. And you had your own troubles to overcome."

"I have learned to live with my scars, if that's what you mean, but only because once a gentle young man wearing an enemy's colors gave me the strength of his own heart when I had none of my own."

Samuel smiled. "It seems we are doomed to roam the roads of the kingdom together in hopeless quests to find peace."

"We still have hope, Samuel, even when events have led us down these dangerous roads." He saw that the town gate was looming ever closer, and he could make out people entering and leaving on their everyday chores. "Tell me, why did you stay away from your family for so long when it's plain even to you that they are the peace that you seek? Is it possible that you would allow this feud with Christopher to rob you of so much?"

"I had good reason," he answered tersely. "And besides, it should be plain to you that there was no place for me at the mill. I just couldn't bear... " After a short silence, Oliver continued for him.

"You thought everyone blamed you for your father's death."

"I know that they do." Samuel nodded painfully. Oliver took his arm and pulled him around.

"If that's what you think, then you take a fool's burden on yourself." Samuel hurried down the road, but Oliver kept close on his heels. "For God's sake, Samuel, can't you see that you're punishing your family for something they haven't done?"

"What about Christopher? The mill is his by right, and I have no place there."

"Is that what this is all about?" Oliver was incredulous. "You're jealous of Christopher?"

"I'm not jealous, damn you. He has a right to his inheritance without my interference, and I must be content with my fate as a servant. That's what my father ordained for me, and what I must accept. For a short time I thought that I could change my fate, that maybe Kate and I could find a normal life together. But God has shown me the folly of that hope." He was on the verge of tears, but forced himself to go on. "Every decision I've made that might have led me down a different path has led to disaster, and I can't continue to bring misery to them, even if it means never finding the peace that I seek."

"Samuel, please…" but Samuel pulled away and quickened his pace toward town.

At that moment, Christopher and Simon Johnson walked together in a long column of men. They did not know where they were, having marched, mostly at night, for the better part of a fortnight, but they had surely reached the Midlands, much further south than he had ever been before. And Christopher was not pleased.

"What in the Lord's name are we doing in this place?" he asked Simon in a low voice. "I joined this troop to fight for the rights of the Percys, but we've been headed south for weeks. And who are those new men?" He indicated the well-armed footsoldiers marching in the front of the column.

"I told you when you joined, it's not good to ask questions." Simon looked around nervously to see if anyone was too close. "Robin will tell you what we need to know, and everything else is none of our business."

Christopher was growing tired of hearing those words. "I don't see why we can't be told where we're going. And I tell you, those new men look like professional soldiers to me. What would such men want with us, and why would they be under the command of an outlaw like Robin instead of some nobleman?"

"I don't know, and keep your bloody voice down." Simon could see that he was not going to be able to shut Christopher up. "I wondered the same thing myself, but I just can't figure it. They wear no colors, but it's sure that they were supplied by someone of means. And Robin hasn't spoken with anyone, except to give a few orders. It's all very odd, I can tell you that."

There was some disturbance at the front of the column and the mysterious fighting men began to break ranks. The word finally came down that they were to make camp. They had come upon a broad valley that was drained by a shallow, meandering stream, bordered by thick willows. Just off the road before them was a small group of cottages, not enough to even qualify as a village. Several had clearly been abandoned and were in such disrepair that Christopher wondered what kept them from collapsing. Behind the handful of cottages that were still occupied, several vegetable gardens were just beginning to bear fruit, and beyond the gardens were a few virgates of cultivated land. Christopher guessed that the yield would barely support the residents through the winter.

The soldiers began to spread out over the valley, staking out a comfortable place to spend the evening. Those responsible for feeding the men began to round up the meager livestock that sustained the farmers, including several pigs and a large number of chickens. And while the farmers and their families stood by in silence, the gardens were stripped clean of anything edible. Without their stock, they knew, they were likely to end their days as beggars in some nearby town or monastery. One farmer ran from his field when the column arrived and, in a last attempt to save his pigs, yelled at a soldier.

"These fields are the king's own demesne."

"All's the better." The soldier shoved him aside. "He'll find himself the poorer for it."

At least these mystery soldiers were Lancastrian sympathizers, and no friends of the king. But the plight of these farmers made Christopher's heart ache. In the faces of these people who had spent their lives scratching subsistence from these lands, he saw his own family and friends.

Simon led him away. They found a place by the stream that was partially protected from the sun by a stand of willows, and Christopher was pleased to finally get off his feet. Removing his shoes and kneading his feet, he allowed himself to relax to the sound of the water trickling past. For once he would not think of Emma and the children.

Samuel and Oliver arrived at a suitable inn in Lincoln at dusk and decided to get their first full night's sleep since leaving York. It was really not a conscious decision, since they would rather have begun making inquiries that very evening, but upon dropping their packs, exhaustion had overcome them both.

The morning brought a steady drizzle that continued for the entire day and made their search all the more unpleasant.

"I think we should separate," said Oliver.

Samuel frowned. "What if we find them? We'll need each other."

"Perhaps, but it would be preferable for one rather than both of us to be caught."

"All right then, you stay out of sight and I'll start asking questions."

"You're the one who should stay out of sight. Being the soldier, you would stand a better chance of coming to my rescue than the other way around."

"I have great faith in your abilities."

"This is no time to be selfish, Samuel. You know that I'm right and for the sake of the women, stop this. Stay secluded and keep a watch on me."

"Where will you look?"

Oliver pointed toward the main gate where they had first entered town.

"I'll start there and work directly down the street. We'll check every inn and alehouse."

"Be careful, Oliver. For both our sakes." Oliver nodded and headed down the road. As the day went on, Samuel stood in the rain following Oliver from place to place. Sometimes someone would remember seeing the people they sought, but had no idea where they had gone. One tip had brought them to a smith who had changed the shoe of a horse belonging to a man clearly fitting Sir Hugh's description, but he had not known where Sir Hugh and his party went after they left. They had managed to cover their tracks, and Samuel could feel Oliver's growing disappointment as the day faded into dusk.

Turning down a side street lined with inns, Oliver wondered how many more such lodging places they would have to search in this market town, where many country folk came to trade their wares. He entered a small alehouse. There were only a handful of tables with three of them occupied. Oliver came up to the man that was serving them, presuming him to be the owner.

"I seek two men, one with a long scar on his face, perhaps in the company of two women. Can you help me?" The owner glanced at him for a second and continued waiting on tables.

"Do I look like one who takes note of who comes and goes? Anyone who fairly pays for food and drink is welcome here, and I give them their privacy. If you'd like to sit and eat, I'll do the same for you." Oliver had found another dead end, and had not really expected anything else. He was headed for the door when he saw a dirty man with large bags under his eyes motioning for him to come over. Oliver walked carefully over to his table.

"Sit down. I may be able to help you." The man's ingratiating smile revealing that he had only a few teeth left in his mouth. "Come, do you want information or not?"

"Have you seen the man with the scar?"

"I have indeed. It's not easy to forget that face, is it?" Despite himself, Oliver shook as the vision came to mind. "No, I see you agree," the man smiled again. "If I were to find him for you, what could you do for me?"

"What is it that you wish? I have very little of value."

The man leaned back and took a pull from his wooden mug. "Tell me, what is your business with that whore's son?"

"That's for me to know, and I intend to keep it that way."

"I can understand that. But I've seen death in a man's eyes before, and I see it in yours right now, so I'll wager my last penny that you hope to cut his life short."

"You would lose that penny."

"Maybe I would," the man mused almost to himself, "but it would be payment enough for me to see harm come to him. So I'll tell you what I'll do. I'll check with a few of my friends tonight, and if you come to the house behind the King's Bridge bakery at first light, I'll tell you what I've found."

"You say that you want harm to come to the man with the scar. Why?"

"That would be my business, wouldn't it? And, like you, I expect I'll keep it that way." Oliver nodded and stood.

"Then we'll speak tomorrow." The man smiled and gave a slight bow of his head. Oliver turned and left. He guessed that Samuel was watching from somewhere, so he made straight toward their inn at the other end of town. Whatever else he had accomplished that day, he was sure that the dirty man in the alehouse had personal knowledge of Sir Hugh. Samuel entered shortly after Oliver arrived.

"What happened?" he asked.

Oliver told him of his encounter and of the appointment at King's Bridge. Samuel thought about it for a while.

"It should hardly surprise us that someone else would have a quarrel with Sir Hugh."

"Not ordinarily, but this seems a little coincidental to me." He rubbed nervously at a protruding ear.

"I agree, but we can't let this lead get away from us, can we? If the women are in this town, it may be our last chance to save them."

"What will you do?"

Samuel thought for a moment. "Hopefully, no one knows you have a partner, and we should make sure it stays that way. Tonight, I'll go to King's Bridge and see what's there. If it's a place that we can use to our advantage, I'll try to devise something before first light. Tomorrow, on your way there, stop outside the Three Lions Tavern, and I'll get a message to you." He began gathering his things.

"Samuel," Oliver called him back as he was about to open the door. "If we don't see each other again... "

Samuel smiled at his friend. "At the Three Lions tomorrow." And he was gone.

At that very moment, in another part of town, the man who had spoken with Oliver entered a dimly lit room, where he found his master in a dark corner. The dirty man closed the door behind him.

"Someone is looking for you, my lord."

"Will she never deliver?" Edward could not hide his agitation.

"At times I think that women deliberately drag the process out to keep us in their power for as long as possible," answered Hastings. "But we cannot wait much longer, Sire. The latest intelligence puts the rebels somewhere near Leicester." Edward nodded.

"Where are our friends?"

"Lord Herbert has gathered a sufficient following of Welshmen to turn back this rebellion. They have gathered at Edgecott, where they wait for their king to join them. But we must not be late, Sire. We know that the Welsh will lose heart without the king to lead them."

"Very well, William, prepare our escort. We leave within the hour."

Hastings bowed and started for the door when the queen's physician, an elderly gentleman with a red face, burst through.

"Your Highness!" He panted.

"Your news, Doctor. Quickly."

"Your Majesty, the queen has given birth and God has granted her and the child a safe delivery."

"Yes, and... ?" Edward had already surmised the news.

"The queen has delivered a princess."

"We thank you, Doctor. You have our leave to return to the queen, and to tell her that we rejoice at the news and will visit her shortly." The doctor bowed and hurriedly left the room.

"A male heir would have been a greater blessing, Sire."

"God has otherwise ordained." Edward knew that he would have to put this disappointment behind him and proceed with the business at hand. "Go, William, and prepare our escort. We leave within the hour."

Edward went to the queen's place of confinement and was shown his new daughter. He marveled that even moments after birth, she so clearly carried her mother's features, and it was easy for Edward to forget his disappointment. He sat on the edge of the bed while the attendants moved to the corners of the room.

"I am sorry, my lord, that the child is not the heir we need." While tired and still recovering from the birth ordeal, Elizabeth was as beautiful as ever. Her golden hair, damp from exertion, hung in strings around her shoulders, and her sharp blue eyes had lost none of their brilliance. He pushed a few strands of hair from her face.

"We have time enough to produce an heir. She is the very image of her mother's beauty, and will be the envy of the court."

"Have you chosen a name?"

"I had thought of naming her Cecily, after my mother, but after seeing her, I believe that she should be named Elizabeth."

The queen smiled and shaded the infant's face from the sun coming through the huge windows.

"We can honor your mother after I have borne you a few sons." Edward kissed her gently.

"And now I must leave. There are matters of state that demand my attention at Edgecott."

"What business calls you to there?"

"It is nothing to concern you, only some rumors of a disturbance that require my attention."

"It must be some disturbance indeed to demand the attention of the king himself. What have you not told me?"

"Elizabeth, please, it is not wise to trouble yourself so. It is nothing, I assure you."

"My condition will only be made worse by the aggravation caused by your silence. I pray you, sir, tell me what draws your attention to Edgecott."

Edward relented. "There is news of an armed detachment of northern rebels headed this way. It is really nothing, my love. I have already gathered more men than I need to put down this rabble, which is all they are. Now do not concern yourself further in this matter, and I'll be back within a fortnight to see to the christening of our new princess." Kissing her once again, he stood to go.

"Do not underestimate your enemies, my husband. Unexpected is this uprising, and your cousin of Warwick has been too quiet of late to give me comfort." Edward squeezed her hand and left.

Samuel had not been able to recover his bow, since the gates of the city had been closed before they formulated their plan. The gates would remain closed during the night, and even if he were able to convince the gatekeeper to let him out, he would not be readmitted before first light. He resigned himself to doing without.

His inspection of the King's Bridge bakery had confirmed his fears that the place would be ideal for an ambush. The streets were narrow and there were nooks and crannies of all kinds where any number of henchmen could stay out of sight. The bakery was also near the south gate of the town, which would be open by the time the meeting was to take place, giving an excellent avenue for a quick escape. As Samuel considered how to proceed, he could only think of two courses of action. He could return to Oliver and call the meeting off, which would certainly result in the loss of any opportunity to find the women. Or he could seclude himself in one of the crannies of King's Bridge Street now and wait to see who arrived toward morning, which would mean that he would miss his promised meeting with Oliver at the Three Lions. Would Oliver keep the appointment if he did not find Samuel there waiting for him? There was no way to know, but it was clear that the latter course of action was his only option.

As he approached the street near the bakery, he could but hope that no one saw him. The night was dark, and Samuel found himself wondering why he hadn't been blessed with his brother's uncanny night vision. He groped along the buildings on the left side of the street, able to make out only the faintest shapes of the buildings on the other side. The bakery was on a narrow alley that paralleled King's Bridge Street, and could only be reached by the side street. He knew that he would need to position himself to command a good view of both the alley and the side street. When he arrived at the intersection, he found a narrow stairway that led to a door below street level. Standing at the foot of the stairs, the street was chest high, requiring that he stoop low to keep hidden. He sat at the bottom of the staircase and hoped that no one would be using this door until after first light.

At dawn, Oliver, who had not slept at all, walked out of his boarding room and headed to the Three Lions Tavern. He could already see that it would be another cloudy day, and a thin mist chilled him. He walked south along the market street, feeling very much like he did when they had fled Northwood years ago. When he reached the Three Lions, he waited for Samuel.

Finally there was enough light to see clearly, and Oliver searched for some sign of his friend, to no avail. After waiting for as long as he dared, it became apparent that Samuel had not been able to meet him or even get a message to him. Praying that Samuel was safe, he pulled his cloak up around his ears to ward off the dampness and walked quickly toward King's Bridge Street.

When he arrived at the narrow street leading to the bakery, he hesitated for a moment and checked for signs of life. Satisfied, he walked slowly to the alley in front of the bakery. Seeing no one, he began to wonder what his next move would be.

"A nasty morning, isn't it?" The voice came from behind and scared him half to death. He spun to see the man with baggy eyes leering at him, still as dirty as the night before.

"Where in God's name…"

"Sorry I gave you a bit of a fright there, but we can't be too careful, that's sure."

"Just tell me what you've learned."

"I've learned that the man you seek is close by." Oliver was suspicious. "Come, I'll show you the place."

Oliver still saw no one else. But then, this wart of a man had managed to appear out of nowhere.

"Why don't you just tell me?"

"It's in a back street with no description that I can give you, you not being from this town." Seeing Oliver's obvious doubt, he said with a frown, "Come now, I'm risking my own life to bring you there."

"Very well," he nodded.

The man led him further down the alley and then turned down another alley even narrower than the last. They had taken but a few steps in that direction when a strong arm closed around Oliver's neck, immobilizing him. A voice that dripped death spoke quietly in his ear.

"I have learned that it is not always a good thing to find what you seek. But found me you have, and I'll know the reason." Releasing Oliver from his armhold, Sir Hugh spun him around, his huge hand still tight around his throat. The long scar on Sir Hugh's face warped his mouth into a sneer that seemed to define him well. Oliver couldn't have been more petrified. Out of the corner of his eye he could see that two other men stood behind.

"I know this face," said Sir Hugh. "You're the wretch who fled from me at Pontefract." Oliver could not have confirmed or denied it if he'd wanted to, so tight was Sir Hugh's grip on his throat. His vision was blurring. "So tell me, if you're here, your friend the traitor must be near as well. Is it not so?" He loosened his grip just enough to allow Oliver to take some air.

"Speak now or my face will be the last thing you see in this life."

"He is with…the king's guard." Oliver thought it best to tell the truth, which might give Sir Hugh the impression that he was extracting useful information.

"A fitting place for a traitor. So tell me, why then do you follow me?"

Glad to have deflected the conversation back to himself, again he decided to speak the truth.

"You have taken…my wife." He found the grip tightening again, and his face began to turn blue.

Sir Hugh began to laugh, then suddenly flung him against the opposite wall of the alley. Oliver tried desperately to keep his wits, gasping hard for air.

"You can be sure that I'll tend to your lovely wife." Then to his men, "He is no threat, just a dog with delusions. Kill him, and join us on the road. We ride at once." Sir Hugh spun and, with one of his followers, disappeared around the corner. Too stunned to move, Oliver watched as the man with baggy eyes produced a small dirk from within the folds of his cloak and leaned over him.

"You should never have crossed the man with the scar. He always gets the last word." The baggy eyes came close to his face, a look of deadly determination displacing the usual grin. Hoping that the dirty man would make a clean job of it, Oliver closed his eyes tightly and prayed that God would take mercy on Sally. Feeling warm drops on his face, he was surprised to feel no pain as he waited to die. He heard a painful grunt.

He opened his eyes and saw the dirty man lying on the ground, half of his skull missing, his baggy eyes bulging out of his head, never to see the light of day again. He felt his throat and was relieved to feel no cuts, though his face was covered with blood. The sound of a scuffle coming from around the corner drew him back to reality. Struggling to his knees, he crawled to the corner of the alley, where he saw Samuel struggling with the other henchman.

"Samuel!"

Distracted for a moment by Oliver's yell, Sir Hugh's henchman took his attention from Samuel to see what danger Oliver might pose. In that second, instincts honed by years of training under Sir Julian, Samuel drove the heel of his hand straight up into his adversary's jaw, the blow rendering him unconscious. Checking to see that the man was indeed dispatched, he ran back to Oliver.

"Are you all right?"

"I seem to be bleeding," he said, still not in complete possession of his wits.

"Stay here!" said Samuel urgently. "Do you hear me? I have to find Sir Hugh!"

When Oliver nodded, Samuel ran off toward the south gate of town. He arrived just in time to see four riders on two horses ride over a ridgeline and vanish from view.

"Kate!" he screamed, falling to his knees in exhaustion. But he drew only the attention of curious townsfolk.

Through the trees, Robin of Redesdale could see the entire field before him, his captain waiting patiently behind. He watched the Welsh soldiers go about routine chores, and reflected on the long road to this point. They had been marching for weeks with so little hope of success that he wondered if any of his men would have followed him if they knew the truth. But when the new men arrived, everything changed. At least now they had a good chance for success, especially since he had seen the enemy with his own eyes.

Backing carefully away, he signaled his captain to withdraw to where their horses were tethered. As they rode toward the camp, he puzzled over what they had seen.

"It hardly seems believable, but it appears that you're right, Captain."

"I've been about this business all of my life, my lord, and I can read an enemy camp as well as anyone, I'll wager you."

"No need, Captain. I'd not take that wager. But why would they camp here without the archers? Unless their leader is a consummate fool." He looked sharply at the captain. "You're certain that this is no trap to lure us in?"

"As certain as the day is long, my lord. It's much more probable that the archers have not yet arrived."

"If that is the case, when they do arrive, they'll find the battle already fought and lost." He spurred his horse to a gallop.

Arriving at their encampment, Robin gave the call to arms and organized his men into two units. The mysterious men who had recently joined them formed one of the bodies, heavily armed with bows and short swords. The other group consisted of Robin's rabble, Christopher among them, some armed with swords, but most with truncheons and pikes best used for close fighting. Robin passed the word that the enemy was a Yorkist column that had been gathered to hunt them down, and this was their best chance to strike first.

Robin's army made smartly through the woods to within striking range of the still unsuspecting Yorkist camp. The perimeter guards were carefully taken out by a specially trained unit of the first column, whose archers then took up position within arrowshot in strategic locations. When the word was given, the first volley of deadly accurate missiles were sent through the air, and before those in the camp even knew that they were under attack, dozens of them lay dead or disabled on the bloody ground. By the time the alarm was sounded and those in command attempted to array them in a semblance of order, dozens more lay dead from the second volley. With no archers of their own to return fire, the Yorkist army was helpless to defend itself, and fell into turmoil. Robin ordered the general charge and the army erupted from the woods. Christopher ran as fast as he could to close ranks with the enemy. With Simon by his side, they swung their truncheons with bloody abandon, crushing skulls and other bones indiscriminately.

In the moment before the first arrows flew, King Edward sat in the royal tent with Lord Herbert, Sir Julian, Hastings, Earl Rivers, and Rivers' son, Sir John, who had recently scandalized the nobility by marrying the aged dowager Duchess of Norfolk. The king was furious, but it was Hastings that expressed his displeasure for him.

"Why in God's name would you agree to billet the archers separately from the rest of your men, my lord? It is a fundamental error in judgment."

Herbert addressed his response to the king. "Sire, there was nothing I could do. Their captain refused to camp in this place and led his men off. But I assure Your Highness that they will join us now that you have arrived."

"You should have agreed to go along with their captain and camp where he suggested. He is a most accomplished soldier," Hastings said.

"I would have lost face before my men," insisted Herbert angrily. "Such is not the face of leadership required by a fighting force."

"Lord Hastings," the king interrupted, "send a messenger to the captain of the archers and instruct him to come at once, by the king's command."

"I'll see to it myself, Sire." He bowed and left the tent, but a moment later came running back. "Defend the king! The camp is under attack! Follow me to your horse, Sire. Quickly!" he yelled.

They ran outside to find the sky raining arrows. Herbert called for his captain, Rivers and Sir John helping where they could with swords drawn. Meanwhile, Sir Julian, Hastings, and members of the guard escorted the king to his horse through the chaos. It was then that the woods exploded with men charging from several sides, and Sir Julian held the king's horse while he mounted.

"Fly, Your Highness, or we'll surely all be taken!"

Edward spurred his horse and fled toward the rear of the camp. But before he got far, his horse took an arrow in the hindquarter and stumbled to the ground, throwing the king head over heels in front of him. Sir Julian, Hastings, and a few members of the guard, including Stanley, saw the king fall in the distance, and Sir Julian was about to spur his horse in that direction, but was restrained by Hastings.

"The king is taken. We can't help him by dying in this place."

"We have a duty, my lord!" Sir Julian was shocked.

"If he lives yet, they will not harm him. He's too valuable to them as ransom. If he's dead, then we serve no further purpose here. We must flee to serve him again another day."

Dozens of men swarmed between Sir Julian and the place where the king had fallen. He could not have reached him now if he tried. Yelling to the guardsmen who were left, he raised his sword.

"Let's send some to hell, and leave this cursed place!"

The battle was over as quickly as it had begun. The Yorkists that held their positions were massacred, as the king's guard and Hastings made their escape. As Robin and his captain entered the remains of the camp, hundreds of bodies lay mangled, and his men interrupted their scavenging long enough to cheer him heartily.

To Christopher's chagrin, Simon ran forward and grabbed the purse of a decapitated soldier. He retained the contents of his stomach only with great effort. He wondered bitterly if it was for this that he left his wife and children. A man ran to Robin, not able to contain his excitement.

"Robin! We have him, we have him!" he panted loudly.

"Calm yourself and give me a proper report," he said as the captain of the mysterious men joined him to hear the news.

"The king, Robin! We have the king himself!" There was an incredulous silence for a moment, before the captain of the first column took the man by the tunic.

"If he's harmed I'll pull your liver out before your eyes."

The soldier's excitement turned to fear.

"He is well, sir, I swear it. Took a nasty tumble from his horse, but he's none the worse for it." The captain released him roughly.

"Bring him here and see to it that he stays that way." The soldier ran off much less happy than when he had arrived. "A word with you in private, Robin, if you please." Robin nodded toward one of the few remaining tents and accompanied the captain in.

Simon turned to find that Christopher had lost all the color in his face.

"God in Heaven, man, what's wrong?"

Christopher was frantically scanning the encampment, horrified to see all the dead bodies.

"Samuel," he whispered, more to himself than to anyone else.

"Samuel? Who the hell is that?"

"Don't you see? If the king was here, so were his guardsmen."

"That's a certainty. What of it?"

"My brother, Samuel. He's...one of them."

Simon was amazed. "Your brother is in the king's guard?"

"If I'd known that we were fighting against the king himself, I never would have..."

Simon put his hand on Christopher's shoulder.

"Come on, then. Many escaped and I'm sure he's fine, but I'll help you look through the dead. They'll be easy enough to find — the guard wear a tunic with a large yellow sun." They began the horrific search of the bloody remains, Christopher turning each face praying that it was not Samuel's.

Back in the tent, the captain turned sharply toward Robin when they were both alone.

"The king and any other noblemen that we find alive are to be placed under my guard and escorted to the earl. Is that clear, my lord?" Despite the captain's lower rank, it was expected that Robin would follow his commands. "The earl's orders to me were specific in this matter."

Robin knew that he had no choice. The earl's instructions could not be ignored.

"You shall have him, captain, and any others that we find. But now I must find an explanation for this to satisfy the men."

"That's your problem, my lord, not mine. We'll be leaving you at first light."

Waiting for them outside the tent were King Edward, Lord Howard, Earl Rivers, and Sir John, all with wounds but none serious. Edward stepped forward.

"We are your king and expect your obedience."

"Sire," it was the captain who responded, "we acknowledge that we are all your subjects and you shall be treated well, but I must insist that you accompany me when I leave this place."

"To where?"

"It shall be made known to you in good time."

The captain signaled his men, who began preparations to break camp in the morning. Some grumbling could be heard from Robin's men.

"Robin," someone shouted, "the king's a valuable bit of plunder. Where's he taking him?"

"I'll explain everything to you this evening," Robin said. "I promise you we'll benefit from this day as you never dreamed possible."

The king and his friends were escorted away a few moments later, which was none too soon for the captain. He had detested every minute of his time with that undisciplined rabble, and he planned to let his master, the Earl of Warwick, know that he was owed a great deal for this assignment.

Back at the camp near Edgecott, as Christopher continued his grim search, one thing became bitterly clear to him: Robin was not what he seemed. Turning over yet another bloodied yellow-clad body who was not Samuel, he wondered if he would ever see Emma and the children again.

"My lady, the doctor expressly requires that you remain in bed." The queen's sister, Joan, who did not particularly relish her role as lady-in-waiting, was growing weary of trying to keep the queen from exerting herself too quickly after her ordeal.

"Be silent," snapped Elizabeth as if swatting at a fly. It had been a week since there had been any news from Edward. Why would it take so long to dispatch these insignificant rebels? But she knew from painful experience that the fortunes of war were unpredictable at best. "Bring the keeper of my wardrobe. I wish to be dressed."

"My lady, you must not!"

"Do as I say, Joan." She was interrupted by the door opening behind them. The dowager Duchess of Bedford entered with an escort of two servants. Always one of the preeminent ladies of the realm, her mystique had grown even larger since her daughter had been crowned. The years had been kind indeed to a woman of her advanced years, not touching the smooth skin of her face. She was lavishly dressed in a low-necked green velvet gown with a lengthy train. On her head she wore a steepled hennin, which trailed a long mist of fine linen. But Elizabeth noticed only the look on her face where she had failed to conceal a worried frown.

"Mother, thank the Lord," cried Joan. "The queen wishes to be dressed. Please speak to her."

"What is it, Mother?" Elizabeth asked.

"Stop this nonsense, and return to your bed," the duchess said softly. She took her daughter's arm and led her back. "Despite the temptations, we are best served by indirect actions, and do not have the authority to act rashly. I have always thought it better that way, since the power of our sex, while less overt, is clearly stronger if we are patient." She helped the queen into bed and brought the coverlet up to her chin. Sitting on the edge, she took the queen's hand and stroked it gently.

"Tell me your news, Mother."

"There was a battle near Edgecott, and the king's party did not prevail." Elizabeth clamped her eyes closed, her worst fears realized. "But there is no need to fear. I'm certain that the king is well, and that he will soon be back."

"How can you be so sure?"

"It is rumored that the Earl of Warwick has him." Elizabeth gasped. "If true, he will certainly be safe enough. But we may find that the earl now wields more power than we would have hoped."

"But what of Father and John?"

The duchess looked away, trying to keep her legendary composure.

"It is said that they were taken as well. I have not heard further of their fate, but we know that the earl holds no love for them in his black heart. I can only thank God that your brother, Anthony, was not with them."

Elizabeth buried her head in the covers, unwilling to hear more. The duchess and Joan did their best to console her.

That night, exhausted and feeling wretched, Christopher staggered against a tree and wiped the blood from his hands. They had not found Samuel among the dead, though many were so badly mangled it was difficult to be positive. He had lost track of Simon some hours ago. Christopher noticed for the first time that he had wandered near the tent where the king and his party were being held, heavily guarded by the captain's men. Something was not right about those men, and despite his need for rest, he decided to look around, though he stayed well clear of the prison tent. He walked casually toward the back of the encampment where there did not seem to be any guards, and looked into one of the tents that had a flap open. The faint candlelight within yielded no information.

"What are you doing here?" The voice from behind nearly stopped Christopher's heart. He spun to see a guard with sword drawn walking toward him. As he came near, Christopher could see that his clothes were soaked in blood, and the rotting smell of it turned his stomach. "I asked you a question," he snarled. Christopher had to think quickly.

"Robin asked that I keep a watch here." He could only hope that the foul-smelling man did not decide to confirm his story.

"We have no need of help from vermin like you to patrol our camp. Be gone or I'll run you through without a second thought."

Christopher took a step back and was prepared to flee as ordered, but his eyes were drawn once more to the gore on the man's jerkin. It was then that he noticed the tear along the front. No one would have seen it when the soldier was wearing his armor in battle, but the armor was now removed and it was quite dark; the soldier was plainly not concerned anyone could see the heraldic symbol under the torn jerkin. But Christopher could. It was the red Ragged Staff of Warwick. Turning away quickly, he ran as fast as he could, hoping the foul man would not suspect what he had seen.

Once he was safely away, he searched frantically for Simon. Asking several of Robin's men if they had seen him, one finally pointed to a bundle underneath a coarse wool blanket near a clump of hawthorn bushes. Sitting as quietly as possible next to him, he nudged the sleeping figure with his elbow.

"Simon!" he hissed. "For God's sake, wake up."

Simon poked his head from under the blanket.

"Christopher? What in Heaven's name…"

"Robin has betrayed us. We must get away from here tonight!"

Simon was now coming wide awake. He narrowed his eyes in hopes of seeing Christopher better in the dark, but it was futile as only a few nearby campfires gave any light at all.

"What are you saying?" he asked sternly.

"The captain and his soldiers are Warwick's men, I saw the insignia on one of them. I tell you Robin has betrayed us to the Nevilles."

The magnitude of this revelation was almost too much for Simon to understand. Warwick's brother held the earldom of Northumberland, which Robin had claimed he fought to regain for the Percys. That was clearly a lie if he was accepting aid from Neville's brother and had even turned the king over to him. Robin was fighting for the Nevilles, and not for the Percys. "You must be mistaken. He could not do that to us."

"I tell you I saw it. And if you think about it, it's the only explanation for Robin's behavior. Besides, you saw those men fight. They're trained fighting men, not commoners like us. I'd wager they're from the earl's personal guard."

Simon reluctantly nodded his head. It was the only explanation for the odd events of the day. He pulled his meager belongings and the bits of booty that he had collected from the dead into a knapsack.

"Let's get out of here before it gets light. You can use those damn eyes of yours to get us through the woods."

Edward and his friends, Earl Rivers, Sir John Woodville, and Lord Herbert, were escorted to Warwick Castle the very next day. The earl's men were anxious to deliver their prize without delay or incident, and when they crossed the drawbridge into the main court, it was hard even for Edward not to be impressed with the earl's keep. One of the largest castles in the realm, Warwick Castle was built to intimidate. Impregnable walls towered over the moat with pinnacles that commanded unimpeded views for miles in every direction. The earl wanted to advertise not only his power but also his wealth, and the grounds of the castle were impeccably adorned with gardens and statues that gave one the impression that they had journeyed to ancient Babylon. As the king's party and its escort entered the courtyard, Edward found the earl and Clarence waiting for them with several retainers. They all went to one knee. With a sideward glance at his traitorous brother, Edward addressed the earl.

"That knee bends stiffly, it seems to us, cousin of Warwick."

"We are loyal subjects, Sire, and you know me to be an honorable man. But I could no longer brook the corruption of your royal person by the upstart members of the queen's family, and we are determined to correct the wrongs that they have wrought upon the kingdom."

Edward glared at Clarence. "Goes your heart with this as well, brother?" the last word spat like a curse.

"You should have allowed me my proper place in your court. I want only that which is mine by birthright."

"You lost your birthright when you lost your honor to this man."

"You shall see my worth," said Clarence arrogantly. Edward turned again to Warwick.

"What are your intentions with us?"

"Your Highness will be my guest, and will be afforded every courtesy, I assure you. As for these men who have advised you so poorly, their lives shall pay the dearest price."

"They are entitled to the king's justice, cousin."

"They have already been judged by those who are nobler by far." With a nod to his captain, the prisoners were dragged from their horses and bound in a wagon. As the king looked on in horror, Rivers, Sir John, and Herbert were wheeled out toward the main gate. Edward spun on him.

"Where are you taking them?"

"To Coventry for execution. Their crimes demand no less, and the people must see that we have corrected their great wrongs."

"This is a foul deed, Warwick, and there will be retribution, I swear before God in Heaven."

Warwick signaled to the guards. "Take the king to his quarters." When they were alone, he said to Clarence, "We have crossed our Rubicon, my lord, and there is no turning back now."

"I have no desire to turn back, cousin. He has been rightfully served."

Warwick did not even hear Clarence's response, being lost in his own glory. *Now I have imprisoned two kings, and I will not be denied.*

Three hours later, Earl Rivers, his son John, and Lord Herbert were read the charges against them in the central market of Coventry, while a throng of thrill-seeking townsfolk looked on. These lords were not popular among the common people in the best of times, and now, as they were being prepared for death, the town took on a holiday atmosphere. The men's unpopularity aside, there was always a certain satisfaction among the commoners to see such high and mighty lords contemplating their own death and making their final peace with God, for as miserable as a common man's life may have been in comparison, at least they would see the light of another morning.

First Rivers, then Howard, then Sir John were led to the block and without ceremony relieved of their heads, each drawing slightly louder exclamations from the crowd. And when the excitement was over, the heads and bodies were thrown into the wagon, which slowly rolled out of town, children running alongside seeking one last glimpse of the unfortunate lords.

If Castle Colinsworth had been moved to Warwick, it would have fit into the central courtyard of the earl's massive castle, a fact of which Lord Colinsworth was painfully aware. But now he had his prize and with it came hope for the future.

"She doesn't seem so haughty now, does she, Sir Hugh?" They were standing together looking through the small barred window of a stone cell in which Sally and Kate were chained loosely to a wall. A small slit in the outside wall provided the only light to their prison.

"I have delivered as promised, my lord," responded Sir Hugh, "and I will expect the considerations that we discussed."

"And you shall have them, Sir Hugh. Rest assured."

Sir Hugh did not need his assurances, knowing that this man would never dare to cross him. They left the dark chamber and ascended several flights of torchlit stairs until they came out into the great room, light streaming in from high windows along the ceiling. Sir Hugh made himself comfortable in a large chair.

"Now tell me of this news, my lord."

Colinsworth sat in a straight-backed chair opposite the knight. He worried whether his success had come at too dear a price. "Good news, indeed," said Colinsworth, clearing his mind. "It is sure that Warwick has taken the king prisoner and slaughtered his favorites. If we tender our services to the earl, we will surely be handsomely rewarded. It is a rare opportunity, especially since it is well known that Katherine's father, Fitzwalter, has never been a supporter of the House of York."

"Indeed," Sir Hugh said as if to himself, "he will need all the fighting men he can get." Then, having made his decision, he spoke as if making an announcement. "Yes, I will offer my services to the earl. You will keep my prize here, and I will send for her when I'm ready, for I have special plans for the Miller's daughter."

Colinsworth nodded in agreement, not caring what became of Sally. It was Kate who held the key to his future, and indeed a letter had already been dispatched to her father, asking what his wishes were regarding his wayward daughter. But one thing was sure: He'd be damned if he let her get away again.

CHAPTER XXI

Samuel stared helplessly down one road, then another, desperation clouding his capacity to think. Oliver wiped the sweat from his forehead and frowned. It was possible, even probable, that they had already taken any one of a dozen wrong forks they had passed, rendering this decision meaningless.

"We may be headed farther away from them with every step, Samuel. I think it's time we admitted to ourselves that we lost them."

"Are you suggesting that we just quit?"

"Of course not. But this wandering around the countryside is worse than futile. We must try to find news of them."

Samuel collapsed on a large rock by the side of the crossroads, pulling his bow from behind him as he sat.

"If only I'd only had my bow in Lincoln," he said, fingering the bowstring lightly, "the women would be with us now and Sir Hugh would be in Hell where he belongs."

"We probably would have attracted Sir Hugh's attention long before we did, and in all likelihood it would be us who would be conversing with our maker."

Now as the trail grew colder, Samuel wondered if the entire encounter in Lincoln had been for naught.

"We'll continue to the south," he said with new conviction, "and begin inquiries of every villager and farmer we see. He could not have vanished." Oliver offered him a hand up, and together they set off to the south.

Two days later, they found themselves speaking with a sheep herder who swore he saw such a scarred man riding toward Coventry, but he was certain that he rode alone.

"Are you certain that you didn't see other riders, perhaps with two women, coming shortly after?"

"There's no chance of that," the herder said. "I was walking the animals along the road when he passed. He almost trampled one of the sheep." They were crestfallen. If Sir Hugh had left the women with someone else, they would be difficult to find indeed.

"One more question, and we'll thank you for your time," said Samuel. "What is this place here on the hill?" He referred to a small castle that appeared to be poorly kept, wondering if Sir Hugh could have hidden the women there.

"That is Colinsworth Castle," the herder said as he gathered some wayward sheep and continued his journey down the road.

"Do you suppose we should inquire of the castle?" asked Samuel.

"Why? We have our first solid information since Lincoln: We know that Sir Hugh is headed for Coventry. Let's resume the search there."

"Perhaps you're right," he said at last. "Let's head for Coventry as quickly as we can." He adjusted his bow across his back. "And this time he'll find us a more deadly foe," he added darkly.

Hours later, as the last light of day vanished, they found a small rock outcropping not far from the road that would make an ideal place to spend the night where they could not be seen. Samuel had agreed to stand the first watch, and Oliver had quickly fallen to sleep. Sitting in a wedge between two large boulders, Samuel had a good view of the road, and a full moon gave him plenty of light. But he had not realized how exhausted he was, and after only a short while he fell asleep as well.

Knowing within himself that something was wrong, he snapped awake at the sound of soft voices close by. Heart pounding, he cursed himself for falling asleep. Remaining perfectly quiet, he craned his neck to see if he could discern from where the voices had come, and to his chagrin he saw two dark shapes not more than a few paces from where he lay. His bow was at his elbow but the quiver was just out of reach behind him, and it would have been difficult to reach them without alerting the interlopers. Oliver snored, and Samuel's heart sank.

"There! Did you hear it?" one of the intruders whispered. Samuel watched as they separated, each one sneaking around opposite sides of the outcropping. As they closed on where Oliver was sleeping, Samuel knew that once again he had to make a desperate move to save his friend. Lifting himself as quietly as he could to his feet, he picked the stranger on his right and waited until he was within a couple of feet.

"Oliver, wake up!" he yelled as he flew at the dark shape and crunched against the man with all his weight. Together they sprawled on the ground, Samuel landing blows as often as he could.

"Nigel! Help!" his victim yelled, trying to shield his face from Samuel's relentless fists.

Astonished, Samuel recognized that voice and froze. The other man shouted from across the fire pit.

"If you value your friend's life, stop and get off him!"

"Nigel," Stanley called out, beginning to laugh, "it's all right. It's Samuel."

"Nigel?" Samuel was stunned. "Nigel of Devon?"

"Yes, lad, it's me. I thought Sir Julian would have taught you better than to let us sneak up on you." Nigel helped Oliver to his feet. "Sorry to have frightened you, Oliver."

"How in God's name did you find us?" Samuel helped Stanley up.

"Let's light a fire and we'll catch up," said Nigel. "There's much to tell that you must know. These are evil times and we need your help."

They gathered some dry wood and lit a small fire, warming themselves by its meager flames. He saw Stanley's face, and felt horrible that he had raised several welts. One eye was almost swollen closed.

"I'm sorry, Stanley, that I beat you so," said Samuel, "but you took me by surprise, and we have good cause to be jumpy."

"We must press our business," Nigel interrupted. "The kingdom is in evil hands, and the time to act is now." Detailing the battle at Edgecott, Nigel relayed the events that led to the capture of the king.

"One thing is certain, then," said Oliver after Nigel finished, "we will no longer be served by the king's colors on your back."

"That's clear enough," added Stanley. "I've already disposed of mine."

"Tell me," asked Samuel after a moment, "how did you come to find us?"

"I make it my business to be able to find people," said Nigel, "and you were really not that difficult to track." He added a small branch to invigorate the fire. "I had heard of the king's need for men and responded as quickly as I could, but on the road to Edgecott, I met with Sir Julian, who had escaped the carnage."

"Thank God for that," Samuel breathed a sigh of relief.

"There being nothing that we could do at that point," continued Nigel, "Sir Julian asked me to help you. He's quite concerned for your safety, and Stanley asked to join me. So we journeyed to York and heard from your sister what had happened."

"Is she well?" Samuel asked.

"Well enough for a woman with great responsibilities and no help to dispatch them."

"Then Christopher was still not back?"

"She was alone. It was easy enough to follow your path after that. Everyone remembered the man with the scar and the men who inquired after him. I was afraid that you had met your end in Lincoln, but many remembered two men still making inquiries on the road south of town."

"And I have a bloody face to show for my effort," added Stanley.

"I'm glad you're both here," said Samuel, putting his hand on Stanley's shoulder. "We need all the help we can get to find the women."

"I haven't told you the rest," said Nigel. "I just heard from my scouts that Sir Hugh has joined Warwick, and he is there now as we speak."

"But we know that the women are not with him," Oliver spoke for the first time.

"That may be true, my young friend, but there is only one way we'll find out where they are, and that's by hanging the cur by his feet and beating it out of him. And the only way we're going to get our hands on him is by joining with Sir Julian and the rest of the guard and waiting for our chance to rescue the king, which will be soon. I have it on excellent authority that Warwick will move the king to Middleham Castle soon, knowing that its remote location will be more secure. If he succeeds in bringing the king there, we'll not see him again, I'm sure of that."

"It seems we have little choice, once again."

"I promise you, Samuel, that once the king is safe, I'll lend you all the assistance that I can for finding your family, and bringing Sir Hugh to answer for his crimes."

In the firelight, Samuel's eyes found Oliver's, who nodded his assent. They could only pray that the quest to save the king from Warwick would somehow help them find their women.

"It cannot be!" Elizabeth flung a crystal vase against the oak door, where it exploded into a thousand tiny shards. The queen buried her face in her hands, too hysterical to be consoled. Her mother, normally a tower of strength, sat by the fireless hearth, staring into space. Anthony, Lord Scales, who had brought the bloody news to his mother and sister, stood quietly by the leaded windows, engulfed by hatred, but feeling utterly impotent to do anything. He could not find words to console his family; he stood staring at the vast gardens that stretched away from Windsor Castle, clenching his fists.

The duchess had lost a husband once before, but it had not been nearly as painful because the duke had died by nature's course. This, this...murder of her beloved Rivers and her son, at the hands of Warwick, could never be forgiven.

Finally, she straightened her back, wiped her cheeks with her napkin, and stood with dignity. Crossing the room to where Elizabeth still lay in a heap on the carpet, she motioned for Anthony to help her, and together they lifted the queen into a chair. Sitting next to her, the duchess stroked her hair.

"We must have faith that those who have so wronged us and the king will learn the same lesson that has come so painfully to us, and we must be comforted by that." Elizabeth was still buried in her napkin. "Now we must protect ourselves from further insult, and take sanctuary at the abbey in Westminster. We'll be safe enough there."

Anthony was furious. "Run and hide from the man that butchered my father? I'll not do it!"

The duchess slapped him across the face.

"Control yourself," she said firmly. "You are Earl Rivers now, and the Nevilles will not hesitate to take your head as well. We have no friends for the moment who will protect us, and you will not martyr yourself for foolish pride. Look at the queen. Would you have her mourn your death as well?" Anthony could only pace. It was true that he could count on only a few of the noble houses to support him, and even they, with the weakness of his position so obvious, would likely refuse any overt aid.

"What will become of us now?" asked Elizabeth between sobs. "How could this happen? Everything was going so well."

"Perhaps the strength that you sought was best achieved through other means," said her mother. "But these are questions that are better asked in a different place and time. Go," she said to Anthony, "and make arrangements for our swift journey to the sanctuary. We will gather the children and whatever we need to sustain ourselves until fate has shown us a better way."

In the great hall of Warwick Castle, the earl and his brother George, the Archbishop of York, sat at a long table eating the evening supper. The main offering that night was a whole suckling pig surrounded by countless other dishes containing fowl, meat pies, fresh cod and herring, and fruit dishes with apples and peaches from the castle orchard. Warwick still had an ample supply of wine from Bordeaux, which was getting harder to find. The archbishop spoke through a mouthful of bread.

"I wonder that we haven't heard from our brother John since we put the king under our control. I pray every night that he will relent and join with us."

"I have already heard from him," Warwick said casually.

"And you felt no need to inform me? What was his disposition?" George looked at him sharply.

Warwick shrugged his shoulders. "He will not join with us, you can be assured of that. As I feared, he's grown quite comfortable with his new earldom and even went so far as to call our actions dishonorable. This is my thanks for maintaining good government."

"He would make a formidable foe, and we must not divide our family. The scriptures warn against such folly, and for good reason."

"If he had any inclination to move against us, he would have done so by now. No, rest assured that he will not interfere, and, unlike poor Edward, he knows where his loyalties should lie." A page entered the room and crossed over to whisper in Warwick's ear. The earl nodded and he left. "It seems that the nobility is flocking to our banner. The smell of power attracts them from all over the kingdom."

"It should not come as a surprise to you that such people wish to protect themselves from another power shift. Lesser men will always seek to find advantage where the powerful have fallen. It is a lesson that should not be lost on us, Richard."

"I am the greatest power in this land. When men follow me, they can expect great rewards and little risk of failure."

The archbishop took a long drink of wine.

"I only ask that you not underestimate the weakness of your position, and to remember that fate has the constant characteristic of being unpredictable."

The door swung open and two men stepped in. As they approached, the earl and the archbishop stood to greet them.

"Lord Fitzwalter, you are most welcome to Warwick!"

"I thank you, my lord, and hope that I may show my gratitude with service to your righteous cause."

"Your service would do me honor. And you are welcome as well, Sir Hugh. I have heard much of your prowess on the field of battle, and of your service to the Cliffords. It is far better to have you on our side of this brave struggle that we have undertaken for the sake of our realm." Sir Hugh bowed his head in acknowledgment.

"My past service to the Cliffords was honorably dispatched, and I pledge the same to you, my lord, if you are so inclined."

"I am indeed," said Warwick.

"May God be with you, Your Grace," said Fitzwalter to the archbishop, who extended his ring for them both to kiss.

"And with both of you, my sons," he said. "I trust that your journey here was without incident."

Warwick, impatient with the formalities, interrupted.

"Sir Hugh, I have a task of ponderous importance for your first service, and your reputation gives me the greatest confidence that you are the one to undertake it."

"You have only to require it, my lord."

"Good. You shall know of it shortly. Lord Fitzwalter, how many of your men may we expect to help in our cause?"

"Within a fortnight, I can muster a thousand men-at-arms and archers; perhaps more, given additional time."

"Excellent. It may be that we do not need them, but prudence dictates that we prepare ourselves. You must both be tired. You may avail yourselves of any service that I can provide, and I will summon you when the time is at hand." They both bowed their heads and left. Warwick and his brother reseated themselves and continued their supper.

"These former pillars of the House of Lancaster do not sit well in my gut," offered the archbishop.

"Nor in mine, but it's best that we take advantage of the help until it's safe to discard them for more savory friends." He pulled a piece of meat from the pig.

"If the news were better from Northumberland, we would not need them at all," his brother said. "Perhaps I will journey north and plead with our brother to at least lend us some of his considerable resources."

"You can do so if you wish, but I can tell you now that he will not. He's as headstrong as a mule and I know that it would take more than gentle persuasion to alter his thinking." He filled his mouth with meat and drained his pewter chalice of its contents.

"Still," mused the archbishop, "it may be worth the effort."

"Perhaps," Warwick shrugged his shoulders. "You can accompany the king to Middleham. That way you'll have a suitable escort. These are not good times to be out on the roads alone."

George nodded. The events of the last weeks had contributed in no small way to the general lawlessness that prevailed in the kingdom, and the archbishop could not help but wonder what chain of events they had set in motion.

"What is it you hope to achieve now, my brother? Surely you won't place that fool Clarence on the throne in his brother's stead?" Warwick smiled.

"It is still a possibility. As long as he thinks that he may be king some day, he will support my cause. In the meantime, I will take the reigns of government in my own hands until we can be assured that we have a cooperative king. Edward will still sign the proclamations and royal orders, but he will do so at my will."

"How can you be sure that he'll cooperate?"

"His brother Clarence will assure me of that. Edward knows that if he dies his brother will take the throne, a brother whom he knows will do my bidding."

"A precarious situation, playing the brothers against each other."

Warwick sat back in his chair. Precarious indeed, he thought, but he could see no other alternative.

Elsewhere in Warwick castle, in one of the dozens of elaborate guest rooms, Lord Fitzwalter regarded the man with the hideous scar with revulsion that he made little attempt to conceal. Sir Hugh patiently waited for his lordship to speak his mind, thinking to himself what a small man Fitzwalter appeared to be when compared to the mighty earl whose company they had just shared. He was delighted to be once again in the service of one of the great lords, from whom great rewards could be gained.

"I have just received a communication from Lord Colinsworth confirming your news. I trust that my Katherine is safe and unharmed?"

"She is, my lord," responded Sir Hugh.

"And I presume that you have the letter in your possession?"

"She did not have it on her person or in her belongings when we found her in York." Fitzwalter looked sharply at him.

"Your search was thorough?"

"She did not have it, my lord." The response was terse.

"Then she has entrusted it to someone. Who has she been with? Your instructions were to watch her closely before taking her, to prevent exactly this eventuality."

"We searched the man that she was...with, my lord," he was now openly angry, "and it was not among his possessions either."

"Tell me of this man."

"When she left Durham, she was in the company of a soldier who was once employed in Northumberland's guard, but deserted at Wakefield. I was sent to apprehend him, and did so, but he escaped my guard when we were ambushed north of Pontefract. Somehow he managed to make his services available to the king, and has been out of my reach since then, but I assure you that under the current circumstances, he will be mine again before long."

"A soldier in the king's personal guard?" Fitzwalter frowned. "Now that the king is in no position to protect him, I suggest that you find him quickly and ascertain with certainty if she gave him the letter. I should not have to tell you that our support of this haughty earl is only a pretense to destabilize the throne until Queen Margaret and the prince are able to invade. We are closer than most people realize, but our success could hinge on finding that letter. Do you understand that?"

"You needn't fear, my lord. I will find the cur, as God is my witness."

And when I have what we seek, I'll dispose of you and your bothersome daughter.

Kate walked through the dingy halls of Colinsworth Castle escorted by a serving man. She needed to know who was behind these outrages visited upon herself and the Millers, but she was afraid of what the truth would reveal. She would never be able to forgive herself if Sally were harmed on her account. The abduction from York and hellish journey through the country was nightmare enough for a lifetime, and of course Sir Hugh had told them nothing, preferring instead to enjoy their terror.

Once they had reached this dreary castle, they were pushed into a small room somewhere within the rampart wall, where only a small slit for a window allowed any light.

As she was escorted into the central courtyard, she shielded her eyes against the light. There was little activity in this place that, in a typical castle, would be a center for the daily business. Here there was only a single kitchenhand plucking a chicken, and on the allure above the gate a single guard watching them as they walked toward the main keep.

"In here," her escort ordered as he opened the doors leading into the great hall. She stepped into the shadowy hall lit only by the high window openings and saw a dark shape of a man standing by the end of the dining table. Her escort pushed her toward the table. The man stepped into a shaft of light. Her fear dissolved into anger.

"You!" She strode quickly to him and struck him sharply across his cheek. "I should have known you were behind this outrage." Lord Colinsworth smiled thinly.

"I can't tell you how pleased I am to see you again, Katherine, my love."

"You do not have my leave to call me that."

"Ah, but I think that you'll find you have very few rights any more, my love. You see, you are nothing but a common serving girl." Taking her arm, he pulled her roughly to him so that his face was inches from hers. "Such wenches do not have rights, and so I will take what liberties I wish."

"Let me go!" she said, trying to loosen his grip. He released her abruptly so that she fell back into a chair, then took his seat at the head of the table.

"You see all that's left to me here in this room, don't you, my dear? I have paid dearly for my father's allegiance to the House of Lancaster." His family had always obeyed the dictates of their oath to the Lancastrian king, as should have been the sworn duty of all men, but the politics of the time had made that a deadly crime, and now he was lucky to be in possession of his life and this pitiful castle. The look in Kate's eyes repulsed him. "I prefer your hatred to pity, my love," he said bitterly. "After all, you bear no small responsibility for my present state."

"Choices are not always easy to make."

Her response left him feeling empty, like the day she turned from him so many years ago and fled from his life.

"I could have loved you once, Roger, but you left me no choice."

Colinsworth looked at her longingly for a moment before the cloud descended once again.

"I want the letter, Kate. Tell me where it is."

"You already know that I would not give it to you if it were my last mortal act."

"That act may be a great deal sooner than you think, my dear. I will not live in this pisshole of a castle any longer. As soon as I get my response from your father, we will talk again, and make no mistake, I will have my reward. Take her back!" The sentry took her by the arm and shoved her roughly toward the door.

"You already have your reward, Roger," she shouted.

Once again she was led through the dreary walkways and halls of Colinsworth Castle. But the return trip seemed different, for instead of fear of the unknown, she felt anger and guilt. Anger at the men who, by putting their own interests above the truth, had made so many innocents suffer needlessly, and guilt about the poor young woman in her cell who had been drawn into the maelstrom with her.

She was shoved back in her cell and sprawled off balance until she hit the cold stone floor with a thud.

"Kate! Are you all right?" Sally helped her to her feet.

"As well as I can be in such a place as this," she said. "It's time I was completely honest with you, Sally. I owe you that and much more. Please, let me tell you my story and try not to judge me too severely. You must know that I'd rather die than be the cause of any harm coming to you or your family. If I had known they might find me, I would never have let

Samuel get close to me."

"Find you? Who?"

"I am not what I pretend to be, though I wish to God I were. My father is Lord Fitzwalter, a loyal supporter of the House of Lancaster, and one of King Henry's most trusted advisers. We spent much of my youth at court." She became wistful, remembering those comfortable days. "My mother died when I was very young, and my father enjoyed having me with him, tolerating all kinds of selfish behavior from me. I am ashamed to remember what I was like. I think I was simply insufferable, but my father could not bring himself to correct me. It was only the kind act of a young girl who risked her life to save mine that shamed me into becoming a wiser person." It took a moment before she could continue. "When I came of age, I became a lady-in-waiting to Queen Margaret. I found that things were not well at court. The king suffered from bouts of insanity, and the absence of a king's strong hand gave rise to much disorder. I saw it grow worse every day, and the hatred between Queen Margaret and the Duke of York was at the heart of every evil deed. It was clear that if Margaret did not bear Henry a son, the Yorkists would inherit the throne, a fate the queen would have sold her soul to avoid. And perhaps she did."

"You see, Henry was impotent, or at least unwilling. Even when he was of his right mind, he refused to visit her bedchamber. Perhaps it was not always so, but certainly he never went to her in those days that I was lady-in-waiting, and I knew her anguish."

"These days the queen only consults French priests in spiritual matters. She is deeply devout, you know. But at that time she had an English confessor, Father Stephen, whom she trusted implicitly, and it was to him that she confessed the great sin she had committed, a sin even her ladies-in-waiting did not know. She confessed to Father Stephen that in her desperation to bear an heir for the House of Lancaster, she had bedded the Duke of Somerset, father to he who was recently beheaded at Hexham, and it was by that duke, a cousin to King Henry, that the Prince of Wales was fathered."

Sally was incredulous. "If that's true, there is no heir to the House of Lancaster."

"An even greater folly was to follow. She gave a letter to Father Stephen to deliver to Somerset in which she asked him for military assistance against the Duke of York, for the sake of the son they had conceived together." Kate paused to let the significance of her words sink in, and wrung her hands. "By telling you, I may have jeopardized your life, but I don't see how your knowing can make matters any worse than they already are."

"How did you come to know of the truth?" Sally was dazed.

"Father Stephen could not tolerate the thought of a bastard on the English throne. I assume he felt divulging the contents of the letter was a way of getting the truth out, while not breaking the seal of the confessional. He intended to hand it over to the Bishop of Bath, one of King Henry's closest advisors. But he chose poorly, because the bishop is an ambitious man. When he heard of the letter, the bishop knew if he were to expose Father Stephen's actions to the queen, the rewards would be great. The bishop's manner made the priest suspicious and he insisted on presenting the letter to the king directly, upon which the bishop called for the guards. Father Stephen fled." Kate paused as the memory became more painful. She remembered the events as if they had just happened. She told Sally how Father Stephen had come to her room and left his burden with her. "He was captured in another part of the palace and was tortured for days before he died, but they were never able to rip from him the location of the letter. He sacrificed his life to protect me." Tears welled in her eyes. "Of course, there was no way for me to get the letter to the king. He was bereft of his wits, and isolated from everyone by the queen's command. I left the palace as soon as I had a good excuse and went directly to my father, whom I had always known to be a loyal supporter of the king. But when I told him of the letter, to my surprise, he berated me for even considering turning it over to the king, insisting that it would be the end of the House of Lancaster and demanding that I give it to him to destroy. But how could I have done that, knowing as I did the way Father Stephen had been made to suffer in his final hours? Instead of revealing where I had concealed the letter, I had a horse saddled and fled his house, to the only other men I thought would help, Lord Colinsworth and his son, Roger, whom my father had contracted me to marry."

"I admired Lord Colinsworth and knew him to be an honorable man, and Roger was kind enough when we were introduced. But when I arrived, desperate for help, Lord Colinsworth was off on one of the queen's campaigns. Roger allowed me to stay with him. Finally, I told him of the letter. He agreed to help, and offered to let me stay as long as I needed, but I did not truly know Roger. The next day, as I was walking in the courtyard, I overheard him tell a stablehand to dispatch a rider to my father. I fled in the guise of a serving girl and left my life as Lord Fitzwalter's daughter behind me. I wandered north away from those who knew me, taking charity to survive until the Bishop of Durham gave me a job in his kitchen."

"How difficult it must have been for you all these years." Kate smiled thinly at her gentle cellmate.

"Being a serving girl instead of Lord Fitzwalter's daughter was much easier than I had expected, though I should never have worked for the Bishop of Durham since it was inevitable that someone would recognize me sooner or later. But I fell in love. It was foolish of me to think that I could start a new life with your family, but you were all so kind, and I thought that I could live that life and forget the past. Instead I brought this fate upon you."

"You have no cause to feel that way," Sally brushed Kate's thick brown hair from her face. "Samuel's love for you makes you one of us, and the burden that you carry is our burden as well. I am glad to share this pain with you."

Tears ran down Kate's cheeks as she embraced the woman she prayed would one day be her sister. The weight that had tugged at her soul was lighter for the first time in years.

Sally did not ask where the letter was. She knew that was a cross Kate would have to bear alone.

"Tell me of the young girl who saved your life."

Kate smiled. "It was the Lady Elizabeth Woodville, she who is now our queen."

The Tower of London was the great fortress built by William the Conqueror on the shores of the River Thames in London four hundred years before Edward became king. Many additions had been made, but the imposing square keep that the Normans built for William, called the White Tower, was still its most striking feature. Surrounded by two more or less concentric walls, it contained the royal apartments that every monarch since William had used as a secure stronghold within the city.

Prisoners were brought into the fortress through the Traitor's Gate, which opened to the river, away from the curious eyes of the public. Behind the Traitor's Gate, within the inner wall, stood the Wakefield Tower, a round keep with no openings except for the heavy wooden doors leading to the lower chamber, and a single set of long, narrow windows that looked out from the upper chamber. It was the first imposing structure seen by incoming prisoners. Added by previous monarchs as part of the royal quarters, it had been converted to a secure prison for wayward nobility some two hundred years past.

The upper chamber of the Wakefield Tower was a high vaulted room with eight stone ribs supporting the ceiling. Along the walls were alcoves for three doors, the windows, a fireplace, a sleeping area, and a small chapel. One of the doors hid the spiral steps leading to the lower chamber, and the other two doors led to the opposite sides of the allure atop the inner wall. All were securely locked.

The dim light revealed a man lying on a pallet of rotting wood. His tattered clothes disguised the fact that this was Henry VI, once king of England and France.

The days had passed anonymously since his imprisonment. But he knew where he was, and who he was. A tin bowl of uneaten slop and a stale hunk of bread rested by one of the heavy wooden doors that separated his kingdom from the world outside.

Henry noticed something in the room and rubbed his eyes to clear his vision. A mist had formed into a shimmering shape. He could see a man coalescing within his cell, silvery at first, then gaining definition. Henry propped himself on one elbow and stared at a young man with fair hair and gentle countenance, wearing a white tunic with the Falcon-and-Fetterlock crest emblazoned on the chest, with white leggings and bare feet.

"Do you know me?" the vision asked in a voice as soft as silk.

"I know the crest you wear is that of the House of York," answered Henry, still trying to focus.

"I am Edmund, Earl of Rutland."

"I was told you were dead." He pondered the problem for a moment, then shrugged his scrawny shoulders. "No matter. Have you come to execute your brother's awful justice on my person? I wish you would, as I have suffered this wretched place too long, and have heard the king is a just man."

"I have not come on my brother's behalf."

"A pity." Henry said. "Then I wish you would leave me in peace."

"Sit up and look on me, great king. I have come to give you strength."

Henry struggled to sit up, not certain why he felt compelled to comply.

"Why would the brother of York wish to give me strength? Are we not enemies?"

"You have already seen that you will rule the land again. You must prepare yourself."

"I was hoping that vision was flawed, or that its true meaning was hidden from me. I have no wish to rule again. Please, I am content with my condition."

"Your fate is sealed, and my brother will come for you when the struggle is done and the night is cold. But before then, there is still one who will need you, and you must be strong."

"I can do nothing for you." Henry stretched his tired back and yawned. "Seek out your brother who sits upon my throne."

"Within each of us dwells the power to achieve our dreams, if they are worthy of achievement. I am only here to remind you of that which you are already aware. The day will come when our houses are united, and these struggles will occupy meaningless pages of history. But you will be remembered fondly by your people, and what better legacy could you hope to leave?"

"You have chosen to be my enemy." Henry waved his hand as if to dismiss him.

"I was never your enemy, great king. I only followed the path that I considered to be God's will, and only at the final judgment will we know the nature of truth. Before that day, we are all united only by our common fate."

"I never asked to be king, but for that crime I am held in this wretched place. How can you speak of a common fate when your brother sits on my throne and you can go as you wish to feel the warmth of a summer breeze on your face and to walk in the forest when the flowers carpet the soil?"

"We are the same. You must never doubt that." Slowly, Edmund lifted his tunic, exposing a deep gash below his sternum, the torn tissue within still oozing blood.

Henry looked for a moment at the awful wound, then squeezed his eyes closed and lay back on his bed.

"Will I suffer?" he asked softly.

The next day, the morning shift guard was surprised to see that the food in Henry's cell had been consumed for the first time in many days.

CHAPTER XXII

"**I**t joys me to see you again, my boy."

Sir Julian clapped Samuel on the shoulder. Although he was not happy to be back among the guardsmen when Kate and Sally were still missing and in danger, his heart was glad to see his old mentor again. Indeed, the welcome he received from everyone in the small camp near Nottingham made him feel as if he had been away too long.

The journey south from Lincoln had been slow due to the deplorable condition of the roads. Samuel was accustomed to roads that were not maintained and horribly rutted, but early spring storms had taken an even harder toll this year, and his small party had frequently found themselves leading the horses through knee-deep mud. Nigel told them that most of the common folk were not inclined anymore to risk the lawless roads, frequented as they were by bands of cutthroats.

Use of the old Roman road that led north to York made the way easier, but even that marvel of ancient achievement, which had carried travelers for more than a thousand years, was now badly decayed. It had taken them a fortnight to make a journey of a few days, and they had arrived later than they had hoped.

When they arrived, they were relieved to hear that the earl's party had not yet passed through the deep copse where they waited. Nigel's informants had reported that a party of several hundred men were on their way, escorting the prisoner king from Warwick Castle to Middleham Castle, another of Warwick's magnificent holdings in the northlands near Richmond. It appeared that the horrible condition of the roads had slowed their progress as well.

Hastings, who had remained with the remnants of the guard since the king's capture, had raised about a hundred archers from nearby towns, still no match for the earl's small army. Only a surprise could even the odds, and the woods made that possible. While Nigel and Hastings huddled in a tent devising a strategy, Sir Julian, who had no mind for such things, preferring instead to meet an enemy honorably on an open field, found Samuel for a talk. They sat beneath an enormous oak that dominated the road.

"Thank you, Sir Julian. I am pleased to see you all again. I only wish that Kate and my sister were safe. Concern for them saps my resolve for these matters."

"You needn't explain yourself to me, lad. I know these have been difficult times for you, and, God knows, I've tried to help when I could."

"Please don't think me ungrateful. I will never forget what you've done for us. But I'm just one man of thousands to the king, but to my family…" He found himself unable to finish, caught by the irony of his situation. After all, it was he who had avoided his family for three years.

Sir Julian fidgeted with his thick white beard. "The realm has not been healthy for many years, lad. Probably not since the Lancastrians first usurped the throne from Richard II some seventy years ago. Since then, the noble houses have feuded for any advantage, and those who have been the most successful have paid the dearest price. You can take some solace in that, for the pain that they've caused you."

"Unless Kate and Sally are returned to us safely, I can take solace in nothing."

The old knight nodded in understanding.

"Sir Julian," a voice came from behind. Oliver approached from the camp. The sun was setting behind him, and his protruding ears cast shadows along the sides of his narrow face. "Sir Julian," he repeated. "Lord Hastings requests that you join him in his tent." The old knight sighed and lifted his ample body heavily from the forest floor.

"You should both get a good rest this night," he said as he brushed the dust and leaves from his leggings. "Tomorrow we tangle with Warwick, and we shall need all our wits about us.

Oliver took the spot next to the old oak that the knight had vacated.

"I don't want to be here either, Oliver," Samuel said, noting his friend's unease. "I just don't know what else to do."

"Nor do I, so you needn't mind me. And for God's sake, if you start to blame yourself for all of this again, I'll not listen."

"Who else could I blame?" Samuel said bitterly. "If I hadn't sent Kate to you, you'd be safe in York right now with Sally and the children by your side."

"You haven't learned anything, have you, Samuel? Are you so full of yourself that you assume that all the world waits upon your actions? Our decisions shape our lives. It's who we are. If we can't change what has passed, it's pointless to dwell on it. All you can do is remember and learn." Samuel looked up at the green leaves and watched as the setting sun cast the last rays of the day.

"Perhaps," he said after a moment. "But living with past mistakes also requires that we atone for them in the end."

"Only if you accept that they were mistakes in the first place. I see no such flaw in your past actions."

Samuel began to feel the fatigue of the long road. He closed his eyes and took a deep breath.

"You're a good friend, Oliver," his voice became slurred.

Oliver watched as Samuel slowly drifted into sleep, taking his cloak and gently putting it over him. Events had indeed been cruel, he thought, and he wondered if it were their fate to die in the morning, in the impossible attempt to capture Sir Hugh and extract their women's location from him. If so, he knew his soul would never rest, and at that moment, he knew exactly how Samuel felt.

In the morning they were awakened by the morning watch, the camp already alive with activity. Some of Nigel's men had returned with news that Warwick's column had camped only a few hours away and would soon be upon them. No cooking fires were lit and Hastings and Sir Julian arranged the men into two groups, the guardsmen in one group with half the archers, and the remaining archers in another, to be commanded by Hastings.

Sir Julian arrived, already fitted in his armor, a page by his side carrying his family colors.

"Samuel, I ask that you join the guard and myself. We are the ones who will most likely cross swords with Sir Hugh." Samuel nodded tightly and, suddenly feeling fully awake, set about organizing his quiver. "Oliver, you must quiet the horses while we spring our surprise on the earl."

Oliver nodded his agreement.

Sir Julian motioned them to join his group where the men waited. The first group to move was Lord Hastings' archers. He led them out of camp on foot and, to Samuel's surprise, directly away from the road, onto a narrow and ill-defined footpath that they followed in single file, dodging low branches and thick underbrush all the way. When the last of them were gone, the guard and several dozen archers began to dig themselves into places of concealment.

When he had everyone where he wanted, Sir Julian went from group to group giving them directions. Oliver was placed well down the footpath where Hastings had led his men, holding three horses by their reins and comforting them into silence. They were the only horses in camp, except for the one Hastings rode at the head of his column. When Sir Julian was satisfied that everyone knew their role, he found a place of close concealment for himself directly between the guard and the archers stretched out along the footpath.

The Earl of Warwick, the Archbishop of York, and the Duke of Clarence rode directly behind the vanguard of their column, feeling reasonably comfortable now that they were approaching Middleham Castle, which was only another day's ride. The earl made a mental note that he would have Edward sign an order to make a priority of improving the roads between Warwick and Middleham, his two favorite castles.

Edward rode several hundred yards behind, bound to his horse and guarded by Sir Hugh and, behind them, the remaining few hundreds of his column. Warwick would soon have the king safely ensconced at Middleham, where he would decide the king's fate, just as he had when he created him king. He watched as the vanguard entered the deep copse and called for his mounted messenger.

"Ride to the captain and warn him to be vigilant through these trees."

"Yes, my lord," he replied and was gone.

"I've never seen you so edgy, Richard," said the archbishop. "If I didn't know better, I would suspect that these proceedings are beginning to take their toll on you."

"I'll feel well enough when we get to Middleham. But there is much to be done and I must have more support."

"I'm sure Lord Fitzwalter's men will be with us soon."

"Yes," Warwick nodded, "but we both know that if John were to join us, the battle would be won." The Earl of Northumberland had not answered any further communications, but they still had hopes that he would side with his family and raise armies in the north. Perhaps when he saw that Edward was securely under Warwick's control, John would have no choice.

"At least it appears that he has not raised troops against us, or we would have known by now," replied Clarence.

The vanguard had been swallowed up by the woods and they themselves were now entering its fringes. The trees thickened quickly as they went on, blotting out the early morning sun.

Further back in the column, Sir Hugh placed the king directly in front of himself. When the road was straight, he could see the earl and his party riding well ahead of his position, but most of the time only a few hundred feet of the road were visible. Behind him, hundreds of footsoldiers followed, laboring through the thick mud that lay deep on the road. Suddenly the dreaded sound of arrows whizzing through the air assailed his ears.

So unexpected was the strike that Sir Hugh could not identify from which direction the airborne death was coming until the next volley fell on them. The arrow from that volley that would have killed him bounced harmlessly off the breastplate of his armor, but the path around him was already littered with dead soldiers. Screaming for support from the soldiers in the rear guard, he knew that a third volley was already on its way. Quickly dismounting, he avoided two arrows that sailed directly through the space that he had just vacated. His horse, however, was not so lucky. Taking an arrow deep in the ribs, it reared in agony and then fell thunderously to the ground.

It was then that he finally saw the enemy. A small group burst from the woods on the opposite side from where the arrows had come. They wore the Sun-in-Splendor emblem of the king's personal guard, and Sir Hugh knew that these were formidable fighters. He drew his sword and prepared for the attack, but instead, they seized the king's horse and fled into the woods.

"After them!" Sir Hugh's scar turned vivid red with anger. The attack had been so precisely executed that very few of the hundreds of men in Warwick's column even knew of the strike, much less had been able to help. "After them, you fools!" he screamed again. But as the soldiers ran into the woods, they were cut down by renewed arrow strikes, and made no progress forward until new waves of soldiers were brought up from the rear. Sir Hugh could see the archers peeling off further down the path that had swallowed the king, and knew that they would soon be out of reach. It was then that he spotted Samuel among the archers in the trees. He was not accustomed to being the hunted, especially when the hunter was one that he should have seen hanging from the gallows long ago. Hiding behind the carcass of his horse, he frantically ordered the soldiers into the face of the wilting enemy fire.

Samuel had picked his targets carefully. With his first shot he killed the footsoldier closest to the king, and then looked to find Sir Hugh. At this range he could easily have ended the devil's life but knew that he would never find Kate if he did so. Instead, as he was instructed, he killed another soldier near the king. With his third shot, however, he wanted to bring Sir Hugh to the ground. He aimed at the hinged area between the plates of his horse's armor and let loose a precision shot that found its target. An instant later he stared horrified as Sir Hugh dropped off the side of the horse just before it went down — had one of his fellows shot him? After a moment, Samuel saw he was still alive. It would take more than a chance arrow to kill such a person.

The guardsmen on the other side of the road made their bold attack and charged past Samuel with the king. Sir Julian gave the order to begin falling back, and when Samuel saw the reinforcements gathering, he knew that he was not going to have his conversation with Sir Hugh on that day. He fell back with the rest of the archers along the path and then began to run through the woods with the others. They broke out into a clearing and immediately saw the rest of Hastings' plan. There, on the other side of the clearing, were several dozen archers protected by the trees. The guardsmen crossed the clearing and took up position behind them, and the earl's men who ran into the clearing after them were slaughtered by the dozen. They broke and retreated.

Knowing that it would take time for them to regroup, the guard vanished into the woods to a prearranged meeting place, where it would have taken a miracle for the earl's men to find them. Further past the clearing where the carnage had taken place, Oliver was holding three horses, as was his charge, when two mounted members of the king's guard came trotting down the path leading Edward's horse by the reins. The guardsmen helped the king from his horse and cut the ropes that bound his hands.

"Oliver," said Edward with a smile. "We are glad to find you well."

"I thank Your Highness, and am joyed to see you delivered from your enemies." At that moment, Sir Julian, Hastings, and Nigel came running down the trail with several more guardsmen.

"Sire, we must be gone. Warwick will surely pursue and we are still greatly outnumbered."

"Where will we go, William?" asked Edward.

"I suggest we make all speed for London, where we will fortify ourselves and reclaim what is rightfully yours, my lord."

Edward nodded and remounted his horse, while Hastings, Sir Julian, and Nigel mounted the horses that Oliver had held.

"We hope to see you again in better times, Oliver," Edward said kindly. The former page bowed and the king's party was gone.

Back at the road, Sir Hugh returned from his search of the woods, mortified by what had happened and dreading having to make his report to the earl. Warwick was impatiently waiting with the archbishop and Clarence.

"Well?" he asked sharply.

"My lord," said the knight, "we continue the search, but the woods are deep and archers hide behind every tree."

"Fool!" hissed Warwick. "You let them take the king right out of your hands."

"There was little that I could do, my lord. The attack was well planned." Sir Hugh knew the earl was right, and that he had failed miserably to dispatch his duty. A rider came galloping up the path from the south.

"My lord, you must flee! The Duke of Gloucester has raised an army and is moving quickly to where you tarry."

Warwick could not have been more surprised. He had been given no news that the king's other brother was raising an army. He had underestimated the young duke.

"How strong is he?" he asked quietly.

"Their number was not reported to me, my lord, except that they are from the Welsh marches and make their way here with haste."

Welshmen. He shuddered to think of the fierce fighters who had been unfailingly loyal to the House of York, a fact that had given him great comfort in the days when he had also been a Yorkist supporter.

"We must make quickly for Middleham," said Clarence. "We will be safe enough there until we can raise more men. If my brother can raise an army, then so can I."

"From behind castle walls that are besieged by the king's men?" The archbishop was amazed by the duke's stupidity.

Warwick was brooding on his horse, stunned by the rapid turn of events. An hour ago he was the master of the realm; now he was but hours from losing his life to the headsman. Of course, his brother was right. To retreat behind the walls of Middleham would secure their safety, but while they were holed up in fear for their lives, the king would secure the throne and have them declared outlaws. None of the noble families would come to their aid in such a state, and it would only be a matter of time before they were Edward's prisoners.

"We have only one course left to us," he said at last. "We must flee to France. Louis will not deny me, and I am still the captain of Calais. We can land safely there."

"We'll be attainted and lose everything," Clarence objected.

"Louis will give us aid to retake the kingdom, and then we can reverse any attainder. It is our only hope." His manner made it clear that he would not entertain any further discussion on the topic.

"I agree," said the archbishop, "you must go. But I will remain here. My office will protect me from the king's wrath, and though I'll be closely watched, I can be of greater assistance to you here while I await your return. But now you must make haste, as many preparations must be made for your passage to France before the king has time to regain control."

Warwick nodded and spurred his horse to the north. As he rode with the few men that remained of his escort, he glanced through the woods that had swallowed up his great prize, and allowed bitterness to grip his mind.

Think not, Edward, that this is how it will end. I will not be so easily deprived of my destiny.

Sir Hugh was equally angry. He was to have been the earl's trusted assistant. Now he could only follow an outlaw to a foreign land. Remembering the face of the miller's son among the guard during this attack, hatred consumed him. The miller's women were safely bestowed, he thought, and Colinsworth will not dare release them, on his life. *No, I will have my revenge for this day, be assured of that, young guardsman, and all your arrows will not save you.*

That evening, a cool spring night in York, Emma sang a gentle song to Alice, easing her youngest into sleep. Sarah and John shared the back room nearest the mill and had put themselves to bed. They were old enough to see how difficult times were for Emma and were doing their best to shoulder burdens that were never meant to be borne by ones so young. Still only four and five, John and Alice spent the day cleaning the winter's debris from the vegetable garden that would soon need to be planted with the early lettuce, carrots, and radishes.

Emma snuggled the blanket around Alice and gently kissed her cheek. The girl was developing her mother's round face, but her hair was dark, like her father's. Emma moved to the cooking area, where there was still a small flame in the hearth to provide some heat in the room, and began her usual routine of preparing the maslin for the next day's bread. This mixture of rye and barley was a favorite of the children, probably because it was such a common part of their diet. Doing her household chores gave her a sense of continuity, and therefore comfort, that she sorely needed these days.

She stopped abruptly when she heard the unmistakable sounds of footsteps approaching the door. Ever since Sally and Kate's abduction, she feared anything that came through that door. The steps stopped and someone pulled the latchstring. The door swung open and Christopher stood on the threshold.

At first Emma was so stunned she could not move. Christopher stepped inside, so obviously exhausted that his knees almost buckled from the exertion.

"Emma...," he said, lost for further words.

She rushed to his arms and they embraced until Christopher had to sit. She led him to the table and found the basin of water that she kept by the hearth. Filling a wooden bowl, she handed it to her husband, who drank deeply as if he had not tasted any in days. It seemed to give him strength, and Emma filled the bowl again. They sat together at the small wooden table and said nothing, until Christopher made to speak. But before he could say anything Emma put her fingers on his lips.

"What could you say to me, husband? Perhaps it is best that you let me assume the best and leave it at that, for my heart is damaged and I fear...that there may be no way to heal the hurt."

Her words, spoken with such difficulty, wounded Christopher more deeply than any sword could have. He hung his head, unable to look at his wife. But he knew for certain that if the healing did not begin at that moment, it never would.

"I know now what a fool I've been, but I cannot change what has passed. I wanted only to make a difference...to do something to make things right."

"And what of your family? What of the difference that you made here?" She tried to keep herself from dissolving into anger.

"I know. I had to learn the hard way." He was consumed by the weight of remorse. "I came back only to see if I learned in time."

"Those are still your children in there, and your nephew who can only pretend to be brave while he prays for the safe return of his parents some day."

"Safe return? Safe return from where?"

"My God, you don't know."

"Know what?"

"The devil who took your father from Northwood took Sally and Kate. He came right here and took them both." She had replayed the horror in her own mind so often that she could retell the story without breaking down. Christopher was not so well shielded.

"Sir Hugh? God's angels help them." He buried his face in his hands.

"Samuel and Oliver went after them, but I've heard nothing for months, and I fear the worst."

"Samuel? He was here?"

"He came to get Kate, but was too late. Surely you knew that he would come after her sooner or later?"

The weight he'd been feeling before was now a millstone that had fallen on him.

"How in God's name did you manage by yourself?"

The memory of the past months made her tired just to think of them, but she straightened her back.

"By doing what had to be done. I took on an apprentice to help with the mill, and the children helped where they could. We found ways to survive."

Christopher stood and walked to the linen behind which Alice slept. Pulling it slightly aside, he peered in on her, barely able to see her through the darkness. He listened for her gentle breathing as he had those days when she was so ill, right before he had deserted his family.

"What have I done?" he murmured softly to himself. Then returning to Emma, he said, "I cannot change what has passed, but my course is clear to me at last, if you'll have me."

"Have you been away so long that you do not already know the answer?" she said.

"Yes, perhaps I have," he answered pensively. "But at least this much you have gained: to know that I will never leave you again, though the devil himself calls for me."

Emma knew her husband well enough to know that he would rather die than break the pledge he made, and it was the only thing he could have said that would have made a difference.

The people of London were only too pleased to open their gates and welcome King Edward back. The city had been racked by disorder and violence since Warwick's revolt. The sheer magnitude of the unrest had been more than the civil authorities could control, and the strong hand of a king was needed. Once news spread that the king was again free and supported by the Duke of Gloucester, whose army had chased the Earl of Warwick from the kingdom, Edward had no problem raising support from among the nobility. John Neville, the Earl of Northumberland, had even come to him with fresh troops, demonstrating at last to whom he was loyal.

On his way to Westminster Palace, Edward first stopped at the abbey and collected the queen and her family, who had taken refuge within the sanctuary. He had gathered several thousand men-at-arms to accompany him as he rode toward the city, and now they had been posted around the city to bring order.

Edward hastily called for a meeting of the Privy Council, and as he sat before them, he wondered if he could trust any of them. But he knew that if he couldn't, his throne was doomed anyway. With him were his brother Gloucester, Northumberland, Hastings, Lord Scales — who was now Earl Rivers upon the death of his father — Nigel of Devon, and Sir Julian.

"Lord Hastings," Edward said, his manner still confident, "send quickly to our garrison in Calais that the traitor Warwick shall not be admitted upon pain of death. I'll not have him given comfort on English soil."

"It shall be done, Sire," Hastings said forcefully. He could see that Edward was not the same young man to whom he had been a companion for so many years. The easy smile and warmth were gone.

"Rivers, to you we entrust the safety of London. Take what men you need from our troops and see to it that the city is secure." Rivers bowed his head in acknowledgment. "Come and receive our dearest thanks, our brother of Gloucester, for you have given us hope for the future, and have incurred a debt of us that can never be repaid." Gloucester embraced him. "With loyalty such as yours in the face of such dishonor, we may always know security. Your rewards will be commensurate, you may be assured."

"My reward is to see Your Highness safe from his enemies and to be the scourge of those who would oppose your Holy claim."

"And you always shall be, we know it. For now, be content with all those titles and lands that before this day belonged to your false brother, Clarence, for never again will he stand in our good graces." The lords in the room looked at each other with surprise. The gift of Clarence's lands and titles was an immense one, and would make the young duke certainly one of wealthiest men in the realm. Most assumed that Edward would keep the wealth from those lands to help pay off some of his many debts. Turning his attention to Nigel, Edward said, "Nigel of Devon, approach and receive our thanks as well. Be it known by all those present and by our pronouncements hereafter that we create Nigel of Devon a knight of the realm. Rise, Sir Nigel, and accept our loving embrace."

It was an honor that Nigel had not expected, and for which he was extremely grateful. But he had risked everything supporting this king in the face of great danger, and knew that he had earned this new title.

"When our time serves us better, we will make due note of all those who have helped us in these trying times of treason and thank all who have deserved our love. For now, we must look to those who need us. So please you all to attend us here again when we have further news of our dangerous cousin of Warwick. Lord Hastings, we have further need of your counsel." Edward stood and left with Hastings close on his heels. Sir Julian and Nigel waited until they were alone.

"I have never known a knighthood more deserved, Sir Nigel. May you wear the title well for many years."

"My thanks to you," he said. "But I fear greatly for us all that toil in King Edward's service. This was a strange gathering of lords indeed."

Sir Julian nodded. "I had the very same feeling. While I admire Northumberland for deserting his brothers in favor of the king, I still cannot bring myself to trust him. And everyone knows he cannot stand the sight of Earl Rivers, much less fight by his side if the need arose."

"That's true enough, and I think young Gloucester shares that sentiment, though he has no use for Northumberland either." He shook his head. "This is no fellowship on which to hang the fate of the crown."

"Even Hastings, the king's closest friend, distrusts the queen and her kin. And she will not fail to recognize that fact. I fear there are too many winds among the king's friends, and soon he will have to choose a direction. When he does, there will be more bloodshed. Of that, I am certain."

"I cannot disagree, though I wish it were otherwise," Sir Nigel concurred sadly. "To make matters worse, the queen will not be in a forgiving mood after the murder of her father and brother, and being a Neville, Northumberland is likely to feel the sting of her animosity."

"Her wrath is not likely to be felt for a while. The king needs Northumberland and his resources desperately."

"Are you sure of that? With Warwick and Clarence in exile, Northumberland would not find the kingdom a friendly place were he not in the king's good graces."

"The earl is needed to keep order in the north, and watch for any treachery from the Scots. This is not the time to make new enemies, God knows, and he has proven to be loyal even when it would have been quite easy for him to follow his brother. And had he done so, we would be the ones in exile. Or worse."

"You and I understand that," agreed Sir Nigel, "but what motivates the queen is altogether a different thing. She will never forgive the Nevilles, and Northumberland's loyalty will gain him little if she sees an opportunity."

Sir Julian suspected that his friend was right and realized that since nothing could be done about the queen's behavior, it would behoove them to keep a sharp eye on the Earl of Northumberland.

"It shames us to treat the earl in this manner when he has behaved honorably in every way."

"Unfortunately, his family has given us little choice, and we both know that honor is a frequent casualty of conflict."

Sir Julian looked at the marble floor of the council chambers.

"Perhaps I am too much a relic of a past time."

Hastings' lack of respect for the Woodvilles was not lost on Edward. He hoped that there would be plenty of time to reconcile his friend with his wife and her family when time better permitted. For now, it was enough that they all knew that they were on the same side.

"Tell me," Edward asked, "what have you found out about the rabble who surprised us at Edgecott? They did not behave as if they were under orders from Warwick."

"Some clearly were, Sire, or you would not have been so quickly brought to the earl. The rest, it seems were northmen who have always been loyal to the House of Percy, and are very displeased with what has happened since the death of the old earl at Towton."

Edward clenched his fists. "We must bring the north into our fold if we are ever to see peace again. These uprisings must stop." He paced the floor. "Do you think that it would be as simple as giving the earldom back to the Percys? Would such an act of faith with them stop this senseless rebellion?"

"I suppose it would remove their principal reason for rebellion, assuming that the House of Percy became loyal to the throne. Forgive me, Sire, but is not the earldom already occupied by one who has shown only loyalty to your person?"

"John Neville will understand that sacrifices are sometimes necessary for the good of the realm. And I can always reward him for his coopera-tion." Edward went back to pacing, then put his arm around Hastings and led him toward the door. "Thank you, my friend. I'll think on what you've advised." Hastings bowed and left the room, wondering what he had advised.

Edward went to see the queen. She was in her closet, attended by sev-eral ladies who were fixing her hair and helping her undress. Edward waved them out of the room and sat next her, still amazed at how the mere sight of her stirred his passion. He stroked her long golden hair that cas-caded freely over her shoulders and down her back like a river at sunset. The flawless skin of her face was marred only by her frown.

"I am sorry, my love, that I was unable to save your father and brother," said Edward, "but there are times when even a king stands impotent in the face of fate."

"Was that what killed my family, my lord?" she asked sharply. "Fate, you say? I heard that it was the traitor Warwick."

"You know that it was, Bess."

"Than why has he not been brought before the king's awful judgment? The blood of my father and brother cry to me from the grave, and they will not rest before their murders have been avenged." Edward took her in his arms and hugged her tightly.

"Warwick will pay for his crimes, I promise you. For now, my love, we must be content that they are banished and can do us no further harm."

"France will give him succor, you can be sure of that."

"We are taking precautions. You must not concern yourself."

Elizabeth separated herself.

"Do not treat me as a child, my lord. It is my father who lies headless in his grave, and we are no more secure on the throne than when he was mur-dered."

"Please, my love, you must have faith. There are some things that are beyond a mortal's ability to achieve unless God is willing. What I can do, I will. That I pledge to you, though I die trying." His words disarmed her. She took him by the hand and led him to her bed.

"Perhaps the most important precaution we can take depends on me after all," she said pulling him down on top of her. "I must bear you a son, and it must be soon."

He pushed the golden hair from her face and kissed her gently. It always delighted him how quickly his passion was aroused by the feel of her body, and the surprise was the same no matter how many times they made love.

"Yes," he said, kissing her harder as they tugged at each other's clothing, "Yes, I must have a son."

In the morning Edward summoned his Privy Council once again, but this time held the meeting in the throne room. Although Windsor Castle was Edward's favorite residence in London, it was here at Westminster Palace that the business of state was conducted, and the throne room was opulently suited to carry on such affairs. The high ceiling was constructed of a series of vaults, each elaborately decorated with floral designs around dozens of supporting stone ribs. The stone walls flowed thickly to the floor, decorated with huge tapestries. The room was long enough to give visitors the proper awe as they walked from the only entrance along its length toward the throne that sat atop a marble dais.

John Neville, the Earl of Northumberland, was the last to arrive at the meeting. Walking toward the throne, he was feeling decidedly uncomfortable. He had been overjoyed at his elevation to the earldom and could not have wished for more from this king as payment for his loyalty. But Warwick put him in a most uncomfortable position, making him choose between his family and a king who had treated him honorably. In the end it was not really a decision at all, and he thought he had made it clear to his brother that he would not dishonor himself by turning on King Edward. On the other hand, he could not war on his brother either, so he chose to remain silently busy in the north when Edward was imprisoned in Warwick Castle, and that action would surely not sit well with the king.

He noticed that his other brother, the Archbishop of York, was in attendance, and wondered why he was present. He saw the Duke of Gloucester, Lord Hastings, and the detested Earl Rivers, along with other courtiers, members of the king's personal guard, and a man whom he could not immediately recognize.

"Welcome, my lord of Northumberland," said the king when the earl arrived at the throne and bowed.

"God save Your Highness," he responded.

"And now," the king turned to Sir Nigel, "what news of these traitors?" he asked tersely.

"Sire, my sources inform me that Clarence and Warwick have attempted a landing at Calais, as you suspected, but the garrison commander, Lord Duras, turned them away, forbidding them entrance to the harbor. However, they were permitted a landing at Honfleur and given asylum by the French king. This is all the information we have." Edward sighed. He knew that there was little he could do while Warwick and Clarence were sheltered by Louis.

"Lord Hastings, send to the King of France and demand that the traitors be returned to us for crimes against our person."

"As you wish, Sire," said Hastings, "but I hold little hope that he will comply."

"Nevertheless. We shall also entreat the Duke of Burgundy. Let Louis know that a joint move against him is a possibility. Such a threat may keep Louis from lending any military aid to Warwick." He nodded to Hastings, who turned and faced the archbishop.

"George Neville, Archbishop of York, I arrest you here for foul treason against your lawful monarch."

The archbishop bowed his head. "I freely submit myself to His Highness' mercy."

Edward's look betrayed no mercy. "While it is true that only the Holy Father in Rome can remove you from your clerical honors, let it be known that no longer will you hold the Great Seal of England and be our Chancellor. And until your dangerous brother is brought to answer for his crimes, you will stay here under careful watch. Sir Julian, see that he is conveyed to the Tower."

"I shall see it done personally, Your Highness," he said.

Edward then turned his attention to the other Neville who was in attendance, for business that was considerably more troublesome.

"My lord of Northumberland, know that we value your service and have well noted your loyalty in this recent rebellion. We wish to reward you and therefore grant you the Marquisate of Montagu. In exchange for your new title we transfer the Earldom of Northumberland to Sir Henry Percy, here in attendance."

The king's decree was like a knife in the ribs of John Neville. While it was true that as a marquis he would be of a higher social rank than an earl, the Marquisate of Montagu held only a fraction of the prestige of the Earldom of Northumberland, and more importantly, significantly less revenue. He looked over to the man he had not recognized before and saw that it was indeed Henry Percy, the rightful heir to the earldom, who had been imprisoned by Edward ever since his father died at Towton. And now he stood here, forgiven of his father's transgressions and possessed of the earldom that Neville had earned with his blood.

"Sire," he stammered, thinking quickly how to best respond to this unexpected turn of events, "I looked not for this new title, and was quite content with my current state."

"We have decided," said Edward, "and we know that we can count on your continued loyalty." The new Marquis of Montagu bowed, seeing that further argument would be futile.

"I remain Your Highness' loyal servant." Thanks to Warwick's rebellion, Neville knew that he had no friends in this room anyway, and it was best that he hold his tongue and choose a better time to express his displeasure with the new arrangements.

After a few more minutes of routine business, the king dismissed the Privy Council and left the throne room, as did the rest of the lords. Montagu stopped Sir Julian before he could escort the archbishop out.

"Sir Julian, I wonder if I might have a word with the archbishop before you take him hence?" Sir Julian did not like the idea, but had little choice.

"As you wish, my lord, but we depart forthwith, and you must be brief." Montagu nodded in agreement and Sir Julian withdrew out of earshot.

"It seems we have done ourselves little good, my brother," said the archbishop.

"The king is deluded if he thinks I'll accept this. Does he imagine that I would be content with this new title?"

"I believe that he knows exactly what he's doing. Besides, you are a Neville, and that's sufficient for the queen, who lost a father and a brother at our hands."

"At your hands, George, not mine. I begged you both not to proceed with this rebellion, but you chose to ignore me. Now you have sucked me into your trap, though I looked not for it and have lost the honors for which I spilt my blood."

"You must be patient, John. While events have turned against us for now, it need not remain so, and I am confident that France will help. When they do, if we stand together this time, we will not be denied. I will not likely be of much use from the Tower, but I'll pray for the moment when you come to liberate me."

"I should have stopped you before. Now I have very few options left to me. Damn you both." He turned and stalked from the room. The archbishop watched him leave, then waved to Sir Julian.

"I am ready for the Tower, Sir Knight," he said boisterously, "and God grant us a safe journey thither."

"You may rest assured, Your Grace, that I'll see you safely there, and presently," Sir Julian responded with conviction.

As Sir Julian was escorting the archbishop to his new place of residence, Samuel, Oliver, Stanley, and Sir Nigel walked together toward the inn where quarters had been arranged for the king's guard, all more or less in awe of the remarkable bustle that characterized the great city of London. Home to seventy thousand souls from every walk of life imaginable, it was the very center of the realm's commercial activity. Surrounded still by the old semicircular Roman wall, the city sprawled on the north bank of the River Thames, the artery that brought the world and its goods to England. Ships from ports all over Europe offloaded their cargoes from dozens of piers along the river's shores, and the resulting commerce fueled an unrivaled hive of activity. The city streets were mostly unpaved and narrowly lined with buildings of every sort and design. Some were timber and plaster, some brick, some squalid huts with thatched roofs, mixing easily with opulent mansions of stone. The most distinctive structure was the massive cathedral of St. Paul, its Gothic walls and buttresses easily seen from almost any point within the city. Most streets meandered senselessly through the turmoil, and were covered with discarded human refuse that was often home to rats and ravens.

The four men walked along Thames Street, the closest street to the river, and one of the few paved with cobblestones. It spanned the length of the city, from the Tower all the way to Blackfriars on the western edge. Easily the busiest street in London, it was packed with fishmongers and purveyors of goods of all description from honey and grains to baked goods, wines, and wax. It was from Thames Street that a majority of the goods that came to the city from abroad were dispersed into the local economy, making their way into the lives of the common Englishmen, and from where luxurious items such as satins and silver from Italy and fine furniture from the Hanseatic towns of Germany came to the nobility.

Through this barely controlled chaos, Samuel walked with his friends, in a mood so black he barely noticed any of it. The king was safe, but in the process they had lost any hope of finding the women, since their only connection to them, Sir Hugh, had fled to France with the Earl of Warwick. At that moment, he had no idea how to proceed, and the helplessness of that feeling was oppressive.

"I know you think we've lost them, Samuel," Sir Nigel put his arm around him, "but I swear to you that I will not forget my promise. Though the king has required my presence here in London, some of my eyes are searching for your family, and what they seek they will find, you know that to be true." Samuel looked at Oliver, who seemed equally unimpressed with Sir Nigel's assertions.

"You'll excuse me if I seem ungrateful, but once again we did what was expected of us, and find ourselves worse than when we started."

Sir Nigel did not take offense. "It only seems that way, my friend. When my men get word of them, and I tell you that they surely will, I'll drop whatever I'm doing, even if I'm at the side of the king himself, and help you to rescue them. This is my pledge to you both."

"As will I," added Stanley. "Sir Julian has already given me leave to stay with you until this business is finished, though the king needs all his guard and will surely be displeased."

When Samuel said nothing, his bitterness still unrequited, Oliver put his hand on his friend's shoulder.

"We both recognize that you are committed to help, and we appreciate it. We have traveled too far to give up now, and we won't, though Hell's gate opens before us. Sir Nigel, we'll stay with you here until we hear from your men, and when we do, our resolve will be great to correct the wrongs that have been done to us."

Samuel was at first annoyed at Oliver for presuming to interpret for him, but realized that he was venting his frustration at the wrong people, and was grateful to his friend for saying what he should have said himself.

"Sir Nigel," he said at last, "when could we reasonably expect to hear something?"

"Soon. My men have been out since the king was freed. We will pick up the trail before long, you can be assured." Samuel nodded and said nothing, but as they continued their walk along the bustling street, it occurred to him that his luck would seem to forebode otherwise, and somehow he knew that Oliver was thinking the same thing.

CHAPTER XXIII

The throne room of the King of France was smaller than that of Westminster Palace, but the opulence of its decor was second to none. Intricately carved columns of oak supported a gold-encrusted ceiling frescoed with cherubs. Candelabra of cut crystal adorned every cove along the walls and lit the room brightly.

Louis XI sat on a throne of mahogany cushioned with lace pillows. Pierre de Brezé and François Lascombes waited as the king considered his choices.

"My lords, the Duke of Burgundy must never again be permitted to side with the English against us," said Louis at last. "It is our principal concern in these matters. Too often, the English have arrived on our shores and shed our dearest blood. I swear I would sooner die than to bend my knee to an English king as my grandfather did." He clenched his fists as he spoke.

"As you say, Sire," agreed Lascombes. "But we cannot miss this opportunity. The English throne could remain weak for another generation."

Brezé cleared his throat. "Perhaps we can accomplish all we need." The king nodded for him to continue. "I'm sure that the Earl will agree to anything that we ask, in return for our assistance."

"We agree," Louis said after a moment's reflection. "Summon Margaret of Anjou to us."

Lascombes bowed his head and left.

Warwick had arrived at the French court a month earlier and had waited impatiently for an audience with the king. When Louis had finally seen him, it was without the pomp and honors with which he had greeted him the last time he came, as ambassador from Edward. But then he had not come as a beggar. The king had made him no promises, except to consider his request for aid.

"My lord de Brezé, what think you of Warwick's strength in England? We would not wish to send our troops on a fool's errand."

"Majesty, he still commands significant resources, and could if needed gather a strong puissance were he to land in England with some hope of success."

"By that, I assume you mean if he is well supplied by us."

"Indeed, Highness. He is not so popular that the nobility will blindly follow him. And we have already seen that they will not accept him as king."

"We may need your help to convince Margaret to accept our conditions. She values your counsel."

"As you wish, Your Highness, but I should point out that Margaret is not easily convinced of that which she disapproves."

"We do not think that Margaret is in a position to defy us. But if she is ruled by us," Louis continued, "we all stand to gain a great deal."

"I will do as you say, Your Highness."

Lascombes returned with Margaret, the exiled queen of England and native daughter of France. The years of exile and Louis' pitifully inadequate financial assistance during that time had not lessened her will, nor did she hold herself any less majestically. She had raised her son, now sixteen, with the knowledge that he was the rightful heir to the English throne, and had done so with barely enough money to feed him, much less train him to be a great ruler. She wore her graying hair in a single braid that was wrapped tightly to the back of her head.

"Your Highness has sent for me?"

"Rise, Margaret of Anjou, we are glad to look upon you again."

"I thank Your Grace, though I wonder that it has taken this long for your invitation."

Louis smiled. He knew she had a right to be upset, but he was not inclined to waste precious resources supporting a queen in exile. However, now that he smelled an opportunity to use her to his advantage, he would tolerate her rebuke.

"Our time serves us now to be more attentive."

"Forgive me, my lord, but I have heard that your great enemy, the cursed Earl of Warwick, has been granted an audience. I am curious to know what such a traitor can hope to gain from the French people."

"Has it not occurred to you that perhaps he can be of great service to us both?"

"The only service that I wish of the earl is to see his trunkless head at my feet." Her hatred had caused her to temporarily lose her civility.

Louis paused for a moment as she regained her composure. He had known that his plan would be hard to sell, but upon her cooperation depended the success of his hopes. He stood and descended from the dais.

"We ask only that you hear us and tell us what you think. Will you agree to that?"

"As you wish, Your Highness." She had little choice.

"Good, good. Warwick has asked for our aid, which we are not inclined to give except in return for great services to us and France. You both have been wronged by the Yorkist pretender and as such have a great deal in common. Instead of enemies, you should become friends."

Margaret crossed her arms defiantly. "While we have both been wronged, it is at Warwick's hands that my son was deprived of his birthright. I cannot ever forget that. If I may be so bold, what can he offer you in his present state?"

"He can be the tool by which your son's birthright is restored."

"I am skeptical, my lord. How would this be accomplished?" Louis smiled and sat again on the throne, knowing that he was now more in control.

"We will offer the earl our support only on condition that he recognize our cousin Henry, your husband, as his lawful and rightful king, and your son as heir to the English throne. Would that not accomplish what you have hoped for?"

She knew only too well that even if Warwick were to defeat Edward in the name of the Lancastrians, her husband would be a puppet at best, and she and her son were being shamelessly used by Louis to attain that end.

Her old friend Pierre de Brezé, knowing at that moment that the king had anticipated Margaret's need for friendly advice, quickly stepped forward.

"Majesty, if you would permit me?" Louis signaled his assent with a nod. "My lady, let me add my endorsement to His Highness' gracious offer, and I am pleased to know that you will soon retake your place as England's queen as God in Heaven has ordained."

Margaret considered his words. Was this how he truly felt, or was he also a pawn of the king? She knew that Brezé was not so practiced in the art of deception as was the king, but there was a sadness in his voice. Finally, she responded directly to Louis.

"Your Highness, I must see the earl myself before agreeing to this plan. I must know his soul. It is my son's life that we risk in these matters."

Louis smiled. "A wise request. We will arrange the meeting for tomorrow. You may return again in the morning."

Margaret bowed and left.

"My lord de Brezé, what support can Edward expect from among the nobility?"

"Of the great magnates, only that of Warwick's brother, and his own brother, the untried Duke of Gloucester. It is not an enviable position."

"Strange how these enemies have traded brothers," mused the king. "Perhaps the time is ripe for us to obtain a lasting advantage over the squabbling English, and we may even, at the same time, extricate the thorn of haughty Burgundy from our side at last. Monsieur Lascombes, draw up terms of alliance between us and Warwick, and take care to include the certain downfall of Burgundy in our terms of treaty. It is our most cherished demand."

"It shall be as you say, Sire."

Louis allowed himself a smug moment. Could it be that before the year was out, he would have a pliant and weak king on the English throne, and that Burgundy would once again pay him homage as all vassals should to the king of a united France? It would be the culmination of his dreams.

The following day, Margaret arrived back to the royal palace. The Earl of Warwick greeted her in a royal waiting chamber where Pierre de Brezé was also present.

"Majesty, though you have good cause to hate me, I beg forgiveness and a moment to prove my worth."

"It is right for you to kneel before your queen, my lord. But you are too late to gain advantage by the act. We are banished from our own land by your rebellious acts, and have no boon to give."

"It is for that very reason that I beg a moment of your time, Highness, for it is my greatest desire to right the wrongs that I have wrought on you and your family. Your Highness, I was misled by the House of York, for which I am truly regretful." That much, at least, Margaret could believe. "I am now willing to make amends. Between us we can and will reverse our fortunes."

"My lord, we both know that this attempt at reconciliation is motivated entirely by your present state. If we were to accept your apology, what would keep you from your treacherous ways once we are back in England?"

"My lady," interjected Brezé, "there is a way for the earl to show his sincerity in this matter and give Your Grace the assurance that she needs."

"You have always been dear to our heart, my lord, and we value your advice. Tell us what you suggest." Brezé bowed his head in thanks.

"My lord of Warwick must make an offer to Your Highness that shows his devotion and sincerity. An offer that cannot be withdrawn or besmirched were the earl to regain his former prominence. A gesture, if you will, that would be blessed by the Holy Church, and therefore sacred." Margaret's interest was piqued.

"And you have a proposal for such an offer?"

"My lady, the earl has a daughter still unmarried and, as I have heard, virtuous beyond question. Is it not so, my lord?"

"As virtuous as any in the kingdom, my lord," interjected Warwick. "I'll swear to that by all that's holy. Her name is Anne."

"And the young Prince of Wales is in need of a wife, is it not so, my lady?"

Horrified as she was by the suggestion, Margaret could not dismiss the idea. If the earl were to regain his estates, Anne stood to inherit a vast fortune. Warwick had no sons, only two daughters, the eldest of whom, Isabel, had recently wed the Duke of Clarence over the objections of Edward. Upon the death of Warwick, English law would split his estate between the two daughters equally, and even half of such an estate would give her son the wealth he would need if he were king. Moreover, as Brezé said, such a marriage would make the earl less inclined to turn his back on them once he was restored to his former power, being content instead with the knowledge that his grandchildren would be rulers of England. Warwick was weighing his options as well.

"What say you to this proposal?"

"If His Majesty the Prince will have her, then with all my heart the union has my blessing."

"My lord. You will have our answer in the morning. Now, there are details that we must discuss with my lord de Brezé." Warwick kissed the queen's hand and left.

"We tell you frankly, Brezé, we fear this union," said Margaret. "Upon our soul, it does not sit well. But for our son's sake we must take this risk."

"My lady, soon your son will be back where he belongs. As for the earl, once you have reclaimed the throne, you will have your destiny back in your own hands."

"But we have seen that the Yorkist pretender is an able general, and we cannot risk our son's life, even for the throne." It was the first time he had ever seen her close to tears. "And Warwick cannot assure us of victory. He may be so deluded, but we are not."

"My lady," he responded after a moment of thought, "perhaps there is no need for your son to be risked in such a battle. I will suggest to Louis that the invasion force be split in two parts, one under the earl's leadership, and one under yours. The earl will go first to see what support he has, and if he is successful, you will follow later with the prince, but only after Warwick has secured a safe kingdom for you both."

Margaret was delighted by the strategy. "It is very agreeable to us, my lord. Let Warwick take the risks and we shall enter triumphantly afterwards if he wins. Will Louis agree?"

"I will see that he does, my lady. He will accede to my superior understanding in these matters. He has too much to gain."

The following day, Warwick, having already started planning an invasion fleet with Lascombes, was not pleased to hear about the king's decision to split the small army. He would need every man. On the other hand, he was relieved to hear that the queen would not accompany them, as she would have been a terrible distraction. But the decision was made. A servant entered.

"Well?"

"My lord, Sir Hugh wishes an audience." The man was a fool, thought Warwick, but he would provide much needed help in the coming conflicts.

"Very well," he waved the man away.

A month in exile had made him irritable in almost all things, but it had not clouded his judgment. It would take at least another month to make all the necessary preparations, and the time would go by slowly. In the meantime, he had to take precautions that intelligence of these plans did not reach Edward.

Sir Hugh entered wearing the same clothes that he wore the day he arrived in this hated land. If the exile had been hard on Warwick, it had been horrendous for Sir Hugh and the rest of the earl's retainers. They had been billeted as common footsoldiers with the private guard of the lord constable, and many were the times that he could have killed the first detested Frenchman he saw. Now, however, he had reached the end of his tolerance, and while he had no desire to alienate himself from the earl, he had come to make it clear that the status quo could no longer be permitted. But Warwick did not give him a chance.

"Sir Hugh!" he called jovially. "I was going to send for you. I have excellent news. We have all been treated deplorably, is it not so?"

"Yes, my lord," he answered, disarmed by the earl's manner.

"King Louis has given us what we sought, and soon we shall see the white shores of our own land again."

"That is good news indeed, my lord." Sir Hugh smiled.

"And you will be pleased to hear that we will fight to place your old master, King Henry, back on throne."

This was a surprise indeed. Sir Hugh commended his own wisdom for the decision to remain on good terms with Lord Fitzwalter.

"When will the invasion begin?"

Warwick shrugged casually. "In a month perhaps. There is much to be done. But you will leave much sooner than that. I want you back on English soil within a fortnight, as there are several tasks that you must see dispatched in preparation of our arrival."

Sir Hugh smiled again.

"I am your servant, my lord."

That evening, Warwick received another visitor, one whom he had been avoiding since his last conversation with the king. But now was as good a time as any to reveal Louis' plan to his son-in-law. Clarence had been hosted by an insignificant member of the king's court, and had been living in a state of despair since his exile with the earl. He had never imagined that his brother Edward could have defeated the mighty Earl of Warwick, thereby making him a beggar instead of a prince. Warwick greeted him with the news of Louis' assistance.

"Louis has asked a price for his assistance, however," Warwick continued, "and though it is not what I wanted, you can surely see that we have little choice in the matter."

"What has he asked?"

"That King Henry be restored to the throne and his son to his birthright."

Stunned that Warwick had essentially bargained away what Clarence had risked his life to gain, he could not at first respond. He was furious, but he knew that it would gain him nothing to protest at this time.

"At my insistence, Louis has agreed that should the prince die without heir, you shall be next in line to the throne." Warwick had hoped that this would appease Clarence enough to keep him from deserting them. "And of course, all of your lands and titles shall be restored to you immediately." He leaned closer to the duke. "I know this is not what you hoped for, but at present, we must accept what we are given. No choice has been offered."

"I see." Clarence was now in control of his anger, and needed to be away from Warwick to collect his thoughts. "You have my support, of course. The thought of my little brother enjoying my domains, and my older brother controlling my life, is galling, and I'll not abide it any longer. Let me know how I may be of assistance with your preparations."

"I shall call on you shortly." It had gone better than Warwick had dared hope, but he shouldn't have been surprised, knowing how greedy the duke was. His wealth in England would be more than enough to keep him happy after they had accomplished their mission.

As he left, Clarence knew that Warwick considered him a fool, but if he had learned one thing during this atrocious exile, it was patience.

Lord Roos greeted Margaret in another of Louis' waiting rooms. The planned invasion of England renewed his hope. He longed for the blood rush of battle once again. When he met the queen, he expected her to be as excited as he was, but instead, she was clearly agitated.

"Lord Roos, God willing we will soon retake our place on the English throne."

"My prayers and hopes are with you, Highness." Ignoring his response, she spun to face him.

"That cursed letter has still not been recovered from Fitzwalter's daughter, and we cannot sleep until it has been. Can you understand that, my lord?"

"I can, my lady, and when we are back in England it will be my primary concern."

"It must be more than that, my lord. We shall instruct the Earl of Warwick to release you from further duty after you have landed, and you will then make it your only desire in life to recover the letter."

"My lady, would it not be advisable to ensure that we have regained the kingdom first?" He hated the idea of leaving the troops like a coward just when a battle loomed.

"Without that letter, the kingdom is meaningless. Can't you see that even those noble families that have supported us will turn their backs if they see its contents? They need little enough excuse to hate us. We must see it destroyed before Warwick lands. He is sending a knight by the name of Sir Hugh to make his secret arrangements tomorrow, and we want you to accompany him. We have already informed the earl."

"It shall be as you say, Your Highness."

Two weeks after that conversation, on a dreary evening in London, Samuel and his friends greeted Sir Nigel in an alehouse that had served the members of the king's guard since they arrived in the city. The knight removed his cloak and shook the rain from it before hanging it on a hook by the door, then kicked the mud from his soles.

"If this rain continues," said Sir Nigel after draining his first tankard, "the roads will be in ruins again, and I would hate to have to assemble an army in such mud if Warwick were to invade."

"Have you heard that he will?" asked Stanley.

"Oh, he will, my friend. Let there be no doubt about that. We would be fools to think that Louis will not leap at this opportunity. The only question is when and where." Nigel was not alone in that opinion. In the recent months rumors had been thicker than flies on Fleet Street, some guessing that Warwick had already landed and was secretly gathering his friends, and others betting that it was Clarence who would soon be marching against his brother. The citizens of London were living on the edge, afraid that French mercenaries would soon be sacking their shops and homes.

Cheerful news did come to the people from Westminster Palace, however. The king announced that the queen was once again with child. They prayed that this time it would be a male child to bring some welcome stability to the succession, and therefore to the king himself. And for the first time in years, there had been no significant uprisings or disorder anywhere in the realm for the past five months, as the new Earl of Northumberland and Warwick's brother, the Marquis of Montagu, exerted firm control over the northern counties, and the Duke of Gloucester patrolled the Welsh marches with equal diligence. But few in the kingdom felt that the calm would last.

Sir Nigel downed another tankard of ale and regarded Samuel, who had been withdrawn and morose since they arrived in the capital.

"I may have news for you, lad. I know it's been long overdue." Samuel looked up from his mug. For weeks, he and Oliver had waited for some word from Sir Nigel's men, each day of silence another dagger in their hearts. They had gone about the daily chores of the guardsmen mechanically, hoping that soon they would be on their way to save their women, but the answer was always the same. "My men cannot be sure," Nigel continued, "and I was hesitant to even bring it up, but I know that any glimmer of hope would be welcome. Have you ever heard of Lord Colinsworth?" Samuel shook his head. "I'm not surprised. His title is a lot grander than he, by all reports. There are farmers who command more wealth. A few weeks ago, a servant, his only one for all we know, entered town and drank his weight in ale at the local tavern, where, as fate would have it, one of my men was listening. I'm told he babbled for hours to anyone who would listen, and my man all but ignored him but for a quick reference to two sorry bitches that he had locked up in the castle."

"Colinsworth?" It came from Oliver. "That's where we were when you found us."

"The same," answered Sir Nigel. "If not for that fact, I probably wouldn't have mentioned it."

"Damn you," Samuel startled everyone. "We were going to inquire there when you talked us into saving the king's hide again. We could have found them months ago!"

"And you would most likely be dead if you had," said Stanley. But Samuel was in no mood to be appeased.

"You don't know that. You have no way of knowing what hell they may have been exposed to in the last three months."

"On the other hand, you may have jeopardized their lives if you had moved too quickly."

"They may already be dead, you fool!" Samuel shouted.

His outburst silenced the room around them, until Oliver finally intervened.

"Please, Samuel, this bickering won't change anything. What has been done is done." For a moment, Samuel did not seem to hear him, but after an awkward glance around the room, he slumped back in his chair. Conversations started up again around them.

"Sir Nigel, what do you propose we do now?" asked Oliver.

"Samuel, I owe you a debt that can never be repaid. When the time comes, you will not find fault with me, of that you may be certain." Their eyes met. "At first light we will travel together to Colinsworth Castle, and by God's breath, we will know the truth." He looked from face to face, Stanley and Oliver each signaling their affirmation with a nod. When he looked to Samuel, he waited.

Samuel, getting an encouraging smile from Oliver, nodded once and drained his mug.

Colinsworth Castle stood on a low knoll, by a deep, narrow stream that formed a rough semicircle around its walls. The nearby country was flat with thickets of trees scattered for miles around. By contemporary standards, the castle was a small keep enclosed by a perfect square of high walls and a moat that did not abut the stream. The approach lane entered through a modest barbican, the narrow path blocked by a single portcullis, a heavy iron grate raised only to allow the occasional guest or servant to pass. The walls contained two towers, one guarding the entryway, and the other on the opposite wall next to the great hall. In between was a small courtyard that housed the servants' quarters and the kitchen. Above the great hall were the master's private rooms, which contained the only windows looking in both directions, allowing views of the surrounding fields, the produce from which supplied food for the castle.

Samuel and his friends arrived at sunset at a rise in the road that allowed them their first view of the castle from a safe and unnoticed distance. It looked like a good place to camp and study how to attempt an entry to that dark and lifeless place. The journey had taken an entire week, four days longer than it should have, over rain-ruined roads. But on this evening, the rain had let up and there were even stars to be seen.

With Samuel, Sir Nigel, Stanley, and Oliver were two of Sir Nigel's retainers. The six of them huddled some way from the road behind a hedgerow that would have to suffice to keep them concealed, though in the daylight they could have been spotted by any passing traveler. They could not start a fire, but had carried with them an ample supply of dried venison.

"Well," said Stanley, "now that we're here, how do we get into that place?"

"I've always said that with a strong heart and clever mind, a man can walk through walls. And that place will be easier than most, I'd wager," responded Sir Nigel. His retainers nodded in agreement, having seen him get into and out of places that they had never thought possible.

"I believe our hearts are in the right place. Perhaps you'll tell us your plan," Oliver said skeptically.

"I have nothing in mind at the moment, my friend. Observation is the cornerstone of planning. We may be here a while simply watching, but we will get in eventually, I promise you that."

They all knew that Sir Nigel had unique skills in these matters, so there was little to be gained by further conversation. Samuel took the first watch. The starlit castle in the distance, he bundled himself against the cool night wind and wondered if Sally and Kate were within that dreary place. The vision of his father dying in the dark dungeon of Pontefract came to him like a knife to his heart.

During the next three days, some went to a nearby village to see what information they could gather, while others watched the activity within and around the castle, carefully making note of patterns of behavior that might aid them. Knowing that Samuel would be far too impatient for the latter duty, Nigel gave him and Stanley the job of gleaning what information they could from the village. While there was no alehouse in the usual sense, the blacksmith typically opened his home to neighbors and strangers who desired libation. One or two drinkers were always ready to talk an ear off in his front room. It was there that the two guardsmen, dressed as common travelers, presented themselves as pilgrims headed for Canterbury and the shrine of Saint Thomas. There was little chance that anyone would suspect that story, since thousands from all over the realm made the same trip every year.

The smith's home reminded Samuel of any of a dozen similar ones in Northwood where he grew up. The furniture was sparse, with only three small round tables and several stools for the guests. The cooking area against the back wall consisted of a hearth with pothooks and a small bench where the cook could sit while stirring. The floor was dirt, packed hard as rock by years of everyday traffic. The blacksmith was affluent enough to have a milk cow, several pigs, and about a dozen laying hens, all occupying the same pen, which was encircled by a combination hedge and rail fence behind their cottage. A separate shed housed the tools and bellows of the smith's trade.

"Will you be moving on today, or spending the evening in the village?" the smith asked Samuel after serving two large ales. The travelers glanced at each other, silently electing Samuel the spokesman.

"We've been a fair distance and need a bit of rest. We plan to spend a day or two to get our legs back beneath us."

"The roads are hard on honest men, I know that," he said. "I can give you a place in the shed for the night, but I'll have to ask you for some honest work." The smith was used to pilgrims wanting shelter and even food, and knew that all they could usually pay was a morning's chores.

"You are most kind," Samuel agreed to the terms with a nod. It would provide a good excuse for them to linger in the village. "If you please, who is the master of that castle?"

"Lord Colinsworth, though you'd hardly know it by the trips he takes. You'll not find five of us here in the village that have seen him since last

Christmas. The elder Lord Colinsworth died fighting for Lancaster and lost everything but that pitiful castle to King Edward, leaving his son with almost nothing." He shrugged his shoulders. "Not that many of us care what becomes of the new master. He was never one to show much concern for us, though we mourned the death of his father."

"Surely the new master comes to town on the holy days?" Stanley asked.

"Not one since his father died. The castle gates stay down all the time."

"How is it provisioned then?" Samuel was pleased that they had gotten the smith to talk about Colinsworth without raising any suspicions.

"Once each week, his steward comes to collect the lord's share of our produce. If our services are needed, to shoe his horses or do some repair work, the steward summons us to the castle. Other than that, we see nothing of him and prefer it that way."

"At least the crop looks to be a fine one this year," said Stanley. The blacksmith nodded in agreement.

"It will be one of the best in memory, God willing the rain stops until the harvest. And the extra grain will help many in this village recover from near starvation, I can tell you that." In good years, the payments to the lord of the manor did not increase, allowing the farmers to keep a greater amount of their own produce. It was the only time when their lot in life permitted more than a diet that barely sustained them, when more grain could be stored for use in the winter or traded at town markets for commodities that were otherwise rare in their lives, such as dried fruits, honey, and mackerel or cod.

The smith's wife entered from the rear door hefting several faggots for the cooking hearth, which she dropped loudly for effect before the fireplace. Adjusting her bosom beneath a bulky dress, she scowled at her husband.

"If you're done with your idle chat, there's some pigs that need sloppin' out there, and two of the chickens jumped the hedge again. I told you a dozen times that you need to tie that hole in the hedge together, but I might as well be talkin' to meself. And you haven't cleaned out the…"

"All right, woman. You needn't nag the whole night long." The smith knew that she wouldn't stop listing chores until he started doing them. He smiled at his guests and pulled a wool coat over his head before heading for the door. Samuel and Stanley knew that helping the smith would be far more desirable than staying in the kitchen with his wife, and they both jumped up to accompany him.

As promised, after spending relatively comfortable nights in the blacksmith's shed, Samuel and Oliver spent the first hours of each of the next three mornings performing routine tasks around the cottage. The animals were fed and the cow milked, and the two men made numerous small repairs around the yard. The smith's wife was pleased with their work and fed them a hearty meal of vegetable and grain stew, with ale and heavy bread.

The friends took their leave on the third day and walked back to the edge of the woods near town where Sir Nigel and the others awaited their report. Not that they felt they'd learned anything that would be of vital importance to their mission, but it was hard to assume what would be of use to Sir Nigel.

When they were still a few minutes from the camp, they met Oliver waiting for them on a large boulder by the roadside.

"Any interesting information?" he asked after greeting them.

"I don't think so," Samuel said. He could see that Oliver was nervous. "Is there something wrong?"

"I think you'd better see for yourself," he answered. "I just wanted you to know that I did what I thought was right."

When they arrived at the camp, a small, practically smokeless cook fire was burning in a pit away from the road over which two rabbits were cooking on a spit. Sir Nigel and his two henchmen were warming their hands. Someone else was with them.

"Did you think that you would never see me again?"

"Christopher!" croaked Samuel in shock. "How…"

"It was my doing. lad," said Sir Nigel. "My men informed me that he had returned to York and I told them to bring him here. I thought you'd be happy."

"I suppose we can use the help," Samuel said reluctantly. His lack of warmth was evident to everyone. He turned and moved away from the camp and the others, Christopher following.

"It's just like you to sulk, brother." Christopher joined him in the dark.

"The word comes hard to your lips, Christopher, but you never needed a brother anyway."

"It comes no harder to me than to you. It wasn't I who deserted the family for all these years."

"But you did desert the family, on some damn self-righteous quest. And now Sally and Kate are paying the price. And Emma and the children have suffered as well."

Christopher hung his head. "I admit my mistake. Perhaps I was trying to right the wrongs that I saw in you." Samuel's accusation had wounded him deeply. "But let me say that it's kind of you to show concern for children that you did not even know existed until recently."

"I was the one sold into servitude." Samuel's face reddened with anger. "And I had other sworn duties. You were given everything, and only had to be there for the family when they needed you, but you couldn't even manage that."

"Listen to yourself, Samuel. Was it so easy to dismiss your responsibilities to us simply because of your duty to the Percys, or was it really some demented need for revenge against Father that you visited on us instead? And don't speak to me of your duty to the earl. You deserted him quickly enough."

Samuel had no rebuttal. He had allowed his own insecurities and self-pity to keep him from his family.

"If you find me so repulsive, I'll find my own way in life as I always have. You needn't concern yourself with me after we correct the results of your actions."

"If that's the way you want it, Samuel, there's nothing I can do." He turned back toward the fire. "By the way, I have a message for you from Emma. She said to tell you that she hopes that you'll remember your promise. She didn't tell me what that means, but I expect that you'll disappoint her again."

Oliver had watched them intently from a distance, hoping against the odds that they could find some common ground. When Christopher returned, he could only shake his head sadly.

Later, when the cook fire had been extinguished, Sir Nigel told the men that he had finally devised a way into the castle, though even he was amazed at how difficult it would be.

"I've never seen a castle so tightly shut that wasn't under siege," he shook his head. "If I didn't know better, I'd think that he knew we were out here, but from what Stanley and Samuel were told by the blacksmith, it seems that it's always that way. I can't imagine what he's so afraid of."

As Sir Nigel unfolded his plan, Oliver felt certain that they would not all return from the brooding castle on the distant knoll.

About an hour before first light, Stanley and Sir Nigel's men secluded themselves where they could watch the castle and cover the escape. Oliver and Samuel, Christopher, and Sir Nigel headed for town armed only with short swords and hoping they would not need to unsheathe them. Sir Nigel's information promised that on this day the steward of Colinsworth Castle would venture forth to seek the week's supplies and hay for the lord's stable. The hay was collected by a farmer who lived near the edge of town. They groped their way through the dark toward his cottage, and carefully crept across its crowded yard toward the hay wagon.

Christopher's night vision made it possible. Without disturbing the animals, he negotiated a path to the loaded wagon, and the four burrowed in. It was full of loose hay and easily concealed them. In the musty warmth, they waited for the steward.

At about noon, when their patience was all but exhausted, they heard horses approach, felt a lurch, and were suddenly on their way to the castle. It became increasingly difficult to breathe through the dusty, shifting hay, but finally they felt the wooden planks of the castle drawbridge beneath them, and heard the unmistakable sound of the iron portcullis being raised. They endured another long wait in the courtyard before they were finally pulled into the stable. They had been fortunate.

"Let's go!" said Sir Nigel. Throwing the hay from his face, Samuel and the others jumped down and hid around the stable. The horses were agitated but made little sound, and now, for the intruders, it was time to wait again, this time for nightfall.

By sunset, the hay wagon that had delivered them had not yet been unloaded, giving them reason to believe that very few servants tended to this castle. They gathered before the stable doors and peered into the courtyard. Christopher pointed out each of the guards that he could see, and then Sir Nigel motioned them to follow the wall around the kitchen to the tower over the barbican. Sir Nigel expected prisoners to be held there. It was usually the most secure place.

They found the steps that led to the allure where the guard was still standing. Sir Nigel peered from behind the wall that shielded the steps and measured the distance to his adversary. Signaling the others to be silent, he steadied himself, then jumped the guard and thrust his blade into his throat. There was a gurgling sound, and Sir Nigel lowered him silently to the ground. Motioning for the others to follow, he took the guard's keys and entered the tower, quickly followed by the others.

Inside, a single torch lit a narrow hall and two doors, one with a barred opening, and the other without. He decided to chance a look into the room with the opening, for no other reason than it was safer than opening the other. He motioned Christopher, the closest, to take a look.

Christopher nodded and carefully looked through the bars, waiting for a moment for his eyes to adjust to the darkness. Without warning to the others, he called Sally's name in a loud whisper. A voice answered from within.

"Christopher?" And then louder. "Christopher, is that you?"

Sir Nigel frantically silenced them with a "shhhh!," then tested the guard's keys until he found the right one. Oliver pushed past the others and ran in as soon as the door was open. A moment later he came out with Sally in his arms, holding her tightly to himself. She seemed dazed at first, but at the sight of her brothers she began weeping.

Samuel squeezed her arm, then entered the cell himself. Coming back, his expression was desperate. Gently stroking his sister's hair, he asked a heart-rending question.

"Sally, can you tell us where Kate is?" She answered through sobs that made speech difficult.

"They took her...they took her away not long ago. I don't know where." Sir Nigel pulled Samuel away.

"We can't stay here. There aren't many other places for her to be." He signaled to the others. "Come, quickly!" He led them back out onto the allure, past the dead guard, and down the stairs to the gatehouse within the barbican. He cursed their luck, for if Kate had been in that cell with Sally, they would surely have made a clean escape by now. Instead, they huddled before the portcullis.

"I'll go with Samuel, the rest of you stay here and wait for our return. If we're not back shortly, leave without us. My men will see you clear."

"You'll need me as well." Christopher stopped him. Sir Nigel shook his head.

"If we don't make it back, they'll need you to lift the gate. Come, Samuel, someone will surely find the guard before long."

Samuel hesitated for a moment, looking at Christopher as if he had never seen him before, then turned and left with Sir Nigel.

Sir Nigel and Samuel made their way past the kitchen again and found a servants' entrance to the great hall. Standing in a vestibule where the servers normally arranged the food before entering, they heard a man's voice but could not make out the words.

Sir Nigel pulled the drape slightly aside and they both peered in. There, at either end of a long dining table, were Kate and a man they assumed to be Lord Colinsworth. Kate pushed the food around her plate but did not eat. Colinsworth pulled meat from a suckling pig. There appeared to be no one else in the room but for the steward, who stood silently between them and the table.

Sir Nigel motioned for Samuel to follow, and drew his sword. Running straight to the steward, Nigel dispatched him with a single stroke while Colinsworth jumped from his chair, too frightened to say anything. Samuel moved quickly to Kate, who ran to his arms.

"I knew you would come, my love," she laughed and kissed him frantically. At that moment, a guard entered the hall, emboldening Colinsworth.

"Take them, you fool!"

The guard pulled his sword and advanced while Colinsworth shouted to raise more of the guard.

"This way, lad. Quickly!" shouted Sir Nigel. Samuel and Kate ran to the door from which they had entered, Sir Nigel close on their heels. Once in the courtyard, Sir Nigel allowed the pursuing guard to come to within a few paces, and then suddenly spun and catapulted himself into their pursuer, the collision sending them both sprawling across the courtyard. Without armor, Sir Nigel was quicker on the rebound and leaped onto his adversary, who had only managed to get to his knees but could move no further before the point of a sword pierced his neck. Blood pumped from the wound. Without pausing, Sir Nigel ran toward the barbican, knowing that in moments the castle would be roused against them.

Christopher and Oliver were already turning the wheel that lifted the portcullis, and by the time Samuel arrived they had secured it high enough to allow the raiders to pass beneath. An alarm bell sounded and several armed men gathered in the courtyard waiting to discover the nature of the alarm. Sir Nigel knew they had run out of luck.

He ran to the gate where Sally and Kate had already been pushed beneath the teeth of the portcullis, and Oliver was just sliding under.

"I'll stay behind and lower the gate. If I cut the rope, you'll have time to get away. My men will be waiting for you."

"They need you to help them find a safe way away from here," Samuel said. "I'll stay and cut the rope."

"Samuel's right," added Christopher. "Even if we have a few hours' start, you're the only one who can find a safe place for them. But I'm the one who will stay."

"For God's sake, Christopher," chided Samuel, "for once think about your family." Colinsworth was already headed toward them with several men. "If you don't leave now we'll all die for nothing!"

Sir Nigel pulled Christopher through the gate. Samuel jumped up to the giant wheel that held the portcullis rope and hacked away with his sword.

"Where's Samuel?" Oliver asked frantically.

"Come," responded Sir Nigel, pulling them across the castle walk. "He's purchased our lives with his own."

Kate screamed his name and started to run back, but Sir Nigel picked her up and ran from the castle. Oliver followed for two steps, then stopped and dashed back, diving under the portcullis just as Samuel severed the last strands. It crashing down between him and his fleeing family. Colinsworth seized them both.

"Get this gate up and go after them!" yelled Colinsworth. "If they get away, it will mean the gallows for all of you." He stared through the bars. "Take these two to the darkest hole you can find, and forget you ever saw them." A quick death was too good for them.

Two guards pushed the friends across the courtyard. Samuel glanced sideways at Oliver.

"Why in God's name did you come back?"

"I could not let you die alone." They were led to the tower opposite the gateway and into the darkness below.

CHAPTER XXIV

"Why did Sir Nigel depart without our leave?"

The news had disturbed him. He needed Nigel now. Pamphlets had surfaced in many towns in which Warwick's grievances were enumerated and his virtues extolled to the commoners. Such propaganda typically preceded invasions.

The Duke of Gloucester cleared his throat. "Sire, I'm sure that Sir Nigel is about the king's business and will return shortly with his intelligence."

"We pray that you're correct."

"Highness, we are prepared for Warwick," interjected Earl Rivers. "We have assembled a standing army and billeted them within an hour's march of London. Our ships patrolling the channel will give the traitor enough to handle before he places a treasonous foot on Your Highness' soil."

"You can be sure, Lord Rivers, that Warwick has anticipated those moves. William, in your estimation, what power could he muster on short notice? I'll wager my kingdom that Louis will give him only a small force, for such is his nature."

"Only the Marquis of Montagu has the means to assemble a large enough army to threaten us, Sire," said Hastings. "But Sir Julian has kept a close watch on him."

"What of the marquis, Sir Julian? He has shown no inclination to be disloyal, but we fear his heart."

"Majesty, I have watched him carefully, but he has only performed those duties assigned to him by Your Highness and nothing else."

"Mind him well, Sir Julian," said the king. "If Warwick invades, his loyalty will be sorely tested. My lords, we will retire for now, but keep a sharp ear to the winds that blow from France, for time alone stands between us and an accounting with the Earl of Warwick. And, Sir Julian, find Sir Nigel and summon him to us." They all bowed as the king left the room.

"I also marvel that Sir Nigel would leave us at such a dangerous time," Hastings scowled at Sir Julian. "It fills me with wonder at his loyalties. Did he give you any indication of his destination before he left?"

"No, my lord, I was not aware that he had left until the king was informed. But I will stake my life on his loyalty, and I assure you there is a good reason for this." His forehead wrinkled as a thought occurred to him.

"What is it?" asked Hastings.

"It's nothing really, my lord. Perhaps there's no connection at all."

"Connection to what?"

"Two of my guardsmen are also missing, but they are good friends and have been greatly bothered by other matters lately."

"I marvel that you would have so little control over members of the king's personal guard, especially when he needs them all most urgently. What connection did they have with Sir Nigel?"

"They are well acquainted with Sir Nigel, and frequently kept his company, my lord," he responded, stung by the rebuke.

"Then it is sure in my estimation that they departed together. I suggest that you find them all, or I'll have them all declared traitors."

"I will find them, my lord." He had tried to warn Samuel that this could happen, and events may already have progressed beyond his ability to protect his young protégé. His only hope was to find them quickly.

Edward put his hand on the queen's stomach. It was a wonder to him how a woman could carry such a burden within her womb and still lead an almost normal life. Of course, Elizabeth had a small army of doctors, handmaidens, and servants of all kinds to help her through her pregnancy, and she drove them all to distraction with her constant vile mood. Remembering similar problems during her first pregnancy, Edward had avoided his wife during the past few months, believing it was easier on both of them. It was the servants' lot to take the abuse. The king's evenings, on the other hand, were better spent in the company of the young maids that Hastings was able to supply. On this night, however, Edward felt a need to be with his wife.

"I have prepared the royal quarters in the Tower for your confinement, and I think that it would be best if you moved there at once," Edward said, lying next to her in an elaborately carved bed hung with flowing silk drapes. From the windows of her chamber, the vast farmlands and isolated cottages stretched away on the south side of the river, distant thatched roofs glistening with moisture from a recent rain.

"How I detest that place," Elizabeth said. "It reeks of…well, I know not what, but it's horrible. And those filthy ravens that have the run of the place make my skin crawl. I really do not believe that it's the best place for me to bear the future king of England, my love."

"You know as well as I that it may be necessary for me to leave at any time, and the Tower will be the safest place for you."

"I would be perfectly safe at Windsor Castle, and I would prefer to be there. You know that."

"The city garrison wouldn't be able to protect you there. The royal chambers are most comfortable at the Tower, you'll see."

Elizabeth could see that she was not going to prevail this time.

"There's something you're not telling me, isn't there?"

Edward rolled over on his back and gazed out the window.

"It is only by God's grace that I have kept the throne this long. I think we both know that. In my present state, I doubt that I could prevail against Warwick if he comes with any kind of power."

"You are the anointed king. I refuse to believe that the noble houses will not give you the support that they have sworn to give before God."

Edward smiled tenderly. "It is you, our daughter, and unborn child for whom I fear most. If it were only me, I'd struggle with the devil himself."

"My husband," she took his hands, "these fears will make you weak, and I will not have it said that I or my children helped to pull a king from his rightful place. It is that which you should fear, for as God is my witness, I shall do what I must to go on. What will happen is only God's to know, and I would rather be ignorant of His plans than live my life in fear of them." He smiled again and kissed her.

"You have always been my strength, Bess. From the first day I saw you in the woods with your children, I knew somehow that you would be the rock beneath my feet." She pulled Edward tightly to herself, as if to unite them into one.

"Together we shall prevail, my love. I know it as sure as I know the sun rises in the morning."

The next morning a post arrived from the Marquis of Montagu. Hastings brought the message to the king in the Jerusalem Chamber of the palace. Legend held that Henry IV, grandfather of poor Henry in the Tower, had died in this very chamber. The guilt of having usurped the throne enticed Henry to undertake a crusade to the holy land, and early in his uneasy reign, it had been foretold to Henry that he would die only in Jerusalem. Alas, the crown proved difficult to hold and rebellion dogged his days, making it impossible for him to leave England. When the sickness of death came upon him, he ordered that he be carried to the Jerusalem Chamber of the palace in order that the prophesy be fulfilled. Edward performed his business there to remind him always of the fate of kings.

Hastings was waiting when the king entered.

"Forgive me, Sire, but there is news of a new rebellion by the one who calls himself Robin of Redesdale. The Marquis of Montagu has sent sure intelligence."

"What are their numbers?"

"Montagu estimates two thousand."

Edward could not contain his anger. "We had presumed that we had heard the last from that traitor when we gave Percy back his earldom. Why has he been allowed to continue to threaten the peace?"

"As Your Highness knows, we've concentrated our troops around London. Until Warwick's threat is extinguished, it will be difficult to bring these petty rebels to justice."

"Send to Montagu and give him permission to levy an army against this fool of Redesdale. I will travel to York myself and meet him there, where we will finally put an end to this rebel. See to it quickly, William, as I do not wish to be away too long."

"Sire, does your Highness think it prudent to leave London? I would be honored to carry your banner on this mission."

Edward shook his head. "We cannot trust Montagu with an army, as I think he will be sorely tested with such power. If I am there with him, I can eliminate that danger. Go now, my friend, and make the necessary preparations, and together we'll make quick work of the traitor."

"As you wish, my lord."

A fortnight later, Sir Nigel had entrusted the Millers into the care of a priest in a small village near Lincoln. They could not go immediately to York, since Colinsworth would surely seek them there. Nigel sent someone ahead to York to bring Emma and the children to their family. He hoped that their need for such caution would last for a short time only, as he planned to ask the king for aid against Colinsworth, and to return to Colinsworth for Samuel and Oliver, if they were still alive. In any case, he would bring Colinsworth to the king's justice for his crimes.

Sir Nigel began his journey back toward London. The weather had turned colder on the morning that found him walking along the decaying old Roman road that led south. At midday, he found a large boulder within sight of the road near a small brook, from which he refreshed himself with a long drink. Settling on top of the boulder, he lowered his pack and took a few bites of dried venison.

He heard a cantering horse approaching and listened to confirm that the rider was coming from the south, then leaped from the rock and hid behind a group of holly shrubs watching as the horse and rider came into view. It was Ralph, one of his own scouts. Sir Nigel shouted and waved. Ralph drew his short sword the instant he saw the waving figure, and was ready to defend himself until he saw who it was. Sir Nigel was glad to see that at least his man knew the dangers of riding these roads alone. Ralph jumped from the saddle.

"Sir Nigel, you have saved me the difficult task of finding you! I was sent by Sir Julian to give you a most urgent message."

"Then I'm pleased that I could make your task easier. Let's hear this urgent message."

"The king has summoned you to his presence, but Sir Julian requests that you meet with him first at the White Swan in St. Albans."

"Is that all?" Sir Nigel's expression did not betray his concern. He had left without the king's permission, and he knew he would have to answer for that.

"That is all I was asked to convey," Ralph responded.

"Come. We'll share your horse."

Together, they rode straight to St. Albans, arriving an hour before sunset. The White Swan was located on the principal street through town and was always crowded with patrons who traveled to and from London, the town being located strategically a day's walk from the capital. Leaving Ralph to tend to the horse, Sir Nigel entered into a cauldron of noise and bustling activity, dozens of patrons engaged in as many animated conversations and various games.

No one took any note of Sir Nigel's arrival that he could tell. Taking a seat near the wall opposite the bar, he scanned the room without appearing to be too interested. He found another of his scouts sitting with a group of rowdy card players, their eyes meeting and silently acknowledging each other's presence. There was no sign of Sir Julian.

Several logs were added to the fireplace and were reduced to shimmering coals before a man wearing the Sun-in-Splendor livery of the king's personal guard entered. He joined Sir Nigel and waved for ale.

"I assume that Sir Julian sent you?" asked Nigel.

"He regrets that events have kept him away and offers his apology," said the guardsman quietly. "Sir Julian asked that I inform you that the king himself is traveling north to York to put down a rebellion led by the one who calls himself Robin of Redesdale, and that you, Samuel, and Stanley have been missed from the ranks."

"The king has led the army north himself?"

"Yes and we're to join him forthwith at Doncaster."

Sir Nigel took a drink and wondered why the king felt it necessary to travel north himself, unless he suspected that Montagu was behind the rebellion.

"Very well. Go and tell your master that I will arrive within the same hour as yourself." The guardsman nodded, finished his drink, and left without further conversation.

Sir Nigel found Ralph waiting outside. "Get us two fresh horses from wherever you can and meet me here." He walked across the cobbled street and waited by the side of a large oak, until his scout at last emerged from the Swan and joined him in the darkness.

"I saw no one follow you out," he said softly. This was Jonathan, his most trusted and skilled follower. "It is provident that I find you here. This very evening I have received certain news that Warwick has landed at Plymouth." Sir Nigel felt his skin crawl.

"This rebellion that has drawn the king north is too perfectly timed with Warwick's landing to be a coincidence, and I fear…" He had to think. "What does the earl bring with him?"

"The complement of sixty ships, the Duke of Clarence, the Earl of Oxford, and Lord Roos. A storm has scattered the English fleet that was guarding against his crossing, and his friends in Kent have already rallied to his side."

"Take the north road to Pontefract, my friend, as quickly as you can and bring me word of any dangers there. I'll ride to Doncaster this night and warn the king myself." Jonathan disappeared into the night without another word. Sir Nigel prayed that his suspicions were unfounded.

The dungeon of Colinsworth Castle was somewhere beneath the walls of the barbican tower. In suffocating blackness, Samuel and Oliver were chained to an unseen wall, the dripping condensation chilling them to the bone. They had no idea how long it had been since they had been imprisoned, but they had been given no water nor food. Samuel's legs no longer possessed the strength to support him, and blood trickled down his arms from his cut and chafing wrists.

"Oliver, where are you?" Even the act of speaking was painful.

"I am here, my friend."

"Damn you, Oliver, now I have caused your death as well."

There was no response. Samuel tried to moisten his lips.

"You shouldn't have come back. We all die alone anyway."

Sounds came from somewhere. At first, Samuel was not sure if they were real or imagined, but then he saw a flicker of light and heard heavy footsteps on stone. Three men holding torches unlocked the iron grate between the dungeon and the spiral steps beyond. The first two placed their torches in mounting brackets on either side of the room, shedding light on the dreary place for the first time since their imprisonment. Samuel saw where Oliver hung on the adjacent wall, his face pale as death. The third man brought his torch to Samuel's face and stood within a few inches. Squinting against the light, Samuel saw the hideous scar that ruined the side of Sir Hugh's face and closed his eyes, knowing that the devil himself had come to call.

"We meet once again, my young tormentor," Sir Hugh said almost pleasantly, bringing his face even closer. "Unfortunately, I haven't much time to stay and get better acquainted, so if you will tell me the whereabouts of the girl you call Kate, I'll be on my way." Samuel twisted in terror. Kate was still hunted by this foul man. What had she done to bring this wrath upon herself?

"I have no knowledge of where she is," he said, his mouth as dry as sand. He took comfort in knowing that the truth would make it impossible for him to betray her.

"Then you can tell me the names of the others who were with you." Sir Hugh motioned to one of the other men, who ripped Samuel's shirt away and pulled a short leather whip from his belt. "You can stop my assistant anytime you wish by divulging the information." The first stroke fell across his chest, so shockingly painful that it took a moment for Samuel to think clearly again. Each new stroke came only after the pain of the previous one was allowed to fully mature. After five blows, Sir Hugh signaled a pause.

"Is she worth your life, dog?" When the question brought no response, more blows fell, but each new shock of agony only took him closer to unconsciousness. Oliver begged them to stop.

Sir Hugh signaled for his henchman to stand aside. He pulled Samuel's head up by the hair, saw no signs of understanding in his face, and dropped it roughly.

"Force some food and water into both of them. I want them alive."

Sir Nigel was recognized and allowed to pass. When he entered town he found Sir Julian guarding the entrance to the king's temporary residence in Doncaster.

"I thank God to see you safe," Sir Julian greeted him. "But I think the king will not be as pleased as I."

"He will have greater problems to deal with, I'm afraid. Warwick has landed and has already begun to gather a following."

Sir Julian was shaken.

"We must return to London before it's too late! I'll begin the preparations now."

"Good," agreed Sir Nigel. "When will you inform the king?"

"I'll wake Lord Hastings now and leave that to him." The old knight ran into the house where the royal party was sleeping. Moments later, a rider arrived.

"You are, I think, Sir Nigel of Devon?"

"I am."

"A man unknown to me was apprehended attempting to enter town, saying that he had urgent news for you. He gave me this button to show you." It was a brass button with Sir Nigel's family crest embossed in its center.

"Bring me to him immediately." He was led to a tent on the north side of town where two guards stood sentry by the flap. Inside, Jonathan paced impatiently.

"Nigel, for God's sake, the king must flee. They are only hours away as we speak!" Nigel could not understand why Jonathan had returned so quickly.

"Who? Who is only hours away?"

"Montagu, the wretched traitor! With an army of thousands."

"Is this confirmed? How can you be sure he doesn't bring them for the king?"

"Members of his army who refused to follow Montagu when he made his intentions known broke away and sent messengers ahead. I tell you there is no question."

"Leave this place, my friend. May God grant we meet again some day." Sir Nigel sped from the tent and galloped back to the house where the king's party slept. "Raise the house! You in there, call the king and stand ready." Guardsmen came streaming out with swords drawn. Sir Julian, Earl Rivers, and Hastings followed a moment later.

"My lord," he addressed Hastings, "treacherous Montagu lies nearby with an army that he will use to take the king. We must leave here at once."

"Sir Nigel," Hastings was frightened and angry, "where have you been?"

"It does not matter," interrupted Edward, stepping from the house.

"I regret that there is worse, Sire. The Earl of Warwick has invaded your realm and marches on London at this very moment."

Edward knew when a battle could not be won, but he did not show his despair in front of his men.

"What do you suggest, William? Are we to spend the rest of our days as a pawn of the haughty Earl of Warwick?"

The Duke of Gloucester, who had just joined them, answered instead.

"Sire, I have heard the news, and I beseech you to flee. We will live to fight again."

Edward smiled at his young brother, and hoped that he would see the day that he could prove his valor.

"Sire, I must agree," said Hastings. "It vexes my very soul to run from a fight, but my lord of Gloucester has spoken well. The Duke of Burgundy will surely give Your Highness aid."

Edward thought of Elizabeth, the princess, and his unborn child. Would they be safe? If he stayed and fought such a hopeless battle against far superior odds, he would only waste the lives of these noble subjects and those of his army. Elizabeth had sought sanctuary before when Warwick imprisoned him. Now she would have to be brave again.

"Very well then. We shall leave our realm, and God save Warwick if ever we meet again."

Within an hour, King Edward's small army was dismissed and a band of desperate men rode toward the coast.

Two days had passed since Samuel had been beaten to within a few breaths of his life. In accordance with Sir Hugh's orders, they had been released from their chains and were fed water and bread. Oliver was quick to indulge, for he knew that he would need his strength in order to help his friend. Still in great pain, Samuel had been able only to drink some water, and Oliver still feared for his life. He had done his best to clean the blood from Samuel's wounds but there was little else he could do.

The sound of the door clanging open startled Oliver out of a thin slumber, and seeing men with torches again beyond the grate of their cell made him wonder what new horrors awaited. Three guards entered.

"Get them up," said the first one. They grabbed Samuel and roughly pulled him to his feet, bringing a sharp cry of pain. Oliver stood on his own, legs wobbling. "You're being moved," said the first guard gruffly. "Bring them up."

Both were half carried, half dragged up the stairs and into the courtyard. Blinded by the light, they were dumped in a heap on the grass before the doorway, where a wagon pulled by two horses waited for them.

The great relief of seeing the light of day again was tempered by the sight of Sir Hugh.

"A pathetic sight if I ever saw one," he sneered. "Get them in."

They were both tossed into the wagon and tied by the wrists to the corner posts, the rope bringing new blood from the raw sores left by the chains. "There will be no escape for you this time, be assured of that. And do not hope for help from your friends in the guard. The usurper Edward has been banished and Henry of Lancaster sits once again on the throne. We travel to London where the rightful king will sign your death warrants and those of your entire family, and I will take the pleasure upon myself to tie the rope around your necks." Samuel tried to struggle against his ropes. Sir Hugh's words were carefully crafted to bring as much despair as possible, and they had succeeded.

The painful confrontation was interrupted by Lord Colinsworth coming from the stable, leading his own horse.

"Sir Hugh, I still object to your taking my prisoners, and I will accompany you to the king to seek retribution for my losses."

Sir Hugh slowly shifted his glare from the prisoners to Colinsworth, who was preparing to mount his horse.

"The queen will not wish to speak to one who allowed the girl for whom she has been hunting for years to escape. In fact, I have Her Majesty's leave to give you this message." He drew his sword and plunged it through Colinsworth's heart, letting him collapse to the ground in a bloodied heap. "Accept Her Majesty's thanks for your incompetence." Wiping his sword clean on his victim's tunic, he mounted his horse and signaled for the wagon driver to follow. The wagon rolled slowly past Colinsworth's bloody corpse, and Samuel painfully shifted to get a better view.

"You have your reward now, fool."

Queen Elizabeth, eight months pregnant and trying to endure her period of confinement in the royal chambers of the Tower, was anxious to receive the messenger, as was her mother. The duchess signaled for him to be admitted. A young man barely out of his teens, dressed in a leather jerkin and heavy leggings, entered and bent one knee to the ground. He was clearly distressed.

"What is your news? Speak quickly."

"My lady, forgive me, for the news I bring is evil and fouls my tongue to speak of it." Elizabeth pulled herself from bed, supporting her back as she rose.

"What is this evil news you bring to my chamber?"

"The Earl of Warwick has claimed the realm for Henry of Lancaster, and King Edward has fled the kingdom. Forgive me, Highness, I would rather have cut out my tongue than speak of such evil things."

"And were I not in so difficult a state, I would cut it out for you," Elizabeth responded angrily. "Leave my sight at once." The messenger fled without another word. She glared at her mother. "Once again, I am without my husband and damn Warwick has our kingdom at his feet."

The duchess pushed a lady-in-waiting toward the door.

"Go and summon help from anyone who will come. We will leave the Tower this very night. If Henry has the throne again, Warwick will have command of the Tower. We must make our way quickly to the sanctuary at Westminster once again." The queen placed her hand on her stomach.

"Warwick will not abide Edward's heir to live freely in the realm, a constant danger to the Lancastrians. He is a traitor, not a fool."

"All the more reason to move swiftly to sanctuary, my love."

"But what kind of life would it be, cloistered in the abbey?"

"Better than to live his life shut within the walls of Middleham Castle, never to be heard from again, or worse. Now please, dearest, we must make hasty preparations."

"But what of the family?"

"We will stand strong within ourselves. It's all that we can do."

Elizabeth looked around the room. Though the royal chambers were plush enough, she still hated this place. It left a lasting impression of decay in her mind.

"Let's depart. I never wanted to come here anyway."

The lady-in-waiting brought the urgent order to the Tower's steward to pack the queen's possessions for a hasty departure to Westminster Abbey. The activity was frenetic, with servants preparing wagons and horses, orders shouted in every direction. One of the last items to be packed was the porcelain angel that had been given to her by Lord Fitzwalter's daughter, Katherine. She watched as it was carefully placed in its gilded box and packed with straw to cushion it from the rough ride ahead. She had gone nowhere without the intricately crafted Italian porcelain, perhaps because it reminded her of the time in her past when she was most happy.

Soon the royal family was on its way past the gates of the Tower, over the moat and out toward the sanctuary at Westminster Abbey.

A scant forty-eight hours later, the heavy doors that guarded the east entrance to Henry's chamber in the Wakefield Tower opened with a clang. The Archbishop of York and several servants entered with the Constable of the Tower, Sir James Brackenbury, to find Henry kneeling at the altar alcove, lost in prayer. He was clothed simply, in wool leggings and a plain white shirt, barefoot.

"Your Majesty, the usurper Edward has fled, and we have come to greet you once again with your former titles and dignity." If there was a reaction from Henry, they did not see it. "My lord, your loyal servant the Earl of Warwick has bid me to greet you once again as our king, and to bring you from this place."

Slowly, Henry's hands fell to his sides and he hesitantly rose to his feet, supporting himself against a railing on the wall.

"Only God may fetch me from this place," he said softly. "However, I will do as you ask." The archbishop motioned for his men to assist, and they led Henry out into the adjoining Garden Tower. Half-carrying the newly re-acclaimed king, they led him to the very royal chambers that Queen Elizabeth had vacated in the White Tower, which had been lavishly arrayed for her confinement. His emaciated body was bathed and new clothing brought from Edward's wardrobe.

After several days of care, Henry was informed that it was time for him to hold an audience. The first visitor was, of course, the Earl of Warwick, who until now had been busy quelling the Yorkist uprisings inevitable after such a coup. Warwick had not spoken to him since arriving back in London, and was barely bothering to hide the fact that no decisions were actually coming from Henry. But soon he would have to deal with Queen Margaret, still in France waiting for word of his success. She would prove a thornier problem.

When he entered the audience chamber of the White Tower, Warwick led a large contingent of nobles, including the Marquis of Montagu, the Duke of Clarence, the Archbishop of York, the Earl of Oxford, and Lord Roos, to greet the new king and to once again swear their allegiance. Among them Henry noticed a man with a hideous scar on his face. Sir Hugh averted his eyes under the king's questioning gaze. Also among the earl's party was a young man in his early teens whom Henry did not recognize. Warwick bowed and addressed the king with his booming voice.

"Your Majesty, from your queen who will join you shortly from France, I am sent to impart greetings and to rid you of the Yorkist pretender, Edward. Be comforted to know that your adversary will trouble you no more."

"We thank you, my lord, for your pains, though we marvel that when last we sat upon the royal chair, it was you who were our most able enemy."

Warwick had hoped the old fool would be too feeble-minded to remember who his enemies were, but he was prepared.

"I regret, Sire, that I was led astray by the House of York, and do beseech Your Highness' forgiveness. I believe that I have atoned for past blunders with my latest actions, and am here today to swear my allegiance." Ignoring the earl, Henry pointed to Clarence.

"You, sir. Our memory is weak from years in prison, but we recall that you are a brother of York, is it not so?"

"It is, my lord," said Clarence, chagrined to be swearing allegiance to this fool whom his brother had dethroned. It was not for this that he had turned his back on his family. But for now he would play along. It was better than living as an insignificant peer in France. "I too was led astray, and crave Your Majesty's forgiveness."

"Where is your brother?" Henry sat back and closed his eyes.

"He has fled the realm, my lord. It is thought he will seek shelter at the court of Burgundy."

"Where is your brother, Rutland?"

Clarence frowned and looked to Warwick for guidance.

"He is dead, my lord, since the battle at Wakefield."

Henry nodded. After long moments of strained silence, he opened his eyes to see the young man who had caught his attention earlier.

"Come closer and let me look upon you." The hesitant boy obeyed. "Who is this youth?" Henry looked for someone to answer. Jasper Tudor, a knight in the service of Oxford, stepped forward.

"My lord, he is my nephew, Henry Tudor, formerly heir to the Earldom of Richmond." The answer brought a smile to Clarence's face, since he was the current holder of that title, given to him by Edward when the young man's father was beheaded for fighting on the side of Lancaster. Henry placed his hands on the boy's head.

"It is a goodly head," he said absently after a moment, "a head on which to place a crown, where it will find peace." The meaning of the king's attentions was lost on the young Tudor, as it was on everyone in the room. His uncle motioned him back and waited for Henry to regain some semblance of sanity, if that was possible.

Warwick had seen enough.

"My lords, the king is not well and requires rest. You shall all be summoned as you are needed." As the courtiers departed and Henry was helped from the room, Warwick retired to an alcove with his brothers.

"These rantings of our new king may prove difficult to control," said Montagu.

"I am more concerned with Clarence," said the archbishop. "He may be content with regaining his fortune, but he is a man with lofty goals left unrequited. Disappointment is the first ingredient of rebellion, and I for one have spent all the time I care to in the confines of these towers."

"You are like a pair of women to prate on so." Warwick could not hide his impatience. "We have achieved all that we could hope for. If you had supported me before we were exiled," he berated Montagu, "we would not have to deal with this old fool, but now we must make the most of what

God has granted. As for Clarence, he is my son-in-law and will not defy me. He has too much to lose."

"What about the queen? She will be more difficult to control," said Montagu.

"We will see to it that she has precious few choices. Furthermore, she will be a great help in controlling Henry's rantings. Come now, forget all these worries and let's sample the contents of the king's cellars. It has been too long since I've enjoyed a fine wine."

The archbishop smiled. "Indeed, prison walls arouse a rare appreciation for such comforts." A thought occurred to him, and he bent his head toward the earl's. "I have heard in the streets the common men call you Warwick the Kingmaker."

Kingmaker! thought Warwick. *If I cannot be king, Kingmaker will suffice.*

In a different alcove, another meeting was taking place. Lord Roos was trying to avoid looking at Sir Hugh and his deformed face.

"You assured me that you had the woman. Now am I to believe that you simply let her disappear?"

"Lord Colinsworth will never fail us again, my lord, I promise you that," Sir Hugh hissed.

"I am not interested in that fool. I cannot tell you more plainly that the queen wants Fitzwalter's daughter more than she wants to live, can you understand that?"

"My lord, now that the Yorkists cannot protect her, I will have her soon. I already have the one who rescued her from Colinsworth, the very one with whom she has apparently fallen in love." The last word was spat like an expletive. "I can use him to coerce her cooperation."

"Where is he now?"

"Safely bestowed here in the Tower, my lord."

"And no doubt to save his life she will turn over the letter?"

"She will, my lord."

"Then all that remains is to find her and acquaint her with the facts. And find her we shall, Sir Knight, or your place in this new Lancastrian order will be short-lived."

Sir Hugh did not like being threatened. He had dispatched mightier men than Lord Roos.

The English Channel had been a formidable barrier between England and France since the earliest Bronze Age farmers braved the first crossings. Its troubled waters had swallowed up more ships and crews than even the most seasoned captains would care to recall.

On a day when, by the grace of God, the weather was pleasant, King Edward and his small party made a safe journey across the dreaded waterway and landed in Holland, a possession of the Duke of Burgundy, near the town of Alkmaar. There was no guarantee that his desperate little band would be welcome, but Edward was again fortunate that the duke's governor of Holland, the Seigneur de la Gruthuyse, happened to be in town. When the governor heard that none other than the king of England had landed on his shores, he hastened to welcome the exiles ashore and offered them every hospitality.

Before leaving the ship, Edward, who had arrived penniless, gave the ship's master his fur-lined coat as thanks for his service and promised that some day he would do better. The Seigneur de la Gruthuyse agreed to help provision the ships to thank the captain as well. Edward and his followers were escorted to The Hague, where the governor resided, and for the next few weeks Gruthuyse entertained his guests while they waited for word from the duke.

Charles the Bold, Duke of Burgundy, having heard of Edward's presence in Holland, was unsure how to handle the delicate situation. Charles had inherited a wealth almost unrivaled in Christendom. Besides the Burgundian homeland in east central France, he also held sway over the wealthy possessions of Flanders and Holland. For hundreds of years, the dukes of Burgundy had remained autonomous from the kings of France, and had even helped to topple the French throne when England's Henry V had invaded.

Now that the English had lost all their possessions in France, Charles was in a more precarious situation, especially since the king of France was slowly gaining enough power to absorb Burgundy. Only the mutual suspicion of the three powers playing against one another had allowed Charles to remain free of the French king's yoke. Indeed, he had agreed to marry Edward's sister Maggy only to assure himself of English friendship.

"Seigneur de la Bard," Charles asked his most trusted advisor, "Will the ambitious Earl of Warwick give aid to Louis against us?"

"My lord, he will have his hands full, at least for a while, maintaining his grip on the English throne."

"Still, should we help Edward, Louis could move against us, a battle that I do not care to fight at this moment."

"I would imagine that Louis would require very little excuse to turn on your duchy, my lord, and I would wager my last florin that Warwick has already promised to provide many of the cursed English archers."

"Perhaps I shall meet with Edward myself. Make the arrangements, de la Bard. We shall meet at Aire."

The Millers sat quietly in a small room near the church's rectory. Located somewhere in Lincolnshire, the church served a small community of farmers. The priest, Father Geoffrey, had been a friend of Sir Nigel's for many years and had sometimes sheltered unfortunates at the knight's request, knowing that such persons were always in dire need. It was his notion of God's calling. There was, however, little to keep the Millers' minds occupied except for prayer, and he could only provide them with meager rations of food, consisting mainly of bread and some locally captured eel and rabbit given to him by his parishioners.

It had been three weeks since their rescue from Colinsworth Castle, though none of them really felt like much had been accomplished that night. Their freedom had cost Sally and Kate dearly.

Christopher felt worst of all. Haunted by the memory of that night, he wondered again and again what he could have done differently, and no amount of reassurance from Sir Nigel or the women could penetrate his mood. Of one thing he was certain: that he should never have allowed Samuel to convince him to run away like he did. He was the eldest and should have protected them all.

Their confinement in the rectory was especially difficult on the children, who could not understand why they were not permitted to play outside and wanted to return to their home. When John asked where his father was, Sally had wept.

Kate watched as the family that had been so good to her — taken her in when she had needed shelter without really even knowing her — continued to suffer. She could not escape the knowledge that it was mostly her fault. In a heartbeat, she decided that she could no longer do nothing while these good people suffered on her account. Pulling a shawl over her shoulders, she gave Sally a hug.

"Thank you ... all of you," she said sadly, "for your kindness, but I must leave now."

"What do you mean? Where are you going?"

"It's me that they want, you know that. I can't hide behind you any longer. I have already caused you too much pain. I only hope that it's not too late."

"You mustn't go. Once you give them what they want, they'll kill you, and then probably do the same to us anyway."

"I won't let them harm you. My father is not a butcher."

"Your father? But you know that he betrayed you once before."

"I know him. He will not do it again if I give him the letter."

"What are you talking about? What letter?" asked Emma.

Sally ignored her. "You will negate everything for which Samuel sacrificed if you do this. His death would be meaningless."

"Why do you speak of him as if he is dead? You can't know that," said Emma.

"We all know the man with the scar," she answered sadly. "He is not likely to let them live after all that's happened, and Samuel's friends can't help him now."

"Don't you see? It's for Samuel that I must do this, if not to save him, then for his memory, for I have no desire for life at the expense of his. And at least I can try to save his family. Please, don't make this more difficult."

"But you're all we have left of Samuel." Sally began to sob, the memory of her beloved brother too much for her to bear. Emma held her.

"Please Kate, you are part of us now."

"Thank you," Kate answered softly pulling the shawl tight and opening the door. "For everything." She stepped through and was gone.

CHAPTER XXV

"My lady, please, the child's time has come."

"Leave me, you fool! The future king of England will not be born in this place." Elizabeth shoved the midwife and leaned against the bedpost, hoping that the pains would pass. The midwife grabbed one of the handmaidens.

"Go quickly and fetch the duchess." Elizabeth was about to forbid her, but was instead gripped by another contraction.

"Go!" yelled the midwife to the maiden, who had been paralyzed by the scene.

Elizabeth cursed softly, knowing well the signs of impending childbirth. She had prayed that somehow Edward would deliver her from sanctuary and reclaim the throne before this one was born.

She forbade herself to even consider that the child could be another daughter, lest her thoughts somehow affect its gender. The door burst open and the queen's mother ran in with several others.

"What, has the time come so soon?" she asked the midwife.

"It has, my lady, and I must prepare."

"Go, I'll stay with the queen."

"Mother, I cannot have this child here." She was almost in tears. The duchess wiped the sweat from her face.

"God has willed otherwise, my love. Now you must be still and let us help, and you shall see, he shall be a glorious prince for all England to admire."

"But what if…"

"Lie still, my love. Only God may know the future. For us it is futile."

Another wave of pain brought a scream that reverberated around the stark walls of the bedchamber. The quarters were provided by the abbot, and were austere compared to the rooms that Edward had prepared in the Tower. The midwife was back with cloths and containers, some empty, some filled with water that had been heated over the hearth. Several of the women helped Elizabeth into position on the bed, and the vigil began.

The queen remained in labor for another hour before the midwife announced the child's imminent birth. The duchess remained by her side, wiping her brow and comforting her through the contractions, until the midwife pulled the child from the birth canal. After the midwife had cut the umbilical, the duchess took the child and handed it to her daughter.

"The kingdom will rejoice with us, for God has given us this beautiful prince," she said, barely able to contain her joy.

Elizabeth breathed a great sigh of relief at the news of her son, and held him close. Ready to sleep after her ordeal, her voice was barely audible.

"He shall be called Edward, in honor of his father."

The duchess remained by her side as she drifted into sleep.

"May God grant him some safe place in this troubled land," she whispered. Those in attendance crossed themselves in agreement.

Sir Hugh and his men ransacked the millhouse in York where Christopher had rebuilt his father's business from scratch. His henchmen pushed a young man out so that he sprawled before the knight's horse. He was trembling with terror.

"Who are you?" The knight's voice lacked all emotion.

"I am called Charles, if it please you sir," he stammered, eyes averted.

"Where are the owners of this place?"

"They all left a week ago, I know not where." The knight leaned toward him on his saddle.

"And what is your relation to these people?"

"I am apprenticed here, sir. They asked that I stay and watch over the mill until their return."

He nodded to the man standing behind the boy, who drew his knife and pressed it to his throat.

"I'll only ask you once, so be sure of your answer. Where did they go?"

"I swear by all that's holy, they told me nothing." He released the contents of his bladder in terror. "They said it was best that I knew nothing." Sir Hugh scratched his scar.

"Your services will no longer be needed here. The millers will never be returning, I can assure you of that." He signaled his men, who threw him onto the street. Jumping to his feet, he ran as fast as he could, hand against his bleeding neck.

"Burn it," ordered Sir Hugh savagely. His men found flames in the hearth that had warmed the young apprentice and used them to create flaming brands, which they threw onto the thatched roofs of both houses. While the millhouse itself was made of stone, the roof and supporting timbers made a satisfactory blaze that Sir Hugh watched with obvious pleasure. When the houses were completely engulfed, he ordered his men to their horses, and turned his back on the ruins.

"I swear on my soul, if he does not give my royal brother what he needs, I'll make his life a hell in his own palace." Maggy had stormed into the room and embraced her brother Edward warmly. She had not been permitted to hear the conversation between the king and her husband, the Duke of Burgundy, but had burned his ear well on their journey to Aire, not comprehending why the duke would hesitate to offer aid.

"He has agreed to help," said Edward with a weak smile, "but I will need a great deal more if I'm to bring down Warwick."

"The noble houses of England will flock to you when they hear of your arrival. They have sworn their oaths and will not forsake you."

"They forswore their oaths to Henry before me." Edward was despondent. "How is anyone to know who to follow, or who to fight for? No, do not expect the nobility to rally behind my colors, or the common folk either. These wars have tried their patience beyond what I can demand."

"How can my royal brother speak this way? To lose hope before even fighting for what is rightfully his. Where is the brash young man that I grew to love and admire at Ludlow? And where the smile that robbed me of so many angry moments?"

He shrugged. "These wars have taken my youth, Maggy. And they have cost me a father and…" His head dropped between slumping shoulders. She put her hand on his cheek.

"I also wake at night calling Edmund's name, and I see his face in every cloud and in the reflection of every misty lake. I long for the sight of his loving eyes, and the days when it was just the three of us, and his laughter filled my heart."

"He tried to warn me. He tried to tell me about the cost of this quest, but I did not understand until now what he meant, now that it is far too late."

"Too late? You have truly lost your way, haven't you? It is never too late, my brother, to correct what has been wronged, or to take back what has been wrongfully seized. Shake off this dangerous mood, Edward, and once again be king, for there is nothing else for you in this life. The ship has sailed that could have borne you to other fates."

Edward turned from his sister and tried to clear his mind of the sadness that had possessed it.

"Of course you're right." His back straightened. "And you need not worry that I'll choose to live my remaining years in a monastery. I will take your husband's small force and return to England, for I will be king of the land that is moistened by its rainy sky until I am dust within its bosom."

"It is well said, Your Majesty." She embraced him again. "And I will pray for you from these shores, wishing that I could be by your side."

"I shall count on that." He kissed her cheek.

She hesitated for a moment.

"I wish to ask a boon before you leave. Will you hear my request?"

"You know that I will," he said tenderly.

"Your brother Clarence still loves you, though he has strayed. If you give him a chance, you'll see that he has a good heart." Edward's face grew hard.

"I marvel that you still favor him after his treachery. I gave him every opportunity to prove his love and he thanked me with betrayal, and now he wallows in comfort while his brother and lawful king suffers the fate of a beggar in a foreign land."

"He will prove a true brother, I know it in my soul. He needs only a chance to prove himself."

"We shall see if God gives me any means to test your faith. Now I must see to our preparations, and will take my leave of you."

"Godspeed, Edward. I will visit your royal throne when, by His will, you have reclaimed what is yours."

"Until then," he agreed with a smile. They embraced one last time and she swept from the room, wiping tears from her cheeks.

"Farewell, my sister. Perhaps when next we meet, Edmund will be with us once again."

The door of Chilton Manor swung open, and the steward of the house looked as if he had seen a spirit from the dead.

"Lady Katherine! I can scarcely believe it."

Kate stood at the threshold, dressed in the garb of a serving girl, shivering from the cold, and wishing she was anyplace but here. Her journey had been long and difficult, walking dangerous roads where evil stalked those who were careless.

"May I come in, Walter?" she asked quietly.

"It is not my place to deny you, my lady. Please come in, and let me take that wet cloak. There is a fire in the great hall. Wait there and I'll get you a dry wrap."

"Thank you, Walter. And will you please announce my presence to my father?"

"As you wish, Lady Katherine."

He escorted her to the great hall. A huge stone hearth with fluted columns on either side contained a snapping fire supported by a shimmering bed of coals. She stepped close, warming her numb hands. The heat raised steam from her wet clothing. Looking around the empty hall, she recalled the lighthearted years of her youth. How she had relished the time when she ran through this room with such abandon. And the banquets! Feasts of unimaginable quantity; jesters and musicians performing their magic to her delight. Her father would allow her to sit on his lap, affording her the best view in the room. He was so young and full of cheer in those days before the wars.

It hardly seemed like the same life to her when, in this very room, he had ordered her to turn over the letter after she had confided in him, an act that felt so like betrayal that she had fled from her life, never to return until this moment.

"My God!" a voice exclaimed behind her. She turned to see her father, Lord Fitzwalter. "It really is you."

She curtsied in respect

"I hope you will forgive my unannounced arrival."

He looked disapprovingly at her clothing.

"So it's true. You have actually lived as a common serving girl?"

"Yes, Father."

"The life I gave you here was so unpleasant that you prefer to live like this?" He waved at her torn shawl.

"We both know why I left." She turned to face the fire.

"Yes we do, indeed. You were shamed by your own act of disobedience, not only to me but to the royal family itself. Is that why you return? Have you finally after all these years seen the dishonor in your actions?"

"Think what you will, Father. I have not returned to debate the past with you, but to offer you a bargain. Will you hear it?"

Lord Fitzwalter sat in a large cushioned seat.

"Very well, what is this bargain? I hope it concerns the letter that you stole from the queen."

"It does." She turned to face him once again. "As you know," her tone was accusatory, "I have been hunted like a wild animal for that letter, and have not had a moment of peace since I left here. I knew that and accepted it when I made my decision, and I regret nothing. But there are others that have been made to suffer for my decision, and I wish for that to stop."

"You refer to your…friend in the former king's personal guard?" Kate could not conceal her surprise.

"You know of him?"

"Your recent activities are well known to me."

"You knew that I was imprisoned by that dog, Colinsworth, and did nothing?" Her surprise was turning to anger.

"You said you had no regrets. Do you wish to amend that assertion?"

She clenched her fists, then seemed to deflate. It was true: Why should he have lifted a finger on her behalf after she had turned her back on him and brought dishonor to his house? And yet she had held some hope that he would relent. Now she knew better.

"Do you wish to hear my proposal?"

"Please."

"I will turn the letter over to you, if you will give me your word that there will be no further persecution of the miller's family. They have nothing to do with what has been done and have no knowledge of any of these affairs. Will you agree to those terms?"

Her father took a while to think.

"Your friend...what is his name?"

"Samuel." The word brought an ache to her heart.

"I understand that he is wanted for crimes against the throne. If so, there is nothing that I can do for him."

"It is his family that I want protected. Samuel has already paid the price for the charges against him."

That information came as a surprise to Fitzwalter. He made a mental note to inquire into its veracity.

"If you turn the letter over to me, I will place the others under my personal protection."

Kate walked over to a small stand upon which a book lay open in the center. The arrangement of the book and its surroundings resembled a shrine. She took the book to her father.

"You will swear it on Mother's Bible."

The Bible was the only possession her mother truly cherished during her life, and was sacred to Fitzwalter, his memory of her being his most valued possession. He laid his hand on it.

"I swear it on this holy book," he said softly.

That very evening, a rider left Chilton Manor with an urgent message for Lord Roos.

"What place is this before us?" asked Edward, pointing toward the low shore off the bow.

"It is the port of Ravenspur, Your Highness," said Hastings. "If our intelligence is accurate, we will find no resistance to our landing."

Edward hoped it was true. He was eager to know his fate. The crossing had been uneventful, taking only one night to reach Cromer off the Norfolk coast, where they had hoped to find a friendly reception. Instead, they discovered that Warwick had anticipated them, and the town was heavily fortified. As they turned back out to sea, the infamous channel weather turned stormy and his small fleet was scattered over the water. One ship carrying mostly horses went to the bottom. The rest of the fleet gathered at the mouth of the River Humber, and longboats were dispatched to seek landing places. Edward sent a portion up the coast with his brother, Gloucester, and another group down the coast under the leadership of Earl Rivers, with orders to land as best they could and make their way to Ravenspur. Sir Julian and Lord Hastings remained with the king and a small following.

"Very well, William. Order the captain to find a suitable landing. God's will awaits us."

Several hours later, Edward's boats had disgorged their men, horses, and meager cache of weaponry. They waited for Gloucester and Rivers to join them while gathering supplies in Ravenspur. He sent to Henry Percy, the man he had restored as the Earl of Northumberland at great cost to himself, to see if he was now ready to repay the favor. He also sent scouts to search for Sir Nigel of Devon.

In one day, his army had assembled and was ready to begin the reconquest of the realm, a lofty goal for so small a fellowship. But the king's spirits were lifted by their high morale, and he would not be the one to lose hope before their fate was sealed. In the morning they set out for York, where, if the Earl of Northumberland was against them, the end of their quest would come quickly. But Edward was, if not the king, the rightful Duke of York, and that town would not deny him entry and provisions. Two days of marching passed without interference from anybody, and it was now clear to Edward as he arrived at the gates of York that Northumberland would not defy him, though his silence meant that he could not depend on military assistance. While not entirely good news, it gave his enterprise a fighting chance.

The mayor admitted them to the city, welcoming him only as the Duke of York. Edward had no desire to press his luck, as Montagu was nearby at Pontefract and would soon raise an army of his own. They stayed only one night and then quickly passed Wakefield on his way south. As he suspected, without the help of Northumberland, Montagu had not had time to gather enough men, and he therefore stayed within the confines of Pontefract as Edward marched by.

Two more days found them at Doncaster, the town from which he had been forced to flee his kingdom, and this time with an even smaller following. But help was slowly arriving: two knights who had received great favors from him in better times arrived with six hundred men, and another hundred and fifty came with him from York.

He knew that to stay in any place too long would be folly, as the process of gathering troops required that the nobility see the king himself with a strong army at his back. Edward marched his men next to Leicester, where Sir William Stanley, a close friend of Lord Hastings, brought three thousand men. Edward was now prepared to march on London.

Later that day, King Henry VI, king for three months now, walked along the inner wall of the Tower, as was his custom on days when he felt that the royal suite of the White Tower had grown too confining. He had been promised that once the queen arrived from France, he would be permitted to move back to Westminster Palace, but for now, his protection demanded that he remain here.

He had felt a need to see his old place of confinement in the Wakefield Tower, and made his way onto the allure, where he paused to enjoy the unhindered view of the River Thames. The guard presented arms when he passed, and then resumed his post with an almost imperceptible shake of his head.

Hearing faint voices, he crossed to the adjacent Garden Tower. Leaning over the wall, he saw two guards below who stood over the river gate.

"Then it's true," said the first gruffly, "he has landed for sure?"

"My brother serves Warwick and he's been called to fight. There's a great rush about it. I'd wager a day's rations that he's headed here as we speak."

"Warwick will make short work of him. He's the Kingmaker, ain't he?"

"That's sure enough. The Yorkists have no friends left. I'd march out with the earl myself if I could only get away from here." The first grunted agreement.

"Now that old Henry's ready to move out, there's no one to worry about here anyway. Who'd want to brave an attack on this place for nothing?"

"Just a few wretches like these two down here," he indicated the base of the Garden Tower. "But I think they have some special fate in store for them." He paused to shake his head in pity. "I'd not be in their place to save my soul."

"Nor I," the other agreed. "What do you suppose they did?"

"No one tells me anything," he shrugged, "but it was that bloody demon Sir Hugh who brought them here, so you can bet they got themselves on the wrong side of the earl. My brother heard that one of them even served the Earl of Rutland, he that died at Wakefield."

Henry, startled by the last comment, tried to calm the voices that shouted to him from the past. Working hard to steady himself, he made his way down the spiral steps that led to where the guards were standing.

"You two, attend us." Recognizing the king, they stiffened and presented arms.

"The one you say served the Earl of Rutland, take us to him at once."

The guards looked at each other.

"The lower cells are not a place that we would choose to take Your Highness," the first one said. "It is most unpleasant."

"We have been to Hell," he said softly. "The cells will not offend us."

"As you wish, Your Highness." They reluctantly led the king to a small door at the base of the Garden Tower, where the first one pulled a set of long keys from his belt and unlocked the door. A torch lit the way down a short set of steps to another door that was also locked. Pulling the torch from the wall, he pushed the door open. Henry saw two men sleeping on the hard floor in a corner, the foul smell of corruption turning his stomach. The guards waited impatiently.

"Wake them," Henry commanded.

The guard gave one and then the other a shove with his foot.

"Wake up, dogs, and kneel before the king!"

They both got to their knees as fast as their emaciated bodies would let them.

Oliver squinted hard. "This is not the king," he said softly. The guard, stunned by his temerity, struck him across the side of his head, sending him sprawling to the ground.

"Stop!" ordered Henry. The guard backed off while Samuel helped his friend back to his knees. Henry stepped forward.

"I have heard that one of you served the Earl of Rutland. Is this true?" Oliver was still trying to regain his wits and did not answer.

"Answer His Highness," the guard threatened.

Samuel answered for him, hoping to shield him from further abuse.

"It is true."

"In what capacity?" Henry asked Samuel.

"I was his page," interrupted Oliver.

Henry regarded Oliver with a dreamy look. He was bleeding from the mouth and filthy from months of abuse.

"When did you see him last?"

"The night he was murdered at Wakefield," he said almost inaudibly.

"Highness, please allow us to take you from this place," pleaded a guard.

"Tell me how he died," the king asked Oliver.

Oliver was angry and felt no fear, even of the hulking guard.

"The bloody butcher Clifford killed him, when he was unarmed and sorely wounded. It was a foul deed."

Henry placed both hands against his own chest, seeming to slip into a trance. The guards waited again, wishing that the king would regain his wits and let them leave.

"Bring them!" he suddenly ordered.

The guards were stunned. "Sire, the constable of the Tower has expressly forbidden us to even enter these cells, much less to take these prisoners out."

"Are we your king or is the constable?" demanded Henry.

They were both terrified at risking the wrath of the constable, whose orders surely had came from Warwick. They looked at each other in desperation, knowing they must obey. They pulled the prisoners to their feet and led them up the stairs to the passageway between the two great walls. Stepping into the open, Samuel and Oliver shielded their eyes from the daylight, unable to see more than just the walls around them. Samuel wore only a pair of filthy torn leggings, his emaciated body barely able to support even those. The welts caused by the beating at Colinsworth Castle still burned angry red. And Oliver looked only slightly better. The sight of them shivering and almost blind in the cold afternoon wind ripped at Henry's heart.

"Both of you, give them your cloaks," he snapped at the guards, who were dumbfounded.

"Sire...!"

"You will obey us."

Reluctantly, they placed their cloaks on the prisoners' shoulders. Henry led them toward the main gate that opened on the bustling city of London. When they arrived, the gatekeepers scrambled in disbelief to attend the king, who waved them away.

"Open the gates and release these men." The gatekeeper looked at the two guards shivering in the cold without their cloaks. He shrugged and gave the signal for the gate to be opened. Samuel and Oliver did not know what to make of these strange events, both suspecting that this was some heinous game. When the gate had been raised, Henry nodded to the opening.

"Go. We give you your freedom. Tell your master when next you see him that we have done his bidding."

They looked at the street beyond, still waiting for some treachery. Finally, Oliver kissed Henry's hand.

"God bless you…Your Highness."

Samuel pulled Oliver through the gate.

"Come on," he pressed, "let's get away from here before someone comes after us. I'll die before I let them put us in there again!"

Minutes later they mingled with the hundreds of souls that were about their business on the bustling streets of London.

Two days later, Warwick and the Archbishop of York surveyed their army from atop the strong walls of Coventry.

"Are you certain?" Warwick asked his brother. "Montagu did nothing to hinder him while he pranced his pathetic little army within a dozen miles of Pontefract?"

"That is the report, Richard, but I think it was his only sensible course of action. He was without any following of his own, and received no aid from Northumberland."

"That earl shall find his new title to be short-lived," said Warwick with conviction. "I'll have him back in the Tower as soon as I deal with Edward."

Moments later, the post for which they waited arrived at Broadgate below them, and Warwick yelled to have him admitted immediately. When the messenger arrived on the wall, he knelt and waited to be recognized.

"Yes, yes," said Warwick, "give us your news."

"My lord, your brother the Marquis of Montagu bids me inform you that he will arrive within a week with four thousand men in good array. He also confirms that the Earl of Oxford will arrive a few days later with two thousand more."

"This is comforting news, and well delivered," the earl beamed. "And here is for your troubles," he threw him his purse. The post bowed and quickly left, clutching more money than he had seen in his life. "Added to the army coming with Clarence, Edward will have no chance. As soon as everyone arrives, we shall make for London."

Margaret waited impatiently for final preparations to be made for departure, her ship full of provisions for a landing in England. She cherished the thought of once again stepping on English soil as queen. With her was Anne, Warwick's daughter, now betrothed to her son.

The prince was a young man of sixteen. The fact that Henry had not fathered him made little difference to Margaret, since he had been conceived to give Henry the heir that he needed. But the boy was stout and broad-shouldered like his real father, the Duke of Somerset, and was bold and daring like Henry could never have been. His sandy hair and hazel eyes belied the fire that burned in his soul — a fire that was fed by the desire to rule England as his mother had taught him was his right and only true destiny. With his new wife by his side, he followed his mother onto the boat. Forty other boats carried men and provisions, a fine company to escort the Prince of Wales, his mother, and his wife back.

With the next tide, they set sail, and were greeted with fair winds for a landing at Weymouth on England's southern shore.

Edward led his army toward London knowing that only a swift and bold action could equalize his daunting odds. If he could convince the people of

London to accept him as king, men would flock to his standard. But if the gates were closed against him, he would be forced to face Warwick and his formidable force. The cruelest news of all was that his brother, the Duke of Clarence, was approaching with four thousand soldiers for Warwick.

That evening, Sir Julian rested in his tent trying to remember if there was any precaution that he had overlooked for the safety of the camp. A sizable portion of pork that had been slaughtered and cooked that night sat on his plate untouched. He had never lacked for courage and, for himself, he felt no hesitation facing an enemy of far superior numbers, but to see the young men that he had trained and practically raised — to see them die needlessly...He stepped from the tent where Stanley stood guard at the entrance. Unable to look him in the eye, he studied the flat land around the camp, much of it being prepared for the coming planting season. The sun was setting over a low hill on the horizon and glared angry red over the land. A fair-sized village lay to the south.

"What is this place that lies nearby?" he asked.

"It is called Barnet, my lord."

Sir Julian had heard of it, and remembered passing through years before on a journey north from London. He had witnessed precious little peace since then. *How easy it is to send these young men to their deaths, and worse, how willingly they rush to comply.*

"Have you prepared yourself for fighting, lad?"

"I have, my lord."

"It will be a difficult day, and many of us will not see another sunset."

"We have faced many such enemies," Stanley said.

"Far too many," Sir Julian agreed. "Try to sleep when your watch is over, lad. You'll need all the rest you can manage." Stepping back inside, he saw the still uneaten meat and thought that he really should force it down, but instead, he sat on a stool and tried to clear his mind. A rider approached and spoke to Stanley, who entered the tent.

"Sir Julian, the vanguard apprehended two men on the road this afternoon, both wearing the livery of the master of the Tower. When questioned, they asked for you by name. The guards wish to know your pleasure."

"Men dressed in Lancastrian garb who wish to speak to me," he mused. "Perhaps I'd better see them. Have them brought." Some minutes later he heard steps approach, and Stanley burst in before the rider had arrived.

"Sir Julian! It's Samuel!"

The old knight snapped to his feet and ran from the tent to see the guard leading two men toward him. He pulled up short when he saw Oliver and Samuel, still robed in the borrowed cloaks of the Tower guards, but so gaunt of face that he hardly recognized them.

Stanley embraced his old friend. Samuel grunted in pain and his knees buckled. Stanley caught him and lowered him gently to the ground. Sir Julian pushed him aside.

"What's wrong with him?"

He spread Samuel's cloak and cringed at the sight of the welts on his body, but could see no grave wounds.

"Bring him to my tent," he barked. "Summon the surgeon and bring proper clothing and food for them both."

The surgeon confirmed that Samuel and Oliver needed only rest and nourishment; both men ate large plates of pork and fowl, many of the guardsmen having donated their rations. Sir Julian let them sleep in his tent. It was a fitful sleep, and the old knight wondered what horrors they had been forced to suffer.

At first light, ale and wheat bread were brought to the tent. Samuel felt some strength in his legs for the first time in…well, he could not remember how long. Stepping out from beneath the flap to the outside, he was greeted by a cool but flawlessly sunny morning. He lifted his head and closed his eyes. The rays felt heavenly on his face. He fought the impulse to weep. Sir Julian's voice came from behind.

"I truly regret that the path has been so difficult for you, lad."

"Is my family safe, Sir Julian?" he asked, his eyes still closed against the sun.

"The last I heard from Sir Nigel, they were together and safe. His courier tells me that he will be here this very day if all goes according to plan, and you can ask him yourself."

"Thank you, Sir Julian. I owe you a great deal, even if it has seemed at times that I didn't know that."

"I know your heart well, my boy, and you need not thank me, I've done little enough." Leaves glowed in the low early sunlight. "Come, lad, and put some more food in your gullet. You must tell me how you both came to be here."

Pure wheat bread was a rare treat, and Samuel ate with abandon. The ale was strong and warmed him deeply. It was only then that he could tell the tale of their imprisonment at Colinsworth Castle and the Tower, of the hopelessness that had consumed them until their unlikely release by the demented King Henry himself. Even then, their journey had not been an easy one, as the gates of London were closed day and night in expectation of renewed civil unrest. A merchant had told them of Edward's invasion, news that had lifted their spirits, knowing as they did that the downfall of the Lancastrians was necessary to end their nightmare. And yet, the vision of poor Henry standing inside the Tower gates haunted them.

"And you have no notion of why Henry released you?" Sir Julian asked.

Samuel shook his head. "We were certain that it was some game he was playing with us."

"He kept asking about the Earl of Rutland," Oliver added, "and I could not understand why. But he seemed quite lucid."

"The Earl of Rutland? The king's dead brother?"

"The same. And when he released us at the gate he said to tell my master that he had done his bidding. I only just now remembered that," he added absently.

"This is not the kind of puzzle that the king needs to hear on the eve of what will surely be a difficult battle," said Sir Julian. "I believe that old Henry perhaps heard the tale of the earl's death and felt that the act of freeing you would somehow settle the score."

Stanley burst through the flap. "Sir Julian, it's Sir Nigel! There is a herald from the Duke of Clarence who asks for a parley with the king!"

They all poured from the tent to see Sir Nigel approach. It was Samuel that the knight addressed first after dismounting.

"My heart is full to see you here, my friend."

"My family?" he asked.

"They are safe." Turning to Sir Julian, he said, "There is a herald here for the king, from Clarence."

"Go," Sir Julian ordered Stanley. "Announce us to Lord Hastings." Stanley ran off toward the king's tent as the rest began their slow walk behind him. "Does Clarence ask for our surrender?" he asked Sir Nigel.

"I have never known him to bring welcome tidings."

When they arrived at the king's tent, Edward and Hastings stood waiting with members of the guard around him. It was important that a herald from the enemy be shown strength. The herald went to one knee.

"Your Majesty, I bring greetings from your loving brother, the noble

Duke of Clarence, who asks the favor of a private meeting before the sun sets this evening."

"Where does our brother wish to meet us?" Edward tried to keep his hopes from rising lest they be dashed again by his inconstant brother.

"Sire, he is camped with his following not four miles to the north. He begs that you meet him halfway between."

Hastings had an uneasy feeling. "Sire, I have seen traps set with more caution. If the duke wishes to speak, let him come here himself."

Edward remembered his sister's request.

"Go and tell our brother that we will meet him there now." The herald bowed deeply and rode away as quickly as he had arrived. "We are not in a position to let any opportunity pass, regardless of the danger. Inform our brother of Gloucester that we require his company. You and Sir Julian will also accompany us with the guard."

"Sire, allow me to bring more men."

"No, William, we shall face our brother alone."

An hour later, the king's party waited in a broad meadow between the camps. Hastings watched the field for any signs of treachery. Sir Julian also kept a sharp look, though if Clarence were planning an ambush, this broad and open field would not make an ideal place. Four riders approached from the north, one carrying the Duke of Clarence's colors. Edward prepared himself for the worst, expecting Clarence to brashly demand his capitulation in exchange for clemency. To his surprise, Clarence dismounted and knelt.

"My Liege," said Clarence loudly, "I beg forgiveness and wish to once again serve Your Highness, if you will have me."

Edward leapt from his horse and pulled his brother to his feet.

"These are the words of a true brother! My heart had not dared hope to see this day." He embraced him firmly.

"To atone for my past transgressions, I present you with my army, four thousand strong and ready to die for their true sovereign."

"My lords," Edward addressed his party, "come and embrace gentle Clarence, for he has our full pardon, and is once again our brother!" Gloucester was the first to obey, smiling broadly.

"Welcome, Clarence. I think I shall never be so happy again as I am at this moment."

After Hastings had also embraced him, Edward put an arm around his shoulders.

"Come!" he said jovially. "Send for your men, and you shall dine with us this happy night." Clarence joined the king's party as they rode back to camp. "Sir Julian! Ride before us and spread the news to the men, for this will gladden their hearts as it has ours."

"As you wish, Sire," said Sir Julian, spurring his horse into a gallop. Knowing Clarence as he did, it only made sense that such a greedy man would feel more secure as the king's brother than as a pawn of Warwick under Lancastrian Henry. And with Clarence's army, the odds were now almost even.

"Flee from my sight, you dog, or I'll have you flogged!" The Earl of Warwick was red-faced with anger. The messenger ran from the tent, leaving Montagu and Warwick alone. The news of Clarence's treachery had left them desperate. "My guts told me to keep a closer eye on him, but I never thought he could debase his arrogant self before Edward."

Montagu, whose own treachery had made Warwick's success possible a few months before, knew they had no time for regret. "Calm yourself, Richard, and forget about what has been done. Edward is only a day's march from here and we had better be ready when we meet, or this time our heads will surely pay the price for our tardiness. We still have superior numbers and will prevail." Warwick's captain entered.

"If I may, my lord?" Warwick testily nodded. "Word has arrived by post that the queen and Prince of Wales have landed and are gathering an army in Cornwall and Devonshire. The news is one week old, my lord."

"Thank you, captain. Return to your post." The captain bowed and left. "This at least is comforting news. Soon many will hear of the queen's arrival and flock to our cause, knowing that Edward is trapped between two armies with no hope. Come, let's make preparations to leave at first light, and find the poor pretender and my wayward son-in-law, for I shall no longer brook these children of York on English soil."

The news of Clarence's shift of allegiance had indeed brought new life to Edward's army. Sir Julian could see hope where before there had been only grim determination, boisterous behavior where before men had sat silently in small groups.

Samuel, Oliver, and Stanley spent the evening together speaking of things that had nothing to do with kings and wars. For that evening, safe and warm before the small cookfire, they told stories of their childhoods and tried to squeeze a lifetime of friendship into the hours before dawn. Nigel and Sir Julian spent the night listening to their scouts , who crept close to the enemy's positions, carefully counting fires and horses.

The next evening, just before sunset, Warwick and his army arrived at Barnet, and by that time Edward was eager to settle the score with his cousin. Knowing that Warwick would array his men and wait for morning, Edward decided to move first. His generals assembled outside his tent.

"My lords, we will move into position this very night under the cover of darkness, so that in the morning Warwick will find an army already within arrowshot ready to defy his arrogance. Inform everyone to make no noise and light no fires, and by God's will we shall give them a sharp surprise at daybreak. Ourself and Clarence will take the center, Gloucester the right flank, and Hastings shall command the left. We shall all fight on foot."

His last command was understood by everyone. It meant that nobility and common soldiers would fight as one, and they would live or die together. It suited them well.

The lords joined their separate commands and began to organize the men. Sir Julian and the guard would fight with the king. As the guard prepared themselves, Samuel approached his old teacher.

"Sir Julian, I wish to resume my post."

Sir Julian hardly recognized the young man whom he had taught to be a formidable soldier.

"You are too weak, lad, and will only get yourself killed. Stay in my tent and get some rest."

"Lord Hastings will not deny me if I ask him."

"For God's mercy, lad, you haven't your strength back. Don't be eager to toss your life away."

"Sir Hugh may be out there," he said. The old knight sighed sadly.

"Very well, but listen to me: You're a member of the king's guard and will obey every command I issue just like every other guardsman. If you endanger the king's life or any of your mates by running off on your own again, I'll take you down myself. Is that clear?" Samuel averted his eyes.

"Yes."

Edward's army crawled its way along the road north from Barnet toward the plateau where Warwick had arrayed his men. Able to see Warwick's cookfires, Edward and his captains positioned their troops less than a mile from the enemy and settled in to wait for morning. Samuel and Stanley found a relatively dry hummock of tall grass. As Samuel huddled in, the fog began to thicken. He could hear the din of activity coming from the enemy camp and realized that only one of those thousands had ever done him any wrong. He was so tired that sleep would have been a godsend, but it did not come.

Finally, the orders were passed to make ready for battle, and the captains hurried from position to position with orders and encouragement. Sir Julian arranged the guard so that the swordsmen were on either side of the king, with archers flanking them. At daybreak, the new light illuminated the ghostly glow of a pea-soup fog that cut vision to a few feet and left Samuel and the other archers feeling useless. They stood and waited while the king prepared.

At last, the sound of the king's trumpets split the fog, and the charge was sounded. Samuel and the other archers fired blindly into the mist, hoping that fate would do the rest, and King Edward's army charged into the unknown.

On the right flank, the young Duke of Gloucester was commanding his first army in a military engagement, and at the first sound of the king's trumpets he also ordered the archers to fire blindly and the rest to advance. As he walked forward with his men, he heard the clash of armor and blade against blade coming from what must have been the center columns off to his left, but found no one for his own men to fight. Continuing their advance, they found themselves marching down a steep slope into a marsh, but they found no enemy soldiers. And now the sounds of battle were coming from behind them.

Something was wrong. Gloucester ordered a halt to their advance, frustrated and claustrophobic in the dense fog. He called for his captain.

"How can this be?" he asked when the captain arrived.

"Your grace, I cannot understand it either. But it is clear that we no longer hold the plateau. Perhaps in the night we outflanked them."

"If that is true, we can attack their rear." Suddenly he was excited. It was possible that fate had unwittingly given them a huge advantage. "Order the men to march left and to climb back up the slope! And be prepared to engage any resistance."

"Yes, your grace." He disappeared again into the gloom.

When Warwick heard the first trumpets of the enemy, he could not believe that they were already hard upon his positions. But his personal guard and best fighting men were in the middle of the line and well prepared for the assault, even if they had expected to do the charging instead of reacting. The arrows that came out of the mist took a heavy toll, and he ordered his archers to return the fire. After recovering from the shock of the surprise attack, the middle of the line was holding firm. Warwick had heard nothing from either flank, the left commanded by his brother, Montagu, or the right under the command of the Earl of Oxford, and that concerned him, since he had instructed them both to send regular updates by mounted courier.

Montagu had sent his courier to report that he had not been attacked at all, but the message died when an arrow shot into the mist found the poor messenger's back. Oxford, like the Duke of Gloucester on the other end of the battle front, found that during the night Edward's army had misjudged the location of the Lancastrian line and as a result, his men were in a position to attack Edward's left flank commanded by Hastings. But unlike Gloucester's, his men were still on the plateau and could attack immediately.

In a short while, Hastings' men were routed and fleeing for their lives toward the town of Barnet, and Edward's army was in grave danger. Had the other segments of the battle line seen the disaster on their left, they might also have broken and fled, but the dense fog kept them from seeing anything but the slashing swords in their midst and they did not lose heart.

Meanwhile, Oxford's men pursued the Yorkists into town and stayed on to loot the village, instead of turning to engage the center of Edward's line.

Samuel had long ago left his bow, knowing that any blind shot into the mist now would be as likely to hit one of their own as an enemy, and was in the thick of the struggle with his short sword. He had already been wounded in the side and was bleeding. It was not long before his strength began to fail, and when it appeared safe to disengage he found a heap of bodies and sheltered himself among them, oblivious to the stench of gore and oozing blood. Panting hard, he struggled to regain his breath and found himself growing faint.

A pounding throb in his head roused him back to awareness. He blinked to clear his vision but the mist made it impossible to tell reality from delusion. When next he opened his eyes — it may have been some time later, he was not certain — he could see Sir Julian's unmistakable armor, the old knight ferociously dealing blows to Lancastrian footsoldiers. He was fighting back to back with another guardsman Samuel did not recognize, and they appeared to be fine until the guardsman was struck down. Sir Julian was engaged by another at the time and in no position to watch his back, from where the soldier who had dispatched his partner attacked him. The double assault proved too much for the old knight and he fell in a large heap, ripe for a deadly final assault.

Samuel leaped to his feet, screaming in rage. In five strides he was running at full speed toward Sir Julian, who lay helpless in the blood-stained dirt. No thought passed through Samuel's mind, only blind rage, which drove him headlong into the first soldier who was in turn driven into the other, all three crumbling to the ground. The wind was forced from Samuel's lungs and he lost consciousness.

As Gloucester's men finally swarmed over the top of the plateau, they found what they had hoped to see: the end of Warwick's left flank, the still unengaged troops commanded by Montagu. When the Lancastrians saw Gloucester's men streaming up the hill, urgent commands went out to reform the lines. But in the confusion they incurred heavy casualties. Montagu sent to Warwick for help.

Warwick knew there was great danger in the deadly assault to his left wing, and he committed the remainder of his reserves to help Montagu, a tactic that at least checked the duke's advance and for the moment neutralized the threat. However, the collapse of the two left flanks had caused the entire battle line to spin on its center so that it was now entirely oriented to the north and south instead of east and west, and it was that quirk of fate that gave Edward an unexpected advantage.

The Earl of Oxford finally managed to reform his men and sent them marching north from Barnet, intending to attack Edward from the rear, an attack that would surely have ended the battle in favor of the Lancastrians. But the earl could not see that the battle line had been reoriented, and the men before him were not Edward's rear guard but Warwick's new left flank. When Warwick's men saw Oxford approaching, in the mist they mistook his Star-and-Streamers insignia for Edward's Sun-in-Splendor and unleashed a volley of deadly arrows.

Oxford's men, thinking they had been betrayed, broke ranks and fled the field, shouting "Treason!" Oxford ran with them. When the confusion on the left flank was reported to Edward, he committed his entire reserves to that side of the line. Warwick's ranks crumbled.

On the Lancastrian left, John Neville, the Marquis of Montagu, was struggling to contain Gloucester's advance and was beginning to push him back when he heard shouts from behind. The center was collapsing. Turning to see what could be done, he found a soldier standing before him, battle-ax raised and poised to strike. There was no time to react before the blade descended on his shoulder, cleaving the armor and severing his spine.

Crashing to the earth, he lay face-down in the mud, and death slowly claimed his body. *Damn you, Richard. I have paid the price for your arrogance.*

The Lancastrian line now in shambles, the ranks broke and fled, hotly pursued by the Yorkists. The news of his brother's death was brought to Warwick by men fleeing the carnage on his left. Knowing that the day was lost, he fled into the woods at the base of the plateau where he had instructed his men to hold his horse.

"Quickly, my lord," one shouted. "There are soldiers seeking blood everywhere!"

Seeing his captain, he smiled. "We will join the queen and fight another day, captain, I swear it."

"Yes, my lord," he responded without emotion and handed the reins to his master.

The woods exploded with Yorkist soldiers. The earl's men fought hard but were overwhelmed, and when the killing stopped, Warwick and his captain lay dead on the rich soil of the forest floor. A shout of jubilation went up from the Yorkists.

Relieved of their armor, Edward and his brothers met at the royal tent and exchanged joyous embraces.

"The hand of God was with us here this day, my brothers, and we have much for which to be thankful."

"It was a glorious victory, Sire," said Gloucester.

"May such fortune grace your throne for many years, Sire," added Clarence. He had fought bravely enough by the king's side, and when the battle was won, he was relieved that he had chosen the right side and would once again take his place as one of the magnates of the kingdom. And now perhaps his brother would treat him with more respect. A page entered and knelt.

"Your Majesty, the herald has arrived with his counts."

"Come," Edward ushered his brothers out, "let us hear what the day has wrought." They stepped from the tent to see Sir Julian and the herald, who had spent the early afternoon taking tallies of the dead. Earl Rivers and Lord Hastings were with them. They all cheered the king and saluted his victory. Behind the herald was a wagon, held by several soldiers. The back of the wagon was covered with a dark wool blanket.

"We thank you all, and recognize that your valiant efforts this day have carried us all to a victory that shall be remembered by our children's children. Herald, what news of the dead?"

"Sire, of soldiers of low birth, fifteen hundred lie dead on the field this morning. Of nobility, Lords Say and Cromwell and fifteen knights of the realm are dead, and here in this wagon lie the bodies of your great enemies, the Marquis of Montagu and the Earl of Warwick." When he said their names, he pulled the tarp from the wagon, revealing the naked and hacked bodies of the two Nevilles, still oozing enough blood from their wounds to cause a steady stream to run from the cart. Edward approached the wagon and crossed himself as he inspected the bodies. When he had said a silent prayer, he turned to his men.

"Let no man report that we are happy to see our cousins in this way. We had always hoped that they would accept our clemency and be once again our friends, but God has willed otherwise, and we cannot change what has been done." With a wave of his hand, he ordered the tarp replaced. "Carry the bodies to London and let the people see the truth of their deaths, for such is the price of treason, and let the heralds spread the word throughout the realm that the Kingmaker will make kings no more." The wagon was wheeled away as the gathered nobility looked on.

"Sire," Lord Hastings said, "we all wish to relish this victory, but our land is still not free of rebellion." Edward lowered his head, exhaustion taking its toll.

"Yes, we must go with haste to the west where persistent Margaret still violates our kingdom." He sighed heavily. "But we will spend the remainder of this day giving thanks to God. Summon Father Dennis to our tent."

Samuel regained consciousness slowly, at first having no notion of where he was. His eyes opened to the sight of a man he did not recognize.

"He's coming around," the man announced. "I think he'll be fine when he gets his strength back." He stepped back and the concerned faces of Stanley and Oliver came into focus.

"I should think that by now you'd be sick of having me nurse you," said Oliver with a broad smile. "God knows, I am."

Samuel tried to move but had no strength.

"There's no use in your trying to get up," said the surgeon. "I don't know how anyone in your shape was able to fight such a battle in the first place, but now you might as well enjoy your rest, because it will be a few days before you're strong enough to be back on your feet." He stood to leave. "Just get him to eat as much as he can. Now there are many who need my care more urgently."

"Where am I?" Samuel asked. Oliver placed a small cushion under his head.

"This is Sir Julian's tent. He insisted that you stay here for as long as you need."

"Sir Julian? Then he's…still alive?"

"Yes," Oliver answered. "He's cut up some, but he made it through the battle alive."

"Thank God," Samuel whispered, drifting into sleep again.

Some time later he opened his eyes again to see Sir Julian gazing benevolently at him.

"Did you have a good rest, lad?" Samuel now found that he was able to move at least enough to lift his hands to his face.

"How long have I been here?" he asked.

"It's morning. You've been asleep for an entire day."

"The last I remember, you were on the ground. I tried to help…"

"You did more than help, lad. You knocked the curs clean off their feet, giving me time to recover and Stanley time to watch my back for the rest of the fight. You saved my life, as sure as I breathe."

"Thank God you're alive."

"Amen to that. Now it's time for you to eat something." He signaled for his page, who brought a bowl of hot stew and held the bowl for Samuel, who had not until then realized how hungry he was. "That's the spirit," smiled Sir Julian. "When you've finished that up, you can get some more rest."

For the next three days, Samuel spent the time slowly regaining his strength, while the king and his advisors busied themselves gathering fresh troops and preparing for another march.

After so much food and rest, Samuel felt almost like his old self again and could even bend his bow with his former confidence. As usual, Oliver had been by his side the entire time, and their spirits were as high as they had been since before they met that hideous night on Wakefield bridge.

The night of the fifth evening after the battle of Barnet, they were tending a cook fire near Sir Julian's tent. Stanley had joined them and was sharing stories of the battle and jokes in the starry night when Sir Julian and Sir Nigel joined them. Samuel did not like their expressions.

"I've seen that look before, and the news was never good. Have the marching orders been given?" They glanced at each other first. Sir Nigel cleared his throat.

"Samuel, I'm afraid that Kate has been taken by the queen's men." Samuel could not have been more surprised if Sir Nigel had struck him with his fist.

"How...?"

"It seems that she went to her father, Lord Fitzwalter, voluntarily."

"Her father?" He was totally confused.

"It came as a surprise to me as well," Sir Nigel admitted, "but she is his daughter. I confirmed it before telling you, though I would never have found out if your sister had not told my man, Jonathan. Apparently she was the only one to know. Kate is the reason that Sir Hugh has pursued you so relentlessly, but for what reason, we still have no knowledge."

"You promised me she was safe!" Samuel was furious.

"When I left her she was. You know that to be true. It was her own decision to leave, hoping that by turning herself over she would buy freedom for the rest of your family."

"Where is she, Sir Nigel? I know that you have the information."

He hesitated, wondering if it was wise to tell. "She has been taken to the queen near Devon, at last report."

Samuel strode quickly to the tent and began collecting his belongings. Sir Julian went to him, speaking softly.

"How could you help her now, lad? We will march to meet the queen at first light, and we'll find her together."

"The last time I heard that, we took care of the king's business and I gained nothing. I will not throw her to the mercies of chance."

"But what can you do? Be reasonable."

"Whatever I can, but at least I'll die trying." Oliver began packing as well, but Samuel took his arm. "Not this time, my friend. You must think of Sally and John. They need you. Go back to them in the morning and be happy. You deserve that at least." Oliver began to object, but Samuel took his pack from him. "In the end, we all die alone, my friend."

Oliver was devastated. After all they had been through, he did not think it would end this way. Samuel gave him a final embrace and shouldered his bow and quiver.

Sir Julian tried one last time. "I promise you, if you stay we'll find Kate together."

"I know you mean that, Sir Julian, but you have other duties that come first. I don't." He turned without another word and disappeared down the road to the west.

No one moved for a long while, the sounds of crickets and voices from other tents made louder by the silence. Sir Julian raised his head flush to the fire, red glow lighting his old eyes.

"I'm going with him."

"What are you saying?" Sir Nigel was incredulous.

"I'm going with him, that's plain enough. I can't leave him alone to fight Sir Hugh, not after everything he's done for me."

"Don't be a fool. You're talking about leaving the king right before a battle. He will have your neck on the block, as sure as there is no hotter place than Hell."

"It's a life that I owe Samuel anyway. I am honor bound, and will hear no more." He stood and stalked away toward his tent. Stanley ran after him.

"You'll have to take me along then, Sir Julian!" he shouted.

A few moments later, Sir Julian pulled himself onto his horse and rode from camp with Stanley. Riding quietly to the edge of camp, he found the road toward the west and spurred his horse forward. A few hundred yards from camp he found Sir Nigel on horseback, astride the road.

"Is it your intention to prevent my passage?" he asked darkly, his old eyes sharp as thorns.

"I owe him a life or two as well," said Sir Nigel. Stanley nodded grim affirmation.

"The king will get the intelligence he needs?" The old knight had not forgotten his duty.

"Jonathan will see that he is well informed."

Without another word, they turned their horses to the west and spurred them forward.

CHAPTER XXVI

The town of Gloucester near the Welsh border had grown rapidly since the plague had taken more than half its population a hundred years before, and while it hadn't regained its numbers, there were many signs of renewed vigor. The markets once again bustled to the sounds of hawkers' shouts, and copious produce flowed to its streets from the fertile land that stretched for miles from its gates.

But on this day the town leaders were contemplating a choice between two warring factions, and the fates of their families would turn on their decision. King Edward had delivered a stern warning to close their gates to Queen Margaret's advancing army. But Margaret was only hours away, and she had sent word ahead that her soldiers were to be refreshed and provisioned. Whatever the mayor decided, if he went with the eventual loser, the town would suffer horribly at the hands of the victor. Punishments such as revocation of royal licenses and punitive taxes could cripple its commerce for years, and its leaders would likely pay for their lack of foresight with their lives. To make matters worse, nobles supporting both sides were in town waiting for the decision to be made. Lords Roos and Fitzwalter and their party were attending the queen's business and had expected to greet her when she arrived. On the other hand, the master of Gloucester Castle, Lord Beauchamp, was a loyal Yorkist and had told the mayor already that the gates were to be barred against Margaret.

Fitzwalter and Kate sat in the bishop's townhouse waiting as Sir Hugh kept watch. It had been a long ride from Chilton Manor, escorted as they were by Lord Roos and his entire entourage of retainers. At this time in the spring, the roads had tried their endurance. But Kate was lost in depression and hardly noticed as the miles passed beneath them, knowing that the knowledge she still kept locked within herself was all that kept her from likely execution.

When they arrived at Gloucester, they were surprised to find Sir Hugh waiting for them with the devastating news of the battle at Barnet and the death of the Nevilles. Sir Hugh's presence was particularly unpleasant to Kate, who despised him for what he done to the Miller family.

"I think it is unwise, my lord, to allow her to be the only one with the information," Sir Hugh leered. "If something should...happen to her, the information would be lost, and the queen would likely have your head in retribution."

"Then I suggest we ensure that nothing happen to her," said Lord Fitzwalter angrily. At some point he would ask the queen to divest herself of this despicable man, but for now every soldier was needed. "I have given my word that she need only divulge the information to the queen herself, and I intend to honor that commitment. I suggest you let me worry about the queen."

"As you wish, my lord." He had a way of making even the simplest courtesy sound disrespectful. Lord Roos entered the room red-faced with anger.

"The fools!" he ranted. "I'll take pleasure in personally placing the heads of those two traitors on the city walls."

"May I assume from this tirade that Beauchamp has convinced the mayor to lock the gates against the queen?"

"And they will pay dearly, I promise you that."

"Be that as it may, my lords," interrupted Sir Hugh, "this will make our duty more difficult. We will have to travel to the queen ourselves with her prize."

"Sir, you will not refer to Lady Katherine as a prize. She is still my daughter and will be treated as such."

"I apologize, my lord," he said. "Are we free to leave the city?" he asked Lord Roos.

"The fool mayor has given us leave to depart as we wish. Beauchamp hadn't the spine to leave his castle to deny us."

"A decision that has bought him a few more days of life," responded Sir Hugh. "However, my lords, I do suggest that we remove ourselves from here quickly. The queen will pass nearby this very night."

Horses were saddled and brought into the bishop's courtyard. When they arrived at the wall, a door in the gate was opened to them and they left town, leaving behind the sure knowledge that if they returned with a victorious Queen Margaret, the mayor was not the only person who would regret this disloyalty.

After two hours of riding, they spotted the vanguard of the queen's army and rode past it to where the queen's carriage was escorted by the Prince of Wales and his betrothed, Anne, who was deeply grieved at the news of her father's death at Barnet. The queen opened the shade of the carriage and, seeing Kate, broke into a broad smile.

"Katherine. You have given us a merry chase." She turned to Lord Roos. "Has she given you the information?"

"No, Your Highness. However, she has sworn to satisfy you at your leisure."

"Has she? And what is the answer from the mayor of Gloucester? Will he yield to his lawful monarch?"

"He will not, Majesty."

"His head will pay the price." She took a moment to weigh her options. Her troops were tired from their long march, and this was evil news. "We do not have the luxury of time for a siege. Order the captains to camp here. Tomorrow we will continue north."

"As you wish, my lady."

"And bring our dear friend Katherine to us when our tent is ready." She smiled at Kate again and lowered her shade.

An hour later, Katherine knelt before Margaret, flanked by Lords Roos and Fitzwalter, while Sir Hugh stood silently by the flap. The Prince of Wales stood behind and to the right of his mother.

"If only you knew the anguish that you have caused us these past years," Margaret addressed her wistfully. "What could you possibly say that would inspire the least portion of mercy from our heart that you have so sorely abused?"

"I seek no mercy from Your Highness," Kate said steadily.

"And yet we are told that you wish to divulge the location of a certain paper containing foul lies about us and our royal dignity. Is this true?"

"It is, Your Highness, provided you can assure me that a promise made to me by my father will be kept."

"You dare to bargain with the queen?" The prince was outraged. Margaret silenced him with a raised hand.

"Lord Fitzwalter, what is this promise?"

"Majesty, in exchange for the speedy deliverance of the letter, I promised only to protect the family of some inconsequential millers from York."

"Forgive me, Your Highness," Sir Hugh was startled by Fitzwalter's promise, "but this family has been charged with treason against His Highness, the king." Fitzwalter was amazed at the vehemence in his voice.

"Only one member of the family has been so charged, Majesty, and I have made no promises regarding him. The rest are blameless."

"Your Highness' courts should determine that, Majesty."

"Enough!" the queen grew impatient. "The letter is our only concern. If Lord Fitzwalter wishes to risk his name in this matter, so be it. We will not interfere. Now, Katherine, tell us what we wish to know."

Kate knew that her life would be forfeit after she told them, but she had no choice. It was the only way her new family would gain their freedom, and as for her own life, without Samuel there could be no happiness. She revealed the location of the letter.

"Very clever, my dear," the queen replied. "Sir Hugh, you will guard her closely until we have the letter in our hands."

"Your Highness," interceded Fitzwalter, "I ask that you place my daughter in my care."

"She will pay dearly for her disobedience, my lord. We will never release her again."

The next day, Edward heard that the queen's army had moved north of Gloucester after being denied access to the city. It was encouraging to know that some of his subjects were still willing to obey his orders, and he made a note to reward Lord Beauchamp for his loyalty. But that news was more than offset by the report that Sir Julian and Sir Nigel had departed without permission. Sir Nigel had left the king's channels of intelligence intact, as Edward was still receiving regular reports from his scouts, so it was clear that he was not deserting to the other side. Still, his behavior was inexplicable.

Edward rode with the vanguard, eager to hear the scouts' reports. He felt confident that his army was well rested, although it had only been a week since the battle at Barnet, and the news of his victory there had encouraged many of the wavering nobility to send reinforcements to replenish those who had been lost.

With him were his brothers, Clarence and Gloucester, and Lord Hastings, who had gone ahead for news. It was a rainy day, though not particularly cold, but the roads were heavily rutted. The front of the column was able to proceed without too much difficulty, but the damage caused by their horses and wagons left the road in even worse shape for those in the rear.

Speed was of paramount importance if Edward was to force an engagement with Margaret before she could gain help. He had suffered these wars for too long, and would have an end to them, even if it meant the end of the House of York, for they were all here and would be victorious or perish in the attempt. Hastings approached at a gallop.

"Sire," he panted, "Margaret lies only an hour's ride from here. She has established her lines in the field before the town of Tewkesbury."

"We are well acquainted with the area, William. Ludlow is not far from there. Edmund and I spent many happy hours of our youth near those fields." For a moment he allowed himself to remember, but the moment passed quickly. "So be it, then. Tewkesbury shall be the place where the final chapter of this struggle is written. Inform our brothers that we shall spend the night where we see the lights of their fires, and God grant that it be not our last."

That night, the armies camped near the abbey at Tewkesbury, two lines of fires separated by a dark abyss. Samuel and his friends watched a tent from a nearby thicket of holly. They had not moved since the early morning hours when they had seen Kate brought there, and if the angels of hell had arrived to summon him, Samuel would not have budged. Earlier they had watched as the queen's army set up camp. Sir Hugh's Black Stallion banner flew over the small group of tents, and his heart leaped when he saw Kate brought in, so tantalizingly close. They found the thicket and waited. Sir Hugh himself had entered an adjacent tent some hours before.

Now it was time, and Sir Julian signaled for them to nock their arrows. Sunrise would be upon them shortly, and the birds had begun their musical welcome to the new day. There were four tents within range, but only two with sentries, Kate's and Sir Hugh's. Looking behind to assure themselves that no patrols were near, they formed a line behind the bushes and placed their arrows on the ground before them. The first priority was to keep the guards away from Kate, and one of the sentries before her tent was Samuel's first target. Taking a deep breath, he let an arrow fly and watched as it completed its short journey by penetrating the belly of the closest guard. The guard beside him saw his companion fall but took a second to fully comprehend what had happened, a second that cost him his life as well, as another arrow came out of the dark and passed cleanly through his throat.

The other guards were running for cover and raising the alarm. Samuel hoped to draw Sir Hugh from his tent, where he would quickly end his detested life. At the first sounds, he did emerge to check the alarm. Other guards who did not know where the arrows were coming from ran in different directions, but were cut down as they came into range. Seeing Sir Hugh in the open before his tent, Samuel was ready and brought him within his sights. But Sir Hugh saw the dead guards before Kate's tent, and he jumped back inside as an arrow sailed through the space he had just vacated. Screaming orders from within, he yelled to his men to get reinforcements.

Watching the arrow fall harmlessly that had been intended to send Sir Hugh to Hell, Samuel cursed and nocked another. A soldier made the mistake of attempting to reach a nearby tent for cover, and was dead before he made it halfway. But now men arriving from the other parts of the camp were beginning to return fire. Arrows landed within yards of their position as Sir Hugh's men advanced, and Sir Julian yelled for them to pull back. Their position was no longer tenable.

Unexpectedly, trumpets sounded from a distance, leaving Samuel to wonder how news of this little skirmish could raise such a reaction so quickly. They grabbed the remaining arrows on the ground and darted toward the trees to the left. The first glow of the morning was now visible, and a guard spotted them, turned, and called for help. At the first tree he reached, Samuel spun and spent another arrow, piercing the guard through the stomach. The plan was to double back to the camp after dealing with the pursuers and rescue Kate.

"Julian!" yelled Sir Nigel, "take Samuel and go back. We'll hold them here as long as we can." Not waiting for a reply, he pulled Stanley away from the others.

After circling behind the approaching guards, Samuel and Sir Julian arrived back at Sir Hugh's tent. Samuel's heart sank when he saw that a horse with Sir Hugh and Kate leapt toward town. There was no hope of an arrowshot stopping Sir Hugh, shielded as he was by Kate. Samuel could only scream her name.

Hearing that, both Sir Hugh and Kate looked back. Kate yelled for Samuel, astonished to see him still alive, when Sir Hugh spurred his horse to a gallop and they disappeared over a low knoll.

At the first hint of light, Edward had ordered his army into action and they fell on Margaret's position with the passion of their king to firm their resolve. Gloucester led the first charge against the center, commanded by Lord Roos, and the two fought to a standstill. Meanwhile, Edward had to respond to a flanking action directed by the Prince of Wales, whose army drove the Yorkists back to their starting point before the battle had begun.

Edward shored up his line by committing his reserves to that side, hoping that Gloucester could hold the center without any additional men. If his brother failed, all would be lost. His gamble was working for the moment, though.

The ground had been saturated by the rains that had drenched the earth for the past several days, causing the mud to cling to them. The conditions made rapid troop mobilizations impossible for both sides, but Edward was most disadvantaged because he'd committed his reserves early.

When the time was ripe, Edward ordered a careful retreat, and his left wing drew the Prince's forces further toward them, until Edward signaled for the trumpets to be sounded once again. Out from the wooded park further to his left several hundred men with spears commanded by Hastings and Clarence fell on the prince's flank. It was an old trick, but perhaps due to his inexperience the prince had fallen into it, and in a very short time, his men were broken and fleeing toward town.

Samuel and his friends arrived at a small hilltop in time to see Sir Hugh ride with Kate through a party of Lancastrians who were guarding the entrance to the Tewkesbury Abbey. They watched as the horse disappeared into the abbey, and Samuel knew that they would not be a match for the troops that stood between him and Kate.

"There must be another way in there," he shouted desperately.

The sounds of battle grew louder from the left. A force of Yorkists found the Lancastrian guards and fell upon them fiercely.

"Come on," yelled Sir Julian, "now we'll have a fighting chance."

They ran down the hill, joining the other Yorkists in the fray, protecting each other's backs like a small, separate army in the middle of the brawl, slowly making their way toward the abbey grounds. At the low wall that surrounded the abbey, Sir Julian signaled them to disengage and climb over.

Sir Nigel and Stanley went first, then Samuel, who turned to help Sir Julian, whose old body was not as spry as it once was. Reaching for his hand, Samuel heard him grunt in pain. The knight fell toward him, a dead weight in his arms, and both tumbled to the ground on the abbey side of the wall.

Samuel pulled himself to his knees and tried to pull the knight up, but Sir Julian did not respond. Releasing him, he saw that his hands were covered with blood.

"No!" he shouted, trying to find the wound. Able to lift one shoulder, he saw the deep gash in his back. Panic constricted his breathing. Sir Nigel and Stanley, startled by Samuel's cry, rushed back to help, and together they lifted Sir Julian to a sitting position. He clenched his teeth against the pain.

"Please, Sir Julian, get up." pleaded Samuel. "We can't stay here." The old knight used his last strength to clutch Samuel's arm.

"Go," he whispered, barely audible, "find Kate, and...be content." Blood flowed from his mouth and his last words mingled with the sounds of clashing swords still coming from across the wall. They lowered Sir Julian gently to the ground and for the second time in his young life, Samuel wept for the loss of a kind and gentle father.

Sir Nigel took him by the shoulders.

"He gave his life for us and we will grieve for him when Kate is safe," he said, urging him toward the abbey.

Samuel nodded. They had to find Kate, for his old mentor's sake as well as his own. He put his mouth to Sir Julian's ear.

"Sleep with the angels, my lord. I know you will be great among them." He placed Sir Julian's sword on his body, wiped the tears from his cheeks, and ran with the others into the abbey.

They entered a small door that led to the cloister and were greeted by an angry monk who blocked their way.

"Will you bring weapons into the house of the Lord? Leave here at once!"

Sir Nigel pushed him roughly aside.

"I am truly sorry, brother, but the devil himself hides within these walls, and we intend to find him."

"It would be better to hide your own souls from the Dark One!" he shouted as they brushed passed.

They entered into the colonnaded cloister, where Sir Nigel turned to his companions.

"It will be more dangerous, but we will find them faster if we separate. I'll check the private quarters, Samuel the church, and Stanley the rest of the cloister. Shout as loud as you can if you find them. Go." He had given himself the private quarters knowing that the queen herself was within these walls. He hoped that Sir Hugh was with her.

Meanwhile, it took Samuel only a short time to find the church. As large as any he had ever seen, it was lit only by the small windows in the clerestory above and the numerous candles burning around the central choir. There was a single woman in the pews facing the main altar, deep in private devotions, and several guards watching the main entrance to the rear.

"Let me go!" He heard a voice coming from the rear of the choir. He slipped behind the huge columns on the left side of the church and walked quietly around the outside choir. There were no further sounds as he came to the back of the church and saw no one. Staying close to the wall, he continued around the back of the choir until he came to a short wall that blocked his view of the right side of the church. Carefully, he peered around it. There on a marble bench along the outside wall lay Kate, who struggled violently against the ropes that held her arms behind her back.

"Kate!" he yelled as he dashed toward her. But he never arrived. A blow from behind sent him sprawling across the floor into the back wall of the choir. Reeling and gasping for air, he tried to regain his feet, but before his limbs responded, large hands pulled him off the ground and crushed him against a stone wall. Barely able to focus, he saw Sir Hugh, face white with rage, the hideous scar crimson in contrast.

"Once again we meet, my friend," he hissed. "But I assure you that it will be the last time in this life." Another blow to the side of his head sent Samuel into unconsciousness.

When the prince's army broke and fled, the outcome of the battle of Tewkesbury was decided. A few minutes later the center of the queen's line was also in full retreat. Clarence saw the prince's colors withdrawing toward the abbey and yelled for his men to follow, knowing that he was the greatest prize. They overtook the prince trying to cross a small brook just yards short of the abbey grounds.

"Yield, pretender," Clarence shouted as his men swarmed around the prince, killing his guards, "and submit to the mercy of your lawful king!"

Dragged before the duke, he was forced to his knees.

"False and treacherous Clarence. My king, and yours as well, is Henry of Lancaster. Bend your knee to me and I will speak to the queen on your behalf."

"Are you still so bold, though God has decided against you on this glorious day?"

"You have prevailed only by means of treachery and deceit. I will not submit to such a judgment."

Clarence nodded to a soldier.

"Then you may discuss it with Him forthwith." The soldier ran his sword through the young prince's back and withdrew it roughly. The boy dropped to the ground, the others watching as his life seeped away. "Bear him to the king," said Clarence imperiously, "and show him that the hope of Lancaster is dead." They lifted the body onto a horse, and set off to find the king.

Samuel regained consciousness with a start. His hands were bound behind his back and he was sitting in a pew before the altar. Sir Hugh was speaking with the woman whom he had first noticed in devotions when he entered. Kate was bound next to him.

"Kate," he whispered softly. She was in tears.

"I am sorry, my love. I should have told you the whole truth from the start. I thought to shelter you but instead I brought death to you all." Samuel wanted to hold her in his arms but could only lean toward her.

"Don't blame yourself, Kate. There was no way you could have known."

"If you only knew how I suffered when I thought you were dead."

"And you were right, my dear, only just a bit premature." Sir Hugh had seen that Samuel was conscious. "I am pleased that you are not yet dead, however, my young friend," he growled at Samuel, "for we still may have some use for you."

"Yes, we may still need to assure that our dear Katherine has not been false with us." Margaret came from behind Sir Hugh.

The main entrance of the church behind them swung open, and several men entered. They were led by Lord Fitzwalter, looking tired and bloodied from several wounds.

"Majesty, our cause is lost. Your army has scattered and Edward has ordered your arrest."

Margaret grabbed his blood-soaked collar. "My son. What has become of my son?" she cried.

"I have no certain knowledge of his fate, my lady, but I heard that he was taken before he could flee the field." She released him and fell to her knees before the altar, praying desperately.

"Then we have no further need for these two." Sir Hugh drew his sword and stood before Samuel and Katherine, waiting for affirmation from Margaret. Locked in prayer with her eyes tightly shut, she ignored him, which he took for permission to proceed. He raised his sword above Samuel, who waited for the death stroke, wishing that he could have embraced Kate one last time. At least he would die knowing that Edward had prevailed. The clang of iron on iron caused his eyes to snap open.

Lord Fitzwalter had beaten Sir Hugh's sword aside with his own.

"You will not harm my daughter!" he said angrily. Sir Hugh turned on him and they fell violently together. Fitzwalter was already exhausted from the battle and gave ground quickly, until he was pinned against one of the huge columns that supported the clerestory above. Sir Hugh used his savage strength to beat the sword from Fitzwalter's hand, then decapitated him with the next stroke.

From where she watched helplessly, Kate screamed hysterically as her father fell at the foot of the column. Sir Hugh walked slowly back to Samuel, bloody sword at the ready.

"No more reprieves," he growled. Samuel glared at him one more time, ready to spit his last defiance, when Sir Hugh jerked backward, then fell forward, an arrow buried deep between his shoulder blades.

Stanley dropped his bow and ran to protect Samuel against the queen's guards, who were approaching to defend her. Sir Nigel joined him.

But before the first blows could be landed, the main doors crashed open once again and Hastings stormed in with several soldiers.

"In the name of the king, yield up your arms," he said loudly. The queen's guards complied immediately, knowing their cause was lost.

Stanley pushed Sir Hugh's body over with his foot and saw that for the first time, his repulsive scar appeared as white as the rest of his face.

"I marvel that his blood is red like ours."

Sir Nigel prodded him forward. "Untie them, boy!" Which he did. Hands finally free, Samuel took Kate in his arms and they held each other tightly.

Hastings approached Margaret.

"My lady, you must come with me to the king."

"This is a place of holy worship," she glared at him, "and we have been granted sanctuary by the abbot. You disturb our meditations at the risk of your soul."

"These are matters for those greater than I. Now you must come with me to the king." Signaling his men, they stood on either side of her. Finally, she slowly stood, still every part of her a queen, and followed them out. "Sir Nigel, you will answer to the king as well."

"I expected that I would," he said. Helping Samuel and Kate up, they were all escorted out to the front, where King Edward sat on his horse, flanked by Gloucester and Clarence. Father Dennis and the abbot stood before them. The abbot was indignant.

"Your Majesty, the sanctity of this Holy place has already been grievously violated. You risk the damnation of all those present if you proceed with this rash behavior!" He included the king's men to make it clear that their souls were in peril as well.

"Sire," said Father Dennis, "the abbot's position is supported by canonical law. You must stop these proceedings."

Edward became angrier by the moment. In the past year, he had been driven from his throne and forced to debase himself before foreign leaders for their reluctant assistance. The struggle had cost him the lives of his father and of Edmund, his beloved childhood companion, whose death had left a rift in his heart that could never be healed. All of his misery could be laid on the head of the woman who now stood before him with no sign of remorse.

"Remove the abbot and Father Dennis from our presence, so they shall remain blameless in the eyes of God," he said harshly. "But Margaret shall not have sanctuary."

"It will only add to your growing burden of sin," replied Margaret. She knew that it would be unlikely for Edward to have her executed, and as long as she had her life she would defy the Yorkists to the last. Edward clenched his jaw in anger.

"Lest you still keep any hope within your cold breast, poor Margaret, know the fate of your House." He nodded to Clarence, who in turn signaled to his men. The body of the prince was dumped on the ground before his mother, who lost all of her majestic composure and fell atop her dead son. It was the only thing that could have hurt her.

"Wretched Edward," she cried hysterically, "the blood of this innocent boy has sealed your fate."

"None of us can boast a guiltless soul," he answered. "Take them from our sight." Margaret was led away, her dead son carried after. Edward turned his attention to Sir Nigel.

"We wonder at your presence in this church, Sir Nigel. It speaks volumes of evil to us. What can you tell us that would make it harder to pronounce your present execution?"

"Sire, I can only assure Your Majesty that I have been and always will be a loyal subject."

"Your actions belie your innocence," Edward shouted. "When we needed you most you fled as a coward, and now we find you consorting with Margaret."

"Your Majesty, the fault lies with me. Sir Nigel is guiltless." A soldier knocked Samuel to the ground for daring to speak to the king without leave. Edward held up his hand.

"We know you. We allowed you the honor of standing sentry over our brother's tomb, is it not so?"

"It is, Your Highness," he said.

"What could you tell us that would deflect our wrath?"

"Sir Nigel came to my assistance against the queen's men, as did Sir Julian, who lost his life in my defense."

Edward's countenance darkened. "Sir Julian is dead? Why were we not informed?" he turned angrily to Hastings.

"The tally of the dead has not been completed, Sire."

"We have lost much." Edward bent his head sadly. The entire company waited while the king reflected. "We have lost our dearest friends because they put the needs of a peasant before the needs of us and the kingdom. We do not understand, but our judgment must be firm. Take them to their present deaths!"

"We die guiltless of any crime, Your Majesty," replied Sir Nigel.

"Take them away. We will hear no more."

"Was it for this, then, that the Earl of Rutland died, Your Highness?" The voice came from behind a row of soldiers. Edward spun, furious that anyone should speak of his brother in that manner. Pushing his way past the last soldiers, Oliver stepped into the clear and defiantly faced the king. Several soldiers grabbed him roughly and forced him to his knees.

"Stop!" shouted the king. They released him. Edward's anger had been deflated at the sight of his brother's childhood companion and page.

"Oliver?" he said at last. "How...how do you come to be here?"

"Your Majesty, these are my family and if they are to die, then you must kill me as well."

"No, Oliver!" yelled Samuel, but he was quickly restrained.

Hastings had heard enough.

"Sire, you have suffered enough of this effrontery."

Edward was lost in thought, almost as if he had been bewitched by the odd-looking man who had appeared from nowhere, and everyone waited for the expected confirmation of Hastings' advice. For the tiniest instant, in Oliver's eyes, Edward thought he saw the still familiar flare of light that was so characteristic of Edmund's, and it was as if a great weight had been lifted from his heart and lifted his soul.

"It is good to see you again, Oliver." The response stunned the entire company.

"And I you, Your Highness, though I wish it were under better circumstances."

"Perhaps we can rectify that. Bring them all to our tent," he said to Hastings. "We have much to understand."

"As you wish, Sire," Hastings responded reluctantly.

In the weeks that followed, several minor disturbances required the king's military attention, but for the most part England was a land at peace for the first time in the lives of its oldest subjects. Henry Percy, the Earl of Northumberland, now certain of his master, eradicated the last pockets of Lancastrian loyalty in the northern counties.

Edward returned to London and escorted his wife from the sanctuary at Westminster Abbey to the palace. On the way, soldiers scattered hundreds of cheering citizens welcoming King Edward back to his city, and back to his throne.

As the caravan containing all of Elizabeth's possessions made the turn from Thames Street, the horse drawing the wagon behind the queen's was startled by wellwishers who had come too close. He reared up, causing the wagon to overturn. Several crates fell from the wagon, including one containing a fine porcelain statue of an angel. The crate cascaded into the river below and shattered on a half-submerged rock, bits of porcelain swept to the bottom. The queen in her fury at the loss did not notice a paper, which had been hastily stuffed into the hole in the bottom of the statuette by a young lady in waiting named Katherine many years ago. The paper was seized by the rapid current and began its long journey toward the turbulent waters of the English Channel.

A few days later the royals sat in the splendor of their throne room in Westminster Palace, where they received many of the realm's remaining nobility to take their oaths of loyalty once again. The king held his infant son, Edward, for all to see and admire, and required that the head of every noble house swear fealty to the young heir. That night, proclaiming a new era of peace and prosperity for the kingdom, King Edward sponsored a banquet the likes of which had rarely been seen.

Late in the evening, the king's brother, the Duke of Gloucester, left the feast early on a special assignment. With warrants signed by the king, he and two retainers rode to the Tower, where they were admitted through the main gates without question. They climbed the steps to the walk along the inner wall adjacent to the Wakefield Tower. Gloucester stopped at the edge of the parapet. It was close to midnight and the moon rose over London Bridge, casting a long light on the River Thames. There were few lights on the other side of the river, where the darkness blanketed dozens of small farm houses. The duke wondered if they would all be safer after he had completed his mission. He shivered against a cold wind.

"Wait here for me. I won't be long."

The door to the upper chamber of the Wakefield Tower was opened by a guard. The chamber was dark, but a torch on the wall near the tiny chapel illuminated a man kneeling in prayer. As Gloucester approached there was no reaction.

"Henry of Lancaster, I have a warrant from the king."

Henry turned. The dim light cast shadows on the features of his face, like a skeleton.

"Your coming was foretold to me," he said.

Henry's otherworldly abilities were now legendary, but Gloucester was not one of the mewling masses that put any stock in such talk.

"Then you must be aware that your son is dead, and your wife a prisoner." Henry turned and resumed his prayer, his knees creaking against the hard stone floor.

"I was aware," he whispered.

"The time has come for the House of Lancaster to expire," the duke replaced the warrant in the folds of his cloak, "and you with it, my lord." The sound of a sword sliding from its scabbard assaulted the peace of the chamber. Henry's back stiffened.

"I have also seen that the House of York will perish at your hands," he said without turning.

The duke was stunned. The shock of the words raised the hairs on the back of his neck.

"Do you think that such nonsense will prolong your life?" he asked angrily. Henry still did not turn.

"I have no desire to prolong my life."

"Then I will satisfy you."

The blade pierced his heart from behind, and Henry did not feel the stone floor of his little chapel as it embraced his body. In the darkness that enveloped him, he saw the flare of light in the eyes that had promised to show him the way.

Sir Nigel had sent word to the Miller family that it was safe to leave their place of seclusion. It was a blessing for the children, for whom the long days locked in the residence of a church seemed like a prison sentence. Samuel, Kate, Oliver, and Stanley began their journey back as well, but first made a stop in the eastern town of Norwich and watched as the last rites were read over the body of Sir Julian. The king, after hearing their story, granted the old knight a contingent of his guard to escort him home, and ordered that he be buried with all honors due a man who had served with distinction.

Samuel did not weep for his old mentor again that day, though he felt the loss more deeply than before. He prayed that Sir Julian knew that finally he could be happy again. He dropped the first handful of soil on the coffin, and stepped back, his final farewell said. Kate placed a single rose on top and crossed herself, then walked from the gravesite with the others.

A few days later they stood before the ruins of the millhouse with the rest of the family. They had been forewarned of the loss of their home by Sir Nigel, though nothing could completely prepare them to see all that was built to last a lifetime and beyond, reduced to ashes.

But King Edward had granted them funds to rebuild from the estate of Lord Fitzwalter. As one convicted of treason, Kate's father had condemned his estate to the fate of attainder, and all of his goods and chattels belonged to the king. But Edward saw an opportunity to repay Kate and the Millers for their suffering. And to repay Oliver for services that could never be forgotten, the king granted him a lifetime stipend that assured him a place among the prominent merchants of York.

The family spent the next weeks building temporary shelter and clearing the scorched rubble of the old structures. The foundation of the mill itself was still sound and would serve as a fine starting point for the new one. It was satisfying to know that something would remain of the past.

On one warm Sunday, the entire family donned their finest clothing and descended on the local church where they watched the parish priest join Samuel and Kate in holy matrimony. Many of the townspeople joined the celebration, the Millers already having made many friends and admirers, their tribulations almost legendary.

Stanley, who had stayed on to help them rebuild, hoping to settle nearby, was the first to congratulate them. It was an unspoken understanding among them all that Stanley would be remembered always as the man who had rid them of the great evil that had stalked them for so many years, and was owed a debt that lifetimes could not repay. On the front steps of the old Norman church, Stanley took Samuel's hand.

"We'll do better in the future, I promise."

Samuel just smiled and squeezed his hand tightly. Next, Oliver embraced him warmly.

"Perhaps you were right about dying alone," he said, "but it's the living that really matters anyway, isn't it?"

Samuel cleared the lump from his throat.

"It's what you tried to tell me all along. I am sorry I was so thick."

Oliver laughed. "It's a quality that I have always admired in you."

Sally hugged and kissed him.

"Welcome home, Samuel." Wiping the tears from her cheeks, she took young John by the hand and joined Oliver on the path below.

Christopher and Emma were next, Sarah and Alice in tow.

"Emma, could you take the children ahead? I need to speak with my brother."

Emma kissed Samuel. "We'll speak later," she whispered in his ear, then gathered the children and joined the others.

"Will you walk with me?" he asked Samuel.

Samuel looked at Kate who nodded with a smile and ran to join Emma. They strolled for a while before Christopher spoke.

"I know now that the anger between us was my fault," he started, "and I regret it more deeply than you could know."

"I think I can say with confidence that we both lost our way for a while. It's difficult to believe that clearer vision came from such depravity as we have seen."

Christopher nodded in agreement. "If God only knew that we would invariably take the wrong path, I wonder if He would have thought twice about giving us the power of choice."

Samuel thought about it for a moment. "I imagine He felt it was the only way we'd learn the consequences of our actions."

"I can't believe that I left my wife and family to fight in a war. The consequences of that will haunt me forever, I can tell you that. If Sally or Kate had been killed, I would never have been able to live with myself."

"You're beginning to sound like me." They both laughed, and it felt good.

Christopher hugged his brother as he hadn't done since they were children.

"I can't tell you how glad I am to have you home again," he choked out the words.

"Come on." Samuel slapped him on the back. "Let's get back." Savoring the time together, they walked slowly back to the mill, where the celebration was already well under way. Ale and mead flowed into the late hours within the makeshift shelter that would serve as their home until the new mill was finished.

Emma managed to pull Samuel aside to a corner where the noise was less deafening. She took his hands and smiled broadly.

"This is all I ever dreamed for us, Samuel. I wish you could feel how light my heart is at this moment."

"I know exactly how you feel," he said tenderly. "But you were always our strength from the very start."

She smiled fondly at him for a moment longer, then pushed him toward Kate, who was dancing with Christopher.

"Go and tell your new wife to stay away from my husband," she laughed.

A short while later Samuel and Kate retired, eager to start the first night of their new life together.

EPILOGUE

For the rest of his life, King Edward IV would rule England in peace and without further challenge. As a result of his astute dealings with the merchants of his kingdom, it is said he was the first English king to leave the monarchy wealthier than he found it, and his subjects admired their young king for the lavish and rich court that he created. Indeed, he became renowned among European royalty for his hospitality and the grandeur of his palace.

Though he was legendary for his reputation as a womanizer, Edward never strayed far from Elizabeth, the woman he had married for love at great risk to his throne. She bore him ten children, seven daughters and three sons, but would never benefit from the king's popularity, as the Woodville family continued to engender animosity among the nobility with their constant attempts to gain power.

The final business of the civil wars was to determine the fate of Margaret of Anjou, who was imprisoned after Tewkesbury. King Louis of France agreed to pay her ransom and therefore bought her freedom. In payment, however, he seized her father's small inheritance, condemning her to live the rest of her miserable life in destitution in France, never to be heard from again.

The Duke of Clarence would never lose his animosity toward his royal brother or toward the Duke of Gloucester, who became Edward's favorite. The favors and titles lavished on Gloucester would eventually drive Clarence into open defiance once again, forcing Edward to have him arrested on charges of treason. In an act that caused the king great remorse, he placed Clarence on trial, many felt at the insistence of the queen who had never forgiven the duke for the murder of her father. Clarence was convicted of treason, sentenced to death, and, in a private place — to spare him the humiliation of a public execution — was put to death. His body was taken to Tewkesbury Abbey, where it lies interred at the back of the choir together with Margaret's son, the Prince of Wales, whom Clarence had killed after the battle of Tewkesbury.

The death of Henry VI was mourned by the people of England for years. His madness notwithstanding, he had always been revered for his gentle ways. There were attempts to have him canonized, but the Popes of the time demanded high fees for such an honor and subsequent monarchs had never been willing to pay the price. Henry's remains were interred in St. George's Chapel within the walls of Windsor Castle. His unassuming tomb is marked only with the words "Shame on he who thinks evil."

A few yards from his tomb lie the remains of King Edward himself, and there the two great enemies rest together in peace.

THE AUTHOR

A lifelong history enthusiast, David Falconieri first became intrigued by the War of the Roses as a teenager while reading Shakespeare's historical plays. After six years abroad, he traveled to Britain and began researching *The Beggar's Throne* by immersing himself in 15th-century English history, examining ancient texts and visiting battle sites. He was born in Ohio and now lives in Denver, Colorado, with his wife, Danamarie. *The Beggar's Throne* is his first novel.